W9-AHK-063

Let the Dead Keep Their Secrets

LET THE DEAD KEEP THEIR SECRETS

ROSEMARY SIMPSON

THORNDIKE PRESS
A part of Gale, a Cengage Company

A Gilded Age Mystery.
Thorndike Press, a part of Gale, a Cengage Company.

Thorndike Press® Large Print Mystery.
The text of this Large Print edition is unabridged.
Other aspects of the book may vary from the original edition.
Set in 16 pt. Plantin.

LIBRARY OF CONGRESS CIP DATA ON FILE.
CATALOGUING IN PUBLICATION FOR THIS BOOK
IS AVAILABLE FROM THE LIBRARY OF CONGRESS.

ISBN-13: 978-1-4328-9346-0 (hardcover alk. paper)

Published in 2021 by arrangement with Kensington Books, an imprint of Kensington Publishing Corp.

Printed in Mexico
Print Number: 01 Print Year: 2022

To well-remembered friends and relatives.

Chapter 1

Josiah Gregory folded the *New York Times* of February 21, 1889, into a neat rectangle and placed it on his desk so the review of *Aïda* was uppermost. Miss Prudence and Mr. Hunter had been in the opening-night audience. He wondered whether they would agree with the unsigned review applauding the staging of the opera, but not the worn-out voice of the famous diva singing the title role. Josiah sighed. Age and its indignities came to everyone.

"Anything new?" asked Prudence MacKenzie. A puff of frigid air invaded the office as she took off her hat and long, curly black astrakhan fur coat. "It's bitterly cold out. Kincaid put warm bricks in the carriage, but my feet are still frozen."

She peeled black kidskin gloves from her hands and stuffed them into the pockets of the coat, running appreciative fingers over the thick bands of contrasting gray fur bordering the sleeves and running from neckline to hem. They exactly matched the color of her eyes. The coat was an extravagance Prudence would not have purchased for herself; it had been a gift from an eccentric aunt to a beloved and seldom-seen niece. The astrakhan turned heads whenever and wherever she wore it.

"I assume you've seen the *Aïda* review?"

"I agree with it," Prudence said. "The staging was magnificent, and Frau Schröder-Hanfstängl had her moments, but there were far too few of them. We had complimentary tickets, so I shouldn't complain too much."

"How was your supper after the performance?" Josiah had made a hard-to-get opening-night reservation at Delmonico's on Fifth Avenue and Twenty-sixth Street. He prided himself on being able to do the impossible.

"We canceled," Prudence said. The shocked look on her secretary's face prompted an explanation. "Miss Buchanan sent a note thanking us for the invitation, but regretfully declining for reasons she didn't specify. She asked if we would meet with her today instead. Here in the office."

"Shall I start a file on her?"

"She didn't say she was coming as a client."

"She will be," he predicted, writing *Buchanan* across the top of a new cardboard folder.

"Is Geoffrey in?" Prudence picked up the *Aïda* review.

"He wanted to be informed as soon as you arrived."

"You'd better join us, Josiah. I don't think we filled you in on everything that happened while we were in England. If you're right and Claire Buchanan does want to consult us professionally, you'll need background information to put in that file." Prudence crossed to Geoffrey's office, knocked, and entered, leaving the door open for their secretary to follow.

The man who stood up behind his desk when Prudence appeared in his doorway was well over six feet tall. He had broad shoulders, long legs, and an athletic grace that spoke of years spent on horseback. Hunter was a Southerner born and bred, an exile by choice from the North Carolina plantation where his family still lived. Unlike most men of his social standing, he was clean-shaven. Black-haired and with eyes so deeply brown they looked like polished onyx, he inevitably drew the attention of the ladies. All of whom he kept at arm's length. Except for Prudence.

"Claire will be here at eleven," she said, laying Josiah's copy of the *New York Times* on his desk, placing the opera singer's note beside it. Her father had trained her to line up evidentiary artifacts like a row of soldiers on parade. It was a habit of which her ex-Pinkerton partner heartily approved. "Josiah thinks she'll be a client."

"I've never known him to be wrong. Do you have any idea what this is about?" Geoffrey asked.

"None whatsoever. Now that I think back over the conversations we had on the ship, I realize how seldom Claire spoke about herself. I don't think I know much more than what Aunt Gillian was able to tell us. She's been a cover singer in opera companies in London and several European cities. Everyone expects she'll join the ranks of the divas before too much longer."

"Is that what opera understudies are called? Cover singers?" Josiah served them coffee, warm milk, lumps of brown sugar, and a plate of pastries from a German bakery he passed on his way to work every morning.

"Exactly. I hadn't mentioned her before the tickets came because I thought it was likely to be one of those shipboard friendships that doesn't persist onto land," Prudence said. "We met Miss Buchanan when we stayed with Aunt Gillian in London. It was a very long month. I don't think there was an exhibit or gallery anywhere in the city we didn't visit."

"Don't forget all the parks and museums," Geoffrey put in. "I've never been so wet and cold in my life."

"You didn't complain about it then."

"It would have been churlish. And Lady Rotherton is not the type to tolerate bad manners."

"The week before we left we went to Covent Garden to see a performance of Bizet's *Carmen*. Miss Buchanan was the cover singer for the title role, but she was buried in the chorus that night. There are always galas after a performance. Aunt Gillian brought us as her guests to one of the most exclusive. The Prince of Wales was expected, but I don't think he ever appeared. Did he, Geoffrey?"

"You would have remembered if he had."

"The hostess at these affairs usually invites one or two members of the opera company. It's a sing-for-your-supper command performance. Claire told me later that no one turns down an invitation, even though they know they're only there to provide free entertainment. She said there's always the chance someone important will hear her sing and realize she's as good as the diva she's covering. Many of the younger women singers hope to snare a patron or protector. The hostess had requested arias by Donizetti and Rossini, so that's what she sang."

"Her voice is one of the loveliest sopranos I've ever heard," contributed Geoffrey. "Rich and full, but not shrill or heavy. There was very little conversation while she performed. It was a great compliment, given the amount of champagne flowing that night."

"My aunt introduced us, since we three were the only Americans at the soirée."

"I thought your aunt was American." Josiah looked confused.

"She was American a very long time ago. Now she's more English than the English," Prudence said. She couldn't remember whether the topic of her mother's sister had ever come up in the office. She thought it probably hadn't. Josiah was notoriously Anglophile; he would have remembered every detail of Lady Rotherton's story.

"Aunt Gillian married a title twenty years ago, well before Jennie Jerome made it the thing to do. Willie, as she always calls him, was chasing her fortune, and she was in the mood to be caught. He died in a shooting accident and she became the Dowager Viscountess Rotherton within a year of the wedding. Since she hadn't given birth to an heir, the estate and the title passed to a distant cousin, but there was a clause in her marriage contract stipulating the return of her dowry and giving her tenancy of their London house for her lifetime."

"She didn't remarry?"

"Nor did she come back to America to live. Aunt Gillian is the kind of woman who takes carefully considered chances that usually turn out to be sure things. My father told me that within a few years of Lord Rotherton's passing, she'd doubled and then redoubled the value of her portfolio, with no guidance except the financial section of the *London Times* and shrewd common sense. He said she thinks of herself as a Hetty Green, with good jewelry and a title."

"From what I observed while we were there, a wealthy widow can lead a very fine life in Victoria's London, even though the queen herself has been in mourning for as long as anyone can remember." Geoffrey helped himself to one of the pastries.

"Gillian returned to America only twice

after she married, once to dance at my mother's wedding and then to mourn at her funeral. She said she remembered me as a beautiful six-year-old child who reminded her so painfully of her younger sister that she fled back to London as soon as decently possible." Prudence paused. "Nevertheless, she offered to chaperone me here in New York. I couldn't decide whether she's become bored with London society or tired of the winter weather."

"You turned her down?" Josiah's sense of what was fitting and proper had long been offended by Miss Prudence's decision to live alone after her stepmother's fortuitous death. If he hadn't been afraid of unforgivably offending her, he would have brought up the subject long before now.

"Not quite. I left the idea hanging in limbo."

"When we met her, Claire had already made plans to come to New York," Geoffrey said, steering the conversation back to its original subject. "She'd signed a contract to cover at the Met and persuaded the Royal Opera Company to release her. We were booked on the same ship."

"For which I was grateful," Prudence said. "The Atlantic was so rough on the westward crossing that ladies didn't dare stroll the decks. You risked being knocked off your feet by the wind. Geoffrey was the only passenger who consistently braved the weather. We used to watch him through a porthole, loping along like a drunken sailor, veering from rail to rail and then hanging on to the ropes that were strung against the outside walls of the cabins. I'm sure the crew thought he was foolhardy and more than a little crazy."

"It's the best cure there is against seasickness," Geoffrey said.

"Claire and I spent a good many hours together in the first-class lounge playing cards. She taught me the tarot. She said that was how members of the opera company passed the time backstage and in the wings during performances and rehearsals. She gave me a deck of French tarot cards. They're beautiful. I'll bring them in to the office to show you."

"As it happens, Miss Prudence, I'm not unfamiliar with the tarot."

"You always surprise me, Josiah."

"Mr. Conkling insisted I learn what all the fuss was about. He had a client who wanted to bring suit against a fraudulent fortune-teller."

"They're all fakes," Geoffrey said. "With a very limited bag of tricks. Once you learn what they are, you can turn the tables on any one of them. If you want." He smiled as though recalling a particularly enjoyable scam.

"We said our good-byes when the ship docked and promised to see one another whenever Claire could find time between rehearsals and performances. The diva she's covering is contracted for four different operas this season. I've kept an eye on the opera news in hopes of seeing Claire's name, but she hasn't been mentioned in any of the reviews or columns I've read."

"Cover singers are invisible until the night they replace a principal," Geoffrey said.

"It's almost eleven o'clock," Josiah informed them. He balanced his ever-present stenographer's notebook on his lap and took a last bite of German pastry, managing not to spill the sugary frosting on his immaculate white shirt and meticulously brushed black suit.

Clients weren't always on time, but Josiah lived by the clock and the firm's appointment book.

The woman Josiah ushered into Geoffrey Hunter's office was tall and slender, elegantly dressed in a gown that could only have been fashioned in one of the couturier salons of Paris. The highnecked black wool afternoon costume gleamed and glistened with elaborate designs of jet-beaded passementerie, rosettes, twisted cording, and finely worked braid, its severe perfection lightened by a fall of snow-white lace from the interior of the narrow sleeves. The perfectly pointed V waist and naturally contoured bustle were the epitome of the latest European fashion as pictured in *Godey's Lady's Book.*

"It's wonderful to see you again, Prudence," she said. "I hope you'll forgive me for declining your supper invitation last night. The rehearsal schedule has been brutal." The women exchanged kisses on the cheek in the French fashion; then Claire held out a gloved hand to Geoffrey. "I hardly recognize you when you're not lurching about on the deck of a ship." Her speech was lightly accented, as though she had spoken English as a child, then lived abroad for many years.

She accepted the cup of coffee Josiah handed her, settling herself into the chair he placed in front of Geoffrey's desk. With one penetrating look she seemed to take his measure; the slightest of nods indicated he would do.

"Thank you again for last night's tickets

to *Aïda,*" Prudence began.

"It wasn't the best of performances," Claire said. "There's no point pretending otherwise." She gestured toward the folded *Times.* "I see you've read the review."

"Will Frau Schröder-Hanfstängl continue?"

"Everyone gets bad reviews occasionally. There was a rumor for a while that she was considering a teaching position at one of the conservatories, but nothing came of it. All performers grow thick skins. We wouldn't survive otherwise. So, yes, she'll sing for the rest of this season at the Met and probably for years to come."

"I'm sure you can't help but wish it were otherwise," Geoffrey said. He knew that some *artistes* spent their entire professional careers singing minor roles or lost in the chorus, waiting for the chance that never came.

"Prudence mentioned that you're a former Pinkerton agent, Mr. Hunter." Claire Buchanan deftly sidestepped his comment. "The Pinkertons claim to be the best detectives in the world. Is that true?"

"It's a well-deserved reputation," he answered.

"I hadn't realized there were lady detectives until Prudence told me about your partnership and that Allan Pinkerton had hired female operatives," Claire continued. "You were kind aboard ship not to ask questions about my personal life. I'm sure I made it obvious I wouldn't welcome them." She smiled an apology. "I wasn't keeping secrets to be deliberately mysterious. I thought that if I didn't talk about it, the pain would eventually lessen. So I taught Prudence the tarot and avoided all mention of what I've lost."

"How can we be of assistance, Miss Buchanan?" Geoffrey asked. Josiah had been right, as usual. Their shipboard acquaintance had come to the office today with the intention of becoming a client.

The opera singer reached into a velvet reticule whose passementerie matched the patterns on her dress. She took out a black cardboard folder slightly larger than her hand. "Open it," she said, giving the folder to Prudence. "A part of me dies every time I look at it."

The cardboard was of the thickness used to mount and protect photographs, the two covers tied together by a narrow black silk ribbon. On the front was an embossed design of intertwined lilies surrounded by a stand of cypress trees, popular symbols of mourning throughout the Western world.

"Is this what I think it is?" Prudence asked. She'd seen cabinet photos like this one too many times not to recognize what she'd been given. She glanced up in time to catch a twitch of aversion cross Geoffrey's face.

"Please undo the tie."

Prudence opened the folder. Inside, mounted within an oval cutout decorated with the same motif of lilies and weeping cypress trees, was the photograph of a young woman holding in her lap a perfect infant. Eyes open, tiny features composed and expressionless, the child had been posed with its head lying against the mother's bosom, as though to be comforted by the sound of her heartbeat.

Except that both of them were dead when the photograph was taken.

The lifeless woman was Claire Buchanan.

Chapter 2

Prudence passed the cabinet photograph to Geoffrey, not saying a word, knowing that after the initial shock he would make the same connection she had.

"Your sister?" he asked.

"My twin," Claire said. "As children we were inseparable."

"The resemblance is striking. Not all twins look so much alike."

"When did you lose her?" Prudence asked gently. "Lose both of them?"

"Catherine and her child only survived for a day after the birth. She gave the baby our mother's name. Ingrid."

Prudence and Geoffrey waited. Their client-to-be needed time to tell the story in her own words.

"Catherine's voice was extraordinary. Had she not married Aaron Sorensen, she would have been one of the greatest divas the world of opera has ever known. Compared to my sister, mine is a very modest talent." Claire hesitated. "The Met contacted me to cover for Frau Schröder-Hanfstängl this season because I'd done it in Europe and I knew the repertoire. That's what brought me back to America."

"Not this?" asked Prudence, gesturing to the postmortem photograph of Catherine Sorensen and her dead child. There was a New York City address below the photographer's name on the back of the folder.

"I was in Vienna when Catherine died. That was ten months ago. Sorensen had sent a *carte de visite* announcing her passing to my apartment in Paris. I don't have my mail forwarded when I'm on tour. There's no point to it. Any correspondence is more likely to get lost than to catch up with me. So I didn't know what had happened until the tour ended and I returned home. By that time my manager had received the offer from the Royal Opera. I knew no one in London. It seemed the ideal place to hide with my grief."

"Did your brother-in-law also send you this?" Geoffrey tapped his forefinger on the closed cardboard folder.

"I had no idea it existed until after I started rehearsals three weeks ago. I share a dressing room at the Met with another cover singer, Lucinda Pallazzo. We've known each other casually for years. She and Catherine became close after I left New York. This photograph was in a drawer of her makeup table. She had put it away to spare my feelings. When I told her I'd never seen it before, she gave it to me."

Claire handed him a black-bordered envelope she took from her reticule. "This is what was waiting for me in Paris when I returned from Vienna."

"May I?" Geoffrey waited politely. At Claire's nod he extracted a black-bordered *carte de visite: In loving memory of Catherine Sorensen, who departed this life on April 30, 1888, aged twenty-four years, two months, and three days, taking with her the pure soul of her infant daughter, Ingrid, aged one day. Cherished wife of Aaron Sorensen. They are gone, but not forgotten.* The message was engraved in the center of an embossed frieze of winged angels and weeping cypress trees. An elegant copperplate signature had been penned in black ink across the bottom: *Aaron Sorensen.*

Geoffrey passed both the card and the envelope to Prudence.

"As you can see, there's no personal message. Just Sorensen's name. His full name. Exactly the way he would have signed dozens of cards sent to friends, acquaintances, perhaps even business colleagues. He did everything he could to come between my sister and me. Omitting her maiden name from the announcement of her death was the final blow."

"You mentioned business colleagues, Claire." Prudence ran a finger over the black-bordered card stock, with its expensively embossed images, before laying it on Geoffrey's desk.

"Aaron Sorensen was an importer of European antiques when he first came into our lives. Our parents had settled in New York City before we were born, and they maintained a home here, even though they traveled extensively. We grew up in hotels and concert halls. I remember my father joking that sometimes the only way he could tell what country we were in was by the cuisine. We were fifteen when our mother fell ill. She begged to be brought back to America to die. Afterward, we stayed on."

"I know how terrible it is to lose a parent when you're young." Prudence had been six years old when her mother succumbed to consumption.

"My father never recovered. He was a pianist, but for a long time he couldn't bear to hear the pieces they had performed together. He never played another public concert. He turned all his attention to my sister and me, but especially Catherine. She was the finest soprano I've ever heard."

"Aaron Sorensen," Prudence prompted.

"He approached my father when a client asked him to broker a Brazilian rosewood Chickering piano that had been owned and played by Franz Liszt. The provenance had been authenticated, and my father became fixated on the instrument. It was all he could talk about. I don't know why he insisted that Catherine and I accompany him when he went to see it. Perhaps he had some idea we would be his final audience. He still practiced as though he were on tour, just never the pieces he had played as accompanist to our mother. That day he played Liszt's Sonata in B minor."

"Did he purchase the piano?" Prudence found herself captivated by the story Claire Buchanan was telling.

"No. I don't think he had any intention of buying it. He just wanted to prove himself Liszt's technical equal on the master's own keyboard. He was magnificent. It was as good a performance as any of his concerts. Three months later, Catherine and Sorensen eloped. She stopped taking vocal lessons. As far as I know, she never sang in public again."

Claire Buchanan reached for the folder containing the photograph of her sister, the image she had said broke her heart every time she looked at it. She sat for a moment holding the open folder beside the announcement of Catherine Sorensen's death.

"What happened after they eloped?" Prudence asked. "Your father must have been very angry."

"Strangely enough, he wasn't. I didn't understand it at the time, and he refused to discuss it. Aaron moved into our home, and my father gave him and Catherine the suite of rooms where he and my mother had lived. The antipathy between me and my new brother-in-law was immediate and impossible to overcome. He hated the fact that as children Catherine and I had been inseparable, and that as adults we tried never to be apart for very long. We could read each other's minds. Sometimes it seemed we were a single individual. He was jealous. He did everything he could to drive a wedge between us."

"Did he succeed, Claire?" Prudence asked.

"No. One of the reasons I went to Europe was to make life easier for Catherine. She paid a price whenever we went out together in the afternoon or if her husband walked in on us when we were having tea and laughing together. Aaron never said or did anything overtly hostile, but every word, every look and gesture, was calculated to wound. When I felt her pain becoming unbearable, I left."

"When was that?" Geoffrey glanced at Josiah, who nodded as he continued to take notes. He'd mastered Gregg shorthand so as not to miss a word of a client's interview or deposition.

"Less than a month after they married. I think I knew from the first day that Aaron was determined to destroy what my sister and I shared. He had convinced her not to confide in me about the elopement. It was the first secret either of us kept from the other. My father deeded our house in New York to Catherine. He provided me with funds of equal value to buy an apartment in Paris. I was to continue my vocal studies there, and he would join me. It seemed a workable solution to what we knew would eventually become an irreconcilable break if we continued to try to live together."

"Was Sorensen a part of these discussions?" Geoffrey asked.

"It seems strange now, but we didn't talk about what was happening. Not with any degree of frankness. It all took place very quickly and quietly." Claire lowered her head for a moment. When she looked up, tears stood diamond-bright in her eyes. "My father never came to Paris. He fell ill shortly after I sailed at the end of October that year. He didn't recover."

"How alone you must have felt," Prudence murmured.

"To survive I threw myself into my work. I took vocal lessons by day, practiced for hours on end, and joined the first company to offer me a contract. I wrote to Catherine every day. She rarely answered, and when a letter did come, I could tell the words weren't hers. Aaron had dictated them."

"Did you keep the letters?" Geoffrey wanted to know.

Claire nodded. "There are only five of them. Nowhere does she tell me she's with child. Not a word about her condition." She gestured toward the cabinet photo and the *carte de visite*. "That's the first I knew of the baby. When she and Catherine were already dead."

"There were no letters from friends or relatives mentioning her condition?"

"None. My father hadn't encouraged us to make friends, and both he and our mother were the only children in their families to live into adulthood. Lucinda said she never imagined Catherine had not written me the news."

"Sorensen didn't object to their friendship?"

"He didn't discover it until just before Catherine gave birth. They usually met for tea in out-of-the-way places, where they wouldn't be seen by anyone they knew. Sometimes they went to museums. When Sorensen did find out, he was furious. He forbade Catherine to see her friend again. Lucinda received a note that I am certain my sister did not write."

"When did you decide to come back to America?" Geoffrey asked.

"I always knew I wouldn't stay away forever," Claire said. "But I couldn't face returning to nothing. I didn't want to live in a New York that didn't contain my sister. I told you I was in Vienna when Catherine died, and that I didn't learn what had happened until I was back in Paris nearly two months later. But I sensed something was wrong long before then.

"The night Catherine died, in the middle of a performance at the Vienna Court Opera, I felt a terrible pain wash over me. I thought I might be falling ill. I had no idea what caused it. I went back to my hotel after the performance, but I couldn't sleep. The next day I sent a telegram to America. There was never any answer. Then the dreams began."

"Can you tell us about them?" Prudence asked. She wanted to stretch out a hand to comfort, console, and strengthen her shipboard friend, but she didn't dare. Something about the set of Claire's mouth told her that any such gesture might break the singer's fragile control.

"They were vague at first. An image of mist and of a person I couldn't make out hidden in cloudlike swirls too thick for the eye to penetrate. The figure and I seemed to be walking toward one another, but we never met. Then I woke up. Gradually the dreams became longer and more complicated. Sometimes I saw an infant in its mother's arms. The woman wept and held the child out to me, but when I tried to take it from her, both dissolved into nothing. Often there was no visible image. I heard cries of despair and anger, a far-off wailing that became so loud it pained my ears."

"Did you recognize the woman?"

"Not until I read the *carte de visite* announcing Catherine's death. Then I understood immediately that it was my sister I'd seen struggling through the mist. I didn't know what she wanted, only that she was desperately trying to reach me from the other side. I can't explain my reasoning, but by the time the Met offer was made, I had healed enough so that I knew I would accept. It meant a homecoming of sorts, and also the opportunity to find out more about my sister. I thought I knew her as well as I knew myself, but I was wrong. Now I wonder what other secrets she kept from me. I want desperately to know what she experienced during the months before she delivered her child. And I have to know what went wrong. A healthy woman doesn't die without warning. What made her child suddenly cease breathing? Catherine comes to me nearly every night in dreams that verge on nightmares. I have so many questions, and no answers."

"Have you tried talking to Catherine's husband?" Prudence asked.

"I sent him a note the day after our ship docked," Claire said, "inquiring when it would be convenient to call on him. When I didn't hear back in a few days, I sent another. He finally replied, but it was only to inform me that he was going out of town on business and would contact me when he returned.

"I can't tell you how many times I walked

past the house after a rehearsal, remembering how Catherine and I had played and practiced in those rooms. How much we loved coming home every time we accompanied our parents wherever their concerts took them. I stood on the sidewalk staring up at blank windows, picturing our schoolroom; our bedrooms; the music room, where my father's concert piano stood; the parlor, where we gathered in the evening and where sometimes my mother sang French country songs and lullabies by the fire. Finally, two days ago, I could bear it no longer. I suspected Aaron was avoiding me, so I made up my mind to call on him without warning.

"I'd gotten as far as the corner when it started to rain. I put up my umbrella, but my skirts were already wet. I thought I must look a sight and had almost decided to come back another day when a carriage came around from the alley and halted in front of the house. The front door opened and a butler I didn't recognize came out. He held a large umbrella over a woman dressed in mourning and helped her into the carriage. I could see her very clearly. She was only a few feet away from me. She gave the butler some instructions. When he answered, he called her by name. *Mrs. Sorensen.*

"My former brother-in-law has a new wife. Judging from her figure, she's at least seven or eight months pregnant."

CHAPTER 3

"My sister and her child didn't die natural deaths, Mr. Hunter," Claire said. "Whether he did it with his own hands or hired someone to do it for him, Aaron Sorensen killed them. I want you to find the evidence that will convict him. He has to pay for his crime."

"Do you have any proof they were murdered?" Geoffrey asked. Every client who had ever come to him sought evidence for what he or she already believed. They were always sure someone had stolen from them, a spouse had cheated, or undue influence had been used to write them out of a will. Accusations of murder were as common as leaves on the ground when there was money or property to be inherited.

"Aaron Sorensen became a very wealthy man when Catherine died. For his new wife to be as far gone with child as she is, he had to have married again within two or three months."

"What else do you know?" Prudence asked.

"Almost nothing. I'll give you the name of the firm of lawyers who handled my father's affairs. I wrote them when Aaron didn't respond to my telegram. One of them answered very promptly with his condolences and the information that her husband was the sole beneficiary of Catherine's will. I wasn't surprised. In the short time I lived with them, I realized that Sorensen controlled every aspect of her life. If I sound bitter, Mr. Hunter, it's because I am."

"You haven't been to their offices since returning to New York?"

"I made one appointment, which I had to cancel because of rehearsals. There didn't seem an urgent need to schedule another. Until I saw the current Mrs. Sorensen, I didn't doubt that Catherine was another victim of childbirth. I thought the dreams were manifestations of my grief and inability to accept that she was gone. I've been to her grave. I wept my tears and said my farewell. I had begun to believe the dreams would gradually cease to haunt me. I was wrong. I knew it the moment I realized how quickly Sorensen had found another wife."

Geoffrey passed the cabinet photograph

to Josiah, who examined the gold-embossed name and address of the photographer. "Do you know anything about him?" he asked.

"It happens I do, sir. When Mr. Conkling died, there was talk of calling this Bartholomew Monroe in to take memorial photographs. He's considered one of the best in the city at his craft."

"Did he? Make postmortem studies of Mr. Conkling?"

"No. Mrs. Conkling decided there were enough portraits of her husband in existence already." Josiah handed back the cabinet photograph. "There were other considerations as well." Josiah's former employer had had a hard death; weeks of fever and hallucinations had appalled and taxed those who cared for him.

"I did go to Monroe's gallery, but when I saw what was in his display windows, I turned away without going in," Claire volunteered.

"Can you tell us why, Claire?"

"Why I went? I thought he might have taken other photos of Catherine and baby Ingrid. I didn't want my only picture of them together to be the one Aaron chose to have printed."

"I meant why you didn't go in."

"I couldn't, not when I saw what was in

the windows. It's a large gallery, and in the center of each display window stands an easel, draped in black velvet. The photographs resting on the easels are greatly enlarged. A dozen or more smaller photographs are positioned in the folds of the velvet. When I looked beyond the windows, I could see walls and display boards covered with the same type of photographs as were on view outside. I didn't think I could stand it if he had chosen to mount Catherine's likeness there among all those others. So I turned away."

"You told us you had a strange foreboding before you actually knew your sister had died," Prudence said.

"I'm sure you've heard people say that time stood still." Claire read the skepticism on Prudence's face.

"There were men who claimed that occurred on the battlefield," Geoffrey said. "What they meant was they had no sense of minutes or even hours passing. They remembered everything later on, but as though the entirety of what happened to them had been preserved in a single, painful image."

"Something like that happened to me on the stage of the Vienna Court Opera. For a few moments it was as though I were moving through a dream while everyone stood still around me. The following morning I sent the telegram that was never answered." Claire's eyes pleaded with them to believe her. "However distressing it may be, I have to know what happened to my sister and her child that night."

"We won't lie to you, Claire. We won't conceal anything from you," Prudence promised.

"If we take your case," Geoffrey temporized.

Claire stared at him, the rigid facial lines of control slowly turning to stone. "Aaron killed them. Catherine is begging me for justice. I thought you would understand that I intend to see she receives it."

"Nothing will bring your sister and her child back," Prudence said.

Geoffrey nodded at Josiah, who slipped out of the office, returning almost immediately with a copy of the contract signed by all clients of Hunter and MacKenzie, Investigative Law.

"We'll take your case," Geoffrey said, knowing that Prudence would agree with him. His seeming indecision had been a test of Claire's determination and commitment. "We'll find out everything we can about your sister's husband and we'll re-create as much as possible of what happened during Catherine's marriage and final hours. I can promise that much."

Josiah's fingers tapped a rapid count on his stenographer's pad. He frowned. Tapped the count again. Scribbled a calculation.

"I have to know what happened when Catherine gave birth," Claire said. "Something caused her to cry out to me for help, even though we were four thousand miles apart. When there was no response to the telegram, I denied my fears, because no matter how much I disliked him, I had no reason to doubt that Aaron loved her. And she him. I should have known it was all a lie, but I didn't."

"We'll need authorization to act on your behalf when we talk to your father's lawyers," Geoffrey said.

Josiah placed the appropriate form on the desk, whisked it away as soon as Claire Buchanan signed it.

"Does the same firm handle your affairs?" Prudence caught Geoffrey's nod of approval and knew he'd guessed where the question was leading.

"I remember a brief visit to their office before I left for Europe. Father insisted I have a valid will since I was of legal age. Musicians travel so much, from city to city, across oceans and continents. He always said anyone living the way we did was a fool not to keep his paperwork in order."

"Who inherits your estate, Miss Buchanan?" Prudence asked.

There was a long, strained moment of silence before Claire answered. When she did, her voice trembled and her already-pale skin turned ashen. "My sister, and if she predeceases me, her heirs."

"Are the heirs named?"

"No."

"Then I suggest you have a new will drawn up as soon as possible because as things stand now, the man you're accusing of murder will inherit every penny and franc you possess."

"This is where we start," Geoffrey remarked, studying the *carte de visite* and the postmortem photograph of Catherine Sorensen and her child. Their client, visibly upset by his revelation of the legal status of her despised brother-in-law, had given them into his safekeeping when she left the office. "Sometimes photographers arrive while the body is still being washed. They see the death scene before it's set to rights."

"Ghouls," Josiah declared. He shared Geoffrey's dislike of postmortem photography. "I know it may be the only memento a family has of the deceased, but I find the practice too macabre for my taste."

"It's done more often than not," Prudence contributed. "Every parent who loses a child wants to have a cabinet photo or a *carte de visite* made up with the infant's picture on it. Hardly a month goes by that I don't receive one or two of them in the post. It's very sad."

"The gallery isn't far from here," Geoffrey said, reading the name and address printed on the back of the folder. "Bartholomew Monroe, Portrait Photographer. It's on Broadway, south of Canal Street."

"Geoffrey, I'd like to ask Jacob Riis to examine the photograph before we visit the gallery."

"Who is Jacob Riis?" Josiah asked.

"I don't think you've met him," Geoffrey replied. "He's the photographer who recorded the crime scene in Colonial Park for the police department when Nora Kenny's body was found. Riis is a crime reporter for the *Tribune,* but he takes every extra job that comes his way. He goes into the tenements at night to photograph how the immigrants live — it's an obsession with him. He's one of the best there is at what he does. He can tell us how this photograph was taken, and maybe even when, relative to the deaths." Geoffrey took *Thomas Compton's Medical Guide to Anatomy and Disease* from his bookcase.

"I don't understand," Prudence said.

"I'll show you." Geoffrey paged through the *Medical Guide.* "Here we are. Physical changes occurring in the body after death. I'm paraphrasing, but this is the gist of it —"

"I wonder, sir, if Miss Prudence might be spared the details," Josiah interrupted.

"I rather think it has to be part of my investigative education," Prudence said softly. "I'm sure Mr. Pinkerton didn't spare his lady operatives anything the men had to know."

"He didn't," Geoffrey confirmed.

Josiah's face fell. He wasn't as strong of stomach as he liked to pretend he was.

"Immediately after death the body goes limp. Then anywhere from two to seven hours later, depending on temperature, the muscles stiffen into what's called rigor mortis. And this is what's important for us. Rigor mortis starts with the eyelids, jaw, and neck. Then it gradually spreads to all of the muscles, taking eight to ten hours to render the body completely rigid."

"Catherine Sorensen and her daughter

weren't rigid when Bartholomew Monroe photographed them. He wouldn't have been able to pose them the way he did, to look as natural as they do."

"Exactly. Which means he had to have been in the house either before rigor mortis set in or after it passed off."

"How long does it last?"

"As long as eighteen to twenty hours according to this article. But there are variables, temperature of the place where the bodies are found being the most important."

"There's something wrong with Mrs. Sorensen's eyes," Josiah said. He held a magnifying glass over the photograph, his objection to explicit medical details forgotten. "I can't be sure, but it looks like they've been changed somehow."

"Retouched," Geoffrey said. "Postmortem photographers are occasionally asked to paint over eyes that are closed and can't be reopened."

"That's another reason for Mr. Riis to look at it," Prudence insisted. "There has to be an explanation for why the eyes were painted over. He might be able to tell us what it is."

"Sometimes they keep the eyes open with a bit of the adhesive actors use to stick their beards on," Geoffrey said. "We saw that fairly frequently when I was a Pinkerton. I remember one case where a dead child's mother had hysterics when they couldn't get the eyes to close again. They waited too long or the glue was too strong. But the photograph was very realistic looking."

Josiah stared at the image in fascinated revulsion.

Jacob Riis worked out of a small office leased by the *Tribune* in a building opposite the Central Department of the New York City Police at 300 Mulberry Street.

"It doesn't look anything like what I thought it would from its reputation," Prudence said. Danny Dennis's hansom cab had deposited them in front of the five-story building where so much New York City police history had been made, where the Rogues' Gallery was located and the third degree perfected.

"There's another entrance on Mott Street," Geoffrey told her. "They're both watched night and day by reporters, especially when a rumor leaks out that a big arrest is about to be made. Things are quiet right now." He gestured across the street, where the occasional figure wearing a bowler hat could be seen crisscrossing in front of curtainless windows, pausing to look out at police headquarters. "The *Tribune* isn't the only paper with a press office nearby. Competition for a story is fierce." He took her arm. "Are you sure you want to go through with this, Prudence?"

"Of course I am. It was my idea to begin with."

"I'm only asking because reporters without anything to write about will sniff out whatever they can. You don't want them becoming interested in what a proper young socialite is doing this close to Five Points. And if one of them sees you, you're bound to be recognized." The MacKenzie name was not unfamiliar to the press; Prudence's father had been a celebrated judge, his daughter's odd predilection for involving herself in criminal investigations the topic of not-so-subtle criticism in the gossip columns.

"I doubt anything I do will sell papers." It was on the tip of Prudence's tongue to remind him that her ambitions far exceeded anything most debutantes envisioned for themselves, but she bit back what would have been a sharp retort. *"Prove yourself first, talk later."* How many times had her father given that stern advice to his beginning law clerks? "Do you think Mr. Riis will remember who we are?" she asked, neatly changing the subject.

"I had Josiah telephone him. He's expecting us."

The *Tribune* office was a single small room on the third floor facing police headquarters. Their footsteps echoed in the narrow stairwell as they climbed; a door above them opened and Jacob Riis leaned over the railing. "I was about to give up on you," he called down.

Geoffrey stepped carefully around a pile of camera and tripod cases left conveniently close to the door in Riis's crowded work area. Prudence followed behind. Labeled boxes of glass slides stood one atop the other in front of a many-drawered cabinet. A battered table in the center of the room held a shiny black Remington typewriter wedged in among an assortment of photographic equipment. A wide, wooden box telephone had been attached to the wall near the only window. One corner of the office had been partitioned off to make a darkroom. Despite the window cracked open to bring in some fresh February air, the place reeked of chemicals old and new. It was clear that Riis was using the *Tribune* space for his own projects, as well as what he produced for the newspaper.

"I won't shake hands," he said, wiping his

fingers on a stained towel. "I'm used to the chemical emulsions, but I doubt you are." Though only thirty-nine years old, Riis had the worn air of a man who had devoted too much of his time and his health to a cause. He wore round spectacles and a drooping mustache starting to go gray; a leather apron covered his clothing. Once Josiah had prodded his memory, he quickly recalled Mr. Hunter and Miss MacKenzie from their involvement in the strange and horrifying mutilations of two servant girls and a prostitute that had reminded New Yorkers of the Ripper killings in London. The photographs he'd taken at Colonial Park had sold for enough to buy months of supplies for his tenement pictures.

"I'm not sure how much use I can be," he said, a slight accent betraying his Danish origins. "But I'll do the best I can."

He held the cabinet photo of Catherine and Ingrid Sorensen by its edges, careful not to smudge the print, setting aside the cardboard folder. "What am I looking for?" he asked, sliding the photograph beneath the thick lens of an enlarger. "How much do you already know?"

"The mother and child are both dead," Geoffrey began.

"That's obvious," Riis said. "You don't

need me to tell you that."

"We have to know how soon after death the photograph was taken," Prudence explained, "but we don't want to question either the photographer or the family. Not yet. Not until we have more information."

"Look at the eyes," Geoffrey urged.

"I need more light." Riis turned on the overhead gas fixture, a pipe running across the ceiling, then down to two open receptacles secured to a shorter horizontal pipe. "Better." The smell of gas mingled with the heavy acidic stench of the chemicals.

"I think the two of you should take a look," he said, standing back from the table. "Don't squint and keep both eyes open. It's easier to use than a microscope, but it still takes a little getting used to."

At first, Prudence couldn't make out exactly what she was seeing. She closed one eye, then opened it again, remembering what Riis had said. Slowly the image swam into focus, and when she played with the knob to which Riis guided her fingers, it eventually became startlingly vivid. Every hair on Catherine's head seemed separate from every other; even the grains of powder on her skin were easily discernible. The closeness was unlike anything she had ever seen. When she stepped away from the instrument, she wasn't sure what such an examination might prove, only that she had entered briefly into a new world.

"It looks to me as if only parts of the eyes have been painted," Geoffrey said, straightening from the lens. "I have an idea what that might mean, but I don't know enough about postmortem photography to be sure."

"It's both popular and lucrative," Riis said. "Bartholomew Monroe has quite a reputation."

"You're familiar with his work?"

"I'm surprised you're not. He has a large gallery on Broadway, with a studio above it for the live portraits."

"Have you ever done this kind of photography, Mr. Riis?" Prudence asked.

"Only when there wasn't any other way to make the money I needed." Riis took off his spectacles, polishing them vigorously on the towel he'd used to wipe the chemicals from his hands. "Not that there's anything wrong with what Monroe does. For some families this is the only way they have to remember their beloved, especially when it's a child who's died. Monroe usually does all of his own photography, but every now and then he hires help. I've worked for him occasionally, but I'm not the only one. The newspaper business has never paid very well."

"What can you tell us about this photograph?" Geoffrey took one more quick look through the lens, then stepped away from the table.

"Do you know about rigor mortis?" Riis asked.

"I was a Pinkerton."

"Then you've probably figured out that the picture was taken before rigor mortis set in, not after it passed off. The texture of the skin told you that."

Geoffrey nodded.

"And the eyes were open. Both the mother's and the baby's."

"Held open by some kind of adhesive?" Prudence asked.

"No. You'd see a trace of the glue against the back of the eyelid in the enlargement. Their lids are smooth."

"Then why did the photographer use paint to make the eyes look more lifelike? I thought that was only done when the eyes were closed and couldn't be made to stay open."

"Look again, Miss MacKenzie. Tell me exactly what you see."

Prudence bent over the enlarger, confident this time that she knew what she was doing. "I'm looking at the mother's eyes. I can see traces of very fine brushstrokes."

"He probably used a magnifying glass or an enlarger lens to guide the brush."

"The white looks almost luminous."

"Look at the mother's pupils, Miss MacKenzie."

Seconds ticked by as Prudence stared into Catherine Sorensen's eyes. When she finally raised her head, she nodded confirmation at Jacob Riis, then turned to Geoffrey. "Look at the pupils of her eyes," she told him. "I don't want to say anything until you do."

Moments later, Prudence knew she had been right.

"Only the whites have been painted over. And so skillfully that if Josiah hadn't noticed it through his magnifying glass, we might not have remarked on it. Our client never said a word about retouching."

"What does it mean?" Prudence asked. "Mr. Riis, you said you've taken this type of photograph yourself. Would you ever paint over an open eye?"

"If there's been an injury, of course. The only other time I've known it to be done was when a wife whose husband was over-fond of the drink wanted his weakness hidden. The whites of his eyes looked like spiders had spun webs in them."

"A new mother would hardly be drinking whiskey," Prudence said.

"I've been a police photographer for a long time, Miss MacKenzie. I've seen women so drunk they didn't know they'd given birth until they sobered up."

"Not this mother."

"No. I agree. Not this mother. Mr. Hunter?"

"Petechial hemorrhages?"

"Very possibly. If the eyes were closed after the photograph was taken, they probably remained that way throughout rigor, certainly while the bodies were being prepared for burial. If there wasn't a police inquiry, nobody would notice the hemorrhaging. The only way to be sure would be to see the original negatives, before the retouching was done."

"I wasn't a Pinkerton, Mr. Riis. You'll have to explain 'petechial hemorrhages' to me."

"When someone dies from asphyxiation or lack of oxygen, Prudence, the pressure on the tiny blood vessels of the eyes and eyelids causes them to rupture, leaving distinctive red dots. Those are the petechiae."

"Well done, Mr. Hunter. The police look for signs of petechial hemorrhaging when they suspect strangulation. I've seen it dozens of times."

"And photographed it?"

"Yes. The damage is unmistakable." Riis took a set of photographs from one of the cabinet drawers, arranging them in a neat row on the table. "These are extra prints I made for my own records," he explained. He handed Prudence a magnifying glass. "Don't look at anything but the eyes, Miss MacKenzie," he warned.

It was impossible not to glance at the ruined, distorted faces before her, some of them so badly battered and bruised they hardly looked human. *Don't look at anything but the eyes.*

Now that she knew what to search for, Prudence quickly catalogued the types of hemorrhages in her mind; they ranged from barely visible dots that looked like pinpricks, to larger, more extensive bleeds. "What color are the petechiae, Mr. Riis?" she asked.

"They can be a pale pink to a bright red," he answered.

"Do you ever tint the petechiae to make them more realistic?"

"Not for police purposes. It's tedious and expensive work. I don't have time for it and the detectives don't need it. They've seen the bodies, so the photographs are just to jog their memories later on." Riis collected the photographs, handed them to Hunter. "The other thing you have to remember is that hemorrhaging can occur in a long or very difficult childbirth."

"Our client believes the mother and child were murdered," Prudence said. They'd been careful to reveal no names, but Riis was an experienced police reporter used to ferreting out stories someone had gone to great lengths to conceal.

"If you're asking for my professional opinion, Miss MacKenzie, I'd have to say that your client may not be entirely wrong. When did they die?"

"Ten months ago."

"Were they embalmed?"

"Our client doesn't know."

"If you can get me the original glass negative, I can print it up for you. And enlarge it, too. You'll be able to see the eyes before the photograph was retouched."

A sudden rush of heavy footsteps in the stairwell precipitated Riis out the door. "What's happening?" he yelled, untying his leather apron and reaching behind him for the overcoat and hat thrown over his camera cases.

"Two Black Marias pulled away from the Mott Street entrance. Headed toward Five Points." The reporter who answered him was still too young and enthusiastic to keep a story to himself.

"I've got to lock up or there won't be anything left when I get back," Riis said. He thrust their cabinet photograph and its holder back at them, then slid his key in the lock. They'd barely brushed past when he slammed shut the door and took off down the stairs ahead of them.

"He didn't say he thought it was murder," Prudence murmured, taking Geoffrey's arm.

"But he didn't say it wasn't."

CHAPTER 4

Claire sensed a change among the cast members as soon as she appeared backstage at the Met the afternoon following the opening night performance of *Aïda.*

Many a cover singer stepped into a major role for the first time when a review far less critical than what the *Times* had written about *Aïda* crushed an aging star. Frau Schröder-Hanfstängl had reportedly taken to her bed. Bets were being placed on whether she'd recover enough to sing the title role again at next Tuesday's performance.

In the meantime some reblocking of the grand finale of Act Two had to be gotten through; there had been several near collisions between standard-bearers, spear carriers, trumpet players, dancing girls, and prisoners marching in what was supposed to be military precision. Fortunately, the *Times* reviewer had been too bedazzled by the gilt and brilliantly colored costumes to comment on momentary confusion. The sheer number of bodies crowded onto the stage during the triumphal march had overwhelmed him.

The thing audiences never knew about the spectacular scenes they applauded was that there were hours and hours of tedium behind each one of them. Before the entire cast of Act Two, Scene Two finally took the stage, each group of the grand procession had to be rehearsed individually. Over and over again until they got it right. It had already taken most of the afternoon.

"Do you think you'll go on?" One of the superstitions no cover singer ever broke was speaking aloud the name of the role he or she hoped to sing within twenty-four hours of the performance. Lucinda Pallazzo was covering Amneris, not Aïda, but she had hopes for Catherine's sister. It never hurt to be overcautious.

"I doubt it," Claire said. "Frau Schröder-Hanfstängl has never been known to step aside because of a bad review. I don't think anything short of laryngitis or pneumonia will keep her down."

"I'm sorry it was losing Catherine that brought you back to New York. But I'm glad to have you here." Lucinda's lower-soprano register limited the number of important roles she could cover. Like most contraltos, she joked that she seldom sang anything but bitches, witches, or britches. Britches were the roles originally written for castratos, of whom there were mercifully few in this enlightened century.

"I did something today I'd rather you didn't tell anyone about." Claire rose from the makeup chair she was sitting in and closed the door to the tiny dressing room they shared. "I've hired a firm of private investigators to look into the circumstances of Catherine's death."

Lucinda's breath caught in her throat. People said it was best not to ask too many questions, let the dead keep their secrets. She'd acted on impulse, giving Claire the cabinet photo of Catherine and her child. And now this surprising announcement. "What do you hope they'll find?"

"I'm not sure." Claire had decided it would sound preposterous if she accused her brother-in-law of murdering the wife everyone assumed died as a result of childbirth. Not until there was proof positive of his guilt would she confide her suspicions to anyone but Prudence and Mr. Hunter. "I went to our family home. Aaron has put off every request to meet with me, so I decided to take matters into my own hands. I have so many questions, Lucinda. I planned to confront him when and where he would least expect it. But when I got there, I saw a heavily pregnant woman come out the front door and get into a carriage. The butler called her Mrs. Sorensen."

"I should have told you."

"You knew?"

Lucinda nodded. Tears filled her eyes. "Sorensen is on the Metropolitan Opera Board of Directors, an adjunct member. I've seen him from time to time when he's come here for a meeting. We were all shocked when he married again. So soon. I don't remember who told me that the new Mrs. Sorensen was in an interesting condition, but it's become common knowledge."

"I wish you had said something."

"I didn't want to be the one to give you such hurtful news, Claire. I hoped you already knew and didn't mention it out of delicacy. I don't think she was to blame for the lack of a proper mourning period. I'm sure it was him."

"Of course it was. He's capable of anything. He ruined Catherine's life, Lucinda. My sister was destined for a great career. Until she married."

"Most of us marry at one time or another.

Our managers, our agents, our conductors, other singers. It need not be the end of a career if the choice is a wise one." Lucinda toyed with the bouquet of pale pink roses on her dressing table.

"From your latest admirer?"

"He has money, but no staying power. He thinks my voice is beautiful, but he doesn't want to be a part of the world I live in. And I have no intention of giving it up."

"I wish Catherine had felt that way. Opera is a very small community, especially here in New York. She must have studied or sung with some of the permanent members of the company. Have they talked about her?"

"The gossip didn't start until we heard you were coming to cover Schröder-Hanfstängl. People who hadn't heard you sing, but knew you were Catherine Buchanan's sister, wanted to know if you had the same range and power."

"What did you tell them?"

"That I'd known both of you for years and comparisons were difficult to make."

"That was kind of you." Though they had occasionally studied with the same vocal coaches and sung on many of the same concert programs, Claire and Lucinda had never been more than casual acquaintances. Until now. As long as her sister was alive,

Claire had needed no other woman friend. And until Claire went to Europe, neither had Catherine.

"Claire?" Lucinda plucked at the petals from one of the pink roses, arranging them in a circle on the dressing table. "There was a rumor that Catherine had spoken to the Met management about joining the company. When I asked her about it, she said she was waiting until after the baby was born to make up her mind."

"Are you sure? She never mentioned anything like that in her letters to me." The letters, she remembered thinking, were stilted and artificial, as though the writer had been noting down someone else's ideas.

"She was taking vocal lessons from Gertrude Strauss. No one was supposed to know, but the person who told me was also being coached by her. Strauss had the reputation of being notoriously difficult to please, but a genius when it came to training a voice. Your sister was in the habit of coming and going by the rear entrance to the building where Madame Gertrude lived. One day my friend arrived early for her lesson and saw her in the hallway. Catherine begged my friend not to tell anyone. She was very insistent about not being found out. My friend promised she'd keep the secret, and she says she did. I was the first one she told, and that was only because she knew we had sung together and she thought you should know. I pretended that Catherine hadn't already confided in me several months before she died."

"I'd like to speak to her."

"She's in San Francisco, with a light-opera company. On tour for the next four months."

"Do you think Madame Strauss would be willing to talk to me about Catherine?"

"She went back to Germany after Catherine died. Said she was too old to teach anymore. I'm so sorry, Claire. When I said that Catherine confided in me, I meant that she told me she was studying again. Not much more than that. She kept anything to do with her marriage to herself. She never talked about her husband, and if I brought up his name, she shut me out. There's so much I want to tell you, but so little I really know." Lucinda eyed the pink roses with distaste. Talking about marriage reminded her of the young man who had sent them.

"I'll never get over losing her, Lucinda," Claire said, "but when I think about her, when I remember something from our childhood, a kind of peace eases the heartache. For a little while, at least. You don't have to worry about mentioning her name or changing the subject."

"I'm not very good at it."

"I know almost nothing about what Catherine felt and did after I left for Europe."

"She concealed her condition for as long as she could. And when your father died, his services were private. Here at the Met we didn't know he was gone until after the burial. There were many who would have liked to pay their respects, who had worked with him in the days before he retired from the concert stage. But the only announcement was a short obituary notice in the *Times.*"

"He was supposed to join me in Paris. It was one of his favorite cities."

"I always wondered, but now I think I understand. You weren't told he'd died until it was too late to come back for the funeral, were you?"

"That's another loss I'll never forgive Aaron Sorensen for inflicting on me. All he had to do was send a telegram. I would have been on the next boat. At least my sister and I could have comforted each other."

"It was after his death that Catherine and I became close. I wrote her a condolence note, she answered, and we met for tea. I remember her telling me that her husband was out of town on business. I found out later that the only time she left the house was when she was certain he wouldn't learn she had gone out."

"Did you ever meet Aaron Sorensen?"

"At Catherine's viewing. I was struck by what a handsome man he is. But cold, Claire, very cold and correct. He knew who I was because he'd discovered that Catherine and I had become friends and he'd put a stop to our afternoon teas. I never found out how it happened. I assumed he'd come home early and unannounced from one of his business trips."

"Would you be willing to talk to the detectives I've hired?"

"I'll answer any questions I can. Catherine was unhappy. I know that much. She may have been taking the vocal lessons as a way of resuming her career and freeing herself from dependence on her husband."

"The money was all hers, Lucinda. The house they lived in was the one my parents bought when we were children."

"She didn't tell me that."

"We were brought up to be private people. I never heard my mother speak of anything personal, and my father was the same."

"I gave her a gift for the baby," Lucinda said. "She was so pleased by it. Then she said she'd have to tell her husband she bought it herself, and did I mind? That's when I first suspected she was afraid of him. It was such an odd thing to say."

"What was the gift?"

"It's called a carrying pillow. This one was made of embroidered white silk with tassels at each corner. They're used to hold the infant during baptism and when the baby is resting on someone's knees. The shop where I bought it imports them from France. They embroider the child's name on it, but since I purchased the pillow before Ingrid was born, that was going to be done later."

"There wasn't time," Claire said.

"I'd hoped to see the pillow in the baby's coffin with her," Lucinda said, "but it wasn't there. I don't know what happened to it."

Neither woman wanted to speculate aloud that a gift for the first wife's child might well be sitting in a cupboard somewhere, waiting to be used by the second wife's infant, but they both knew that stranger things had been known to happen.

Two sharp raps on the door warned them they needed to start making their way through the warren of narrow backstage hallways to the main stage for the triumphal march that was the most famous scene in *Aïda.* None of the principals had been required to attend this extra rehearsal; their places would be taken by their covers. For most of them it was the closest they would come to playing the roles they had to be prepared to sing at a moment's notice.

"This is the part I really hate," Lucinda whispered as they stood in the wings waiting for places to be called. They were cheek to jowl with dozens of walk-ons carrying everything from wooden spears to square silken banners representing crocodiles, storks, lions, and unidentifiable beasts of Egyptian antiquity. Fanfare trumpets waved above the crowd, dancers jumped in place to flex their feet, and all around was the whispering buzz of bored and underpaid performers complaining about something or other. It didn't matter what. Complaining was as much a part of opera as singing.

"Ten minutes," the stage manager called. "Take ten."

"Now what?" asked Lucinda as the crowd surged out of the crowded wings onto the stage to wait out the ten-minute delay. "Seidl and Habelmann have their heads together. That can't be good."

"Maybe they'll call for a full-voice rehearsal of the entire scene," Claire said. Sometimes, even though she was just a cover singer in this company, singing at a rehearsal felt like the real thing. Other covers must have read her mind, she thought, as she heard throats being cleared and then a cacophony of voices like the discordant sounds of an orchestra tuning up. Chorus members walked in circles, eyes down, running through their harmonies; the walk-ons clustered together, arguing about their blocking. In the pit the orchestra members stood up to stretch their cramped back muscles. Up above, sailors who were hired for their rope-climbing skills flitted along the catwalks, whistling signals to each other as they secured sandbags and the tall set pieces representing Pharaoh's triumphal arch and temple pillars.

Lucinda, covering the role of Pharaoh's daughter, would sit beside him on a gilded throne, while Claire, covering Aïda, would be part of the crowd of captives, breaking free when the Ethiopian princess recognized her father among the new prisoners. If the principals went on, as they almost always did for every performance, both cover singers would blend into the chorus yet again. It hardly bore thinking about, but there were covers who spent their entire careers standing by, never singing a major role except in rehearsal. This afternoon, if the conductor demanded a full-voice run-through, Lucinda and Claire would perform for their peers.

"Break a leg," whispered Lucinda as she began to make her way across the stage to the pair of thrones perched atop a high riser.

"Toi. Toi. Toi." Claire tapped out the good luck charm that no one but an opera singer would understand. She stood beside Lucinda for a moment. "Enjoy your evening with the young man who sent the pink roses."

"I will." Lucinda would dine and dance and perhaps indulge in something more tonight, but the shrug of her shoulders when she had spoken of him told Claire that the flirtation meant nothing. A gift, perhaps a diamond bracelet that could be pawned when times got hard, as they always did. Nothing more. The rich young man had bought a box at the Met because it was what you did, not because he was deeply, passionately in love with the music he heard.

Just before they parted to go their separate ways into the confusion that would become the triumphal march, Lucinda leaned forward to brush a light kiss on Claire's cheek. Catherine's twin looked so wan and bereft; if Lucinda had been fortunate enough to have a sister, she imagined she would have crumpled under the grief of losing her.

When the sandbag fell, it plunged through empty air from flies to stage with a swooshing sound that could barely be heard above the dancers' tapping, the singers' scales, and the walk-ons' squabbling. Down it came in a straight, heavy drop, building deadly momentum with every second and every foot.

Lucinda looked into the horrified gaze of a trumpet player who had swung his head back the better to balance a fanfare trumpet that was more than half his height. Her eyes snapped upward, she thrust hard against Claire's torso, tried to windmill her way out from under what was bearing down on her, and fell to the stage under a hundred pounds of sand that had acquired enough force to break bones and split open skin.

Screams filled the theater. A wave of frightened performers rushed for the safety of the wings and the house, pushing and shoving past the curtained legs, over the apron, and down the stairs on either side of the stage. Blood spread beneath Lucinda's body, lapping slowly outward until she lay in a gleaming red pond. Her fingers scratched feebly at the wooden floor beneath them, then lay still, outspread in a last, abortive grasp at life.

Claire, shoved so hard by her friend that

she fell to her knees, felt the passage of the sandbag as a rush of air and the impact as a shuddering of the boards beneath her. For a moment she didn't understand what had happened; then she heard the screaming and saw a rivulet of blood ooze thickly across the wooden floor. She crawled toward Lucinda. Sobbing, she pushed with all her might against the sandbag until it rolled off the body of her friend. Lucinda's back and shoulders were curiously flattened, her skull split so that the naked brain shone through tangles of dark hair. Her eyes were open, staring glassily at nothing.

Cradling her friend's head in her lap, Claire rocked back and forth in the ancient mourning lament of women of every culture, chants from the dozens of funeral masses she had sung rising unbidden from her singer's heart and belly. One by one, other members of the company crept back to join her, until Lucinda lay in a circle of mourning as bleak and stylized as anything the opera masters had ever staged. No one tried to revive her; one glance and they knew she was dead.

It was supposed to be me. The sandbag was directed at me. Claire reached out to touch the hemp rope that held the sandbag fast to its mooring. Her fingers glided over the shredded fibers until they reached a smooth surface. *Cut. Cut through just enough to be ripped apart with a strong tug. That's all it would take. One tight fist, one determined yank, and the hemp rope would disintegrate.*

The sabotage had been so skillfully done that Claire doubted anyone would suspect Lucinda's life had been taken by anything but chance. She might be the only person in the theater who knew it wasn't an accident.

The sandbag was meant for me.

CHAPTER 5

Claire's hands had to be untangled from Lucinda's blood-soaked hair before she could be lifted away from the body to which she clung.

"Let go, Miss Buchanan," urged the dresser whose responsibility it was to make sure the cover singer's costumes were pressed and ready to be worn onstage every night. "We're going to help you up now. There's nothing you can do for Miss Palazzo. You need to come along to your dressing room and let me wash you off."

Someone laid a soldier's scarlet cloak over Lucinda's body, hiding from sight everything but the edges of the pool of blood in which she lay. The stage manager ordered the company out into the audience seats to await the arrival of the police. He instructed the lighting man to turn off all but the dimmest gas work-lights onstage and to do the same with the houselights.

From every corner of the theater, people's eyes were drawn to the scarlet bundle that had been a living woman. No matter how hard they tried to look away, an awful fascination with sudden death drew them back. As the minutes ticked by, the hum of conversation increased.

"I was standing right next to her."

"I heard the sound of the sandbag striking something, but I never thought it would be one of us."

"Did anyone hear a whistle before it fell?"

Inevitably, the mezzo-sopranos in the chorus wondered whether one of them might be chosen to cover the role of Amneris. What had happened to Lucinda Pallazzo was a terrible tragedy, but it would also be someone else's opportunity.

Beatrice Morgan washed Claire Buchanan's hands as gently as she could; the blood had caked around her fingernails and worked its way into the cuticles. She rubbed the cream used to remove heavy stage makeup into the skin, murmuring comforting words as she worked. Then she held a glass of whiskey to Claire's lips, coaxed her to swallow.

"I'm all right now, Beatrice," Claire said.

"Not yet, miss." The dresser wiped the cream from her hands, then immersed them in a basin of warm, soapy water. The front of Claire's gown was saturated with blood, ruined beyond any hope of cleaning. She had to be held on her feet while it was cut off her. Beatrice bundled it into a basket and threw a makeup towel over it. She wrapped her charge in a dressing gown, dried off the now-clean hands, and led her to the couch, where quick naps could be taken on days when rehearsals ran long.

"One more swallow of this whiskey," Beatrice urged.

"The police are here," called out one of the stagehands, opening and closing the dressing-room door.

"We'll stay here together, Miss Buchanan," said Beatrice. "If they want to talk to you, they can just come find you."

Detective Steven Phelan drew the soldier's cape from Lucinda Pallazzo's body and handed it to the uniformed policeman standing behind him. His partner, Detective Pat Corcoran, careful not to get the victim's blood on his shoes, used one of the fake wooden spears to lift the hair from the side of her face.

"Looks simple enough," Corcoran said. "A hundred pounds of sand dropping from that height was more than heavy enough to kill her."

"The stage manager says they hire sailors on shore leave to work the rigging because they're better at it than anyone else."

"Stands to reason." Corcoran summoned another policeman to the stage. "Make sure the sailors up in the flies don't leave. We'll need to talk to them."

"He also says they've never had a fatality in this theater before today." Detective Phelan pointed at the ragged end of the hemp rope attached to the sandbag. "I don't like the looks of that. It's only unraveled on one side. The other side is smooth enough to have been cut."

"You think somebody helped it along?"

"Maybe. I'll know more when we can get one of those sailors to explain what the hell it is they do with these things. Could be they splice the ropes to make adjustments and one of them got careless."

Corcoran stared into the darkness high above the stage. Nothing moved. If anyone was still up there, he was taking pains not to be noticed.

"Keep everyone away from the body until the medical examiner gets here," Phelan instructed the patrolman holding the soldier's bloodstained cape. "There'll be a photographer, too, on Chief Byrnes's orders." They were all getting used to the chief of detectives' new ideas and procedural requirements, but the changes slowed things down at the scene.

"Let's get everybody out of here except the ones who were close to the victim or who actually saw something," Corcoran said. "That's probably no more than a handful of people, and not enough witnesses to do us any good." He moved off toward the steps leading from the stage to where the audience sat.

"Is there anyone else who might have seen something?" Phelan asked the patrolman who had been first on the scene.

"When I got here, there was a woman kneeling next to the victim. Holding her. She had blood all over her dress and her hands. One of the backstage people took her to a dressing room to clean her up. She looked like she needed a doctor, from the shock of what happened."

"Did you get her name?"

"I did." The patrolman took out the notebook in which he had written everything he thought the detectives might need to know. "Here it is. Claire Buchanan. She's what they call a cover singer, which somebody explained to me means she takes the place of one of the main singers if that person gets sick or can't perform for some reason. The dressing rooms are down that winding metal staircase over there, sir."

"Let me know when the medical examiner arrives. I'll be downstairs until then."

The woman sitting on the couch in the closet-sized dressing room stared at Detective Phelan as if she had no idea who he was or what he was doing here. Haunted, he thought, she looked haunted. He'd seen that look before — when an intended victim escaped injury, but an innocent bystander did not.

"I'd like you to tell me everything you can about what happened onstage this afternoon," Phelan began, keeping his voice low and intentionally matter-of-fact. He pulled a chair from in front of the mirrored makeup table, turned it around, and straddled the seat. He smelled liquor, and realized that an older woman held a glass of whiskey. She'd said she was a dresser by the name of Beatrice Morgan.

"A dresser gets the performers ready to go onstage," she'd explained. "I take care of Miss Buchanan and Miss Pallazzo. I have to make sure the principal costumes are ready in case they have to sing those roles, and also the crowd costumes if they're singing in the chorus." She'd held the glass of whiskey out to Miss Buchanan, who'd shaken her head and pushed it away. "I got a couple of swallows into her, Detective. For the shock."

"Miss Buchanan, can you tell me what happened?"

"We were waiting in the wings. Places had been called."

Phelan had to lean forward to hear what she was whispering. When Beatrice pressed the glass of whiskey into his hand, he nodded encouragingly at Miss Buchanan and held it out to her. "Try to get some more of this down, miss," he said.

This time she accepted the glass.

"One big gulp," Phelan said, tilting his wrist to show her what to do.

When she handed him back the glass, it was empty. Her pale skin flushed a healthier rosy hue; memory and reality brought a flood of tears to her eyes.

"We were in the wings," she repeated, "about to take our places. Then the stage manager called 'ten minutes.' There was a lot of chattering and complaining and everyone started moving out onto the stage. We were so crowded in the wings that you couldn't move and it was hard to breathe. A ten-minute wait onstage is better than ten minutes crushed together in the wings. Lucinda and I were standing next to each other. She was about to climb up to the throne where she sits next to Pharaoh as the processional comes in." Claire shuddered. "Then she leaned forward and kissed me on the cheek."

"Was that unusual? She wasn't leaving for the day. She was just going across the stage."

"Lucinda was always impulsive. And affectionate. She was Italian, Detective. They're a demonstrative people."

"So she leaned forward and kissed you on the cheek. What next?"

Beatrice Morgan slipped a knitted shawl around Miss Buchanan's shoulders. The room was stuffy and fetid, but cold with the chill of a basement in winter.

"She looked up. I remember that very distinctly. Then she pushed me. So hard I fell onto the stage." Claire rubbed one knee, ran a hand over an elbow to soothe the bruises blooming there.

"She pushed you deliberately?"

"I'm sure of it. Her hand came out like this," she said, thrusting her arm forward with a sharp snap. "Then she was lying on the stage near me, but crushed under that sandbag, blood flowing all around her head. It was so red, and I couldn't do anything to make it stop." Her hands twisted in her lap, the intertwined fingers kneading each other.

"Who got the sandbag off her?"

"I did, Detective. I shoved as hard as I could, and maybe somebody else helped. I don't remember. But I felt it roll off her body, and when it did, I could see that her back was broken and her head damaged. There was blood in her hair."

"I washed it off Miss Buchanan's hands," contributed Beatrice, "and cut off her dress. It's in the basket over there."

"The patrolman said you were cradling Miss Pallazzo's body when he arrived."

"Was I? Yes. I remember thinking how glad she'd be to know that her face hadn't been injured. Lucinda cared a great deal about her looks." Claire's speech had begun to slur, her eyes to glaze over again.

Whiskey and the strain of telling what she'd seen and done, Phelan thought. She'd turned out to be a better witness than he'd hoped for, but it was time to let her rest. He doubted she'd be able to talk for too much longer.

"I'll take care of her," Beatrice said.

Detective Phelan stood for a moment in the doorway. Claire Buchanan lay stretched out on the narrow couch, covered with the knitted shawl. Her eyes remained open, one hand curled beneath a cheek. She looked like someone who couldn't decide whether to seek oblivion in sleep or fight to stay awake.

Phelan had always pictured opera singers as stout women of a certain age, commanding presences onstage, domineering harridans off. This one was young and slender, rendered fragile and vulnerable by the terrible accident that had taken the life of her friend. It must be a lonely life, he thought, waiting to sing in a great opera house, being disappointed night after night by the robust health and strong lungs of the principal you were covering.

A life in the shadows.

He'd been a copper for a long time. He'd seen a lot and interviewed more witnesses than he could count. But he'd never felt tenderness before now.

"One of the men who carries a fanfare trumpet says he held the instrument above his head to protect it in the crowd and was looking up to make sure it was still all right when he spotted some movement in the flies. He was trying to figure out what it was when he saw the sandbag swing violently from side to side. They're not supposed to do that.

"He knew right away something was wrong, and then the victim, Miss Pallazzo, leaned forward toward Miss Buchanan. He said Miss Pallazzo saw him looking up and he thinks he probably had some kind of horrified expression on his face that made her glance in the same direction. That's when the sandbag fell. He didn't see the victim push Miss Buchanan, but he's positive Miss Buchanan was standing right under where the sandbag struck. It hit Miss Pallazzo across her back when she leaned forward to shove Miss Buchanan out of the way. He said it happened so fast there wasn't time to think about it until afterward." Detective Corcoran closed his notebook and shoved it into a coat pocket. The best kind of case was when there wasn't a case, just an accident.

"Anything else?" Phelan asked.

"The trumpet guy is the only one who saw anything. It's dark up in the flies and nobody else had a reason to look up."

"Did the photographer get here?"

"Right behind you."

"You know what to do, Riis," Detective Phelan greeted the hardworking Dane who was so oddly fixated on capturing images of the city's poor immigrants. "Same as usual. Chief Byrnes wants everything captured exactly as we found it before the medical examiner or anyone else starts poking around."

Jacob Riis busied himself setting up his tripod and camera, readying the flash pan he used to illuminate the scene, checking the supply of glass plates slotted into a wooden carrying case. In Mathew Brady's day so many things could go wrong in the relatively new field of photography that it was a wonder half the exposures taken during the war turned out to be printable. New advances were being touted all the time now, the best being that photographers no longer had to coat their glass plates individually and develop them within ten minutes of exposure. Riis could concentrate on composing the images he wanted to create without the constant interruption of having to disappear into a portable darkroom. He was getting wonderful slices of dark and desperate tenement life with the magnesium flash that made it possible to photograph his subjects in all kinds of light. Even the absence of light.

What Chief of Detectives Byrnes wanted wasn't artistry, though. It was a faithful and permanent record of what men who had to depend solely on the witness of their eyes would never agree on. Memory was an unreliable documentarian.

The magnesium flash exploded softly every time it ignited, spilling out small chemical clouds that had an acrid odor to them. Riis concentrated on the victim's body, the sandbag, and the pool of blood on the stage floor. He took his photographs in tight sequence, following the invisible path along which the human eye would move from one point to another, pausing to verify the details of what it was seeing.

He had one glass plate left when the sound of footsteps climbing the spiral metal staircase from the dressing rooms made him look up.

A woman with a shawl over her shoulders walked slowly from the blackness of the wings out into the half-light of the stage. The woman was bareheaded, her pale blond hair twisted up off her neck, a few soft curls escaping their pins. Her gaze was focused on the body that lay at Jacob's feet; she didn't seem to notice the photographer or his equipment.

"I came upstairs to say good-bye before they take her away," she said to Detective Phelan. The hand she had been holding to her face dropped away.

Jacob Riis's last glass plate slid from his grip and smashed to bits on the stage floor.

The woman standing not three feet from him was the same woman whose dead, painted eyes had stared up at him through his enlarger.

Chapter 6

"I saw your dead woman," Jacob Riis announced. "Very much alive, though I'm told it was a close call."

Out of breath from hauling his camera, tripod, and wooden case of glass plates up two flights of stairs to the offices of Hunter and MacKenzie, he stood in the open doorway of Geoffrey Hunter's office, panting and shaking his head, an indignant Josiah Gregory behind him.

"He stomped right past me," Josiah fumed. "Dumped all his equipment in the corner and invited himself in."

"I got her name from the police detective on the scene." Riis pulled a scrap of paper from his pocket. "Claire Buchanan. She's a cover singer at the Met this season."

"Mr. Riis?" Prudence eased her way past Josiah to the photographer's side. "Has something happened to Miss Buchanan?"

"I think it's time you told me what's going on," Riis answered. "I dropped a glass plate on the stage when she walked out into the light. I was that startled. Your dead woman isn't dead, Miss MacKenzie."

"Josiah, would you brew up some coffee for us, please?" Prudence steered the photographer toward one of the client chairs in front of Geoffrey's desk.

"What was a detective doing at the Met?" Hunter asked. "And why were you there?"

"She's not dead," Riis insisted. "It's the same woman whose photograph you brought me. She's as alive as you are."

"Start at the beginning, Mr. Riis," Prudence coaxed. "Why were you at the Met?"

Jacob Riis looked from the determined young woman to the former Pinkerton and knew the only way he was going to get information was to exchange what he knew for what they were willing to tell him. He'd worked with Chief Byrnes's detectives long enough to recognize a stone wall when he came up against it.

"I was in police headquarters delivering some prints. A call came in from the Met. Detective Phelan and his partner, Corcoran, were on their way out the door when Chief Byrnes came out of his office and yelled for a photographer. I was the only one there, so I said I'd follow along as soon as I picked up some more plates. Which I did."

Riis accepted the cup of coffee Josiah held out to him. He took a large swallow and tried not to grimace. American coffee bore no resemblance to the thick Danish blend flavored with cinnamon, cloves, and spiced rum.

"By the time I arrived, most of the company had been dismissed. They were leaving the building as I got out of the hansom cab, so I found out what had happened before I went inside. It was all any of them wanted to talk about."

"Go on."

"A sandbag fell out of the flies while most of the company were standing on the stage during a rehearsal break. It landed on one of the cover singers and crushed her. I was taking photographs of the body and the area around it when your dead woman walked out of the wings and told Detective Phelan she'd come up from her dressing room to say good-bye. The victim was a friend of hers who saw the sandbag falling and pushed this Miss Buchanan out of the way. She couldn't save herself, there wasn't enough time." Riis took another scrap of paper from one of his jacket pockets. "Lucinda Pallazzo. The back of her skull was split open. I took close-up shots of the damage."

"Was Miss Buchanan hurt?"

"Not as far as I know. She got some bruises from being shoved onto the floor, and she apparently managed to push the sandbag aside. But it was too late. One of the company said she sat holding her friend's bloody body until someone forced her to go back to her dressing room."

"Where is she now?" Prudence asked.

"That's all I know. The medical examiner came while I was finishing up, and I was sent on my way. Detective Phelan wants prints as soon as I can process them. I've got to get back to my darkroom."

Geoffrey Hunter took a roll of cash out of his desk drawer. "One complete set," he said, counting out bills until Riis signaled that was enough.

"Send somebody to pick them up in a couple of hours."

"Josiah?" Geoffrey asked. "Mr. Riis's office is across from police headquarters on Mulberry Street."

"Detective Phelan knows me by sight," the secretary replied. "I'll get word to Danny Dennis. He can send one of the other hansom cab drivers after them. That way there won't be anything to connect us to Mr. Riis." It probably wasn't a crime to buy a set of police photographs, but Chief of Detectives Byrnes had a fierce temper when information leaked to the press or anyone else.

"Now I think you'd better explain how a dead woman can come back to life," Riis said.

"The mother with the painted eyes was Claire Buchanan's twin sister," Prudence said. "She told us that even their parents couldn't always tell them apart."

"I've heard of twins like that." Riis took his watch from his vest pocket, looked at it, and shook his head. "I'm already late. A few more minutes won't make any difference."

"Miss Buchanan is a client."

"I guessed that."

"I want to put you on retainer, Mr. Riis." Geoffrey laid out more bills on his desk. "If you accept, you'll be bound by the same code of confidentiality we are."

Riis didn't hesitate. He needed every extra dollar he could earn to buy the supplies that would allow him to continue photographing the city's tenement dwellers, and Geoffrey Hunter's cash wages were generous. "You've got yourself a deal," he said, reaching across the desk to seal it with a handshake.

"Good."

"Mr. Riis, how many crime scenes have you photographed for the police?" Prudence asked.

"More than I can count or remember," he answered.

"That's what I was hoping you'd say."

"I don't understand." He wasn't sure what she was getting at, and it was more than a little disconcerting to be interrogated by a woman. Detecting was a man's job.

"What I mean is that you've been to so many crime scenes that by now you have to have developed a feel for them. You'd know right away, as soon as you set up your camera, whether what happened was a deliberate killing or an accident."

"I photographed the end of the line that tied the sandbag to one of the steel pipe battens. Detective Phelan thought it looked like part of it had been cut or maybe a splice had come apart."

"Are you sure that's what he said?"

"My flash makes it hard to hear sometimes, so I couldn't swear to the exact words, but it was something like that. And Phelan had me take several shots of the end of the rope. So he's looking for something."

"What else, Mr. Riis? Anything that struck you as odd?"

"With all the dozens of cast members on

that stage, why did the sandbag nearly fall on the only one among them who's had a reason to hire investigative detectives?"

"That's not something you knew until a few minutes ago."

"No, it's not, Miss MacKenzie, but you asked me if I thought anything was odd."

"I meant while you were there. Before Miss Buchanan appeared and broke your concentration."

"Scared me out of a year's growth, you mean. No, I know what you're asking. Let me think for a moment." Riis closed his eyes, lowered his head, and danced a forefinger back and forth across his mustache. He was conjuring up the stage of the Metropolitan Opera House, his photographer's visual memory nearly as accurate as his camera.

"Miss Buchanan looked frightened," he said. "Saddened and shocked by what had happened, but also very frightened. If her friend had not pushed her out of the way, she would have been the one lying broken and dead in a pool of blood on the stage. I saw apprehension, sorrow, even anger on other faces, but not the kind of bone-deep terror emanating from Miss Buchanan."

"Do you think anyone else would describe her as being afraid?"

"Probably not. The body held everyone's

attention, and Miss Buchanan was only onstage for a minute or two. I saw her touch her fingertips to her lips and then to Miss Pallazzo's forehead. She whispered something, but I couldn't hear what it was. Then she went back down to her dressing room again. That's when the medical examiner arrived, and Detective Phelan asked if I'd gotten all the angles. When I said I had, he told me to get him the prints as soon as I could. I left."

"Frightened. Are you sure that's how you'd describe Miss Buchanan?" Geoffrey asked.

"Panicked maybe. The way people get when they're afraid of something, but they don't know what to do to protect themselves."

"Claire Buchanan hired us because she believes her sister and her child were murdered." Geoffrey paused. "Her sister's name was Catherine, the baby was Ingrid."

"The dead mother in the cabinet photograph. The one with the painted eyes."

"Now you're telling us that our client was inches away from what would have seemed her own accidental death. We don't trust coincidences."

Riis nodded his head and looked at his watch again. "If you can get me the negative to that cabinet photograph, we might be able to tell why the whites of the eyes were painted over."

"There's no other way?" Prudence asked.

"I know people think photographers are magicians, but we're not. We're faithful recorders of reality, nothing more. I can't undo retouching that's been made on the print itself without damaging it. It's just not possible if the ink has penetrated the fibers of the paper. But I'm reasonably sure this print was pulled from a retouched glass plate negative, and I think I know how it was done." Riis gulped down the dregs of his coffee and got to his feet. "Just get me that negative," he repeated.

"What he really meant was steal the negative," Prudence said. "I don't suppose there's any other way to get it."

"Let's think this through. We don't want Bartholomew Monroe to realize that someone is interested in the photographs he took of Catherine Sorensen."

"And then retouched."

"Exactly. If he's hiding something, he'll destroy the glass plate negatives."

"Maybe he's already gotten rid of them."

"I don't think so," Geoffrey said. "Photographers keep the originals of every image that passes through their cameras. Riis told me he spends hours in his darkroom printing and reprinting from the same negative until he gets the balance of light and dark just right. He says that's where the artistry comes in. I'd venture to guess that Monroe has hundreds of negatives in his files. He can't bear to part with any of them, just in case he wants to pull a print."

"Then I'll have to ask to go through all of the negatives of my dear cousin Catherine so that I can decide which photographs I want printed in addition to the one I already have," Prudence decided. "Surely, that's not an unusual request. I can't imagine a postmortem photographer not acceding to a grieving relative's wishes."

"We don't want to do anything that will warn Monroe."

"I'll wait until he's left his studio on an assignment. He must have a clerk to see to the gallery, someone to do the mundane chores of keeping up with files and orders and payments."

"I don't think you should go alone," Geoffrey said.

"For what I have in mind, Josiah would be the perfect companion."

Danny Dennis parked his hansom cab on

Broadway, a block south of Bartholomew Monroe's studio. "It might be a long wait," he said into the open hatch below him.

"We're prepared to remain here until he comes out," Josiah replied. This wasn't the first time Miss Prudence had asked for his help on a case. Mr. Hunter had had a few words with him, too, though they were less about the investigation than about keeping the distaff side of the team safe. Miss Prudence would be furious if she knew.

Danny Dennis listened through the hatch as Miss MacKenzie and her secretary rehearsed what they would say and do once they were in the studio. He thought the plan ought to work. He'd keep an eye out for trouble from across the street, but he'd seen the duo in action before; he had no doubt they were more than a match for the photographer's clerk they intended to intimidate.

"Here he comes."

A smart brougham pulled up in front of the studio, its driver jumping down to help a young man in a dark apron carry boxes of photographic equipment from the studio and load them onto the rear luggage rack. Bartholomew Monroe and a woman dressed in black secondary mourning appeared in the doorway.

"Do you know how long they'll be gone?"

Dennis asked.

"There's no way to tell," Prudence answered. "When I called to make an appointment, I was told the photographer wouldn't be available this morning, but I got no other information. If he knew in advance that he would be taking postmortem photographs, then the deceased must have passed away sometime yesterday afternoon or evening. But I have no idea how long the process takes."

"Families schedule time in advance, Miss Prudence," Josiah said, "as soon as the doctor tells them death is imminent. If you want the very best photographer, you have to put him on notice, so to speak. Everything has to happen very quickly once that last breath is taken."

"Wait until Monroe's carriage is well out of sight," Danny Dennis warned. He jumped down from his driver's perch to pick up and pretend to inspect one of Mr. Washington's enormous hooves. "I can still see it, but it looks as though he's about to turn off Broadway." He gave the ugly white horse an affectionate stroke on his bony withers. "I think it's safe now."

"Wish us luck, Mr. Dennis," Prudence said, lowering a mourning veil over her face. "Ready, Josiah?"

" 'Into the valley of Death rode the six hundred!' " Josiah quoted.

"There are only two of you." Danny Dennis was nothing if not pragmatic.

"Lord Tennyson preferred large numbers. They make for a more stirring image."

"You'd better hurry. Miss MacKenzie is halfway across the street already." Danny watched the little man scurry after the late judge's daughter and wondered what that famed jurist would make of his only child's unladylike occupation and odd companion.

He put a feedbag on Mr. Washington and settled down to wait.

CHAPTER 7

The gallery was empty.

"I told you no one in society leaves home before noon," Prudence said. The success of her plan depended on Monroe's absence from the premises and a dearth of casual visitors to the gallery's exhibits.

"You were right, as usual, miss." Josiah shifted the heavy leather satchel from his left hand to his right. Jacob Riis had brought four exposed glass plates to the office, explaining that every photographer had plates that failed to capture or hold a negative image. To conceal their theft, Prudence had to find a way to substitute the blank plates for the ones she would be taking.

"I can understand now why Claire changed her mind about coming into the gallery," Prudence said. "I've never seen anything like this."

Dozens, perhaps hundreds, of photographs hung from floor to ceiling of the gallery walls. They ranged in size from cabinet pictures no larger than the palm of the hand to photographs blown up to the dimensions of a landscape painting. Men, women, and children with only one thing in common: All had been captured shortly after death in black and white or tones of sepia. Here and there a touch of pastel color enhanced cheekbones or heightened the impact of a bank of flowers, but the overwhelming effect was of a host of shadows, lifeless eyes staring out of an army of solemn faces.

"I'd rather not be photographed after I'm dead," Josiah declared. He didn't like the idea of anything being done to him over which he would have no control. "Someone's coming. Are you ready, miss?" He glanced anxiously at his employer, uncertain how much she could see behind the heavy veiling hiding her features.

"Not to worry, Josiah," she murmured. "If everything goes according to plan, we'll be out of here long before Monroe gets back."

The young man hurrying across the gallery in their direction was the same one who had helped load Bartholomew Monroe's photographic equipment into the brougham. He wore black half sleeves to protect his shirt cuffs, a shade over his eyes, and a dark blue canvas apron that covered his clothing from neck to knees.

"I'm sorry to have kept you waiting," he apologized. "We're a bit short staffed at the moment." Suddenly aware that he should not be wearing his eyeshade and stained apron in the gallery, he hastily removed them. "How may I be of assistance?"

"My niece's cousin passed," Josiah said. He did a near-perfect imitation of the late Senator Roscoe Conkling addressing an uncooperative witness. "They were very close as children, almost like sisters."

"My condolences, madam. Sir."

Prudence bowed her head under the weight of her sorrow.

The quality wasn't usually out and about this early in the day, but there was no doubt in the gallery assistant's mind that the lady in mourning and the gentleman who accompanied her were members of society. Only the gentry used that condescending tone of voice to address their inferiors.

Josiah held out the cabinet photograph of Catherine Sorensen and her child. "We require additional copies to be made."

"That shouldn't present a problem." The young man examined the photograph. "Each of our clients is identified by a number, you see, to protect the privacy of the family. Here it is. All I have to do is match the number to our records and you may order as many copies as you wish."

"My niece would also like to see any other negatives you might have."

"Other negatives?"

"We were not able to attend the funeral, but we understand that this cabinet photo was chosen by our late relative's husband and was the only one made available to mourners. We've been informed by a reliable source that there are always other negatives from which to choose. We would like to see those additional negatives."

"Mr. Monroe is not available this morning."

"We are not asking for Mr. Monroe's time. I'm sure his services are in great demand."

"They are."

"But you are his assistant?"

"Assistant and apprentice. He's teaching me the business of photography. I already do most of the developing and printing." He gestured at the heavy canvas apron spotted with chemical spills, which he had draped awkwardly over one arm. "Samuel Payne, at your service, sir."

"And you hope to have a studio of your own someday, Mr. Payne?"

"I do."

"Then I see no difficulty at all. Since Mr. Monroe is not here, it is within the scope of your duties to assist us with our request. So. You will bring out the negatives of my niece's cousin and we will decide which of them we want printed."

"I'm not sure I have the authority to do that. Perhaps if you came back this afternoon or tomorrow, when Mr. Monroe is here."

"That will not be possible," Prudence said, forcing suppressed sobs into her voice. She leaned toward the assistant, the picture of helpless femininity.

"I wish I could help you."

"You can. If you will." Josiah slipped a packet of folded bills from a vest pocket. The bribe was delivered and accepted so quickly, it might not have happened at all.

"If you will seat yourself at that table, miss, I'll find the negatives for you."

Prudence settled herself into the chair Josiah held, quickly draping a fold of her full black skirt over the leather satchel he set beside her.

The box Samuel Payne brought out from the file room contained a dozen glass plates. "What you'll see is the reverse of what appears in the print," he explained, lifting the lid as he placed the heavy box in front of

Prudence. "Light is dark, and dark is light."

He waited for a moment, but the lady seemed to want privacy. She gestured him away, and then the gentleman, who had already paid him so generously, beckoned from across the gallery. Checking over his shoulder to be sure he was no longer needed, Samuel threaded his way through the display boards to Josiah's side. His client was standing in front of a greatly enlarged photograph of an elderly man holding two small dogs in his lap. All three of them were heavily furred and dead.

Prudence took the glass negatives out of their box, one at a time. She had to work quickly, but accurately. The first negative she looked at was taken too far away from the bodies to be useful. Claire lay in her coffin with her infant, Ingrid, cradled in her arm. Eyes closed, they slept forever. The second negative was the one from which the cabinet photograph had been printed. Prudence slipped the glass plate into the leather satchel, eased an exposed blank plate into the file box.

Choosing carefully, she set aside two more negatives. One appeared to be a close-up of baby Ingrid's face, the second a similar photograph of Claire lying in her bed. Prudence knew a moment of panic when she had to decide on the last glass plate. So much depended on the selections she made. There was one other photograph of Claire holding Ingrid, but this time the child lay on what appeared to be a folded blanket or pillow.

Glancing toward the display that seemed to fascinate Josiah, who was holding the clerk captive with one question after another, Prudence made the final substitution. She coughed to signal Josiah that the exchanges had been completed.

"What I don't understand is how it happened that the dogs died at exactly the same time as their master." Josiah turned from the large photograph he had been studying and walked back toward where Prudence sat. "Unless they were helped along, of course. One has heard of such things occurring." He turned for a last look behind him. "It's amazing how much some dogs and their owners resemble one another."

Prudence had been careful to leave the lid off the box containing the glass plate negatives. She wanted the clerk to be certain that all twelve of them were exactly as he had given them to her.

"Were you able to decide on the prints you want to order?" Simon Payne asked, running a finger over the contents of the box. Each plate stood upright in its own wooden frame. He was used to speaking with women dressed in mourning, but he thought this lady's veiling exceptionally opaque. He could barely make out a pale oval behind the black.

"No, I wasn't," Prudence said, her voice not much above a whisper. "I found it more confusing than I thought it would be. I couldn't make out what the photographs were supposed to look like."

"I don't suppose you made up any extras of the cabinet photo we already have?" Josiah asked. "In excess of what was originally ordered? In case your client needed more of them in a hurry?"

"Mr. Monroe does sometimes do that," the clerk said. "I can check the print files, if you like."

"That would be very kind of you. Perhaps all we'll need, after all, is a few more of the same print. What do you think, my dear?"

Prudence nodded her head, choking back a heartbroken sob. "I can't bear to look at those things again," she said, pointing at the open box of glass negatives, her voice thick with unshed tears.

The clerk closed the box and fastened the lid. The bills he had taken were burning a hole in his pocket, but luck might be on his side for a change. He was fairly certain there were extra copies of the cabinet photograph in the files. He remembered Monroe commenting at the time that he was sure the husband had not ordered enough and would be back for more. He'd put the negative box back where it belonged and never say a word about having shown it to a customer. Fortunately, the lady was wearing gloves. If Monroe did make more prints, there wouldn't be any finger smudges on the glass surfaces.

The photographer was a strange bird, a master at what he did, but difficult to please. Samuel Payne was counting the days until he could leave and set up on his own. Humming under his breath, he patted the pocket where the unexpected bounty of more than two weeks' wages nestled.

"If you do have additional copies, we'll take five of them with us." Josiah assisted his grieving niece to her feet, adroitly retrieving the leather satchel hidden beneath her skirts.

"I'll wrap them for you," Samuel Payne offered, scurrying through the curtained doorway at the rear of the gallery.

"Did you get them?" Josiah whispered.

"The one Riis wanted, and three others. Two of the plates are close-ups of their faces, I think. It's hard to tell what you're looking at when everything is in reverse."

"He's coming back," Josiah warned.

Prudence swayed just enough to suggest emotional distress.

"Here we are." The package was neatly tied with string, a large loop left for carrying. "If you'll give me a moment, I'll write you up a receipt."

"We have a cab waiting," Josiah said. He pressed several bills into the clerk's hand. "A receipt isn't necessary, but there is one other request I would make." He hesitated, as if uncertain whether to trust the clerk with personal information. "We are not on close familial terms with the deceased's husband. I'd rather no one knew we had obtained additional copies of the memoriam photograph. He was deliberately parsimonious with them. I'm sure you've experienced situations like that before."

"You have my promise, sir," Samuel Payne assured them, one stained finger laid alongside his nose to seal the bargain. Josiah repressed a shudder.

Bartholomew Monroe's accommodating clerk ushered them toward the door and assisted them into the hansom cab pulled up to the curb before hurrying back inside. The last Prudence and Josiah saw of him he was carrying the heavy box of glass negatives through the curtained archway at the rear of the gallery.

"We got them, Geoffrey," Prudence announced, taking off the heavy mourning veil that hung to her knees. "Danny Dennis is sending one of his friends to deliver the plates to Mr. Riis. He says Mr. Washington is too easily recognized if we want to keep our connection to him quiet. There isn't a reporter in the city who doesn't know that horse by sight."

"Congratulations to both of you. Was it dicey?" Geoffrey knew that Josiah was that kind of rare bird who thrilled to adventure while presenting himself as the most cautious of men. Prudence might not want to admit they'd encountered any danger, but their secretary thrived on sharing tales of dangerous exploits.

"Not at all, sir," Josiah said. He sounded disappointed. "We had the whole operation too well-planned for anything to go wrong. Danny kept watch outside in case Monroe came back early. But he didn't."

"Were you able to talk to Claire?" Prudence asked.

"I was. She's convinced the sandbag was deliberately aimed at her." Geoffrey had spent most of the morning at the Met. He had the gift of being able to make himself welcome wherever he chose to go.

"If that's true, whoever cut the rope had to have been hiding in the flies until exactly the right moment. It seems a chancy way to commit murder."

"I talked to the stage manager, too. He says it's the first time he can recall anything like that happening. They use sailors on shore leave to work the sandbags because they're good with knots and they're used to heights. He said they scramble around up there like monkeys, yet none of the men working yesterday admitted to seeing anyone who shouldn't have been there."

"Is Claire covering tonight?"

"Not until Monday, when it's *Aïda* again. There's another rehearsal this afternoon. It's probably started by now."

"I'm surprised the management didn't give them a day or two to recover."

"She said it doesn't work like that in opera or the theater. You perform or rehearse no matter what. I got the impression it was a point of pride as much as anything else."

"Theater people and opera singers aren't like the rest of us, Miss Prudence," Josiah said.

"I told her we could arrange for protection if she wants it," Geoffrey said.

"A bodyguard?"

"Nobody could get by the man I'm thinking of."

"What did she say?"

"That she'd consider it."

"I thought she was frightened."

"She is. But something else is going on. If I had to place a bet on what she's planning, I'd say she has the crazy idea that if she lets herself be seen as vulnerable, whoever wants to do away with her will try again. And somehow that will allow her to avenge her sister."

"That's ridiculous," Josiah remarked. He still had nightmares about being trapped under the Central Park Carousel with a murderer.

"She's armed," Geoffrey said. "She carries a small gun with her whenever she travels alone, and she claims to be a good shot."

"Hire the bodyguard," Prudence said. "If he's as good as you say he is, she doesn't have to know he's watching her. Do we have yesterday's prints of the Met from Mr. Riis yet?"

Geoffrey handed her a large envelope stiffened with sheets of cardboard. "One of Danny's cohorts was waiting outside as I came in."

Prudence slit the envelope with Josiah's silver letter opener. The first print she extracted was of the back of Lucinda Palazzo's head, the frayed and cut end of the sandbag's hemp rope lying just beyond the pool of blood. She laid the photographs on Josiah's desk, one by one, each more graphic and disturbing than the last.

"I don't think there can be any doubt about it," she said when the last photograph had joined the others. "This was murder. Someone tried to kill our client."

CHAPTER 8

"I haven't slept," Claire Buchanan said. "All I've done is think."

"That's why we're here," Geoffrey told her, "to do some of the thinking for you."

"I must look terrible." She raised both hands to the masses of pale hair coiled atop her head, patting stray tendrils into place, pushing loose pins back into the curls they were meant to control. Unlike most blondes her deep green eyes were accentuated by dark lashes. The fair skin beneath them looked bruised.

The *Aïda* rehearsal was over, its exhausted cast ending a long day in their dressing rooms, Lucinda Pallazzo's death yesterday on the stage they had just vacated still preying on their minds. Assistants to the stage manager knocked on doors and shouted their message along dark, narrow corridors. "No rehearsal call tomorrow. Lockup in thirty."

"What does that mean?" Prudence asked. She'd never been in a theatrical dressing room before. The smell of greasepaint and sweat-stained costumes was heady, the noise and bustle of hurrying feet enervating, and the close quarters of the small room Claire had shared with the dead woman claustrophobic.

"There won't be another rehearsal of *Aïda* tomorrow and everyone needs to be out of the theater in thirty minutes or risk being locked in," Claire explained. She squeezed the juice of half a lemon into a cup of hot water, added two teaspoons of honey and a dollop of brandy. "For the throat," she said. "The lemon cleanses, the honey soothes, and the brandy relaxes the muscles. Every singer has a favorite remedy. This one is mine."

"Were you singing this afternoon?" Geoffrey asked.

"Just the cue bars," she said, "some of them over and over again. It was a very ragged rehearsal. Every time I looked down at the stage floor, I remembered Lucinda lying there in a pool of her own blood. I wasn't the only one."

"The memory will fade," Prudence promised. "I know it seems impossible now, but I can tell you from my own experience that the horrors we manage to live through gradually lose their power. If you're lucky, one day you wake up and what was bedeviling you is gone."

"I'm going to choose to believe you," Claire said, sipping her concoction of watered lemon juice, honey, and brandy. "I apologize for not wanting to see you last night. It was rude and unforgivable, but after I answered that detective's questions, I couldn't bear to talk anymore about what happened to Lucinda."

"Steven Phelan is very thorough."

"You know him?"

"He's a bulldog detective," Geoffrey said, avoiding a direct answer to the question. "Once Phelan sinks his teeth into a case, he doesn't let go until he solves it. Or the chief of detectives calls him off."

"I didn't mean he was discourteous or offensive. He wasn't," Claire said. "But Lucinda and I talked about Catherine before we went onstage. I kept thinking there had to be a connection." She shuddered, one fist pressed against her lips to still their trembling.

"Did you tell Detective Phelan that?"

"No. I thought it sounded melodramatic, as if I were trying to push myself into the center of attention. I'm not, I promise you.

But I couldn't shake the feeling that the sandbag was meant for me. Does that make any sense?"

Geoffrey nodded. "What did Miss Pallazzo have to say about your sister?"

"She told me that Catherine was planning a return to the opera stage. I had no idea."

"The impression Miss MacKenzie and I got was that your sister abandoned any thought of a career after she married."

"Sorensen insisted. She withdrew from all contact with other performers, some of whom had been friends for years. Her husband feared they might influence her. Catherine didn't say as much — she was loyal to him. But I know that was the case."

"What made Miss Pallazzo so sure your sister intended to sing again?"

"Catherine was taking vocal lessons from a diva who retired from the Met some years ago. A friend of Lucinda's saw my sister outside Madame Strauss's apartment. Catherine begged her not to tell anyone. The friend only broke her promise when she knew I would be coming to New York and she would be leaving for San Francisco. She thought I should know, even though Catherine was dead. She trusted Lucinda to tell me."

"Is this Madame Strauss still in New

York?" Geoffrey asked.

"Lucinda said she returned to Europe perhaps half a year ago. And I didn't think to ask for the friend's name. That was stupid of me."

"You couldn't have known what was about to happen."

Claire squared her shoulders, raised her head, and looked challengingly at Geoffrey. "Mr. Hunter, the sandbag wasn't meant to fall on Lucinda. It was aimed at me."

"Convince me of that, Miss Buchanan."

"Lucinda wasn't a threat to anyone. She was a contralto, so the number of roles she could sing or cover was limited. Most of the major roles for women are written for a higher range."

"You're saying that jealousy would not be a motive to kill Miss Pallazzo, but it might be a reason to want to injure you?"

"You saw the *Times* review."

"The scenery and the costumes made a more favorable impression on the reviewer than the performance."

"I could feel it all around me as soon as I arrived backstage yesterday. There was a buzz of gossip and excitement that usually only happens on opening night. This time there was talk in the company that Frau Schröder-Hanfstängl had taken to her bed and might not perform next Monday. Do you know what that means to a cover singer? It's a dream come true, maybe the only chance you'll ever have to make your mark in the opera world. It's everything, Mr. Hunter, everything."

"You're saying that someone wanted to guarantee you wouldn't be able to sing, no matter what Frau Schröder-Hanfstängl's circumstances."

Claire nodded.

"I understand what happens if a singer can't perform because of illness, but are there other circumstances when a cover might substitute?" Prudence asked. "Someone other than the performer herself who decides she won't go on?"

"Anton Seidl is our conductor. He's also the final authority for any decisions made this season." Claire shook her head. "I won't name names and I won't make accusations I can't prove," she said.

"Have you ever known malicious mischief to be done that would prevent a singer from performing? In all of the companies of which you've been a member, has that kind of thing ever happened?"

She laughed. "Everything from deliberately tainted chocolates to loose heels that break off and make someone stumble. Itching powder in a costume, alcohol in a water glass, cues that are never given. If you can imagine it, Mr. Hunter, someone has tried it."

"But murder, Miss Buchanan? Murder is carrying jealousy and ambition to an extreme."

"That's what every opera is about. Jealousy, revenge, murder. I was terrified last night. My first thought was that what happened to Lucinda was somehow tied to Catherine, that someone found out I had hired you to investigate the truth of her death. But I've had time to think it through, and I don't believe I'm in any danger now. That's why I temporized when you suggested a bodyguard. Whoever let loose the sandbag won't try again. He or she meant to frighten me into breaking my contract so someone else could take my place if Frau Schröder-Hanfstängl can't or won't go on. Murder was never the intention. This has nothing to do with my sister. The timing is pure coincidence."

Geoffrey didn't agree with her, but he hadn't any proof to contradict the argument she was making.

They were too late to catch the last breath, despite having expected the death for more than a week.

"She passed away toward dawn, we think." Pauline Anderson's daughter-in-law had already seen to the external signs of mourning. A black-ribboned wreath hung on the front door of the house, all of the mirrors had been covered, and the servants wore black armbands over their uniforms. She was loath to admit that the family had gone to bed as usual the night before and the maid charged with sitting at the elder Mrs. Anderson's bedside had fallen asleep in her chair.

"You have our deepest condolences." Bartholomew Monroe handed his heaviest cases to a footman, who would carry them up to the deceased woman's bedroom. "May I present my sister, Miss Felicia Monroe? She will be assisting me."

"Then you won't need my presence?" Thalia Anderson had been determined not to shirk her duty, but now that a woman accompanied the photographer, the proprieties would be observed without her having to remain in the room. Mother Anderson had withered during her final illness, and though the housekeeper had done most of the actual washing of the body this morning, Thalia had assisted with dressing her husband's late mother in the gown and widow's lace cap in which she would be buried. She had averted her eyes as frequently as possible from wrinkled, sagging flesh that was already acquiring the odor of decay; it hadn't been a pleasant task.

"Do you have a preference for how Mrs. Anderson will be posed?" Monroe asked.

"My husband would like his mother to be seated in her favorite chair, with an open book on her lap. She was a great one for reading. It was a terrible burden to her when her eyes gave out."

"Of course. We like to remember our loved ones as they once were, and that includes treasured pastimes."

"The wedding photograph that was taken of my husband's parents no longer exists, so this will be the only memento we have."

"I understand."

The house was large and expensively furnished. Dark ancestral oils hung from the walls and Turkish carpets covered the floors. Every corner had its plant, Oriental vase, or Greek bust. The staircase leading to the second floor curved gracefully upward from the marble-tiled foyer, an elaborately carved banister gleaming with polish. All of the drapes had been drawn in deference to the death; gas lamps illuminated the upstairs hallway.

"I'll leave you here," Thalia Anderson said, opening the door to her mother-in-law's bedroom.

An older woman dressed in black with a housekeeper's chatelaine around her waist rose from the chair where she had been keeping watch beside the body. She passed them with a nod of acknowledgment, joining the younger Mrs. Anderson in the corridor. Felicia Monroe closed the door, then listened as two sets of footsteps moved away and descended the staircase.

The room was cold. Both windows had been opened six inches from the bottom sash; the damp chill of late February penetrated into every corner.

Bartholomew Monroe closed the windows and turned on the gas fire in the grate. The body would stiffen faster in the heat, but they'd work quickly. No sense catching pneumonia when they'd already missed the most important moment of the passing. No photographer had yet managed to capture that precious exhalation of soul everyone knew had to be there; the few claimants to that discovery had proved to be charlatans.

Pauline Anderson's favorite chair stood before the fireplace, an embroidered ottoman nearby for toasting cold feet. The book she was to hold lay atop a crocheted shawl.

Felicia took a small hand mirror from one of the cases and held it close to the dead woman's mouth, watching carefully for any clouding of the reflection. She had been surprised and frightened the first time a corpse breathed. Bartholomew had solved the problem without any fuss, though the photograph he took at that moment showed no sign of a soul escaping in a cloud of transparent plasma. A great disappointment, but the deceased had been so freshly gone that the rest of the photographs almost made up for it. The result had been one of Bartholomew's most lifelike set of cabinet photos, a great comfort to the family and the first of the enlarged images to be hung in a gallery now famous throughout the city.

"We'll leave the chair where it is," he said, standing back with hands cupped around his eyes to imitate the shutter's field of view. "Just turn it around a bit to catch more of the light from the window. Good, that's it. And we'll position a drape behind to remove the distraction of the rest of the room. It will look as though she's come into the studio for a live portrait."

"What about the eyes?"

"In this case, since she's supposed to be reading, we'll leave the lids alone and tilt the head downward and to the side a bit.

Taken slightly from above, the face will look less wrinkled, and therefore a bit younger. If necessary, we can retouch later, but I think that will do nicely."

Mrs. Anderson, a small woman in life, was birdlike in death. Bartholomew Monroe gathered her into his arms and settled her into the chair in which she had spent many comfortable hours. "She's gone off a bit," he remarked, taking a camphorated sweet wrapped in a twist of paper from a snuffbox he carried in his vest pocket. The strong odor of the camphor quickly spread throughout the small bedroom.

Felicia crunched a sugary camphor ball between her teeth, taking a deep breath as the fumes spread into her nostrils and down the back of her throat. Then she bent over Pauline Anderson, arranging the folds of her gown, smoothing the long sleeves over her shriveled hands, propping the book where it would lie open in the dead woman's lap, exactly as if she were so absorbed by its pages that she hadn't noticed a photographer capturing her likeness.

"I think a bit of liquid powder will help, and perhaps some Rowland's Macassar Oil on the lips." Felicia busied herself applying a thin coating of face powder mixed with alcohol over Mrs. Anderson's age-splotched skin, shining her lips with the same product men used to slick down their hair. Nothing else looked as natural, gave quite the right sheen. She combed a few stray wisps of hair into place and settled the lace cap to hide the near baldness of the skull. The last touch was a pair of jet earrings left on the dresser to be screwed into Pauline Anderson's ears.

"She's ready," Felicia announced, standing back to view her creation.

"The family will be very happy with this," Bartholomew said. He disappeared under the black cloth draping both him and his camera, muttering to himself as he inserted the glass slide, composed the shot he meant to take, focused, and calculated the exposure time. Every detail of the scene before him would be captured in startling clarity. He was an artist who would take as much time perfecting the final print as he had the design of its negative.

For the five minutes he deemed necessary to obtain a perfect representation of reality, neither of the Monroes moved or spoke. Felicia had long ago decided that during the slow process of securing a life image on glass, her brother was akin to a priest performing the miracle of transubstantiation. Or perhaps a shaman entering the trance state of divination. Whatever or whoever he became, the transformation never failed to mesmerize her.

"Will you take other shots?" she asked when he had packed three glass plates into their holding cases.

"I don't see any point to it."

Occasionally, if the deceased was unusually beautiful or ugly, he took extra photographs for the private collection over which he pored for hours, looking for a clue to the mysterious chasm separating life from death. But this face was old and ordinary. It didn't matter whether she might have been lovely in her youth; Bartholomew was only interested in seizing a likeness of what he believed escaped into empty air at the moment of passing. It would be a ghostlike image, a cloud of swirling vapor, with perhaps at its center a light like the flame of a candle. The departure of a soul was reputed to happen in an instant, but no one knew for certain. No one had been able to prove he'd seen it happen. That's where the promise of photography came in.

Monroe lifted Mrs. Anderson from her reading chair and laid her on the bed. Felicia folded the hands and straightened the lace widow's cap again, removed the shawl and placed it with the book at the foot of the bed. "She's stiffening," she reported, slapping gently on the corpse's cheeks to shape the lips into what would pass for the smile of a Christian woman gone happily to meet her Maker.

"We're finished." He turned off the gas and opened the windows again. Some of the camphor smell drifted out of the room, replaced by the familiar odor of ripe horse dung piled against the curb.

When they had repacked all of the equipment into the boxes, the Monroes left Pauline Anderson in peace. The same footman who had carried the cases upstairs was summoned to bring them down again.

"My mother-in-law will be viewed in the parlor tomorrow," Mrs. Anderson said as she showed them out. "Will you be able to supply *cartes de visite* and cabinet photographs by then?"

"You shall have them tomorrow morning," promised Bartholomew. "I'll have my clerk deliver them."

"I think fifty of the *cartes de visite* for friends and acquaintances and a dozen cabinet photographs for family," Mrs. Anderson decided. "If my husband should want more, we'll send word to you."

"Once again, our deepest condolences." Bartholomew bent over her hand, but did not brush it with his lips.

As the door to the Anderson mansion closed behind them, the Monroes saw a mortuary wagon turn into the alleyway. The coffin had arrived.

Chapter 9

The first thing Jacob Riis did after the package arrived was lock the door. Reporters were a curious and talkative bunch, in and out of each other's offices all day chasing rumors, racing up and down the stairs to find a story, place a bet, or haul in buckets of beer. The story Hunter and MacKenzie were paying Riis to follow might turn out to be nothing, but he wasn't about to take any chances. He'd have to keep his mouth shut and his typewriter silent until Geoffrey Hunter gave him the okay, but if what their client suspected proved to be true, Riis would be the first to break the news. New Yorkers loved to read about spouses killing one another.

He unwrapped the glass negatives and slid them out of their protective wooden frames. You could tell a lot from a preliminary inspection, but you had to know what to look for.

Miss MacKenzie had done a good job. Four glass plates stolen and four exposed blanks substituted. Riis had had to lay odds that he and Monroe were using plates from the same photographic supplier, but since most of the photographers in New York City did business there, the risk had paid off.

Every busy photographer had unprintable negatives in his files, and most of them would have sworn that the negatives had been properly developed and handled and were perfectly fine when they were put away. Since no artist wanted to blame himself for failure, it had to be the fault of the company producing the new dry plates that had made their lives so much easier. With every technological advance, they reasoned, there had to be a period of trial and error. He hoped Bartholomew Monroe subscribed to that theory.

Only one of the glass negatives Prudence MacKenzie had taken bore unmistakable evidence of retouching, the one from which the cabinet photograph had been printed. Examined under the strongest light Riis could manage in his cramped office, it became obvious how the negative had been altered. It was a commonly used method that was both cheap and durable. Varnish was brushed over the glass, sometimes several coats, both to preserve the negative and to provide a surface on which the changes could be made. Facial wrinkles were smoothed out, unwanted backgrounds disappeared, sometimes a pet was added. Anything the photographer could dream up that he or the artist he hired could draw, paint, or etch into the fixative.

If the coat of varnish was thick enough, it was possible to scrape away at it with delicate persistence until tiny flakes danced off the glass. The trick was not to harm the original negative. Before he set to work on the plate, Riis pulled several prints, ensuring that he would have an accurate record of what the negative produced prior to whatever changes he effected. The enlargements he printed were clear, the contrast between light and dark more heightened than in the cabinet photograph Claire had given Geoffrey Hunter. Whoever had painted the whites of Catherine and Ingrid Sorensen's eyes had used the finest of tiny brushes; it was almost impossible to detect the hairlike strokes.

Riis used an ebony-handled medical scalpel to scratch gently at the varnish over Catherine Sorensen's eyes. He didn't dare apply heat, but he breathed moisture onto the surface of the plate as he moved the sharp blade back and forth, barely grazing the varnish with each pass. Infinitesimal bits loosened themselves and were sloughed off. Slowly, slowly, until finally he thought he had entirely cleared the whites of the subject's eyes.

His back ached from bending over; the fingers holding the scalpel had cramped. He stood for a moment stretching and rubbing his hands together, then hurried into the darkroom.

When he came out for the last time, holding one wet print by a corner, Riis was more puzzled than pleased. Four other prints hung on the drying line, each one developed with varying degrees of contrast. He could pull as many as he wanted from that single negative, could change the ratio between light and dark, do away entirely with shadows, but nothing would change the basic fact that there didn't appear to be any reason for the photographer to have painted over the whites of Catherine Sorensen's eyes.

Unless Riis was so tired that he had missed it.

He laid the print on a sheet of absorbent white paper, then went to the minuscule gas stove, where he brewed coffee to keep himself awake when he photographed the tenements at night. He had been so sure he would find spider threads of petechiae in the dead woman's eyes that despite the evidence of his own work, he was having a hard time believing they weren't there. He took off his glasses and rubbed his face. Lit the gas burner beneath the pot of coffee he had boiled several hours ago, and drank a cup of the vile-tasting liquid as quickly as he could without burning his mouth. He was missing something. He knew he was. He would start over, and this time he would find what he knew had to be there.

The print he had laid on the white paper was still damp. He put another sheet of paper on top of it and pressed lightly but firmly. He was about to go back to the darkroom when he glanced at the enlarger where he, Miss MacKenzie, and Mr. Hunter had studied the cabinet photo. He hadn't seen petechiae with his naked eye or with the magnifying glass he kept near his developing tanks, but this new enlarger he had bought with the money he made freelancing had one of the most powerful lenses you could obtain. It couldn't imagine something that wasn't there, the way the human brain could. If there was even a single burst capillary in one of Catherine Sorensen's eyes, the lens would find it. It made a human hair look like a thick shaft of Oriental bamboo.

At first, Riis saw nothing but faint traces of the varnish he had scraped off, but as he turned the focus knob, it was as if he were plunging past what lay on the surface, through the glass onto the eye itself. And there they were. Not like a web, as he had pictured them, but a spray of infinitesimally small red pinpoints. He had looked right past them, searching so intently for the kind of damage he had seen in the violent deaths he had photographed for the police that he had not allowed for what might happen in a slower, more gentle murder. If there were such a thing.

Now that he knew what to hunt for, he could locate the petechiae easily; the evidence of strangulation or suffocation was too plain to be anything else.

Riis took the other three glass negatives into the darkroom, confident he was about to provide the keys that would unlock the mystery of how Claire Buchanan's sister and niece had died.

By Monday, when he took them to the Hunter and MacKenzie office, Riis had made five prints of each of the four glass negatives Prudence had filched from Bartholomew Monroe's studio. From past experience dealing with police detectives, he knew how often a photograph was defaced by notations scrawled across its surface with grease pencils. Arrows, circles, and exclamation points were their favorite symbols. He assumed that Geoffrey Hunter's background as a Pinkerton would have taught him the same destructive habits.

"Let's start with the cabinet photograph." Riis laid the copies on the Hunter and MacKenzie conference table. Josiah Gregory, notebook and sharpened pencil in hand, joined them.

"What you're looking for are almost microscopically small dots on the surface of the eyes," he explained. "I'm going on the assumption that a pillow was used to suffocate them, that the baby was too recently born to struggle and the mother too weak from childbirth to be able to fend off her killer."

"We don't have any proof of that," Geoffrey said, always pragmatic and skeptical.

"That's what I think I can give you," Riis replied. "If not proof that will stand up in court, at least enough substantiation of what Miss Buchanan claims to justify continuing with the case."

"That's all we need at this point," Prudence said. Whether they had two cases or one was a point of contention she and Geoffrey hadn't yet resolved. Their client was convinced that Lucinda Pallazzo's death was entirely separate from whatever had happened to her sister. Geoffrey argued that murderers often committed multiple crimes to conceal their first killing.

"The retouching was done by painting over a layer of varnish that protected the glass plate negative. It's something photographers do all the time. When chemical baths were less stable than they are now, varnish was a way of protecting the negative from deterioration," Riis explained. "What I did was scale off the coating very carefully until I got down to the glass surface. Then I reprinted. The photographs you're holding now are the result."

With the magnifying glass Josiah Gregory provided, Prudence studied the prints, searching determinedly for the tiny pinpoints of broken capillaries Riis claimed to have found.

"Geoffrey, take a look at this and tell me your opinion," she said, handing him her magnifying glass and the photograph she had been examining. "I think I see what Mr. Riis described, but I have another concern. Is the *Compton's Medical Guide* still in your office?"

"In the bookcase behind my desk."

"This is what I thought I remembered," Prudence said, a forefinger keeping her place in the medical book she brought back from Geoffrey's office. She opened it on the table and tapped the pertinent page with an impatient fingernail. "I looked up *petechiae* after Mr. Riis told us about them and showed us the police photographs. They can occur anywhere on the skin or inside the mouth or nose, as well as in the eyes, whenever there's pressure on the capillaries. The author specifically cites the great strain associated with birthing a child. So if a labor is long or difficult, it's very likely the mother will experience the kind of damage associated with great effort or even violence. That's one of the reasons some new mothers are reluctant to see anyone but family members. The petechiae can look like one of those terrible rashes one associates with poison ivy."

"So even after our foray into that ghoulish gallery, we still can't prove anything?" Josiah asked.

"What Miss MacKenzie says about the mother is true," Riis said, "but it's not an explanation of why a newborn would have damaged eyes."

He took a second sheaf of photographs

out of his satchel and handed them around.

"This is baby Ingrid," Prudence breathed. "I had trouble making anything out when I looked at the glass negative, but I could tell that the eyes were open and it was the only plate that seemed to contain a close-up view of her face. Poor baby. Hardly arrived before she was taken away."

Catherine Sorensen's child was lying in the crook of her mother's arm. The photographer had leaned in as close as he could; there seemed to be traces of some sort of salve in a few places around her eyes. Which were wide open.

"What you're seeing on her skin is spirit gum. He's put a tiny drop on her eyelid, then pressed it against her skin to hold it open for the length of the exposure. Which, since he used a dry plate negative, was probably not that long. The spirit gum is taken off with alcohol or grease, and if you use it very sparingly, it's not difficult to remove. Actors hate it because they say it burns the skin, but they all use it to attach false mustaches and beards."

"I can see the petechiae in her eyes," Prudence said. "Even without a magnifying glass."

Riis handed around close-ups of Catherine Sorensen, and then the last set of pictures.

In these, Catherine and her baby lay together atop rumpled sheets, as though the photographer had turned back for one last picture before putting away his camera and setting the room and the bodies to rights again. The infant had been placed atop an embroidered pillow that seemed too big to fit comfortably within the mother's arm. "You could argue that what you see in the mother's eyes is from natural causes, but you can't say the same for her child. If you look closely at them, the petechiae are so alike that they appear to have been caused by the same type of pressure. As I said before, I think someone held a pillow over their faces until they stopped breathing."

In the thunderous silence that followed Jacob Riis's accusation, no one heard the outer office door open.

"I came to see if you had discovered anything yet." Claire Buchanan stared at the photographs scattered on the conference room table.

Before anyone could stop her, she was holding a close-up of her dead sister's face in her gloved hand.

CHAPTER 10

The only other time Jacob Riis had seen Claire Buchanan was on the stage of the Metropolitan Opera when she stepped out of the dark wings and walked toward the body of Lucinda Pallazzo. His last glass plate negative had slipped from his fingers then; today he dropped one of the post-mortem prints of Catherine Sorensen.

"Where did you get these?" Claire asked. Her eyes skipped from photograph to photograph.

"We went to Bartholomew Monroe's gallery," Prudence answered. She started to gather up the prints, but when she glanced at Geoffrey, he shook his head.

"He gave them to you?"

"We stole the glass negatives," Josiah said proudly.

Claire nodded, then turned to speak directly to Jacob Riis. "I saw you at the Met. You're the police photographer." She gestured toward the brown envelope containing the prints he had made of Lucinda's death scene. Enough of one photograph could be seen to identify what it was.

"Riis also works for us when we need him," Geoffrey explained. "He knows we're investigating Catherine's death. And why."

Riis had been thumbing through the photographs in the brown envelope. Now he chose one and placed it in the center of the table. The end of the hemp rope tied to the sandbag had been circled with a grease pencil, and an exclamation point added in case there was any doubt about what was being scrutinized. Half of the rope end looked as though it had ripped and shredded itself free; the other half was neatly cut.

"This is what caught Detective Phelan's attention." Riis placed additional copies of the print on the table.

"Lucinda's death was a warning gone terribly wrong," Claire said. "Someone believed I was a threat to the principal soprano or to another cover singer's career. The sandbag was meant to frighten me out of the company. But as I told Miss MacKenzie and Mr. Hunter, I don't think it has anything to do with Catherine's murder. I believe Aaron Sorensen killed my sister and her child. For his own reasons, one of which must certainly be the fortune she inherited."

"Have you met with the attorney who drew up your will?" Prudence asked.

"I went straight from your offices to his. Aaron Sorensen no longer profits from my death."

"Does he know that?" asked Geoffrey.

"The attorney is sending him a letter to the effect that a new will is in existence that does not name him as a beneficiary. He said it was a very unusual thing to do, but I insisted. In the end he agreed." Claire took off her gloves before picking up her sister's photograph again. "I have a care for my own safety, Mr. Hunter. I've looked out for myself since the first time I was given a company contract."

"Mr. Riis, what is this shadow on the baby's nose?" Josiah Gregory brushed furiously at a print atop which he'd momentarily laid his stenographer's notebook and pencil. "I thought the pencil had rubbed against it, but now I'm not so sure." He passed the photograph down the table.

Riis laid two prints of the same photograph side by side, then reached for the other three. When he had them lined up, he used the magnifying glass to study each in turn. "It wasn't your pencil, Mr. Gregory," he said. "And it isn't a shadow, either. The photographer held the flash gun directly over the subject. There are no shadows anywhere in the picture."

"But there is definitely some sort of darkening there," Josiah insisted. "You can see it more clearly in some prints than in others."

"I varied the contrast deliberately," Riis said. "It's easy to fool the human eye."

"He held the pillow too tightly over the baby's nose, perhaps afraid the child would wake up and cry out," Geoffrey said. "I'm sorry, Claire, but that's how it could have happened. That's how this bruising might have occurred."

Claire's horrified gasp reminded all of them that what they regarded as a fascinating and challenging puzzle would continue to haunt her dreams and nightmares well after all of the facts were known. Even now her brain was conjuring up horrific images brought to life by Geoffrey's assertion of how Catherine and Ingrid's deaths had been managed.

Prudence had been turning pages in *Compton's Medical Guide.* Now she began reading aloud from an entry on the appearance of newborn babies: " 'The nose may appear flattened, but this will usually resolve itself within one to two weeks. In addition, the whites of the eyes may be yellowed or display what seem to be small pinpricks of blood. The jaundice will dissipate more quickly than the blood spots, which may remain for as long as three weeks.' " She looked across the table at the dismay written on Claire Buchanan's drawn face. "Everything we've taken as an indication of foul play can be explained away as a normal occurrence in the newborn child."

"There has to be a logical reason why Monroe retouched the cabinet photograph the way he did," Geoffrey said. "Either he was instructed to do so by Aaron Sorensen, who ordered the prints made, or he did it for his own reasons, without Sorensen's knowledge. From what we've seen here, it really wasn't necessary. Even Mr. Riis had to search to find the petechiae. The naked eye or the casual glance doesn't see them. Miss Buchanan?"

"I didn't notice them. I couldn't even have told you that the photograph had been retouched."

"Mr. Riis, put yourself into Bartholomew Monroe's place," Prudence urged. "Imagine that you've been called to the Sorensen home. What do you find? What do you do?"

"The negative plates were numbered, Miss MacKenzie." Riis arranged the four photographs in the order in which they were taken. "If all of the dozen plates in the box you saw were exposed, we're missing eight of them, but I think I can reconstruct what happened from the four we do have."

Josiah's pencil scratched across the page of his stenographer's pad. No one else in the room moved.

"All right. Strange as it might seem, the cabinet photo was the first one taken. Monroe must have been anxious to pose the bodies while they were still flexible." Riis glanced at Claire Buchanan. Her hands were clenched, the fingers a bloodless white, but she looked back at him with an urgency that told him she would neither faint nor cry out, no matter what he said.

"His sister is his assistant. She's especially useful when the deceased is a woman or a female child. So I would say that the two of them followed someone's instructions about how the bodies were to be posed. Mrs. Sorensen and her daughter had probably already been washed and dressed for the viewing that was to follow. They lay on the bed together or perhaps the child had been placed in her cradle. Monroe has done this so many times that it would have taken no more than a few minutes to place the mother in the rocking chair and arrange the baby in her arms. The eyes would have been closed by whoever had tended to them, but Monroe was able to open them and keep them from closing while he took the cabinet photograph. Either rigor had not begun to set in or he used an infinitesimal and therefore undetectable amount of spirit gum.

"We're missing four photographs, according to the numbering system, then we have the close-up of baby Ingrid. I think Monroe saw something he decided to photograph for his own records, not for the family. I'm going to speculate that when he was leaning over the baby to make final adjustments before he took the first exposure, he saw the petechiae in her eyes, and when he looked at Catherine again, he saw the same tiny pinpricks of blood. He knew that could happen during childbirth because he's taken hundreds of pictures of dead mothers and infants, but there was something else that bothered him. He might have talked to his sister about it, perhaps not. At any rate he uses spirit gum, severe close-ups, and long exposures to capture what he's seen. Then we're missing more photographs. The last plate, the one Miss MacKenzie described as looking rumpled, tells me more about Monroe and what may have been going on in that bedroom than any of the others.

"He and his sister put Mrs. Sorensen and her child back onto the bed, where they were before he posed them for the cabinet photo. He props the baby on a pillow. He wants to look again at the faces he's photographed, so he leans over the bed. Maybe he takes a magnifying glass or an extra camera lens out of his bag and uses it to examine the skin and the features more closely. To do that, he has to straddle the bodies, which means he's disarranging the sheets. Whatever he sees has him so excited he doesn't pay attention to the rumpled bedcovers until after he's taken that last photograph. Then I'd have to presume the two Monroes leave everything in perfect order before they finally leave.

"What I think is that Bartholomew Monroe may not be averse to a bit of blackmail. He doesn't know for certain that the deaths are suspicious, but he's willing to document what he thinks might jar the complacency of whoever believes he's gotten away with murder. In his mind it has to be the husband. He paints over the eyes in the cabinet photograph, but says nothing. You yourself said you never noticed it, Miss Buchanan. He keeps the other negatives unretouched. Just in case he decides to use them. That's what I think happened, Miss MacKenzie."

Riis sat back in his chair. He looked around the table at the faces staring at him. Mr. Hunter had told him to be logical. Miss Buchanan had begged for an explanation of the proof that wasn't really proof. Miss Prudence had encouraged him to put himself in the shoes of a fellow photographer who was probably also a blackmailer. There was one other possibility, but he was counting on Geoffrey Hunter's Pinkerton training to sniff that out.

"What did he see?" asked Prudence.

"Petechiae and bruising. I think he found faint indications of bruising on the baby's flattened nose and perhaps on Catherine also. Either from the force of the pillow on their faces, or in the infant's case from pinching the nose so she couldn't breathe. I think he or his sister discovered the bruises when one of them, probably Miss Monroe, applied liquid powder to make the skin appear more lifelike. At some point they wiped off the powder so he could take photographs for his own purposes, then reapplied it before they left. If the bodies were not to be embalmed, they would have been lifted right away into their coffins for the viewing, perhaps surrounded by flowers. No one is surprised when the skin begins to discolor a bit. Most of the time one of the women in the family pats the face with more powder."

"Is there anything else to be learned from the photographs?" Prudence asked.

"We've uncovered what was supposed to remain hidden," Riis replied.

"There is something else." Claire used one of the grease pencils lying on the table to circle the figure of baby Ingrid lying on a pillow against the side of her mother's body. "Look at the tassels and the embroidery," she said. "This is the pillow Lucinda gave my sister. Catherine told her she would have to pretend she bought it herself. Lucinda expected to see it in the coffin, but it wasn't there."

"What are you suggesting?" Geoffrey asked.

"Look how awkwardly the baby has been placed on the pillow. Everything else Monroe has done looks carefully thought out. I think he needed something to keep the baby from falling off the bed when he leaned over it or when he straddled the bodies, if that's what he did to take the picture. At any rate Catherine and Ingrid weren't meant to be posed this way. Ingrid's gown has ridden up over her legs. There's a dark stain beneath her. You can just make it out."

"Perhaps the pillow was used right after

the delivery," Prudence suggested. "It wasn't washed because someone turned it over to hide the spot and then forgot about it."

"Until Monroe picked it up. Along with what he'd captured on his negatives, he saw something that convinced him he had enough proof of a crime to blackmail the newly wealthy widower. So he put the pillow into one of his cases and took it away with him. That's why it wasn't in the coffin, where Lucinda expected to see it."

No one said aloud what each was thinking. A gift had become a weapon.

"I think we know what has to come next," Geoffrey said.

"We have to find out everything there is to know about Aaron Sorensen," Prudence said.

"And Bartholomew Monroe," her partner added.

"There's a letter here for you from a law firm."

Ethel Sorensen pointed toward the silver salver the butler had brought into the parlor late in the afternoon while she was still reading through the letters and invitations from the day's earlier deliveries. Aaron had told her he rented a post office box for his business mail; this letter in its expensive envelope was disconcerting and out of place in their home.

"Are you perusing the return addresses of my correspondence now?" Sorensen was tall, very blond, wide of shoulder, and narrow of hip. He was no one's idea of what a dealer in fine antiquities should look like; it amused him to see the surprise on the faces of first-time clients.

"Of course not, Aaron. But I couldn't help but notice."

"I'm surprised you didn't open it, being so curious."

"It's inscribed to you."

Her husband had a way of insulting her without ever raising his voice, which Ethel found as disturbing as it was annoying. During their courtship he had been unfailingly polite and deferential; she'd yearned for him to demonstrate more of the forcefulness she admired in heroes of the romantic novels she read. *Be careful what you wish for.*

She no longer recognized herself and her thoughts; being with child was a woman's greatest gift to her husband and most daunting challenge to herself. Young wives talked about it endlessly, their only sources of information each other: *"I burst into tears for no reason whatsoever"; "I'm so tired I can hardly drag myself out of bed in the morning"; "I ache all over, and when my husband approaches me, all I want to do is turn away."* Childbirth, dangerous though it might be, apparently wrote finis to all of these strange and unwelcome changes.

Well-bred wives, like Ethel Sorensen, bit their lips and their tongues, kept silent for the most part, and knitted or crocheted furiously. It was something to do, a way of passing time until they proved their worth in labor and delivery. Everyone wanted a boy, of course, so as not to disappoint a husband, who could never be expected to understand what it felt like to experience an unborn child's kick against the ribs or the anticipatory ache in breasts yearning to suckle.

Aaron's face darkened as he read the lawyer's letter. He folded it up carefully when he had finished and slid it back into its envelope.

The parlor door opened. Lewis, the butler, came in quietly and said something in Aaron's ear that Ethel could not hear. Her husband nodded his head and left the room. No explanation. No apology for deserting his pregnant wife during the important hour before dinner was served. Sometimes it was the only time they spent together throughout a day that seemed far longer than twenty-four hours.

Ethel struggled up from the chair, which was holding her prisoner. Aaron had tossed the lawyer's letter onto the small writing desk, where she crafted polished answers to invitations she was forced to decline. *That's careless of him,* she thought, *if he's hiding something.* She felt a warm flush surge from her rounded belly to her cheeks, and for a moment she wondered why she was doing what no properly submissive wife should do.

The letter from the lawyer was clearly phrased, but confusing. It seemed that someone named Claire Buchanan had rewritten her will and wanted Aaron Sorensen to be informed that he was not included as a beneficiary in the new document.

And then she remembered.

The cabinet photograph of her husband's first wife and deceased child was hidden in the bottom of a box of Ethel Sorensen's monogrammed stationery. She had found it fallen between the wall and the writing desk. No telling how long it had been there. Ethel thought it might be the only one in the house, because Aaron had been adamant about putting away images of his first wife, though he had been equally insistent that

Ethel wear the mourning that society expected of a hastily acquired successor wife.

Ethel had found Catherine's expression particularly touching. There was something poignant and infinitely sad about the mother and child that spoke to an empty place Ethel had believed marriage would fill. It had not. Concealing from her husband what she had found had been her first act of quiet disobedience.

Buchanan had been the family name of Aaron's first wife. Persistent questioning had gotten her few details of her husband's life before they were wed, but she did learn that Catherine had had a sister.

If it had been entirely up to Aaron, that would be all Ethel ever found out about her predecessor. But society loved to gossip; so when the second Mrs. Sorensen showed herself curious about the first Mrs. Sorensen, the women in whose homes she was served tea were only too happy to supply her with the particulars.

Ethel's father had been a man of long and deep silences; early on in her girlhood she had learned how to manage him. When her husband displayed a marked preference for rarely opening his mouth, except to give her an order or comment acerbically on something she had done that displeased him, she knew how to react. Silence met silence. Sometimes several days would pass with only the most mundane of everyday comments exchanged. Ethel knew the pitfalls to be avoided; she was becoming expert at sidestepping them.

This letter from Claire Buchanan's lawyer. Although it revealed very little, she believed she could fill in the background from what had been gossiped about in teatime tittle-tattle. The Buchanan sisters had been beautiful, talented, and very wealthy. What they had not been, unfortunately, was born into fashionable society. The father had been a concert pianist, the mother a singer. *Artistes.* One could admire their musical talents, but they would always remain on the fringes of what was socially proper and acceptable.

Claire had not married. She had achieved a modest amount of acclaim on the concert stage and in various touring opera companies. Her brother-in-law deemed her an undesirable influence on his wife, who had abandoned the expectation of an operatic career at his command. If Claire Buchanan saw fit to instruct her lawyer to inform her late sister's husband that she had written a new will excluding him from inheriting, it must be because in the old will her sister and probably her sister's heirs had been her beneficiaries.

No wonder Aaron's face had turned thunderous when he read the letter. Her husband liked to live well, which meant that he needed a wife whose income could maintain him in the style to which he believed himself entitled. After their marriage it had been a shock to learn how quickly and how deeply Aaron dipped into the considerable marriage portion she brought him.

Ethel refolded the letter and replaced it exactly where and how Aaron had left it. Nowadays she judged everything by what effect it would have on her and her unborn child. She wondered where Aaron kept the marriage contract that spelled out the financial arrangements made for her by her father.

And whether she would understand them even if she could find it.

Chapter 11

"Aaron Sorensen doesn't exist as a business," Josiah Gregory said, hanging up his hat and coat and shaking out his umbrella. "He's never applied for a commercial license of any kind from the city, and he doesn't own or rent any properties other than the house he inherited from Miss Buchanan's sister."

"Claire told us he imported and sold European antiques. He met the Buchanan family because he was brokering the sale of a piano once owned by Franz Liszt. The father insisted his two daughters come with him when he arranged to play the instrument." Prudence turned to Geoffrey for confirmation.

"She said her father became fixated on the piano, although he had no intention of purchasing it," he agreed. "Three months after that impromptu concert, Catherine and Sorensen eloped."

"There are no records of him ever leasing or buying a showroom," Josiah repeated firmly.

"We need bank records and the names of the clubs he belongs to," Geoffrey said, "and everything we can find out about his second wife and her family."

"Sir?" Josiah questioned.

"Inheritance can become a habit," he answered.

Prudence's assignment was to locate someone who had purchased art or furniture from Sorensen. "If he really is doing business, it has to be by referral," she told Geoffrey and Josiah.

"Creating phony antiquities is a cottage industry in Europe," Geoffrey warned her. "The problem is in convincing a client he's been deceived. Most don't want to admit they've been made fools of."

"The new money cares more for glitter than authenticity," Josiah said. "It makes them vulnerable to swindlers."

"Then that's where I'll begin. I have a silver bowl full of calling cards from women whose visits I had no intention of returning. Until now."

Josiah looked pointedly at the black

mourning dress she was wearing for her late fiancé.

"I know," she said. "The one-year anniversary of Charles's death is not until next month. But I've already worn gray on occasion and I'm certainly not in seclusion. People are much less shocked by social change than they used to be. I'll start making my rounds this afternoon."

The first two calls Prudence paid netted her nothing. She had opted for a muted gray dress of half mourning to make things easier for her hostesses, but conversation had been subdued and stilted. Everyone in society had been acquainted with her famous father; her fiancé's family and his tragic death during the Great Blizzard were equally well-known. While good manners dictated that neither topic be mentioned, Prudence's independent lifestyle meant that the women in whose parlors she sat weren't sure exactly how to treat her.

"Keep them off balance, Prudence," Geoffrey had counseled. "Lawyers use all sorts of tricks to get what they need out of reluctant or hostile witnesses."

"I wish you could come with me," she'd told him. "You have a way of sensing when someone is stretching the truth."

"You'll do fine," he assured her.

"Georgina Langston has to have gotten her Louis the Fifteenth pieces somewhere," Josiah commented when Prudence showed him the list of women whose calls she intended to return. The refurbishing of the Langston mansion had been thoroughly covered by the gossip press. "They were certainly not passed down through the generations."

"The family fortunes were made during the war," Prudence confirmed. "*Nouveaux riches* on both sides."

"The *Times* named them the 'shoddy aristocracy,' " Geoffrey said.

"Georgina is desperate to be accepted," Prudence continued. "She couldn't marry into any of the old families, but she did manage the next best thing."

"No one will remember after another two or three generations."

"You're a terrible snob, Geoffrey."

"Family is everything to a Southerner. It's what makes us interesting to outsiders and each other."

"If there is anything to find out about Aaron Sorensen, Georgina will know what it is," Prudence told them. "That's why I've included her, even though we've only been introduced once. She firmly believes that knowing all the city's important gossip will gain her the entrée into society that her husband's money can't purchase."

"I sometimes wonder what the fascination is, or why anyone bothers," Geoffrey said.

"That's tantamount to heresy, sir." Josiah never let a day go by without reading the society and gossip columns. He handed back Miss Prudence's list. "I don't see how you can fail, miss."

"I'm so delighted you noticed my latest treasures," Georgina Langston purred. "I didn't realize until after they arrived how empty the room had been." She beamed proudly at a pair of yellow silk upholstered Louis XV fauteuils squeezed into a place of honor in her overcrowded parlor.

"They're stunning," Prudence said. She couldn't have put it into words, but there was something not quite right about them. She wondered if they might be distressed reproductions being passed off as the genuine article. Geoffrey had described ateliers in the back alleys of Paris where artisans routinely aged the new antiques they crafted. So many came on the market every year it was a wonder the aristocrats of the *ancien régime* had had any room in their palaces and *hotels particuliers* to stand upright.

"I do wonder where you found them," Prudence continued. "Was it perhaps through a private importer? They're much too beautiful ever to have been in a gallery."

"I was very fortunate," Georgina said. "Aaron Sorensen is a genius at finding exactly what his clients need and want. You may have heard the name?"

"I may have," Prudence lied. "It sounds familiar, but I've only recently begun coming back into society again."

"Of course. It must be terribly painful to have had two bereavements so close together. You're being very brave, Prudence."

"I'm out of touch. Wasn't there some scandal associated with him?"

"It's a very difficult situation. Awkward. Embarrassing." Georgina paused to sip her tea and pique Prudence's curiosity. "He remarried two months after his first wife died. Everyone talked about it."

"Were there children?"

"No, and that's what made it so shocking. The first Mrs. Sorensen died within a day of giving birth, and so did their daughter. So it wasn't a case of a baby needing a mother to take care of her."

"I'm surprised the second lady consented

to wed if the proper mourning period had not been observed." Prudence's too-strong tea was getting cold. She hoped Georgina wouldn't notice she hadn't drunk it.

"They married in Philadelphia, not New York. It was hasty, if you catch my meaning." Georgina's pursed-lip disapproval communicated what she was too well mannered to say. "At first, the new bride didn't wear mourning for her predecessor. I had the impression she may not have been aware there was a first Mrs. Sorensen until after the wedding."

"How is that possible?" Prudence asked. "And what makes you think she didn't know?"

Georgina settled in for a lovely bit of pure gossip. "When she made her first round of calls, she seemed very curious about Catherine Sorensen."

"I thought you said she didn't know about her."

"Not at first. Someone, I think it may have been Henrietta Ludlow, mentioned that it was sad, but perhaps a blessing in disguise, that Mr. Sorensen's first wife and child had died together. 'Stepchildren are always more difficult to raise than one's own' was the way she phrased it. Apparently, the second Mrs. Sorensen turned as pale as a ghost and had to resort to her smelling salts. By which Henrietta inferred that the husband hadn't told her about the wife whose place she had taken."

"I can't imagine what she felt. Such a deception, and nothing she could do about it."

"After that, she asked questions at every opportunity. It became embarrassing. We realized it must be because her husband hadn't told her he'd been married before."

"Perhaps he spoke of his previous marriage as though it had happened some time ago, and she was taken aback when she understood how recent it had been."

"That's exonerating him more than he deserves, Prudence. I think he wooed her, seduced her, and married her in one of the most cold-blooded examples of self-aggrandizement I've ever heard of."

"But he must have been a wealthy man in his own right. And wasn't his first wife an heiress?"

"Perhaps when he married her. But he spends lavishly, and there was talk that he lost heavily at cards. There probably wasn't much of the first wife's portion left when she died."

"What club does he belong to?" Prudence asked. A gentleman drank and gambled within the sacred precincts of his private club, where everyone from fellow members to the doorman knew to the penny how much went into other men's wallets every night. Not much of anything else about him remained private for very long, either.

"At least two that I know of. The Lotos Club and the Union Club."

Membership in two clubs was expensive to maintain, but perhaps necessary if a compulsive cardplayer needed to cover the size of his overall indebtedness. What was more telling to Prudence was that the clubs Georgina named were well-known for their private art collections and for the number of art connoisseurs and collectors in their ranks. It was considered bad form to conduct business in one's club, but that was exactly what the members did, of course, using a kind of code all of them understood perfectly.

"I'm sure I heard the name Sorensen during one of my earlier calls," Prudence said. "Could it be that the second Mrs. Sorensen is in the family way?"

"Ethel is her name. She was a Caswell before she married." Georgina offered slices of sugared date-and-nut cake. "The Philadelphia Caswells."

"I don't believe I know any of them," Prudence said. She took a polite bite of the cake and wished she hadn't.

"They aren't a large family," Georgina began enthusiastically. Now that she knew Prudence was neither a relation nor a friend of the Caswells, she wouldn't have to watch what she said. "They're prominent in Philadelphia, though. Old stock, but too many only children in the past few generations. I believe Ethel may be the last of the direct line, and being female, the name will die with her father. Such a shame when that happens." Georgina herself was fertile to a fault, five children under the age of seven, all of them healthy if not particularly attractive.

"Will her mother come for the *accouchement*?"

"Mrs. Caswell passed away some years ago. Mr. Caswell never remarried. And he's not in the best of health himself. One doesn't want to attract ill fortune, but I believe Ethel is afraid he won't live to see his grandchild born."

"How dreadful for her."

"What's worse is that she's often alone in that big house, with just servants for company. Sorensen travels frequently and is absent for weeks at a time."

"Surely, he doesn't leave her for anything

but the most urgent of reasons."

"No one knows. He never reveals where he's going."

"But his wife must be aware of his destinations."

Georgina shook her head. "I don't know what she'd do if she needed him and had to send a telegram."

"I've never heard of anything so callous and uncaring," Prudence declared. "Unless he's traveling on business and can't help it."

Prudence's gaze drifted over to the two Louis XV fauteuils. The more she learned about Claire Buchanan's brother-in-law, the less likely she thought it was that they were genuine. She wondered if Georgina suspected she'd been cheated and was too embarrassed to admit it.

Prudence considered the only other possibility. Could Georgina, with or without her husband's knowledge, have connived at passing off a reproduction as a genuine antique? Decorating one's home with the absolutely right furniture and accessories was as important to someone climbing the social ladder as patronizing the correct dressmaker, serving vintage wines, and knowing all of the arcane social customs that meant nothing to outsiders. There was one way to put her suspicion to the test.

"I simply must see this beautiful yellow silk up close," Prudence gushed. As she walked toward the Louis XV fauteuils, she heard the swish of another gown and knew that Georgina was following close behind.

"I love the whole Rococo feeling," her hostess said. "All the splendid curves and the gilt, ornate, but still so light and playful. Don't you find it so?"

Prudence pinched the corded silk edge of a seat cushion between her fingers. The material was too supple and strong to be more than a hundred years old.

"The clubs will be no problem at all," Geoffrey said, reading over the report Prudence had dictated to Josiah.

He had begun introducing Pinkerton procedures into the office, including the vitally important task of transcribing accurate and detailed accounts of interviews as soon as possible after completion. Prudence had taken to the practice enthusiastically. She had learned to write clearly, succinctly, and with great respect for facts when helping her father analyze briefs and compose opinions from the bench.

"Why is that, Geoffrey?"

"I'm a member of both of them." He smiled at the quizzical look on her face.

Interesting that Prudence obviously did not think of him as the sort of gentleman who would spend his leisure hours at exclusive private clubs. He wondered where she thought he did spend them.

"Won't they get suspicious if you start asking questions?"

"All I have to do is hint that Sorensen may not be paying his gambling debts elsewhere and I'll have as much information about him as we'll need. No club wants to retain a member who might incur disgrace or cause a scandal to be associated with its name. It will be in their best interests to find out everything I know. Which I'll be reluctant to share until they begin to open up to me. That's the way the game is played among gentlemen."

"And among ladies," Prudence added.

"I'll stop in at the Union Club tonight," Geoffrey said, "and I'll ask Ned Hayes to come along if he's free."

"I'd like to be a fly on the wall," Josiah said.

"That's the only way a woman will ever gain admission to the *sanctum sanctorum,*" Prudence declared. "Fortunately, we have other ways of worming secrets out of men."

Josiah was properly scandalized.

CHAPTER 12

"If he's a gambler, especially if he's been losing lately, he'll be looking for a game. It's as much an addiction as laudanum or liquor." Ned Hayes knew what he was talking about. Cocaine and whiskey had nearly cost him his life when a thirst for justice lost him his job as a detective with the New York City Police. Working with Geoffrey Hunter had helped moderate his dependencies, though Ned doubted he would ever be entirely free of them. He hadn't used his membership at the Union Club for years, but he'd agreed to come along with Geoffrey tonight because it was where Aaron Sorensen had led them. Memories of the past be damned. "Do you know what his preferences are?"

"All I'm sure of is that he owes money at his clubs, but he's paid off his debts in the past every time he's fallen into arrears."

"Which means they'll continue to let him

play, and there won't be any shortage of members ready and willing to take his money or his IOUs." Hayes fanned out the deck of cards he'd been shuffling. "Pick one."

Geoffrey obliged, knowing from past experience that his friend Ned was a master at the art of deception.

"Lay it facedown on the table. You picked the ten of hearts. Turn it over."

Geoffrey did, not surprised that Ned was right, but baffled by how he did it.

"I'd say his favorites are whist and poker," Ned decided, shuffling and laying out cards, naming each one correctly before revealing its face. "The stakes can go very high, very fast, in both those games. They take a good head for counting and remembering what's been played and a face that won't give away what the player is thinking or seeing. It doesn't hurt to have nerves of steel and the ability to bluff your way out of a tight spot."

Waiters at the Union Club prided themselves on knowing and remembering every member's customary drink, no matter how much time elapsed between visits. One of them set a glass of French cognac at Geoffrey's elbow and a tumbler of Kentucky bourbon in front of Ned. A carafe of water accompanied it.

"Has Mr. Sorensen come in yet tonight?" Geoffrey asked.

"About half an hour ago, sir," the waiter answered, smoothly tucking away the bill he'd been slipped. "He's in the small card room. Will there be anything else?"

"Mr. Hayes might have a few questions for you later on, Samuel."

"I'll be around, sir."

They watched the dignified Negro waiter weave his way among the upholstered chairs and narrow side tables of the smoking room, collecting empty glasses and full ashtrays as he went.

"He'll know whatever secrets Sorensen is trying to hide," Ned said.

"But will he tell you what they are?"

"He served me my first drink when my father brought me here just before my mother took me South. Samuel is loyal to a fault, and Hayes men have been Union members since the club was first founded. It won't show on his face, but if what we suspect about Sorensen is true, he can't have much respect for the man. He'll do it reluctantly, but he'll tell me."

"I'll make my way to the small card room, then."

"Don't hurry," Ned warned. "Sorensen is probably desperate to win, which means he's twitchy."

"Do you think he'll try something?"

"The only question is whether he's skillful enough to get away with it."

"I don't plan to do anything more than watch him. He'll see me, but he won't know who I am."

"You're sure you've never been introduced? Perhaps in the lounge?"

"Positive. I would have remembered the name. The first time I heard it was from my client a few days ago."

"Watch to see if he drags his arms along the table when he pulls his cards in."

"Allan Pinkerton hated men who cheated. He made sure all of his agents knew what tricks to look out for."

"All I'm saying is that you don't know if he's an amateur or he's been at this for a while. He could be clumsy or very, very good." Ned shuffled and then sprang the deck of cards from one hand to the other; the movement was so fast that all Geoffrey could make out was a blur of motion and a snapping sound. Even with a few drinks of Kentucky bourbon inside him, Ned Hayes was as good as any shark Hunter had ever seen.

The small card room was one of the quietest in the club. The walls were padded with dark green patterned Chinese silk, the floors laid with Turkish carpets. Tables were felt covered, chairs cushioned for the comfort of players who sat in them for hours at a time. Each table was illuminated by a single gas lamp hung low enough to cast light on the cards while allowing the faces of the men to recede into half shadow. There were four tables in the room; a club attendant supplied chips and the occasional paper and pen. He also monitored the waiters who served drinks, lit cigars and cigarettes, emptied ashtrays. Except for the slap of cards, the whisper of bills, and the clink of gold and silver coins, the room was utterly silent. It was bad form to speak for any reason during a game.

Geoffrey chose one of the tall chairs ranged along the wall opposite the door. Idle spectators were discouraged, but members waiting for a seat at the tables often perched on the sidelines after whispering their intention into the ear of one of the attendants.

Sorensen was playing with two men Geoffrey knew by name and sight, and one other he didn't think he'd seen before. Even if a waiter's discreet nod hadn't pointed him out, he would have recognized her late sister's husband from Claire Buchanan's description.

Meticulously barbered and expensively dressed, every inch the wealthy gentleman, he was taller and broader across the shoulders than the other players in the room. New York City's financiers and moguls tended to reflect lives spent in offices and clubs, paunching out from good food and abundant wines as they grew older. Sorensen, blond and as tanned as though he spent every spare moment on a yacht, blue eyes sharp and focused, looked rakishly out of place in these surroundings.

Geoffrey understood immediately the initial effect he must have had on delicate, artistic Catherine Buchanan and the second wife, the Philadelphia heiress who was her father's closely protected only child. Sorensen was the embodiment of the romantic hero popularized in song and prose, the powerful challenger of the gods with whom women fell swiftly and disastrously in love. He knew that Catherine had ceased to have any affection for her husband before her death; now he wondered whether Ethel Sorensen was beginning to have second thoughts about the man she had married.

Sorensen was playing poker, though not with the kind of fierce concentration a desperate gambler might have exhibited. He was smoother than that, holding his cards with a light, almost careless grip, allowing his gaze to leave the table every now and then for a quick glance around the room, something none of the other players did.

Watching, counting off the seconds and then the minutes between those rapid, fleeting looks, Geoffrey soon recognized the pattern and knew what Sorensen was doing. Without being obvious about it, he was checking the concentration of the players and the whereabouts of the waiters and the gaming attendant whose job it was to provide fresh packs of cards and change for large banknotes. It was the kind of prelude to cheating that guaranteed a trick of some sort would be pulled before too much longer.

Geoffrey was watching for a false shuffle or an adroit marking of cards, but Sorensen chose a deception that would be far more difficult to prove was deliberate. He was fast and he was good. If Geoffrey hadn't known it was coming, he might not have spotted it.

It took practice to drop a card so that no one noticed it fall. As soon as it touched the intricately patterned Turkish carpet, it disappeared under Sorensen's left foot. At the same time he raised one finger for another drink, distracting the waiter and disturbing the concentration of the other players. He knew what the card was, of course, and would choose one of two ways to use it.

If the hand was going against him, and the card wouldn't help, he'd pretend surprise and dismay at too few cards. No one would notice his shoe slide off the missing pasteboard; it would be assumed that it had lain there in plain sight all along, its decorated back fading into the Turkish carpet. That round would automatically be null and void. If the hand was going to net him a good win with the aid of the missing card, he would find some pretext to pick it up. A sneeze followed by the drop of a handkerchief, or an ash from his cigar that needed to be quickly brushed from a pant leg. Any one of half a dozen small diversions would do.

As if he'd decided not to wait any longer for a chair to become free, Geoffrey nodded to one of the waiters and stood up. The eagle-headed cane he'd unobtrusively carried into the room and leaned against one of the high chairs fell to the carpet. He took a few steps toward the door and appeared to stumble over it. The glass of cognac he was carrying flew out of his hand, the syrupy liquor splashing against Aaron

Sorensen's pant leg and onto one of his highly polished shoes. The movement of his foot was reflexive, the outraged snarl equally so. The waiter who sprang into action with a linen napkin to wipe up the offending liquid also retrieved the ace of hearts from just beside the sticky shoe.

Geoffrey picked up the cane and bowed apologetically, shrugging his shoulders as if to say that trivial accidents like the one that just happened were unfortunate, but sometimes unavoidable.

"I'm sure you'll want a waiter to sponge out that stain, Sorensen," one of the card-players at his table said, raking in the cards that lay strewn before him and signaling to the gaming attendant to bring paper and pen. "You can leave your IOUs. We know they're good."

Aaron Sorensen had been losing badly, but the cards would have turned in his favor, had he been able to retrieve the dropped card and complete the hand. The bets were high. His eyes met Geoffrey's in sudden suspicion and his handsome face twisted in ill-concealed rage. He scrawled his signature on the notes held out to him, raked the room with a defiant glare as if daring anyone to accuse him of an impropriety, and left with only a perfunctory farewell bow.

He knew. And so did every other person in the small card room. Before the evening was out, the story would be all over the club.

"He told his coachman to take him to the Lotos Club," Ned Hayes said. "There's no hurry. He'll need time to settle himself into another game. What happened?"

"When it was his deal, he dropped a card and stepped on it. The ace of hearts." Geoffrey put the eagle-headed walking stick back into the hollowed-out elephant's leg by the cloakroom. "I spilled cognac on him, and a helpful waiter picked up the card."

"How was he doing?"

"Big losses, but there was a sizable pot on the table."

"He would have used the ace to win it."

"From what I could tell, that's what he was planning to do."

"When did he drop the card? Before or after he looked at his hand?"

"While he was picking it up."

"A cunning man. It could have gone either way."

"But he wouldn't have sustained another loss if the hand was voided."

"He knew what he was doing."

"I wonder how often he's played that trick." Geoffrey allowed the attendant to help him on with his evening cloak.

"Judging by what we know of how much he's been losing, not often enough. He's probably been hoping his luck would change."

"And when it didn't, he decided to help it along."

"He knows what will happen to him if he gets caught." Ned shrugged his shoulders in disgust. "Nothing is ever said publicly, but the man disappears from his clubs and from society as completely as if he were dead. He might as well be."

"He'd have no choice but to leave the city and hope to be able to start over somewhere else." Geoffrey paused, one hand on the door of the hansom cab waiting for them at the curb. "You don't suppose that's why he's so secretive about his affairs, why there aren't any business records at city hall?"

"It makes him very hard to trace, doesn't it? Do we know when he first turned up in New York?"

"Claire Buchanan told us he was dealing in antiques shortly before he married her sister. He would have had to establish a presence here, so that makes it at least two or two and a half years ago."

"Most of the members of the Lotos Club are known to be art connoisseurs and collectors," Ned mused. "I wonder who sponsored him for membership."

"Perhaps someone who had no choice but to do as he requested."

"Every rock you turn over nowadays has some kind of reptile lurking beneath it."

"Another legacy of the war," Geoffrey agreed. "Fortunes were made from first shot to surrender, sometimes on nothing more substantial than the right signature on a commissary contract."

"Don't forget the railroads. They're what's tying the country together. If Sorensen is hiding a shady past, it stands to reason he knows other men who are doing the same thing. Blackmail is an attractive and deceptively easy way to solve problems."

"I think you'd better be the one to keep an eye on him here, Ned," Geoffrey said as they pulled up to the Lotos Club at Fifth Avenue and Twenty-first Street. "He's already suspicious of me because of the spilled drink. If I show up at another card game, he'll call it quits for the night and go home to his pregnant wife. No telling when he'll think it's safe enough to try again."

"Poor woman. Is she rich?"

"According to what Prudence found out,

she's the only child of an old and well-established Philadelphia family. Money and properties on both sides. Her father's health is said to be fragile."

"Didn't Claire Buchanan's sister die soon after delivering a child?" Ned asked.

"I don't trust coincidences."

"There's no such thing. Only repetitions of successful swindles. Or murders."

"He'll leave the city once he inherits from his next widow," Geoffrey predicted. "Sorensen has survived this long because he knows when to disappear. His type can never have enough money. They piss it away as soon as they get it."

"You think there were others? Before Catherine Buchanan and her child?"

"I'd make book on it."

CHAPTER 13

"He won't use the same trick again tonight," Ned Hayes said. "He'll be afraid someone who saw or heard about his game at the Union Club will decide to have his last drink of the evening here at the Lotos."

"I'm surprised he hasn't been asked to resign his membership there."

"The members who would have demanded it left almost twenty years ago to found the Knickerbocker. Too many new millionaires had been inducted into the Union Club after the war for their liking." Ned twisted a heavy signet ring on his left hand, one Geoffrey hadn't seen him wear before. "Sorensen hasn't been challenged openly yet because no one wants to chance a false accusation."

"I saw what he did at the Union Club."

"But could you prove it was done deliberately with intent to defraud?"

"Probably not. That's the beauty of dropping a card. It can happen to anyone," Geoffrey admitted.

"There's something else to consider."

"What's that?"

"As long as Sorensen has expectations of inheriting the Caswell money via his wife, Ethel is safe. If she predeceases her father, I'd lay you odds the fortune will skip the widower and go to a close cousin or to charity."

"Ethel's father has to die while his daughter is still alive for Sorensen to profit more than by the dower amount, considerable though it may be. She has to inherit."

"Our boy is greedy. He'll want it all, especially if Mr. Caswell really is seriously ill."

"Which means Ethel isn't in danger unless we expose her husband prematurely and he has to make a run for it. In that case there's a good chance he'll take out his anger on her before he disappears," Geoffrey said.

"So tonight we let him attempt to cheat, we ruin whatever his scheme is, and nobody is the wiser."

"Except Sorensen. He'll wonder why his tactic didn't work. It won't take him long to figure out that someone else at the table knows what he's doing."

"If I can make him think that one of his opponents is himself trying to rig the game, he might put his defeat down to pure bad luck and coincidence."

"I didn't believe in coincidence when I was a Pinkerton, and I don't now. But every confidence man I've ever run across has a superstitious faith that blind chance will work for him and against his mark."

"If I can carry it off, it will go a long way toward lulling any suspicions he might have that someone is after him." Hayes twisted the ring again, running his fingers lightly and then with more force over the large onyx mounted in a massive gold setting. He emptied his glass of bourbon, then refilled it from a silver flask. "Cold tea," he grimaced.

The club steward wasn't as reluctant to answer questions as Geoffrey had expected him to be.

"I've been worrying about whether to mention Mr. Sorensen's name to someone on the membership committee," Lionel Batters said. Tall, slender, and immensely dignified, the Lotos Club steward was not light enough to pass, but not as dark as the waiters and their assistants.

"What seems to be the trouble?"

"Nothing you can swear to, Mr. Hunter, but a lot of sidelong glances and low-voiced comments whenever Mr. Sorensen's name is mentioned."

"Or when he shows up in one of the card rooms?"

"Especially there. I understand that one evening last week he waited for more than an hour, but no one surrendered a seat. That's most unusual."

"I've heard that he incurs sizable losses."

"Which he eventually pays off. Unfortunately, several members have had to remind him of his obligations."

"How long?"

"Almost two months in one case."

"Did he write a promissory note?"

"He didn't offer to do so at the time, and the member who was carrying the debt accepted his word. He claimed to have forgotten all about it. Implied it was his creditor's fault for not reminding him sooner."

"You'd think someone who loses at cards would eventually decide he's not as good a player as he thinks he is and quit," Geoffrey said.

"He has winning streaks," Lionel explained. "Then his luck changes and he starts losing. His bets get bigger because he's trying to recoup the losses."

"Has there ever been a suggestion of anything unusual about his playing?"

"If you're asking what I think you are, the answer is yes and no. Some of the members are going out of their way not to play with him, but nobody has come right out and disputed a hand or questioned the result of a game. I'd say there's cautious avoidance of the topic, but also a growing feeling that maybe time is running out for Mr. Sorensen."

"He'll be asked to resign?"

"That's how it's usually handled."

"Has anyone ever refused?"

"Not that I know of, and I've been steward here since the club was founded, Mr. Hunter."

"Do you remember when Mr. Sorensen applied for membership?"

"Mr. Buchanan sponsored him about two years ago. It was unusual, because Mr. Sorensen was new to the city and didn't have any secondary sponsors. In fact, unless I'm misremembering, his letters of recommendation weren't from Lotos Club members. They were from gentlemen who had known him in other cities. It was the first time I'd known that to happen. I think the membership committee overlooked the usual requirements because he had married

Mr. Buchanan's daughter."

"On the theory that if there was something wrong with him, Mr. Buchanan would never have allowed the marriage to take place."

"It was probably as simple as that." Lionel nodded his head. "Now that I look back, it seems as though it happened more quickly than usual, too. From proposal to acceptance, I mean."

"I'd like a list of who was sitting on the membership committee then," Geoffrey requested. "And the names of the current members also."

"I can have that for you in a few minutes, sir."

From what the head steward had told him, Geoffrey thought he could construct an accurate picture of Aaron Sorensen's club life. He won substantial amounts of money as long as he could find a way of making the cards work for him. When he couldn't, or when he felt the need to be cautious, his luck varied, sometimes running a losing streak that made him desperate and started rumors flying. He got a little careless. Not enough to be exposed as a cheat, but close enough to make other players wonder.

Whether Sorensen was running good or bad luck tonight, Ned Hayes was more than a match for him.

Five minutes after sitting down at the table where Aaron Sorensen was the next player to deal, Ned Hayes knew what the scam was. One of the oldest, easiest, and still most successful fiddles in the shark's arsenal. Card marking.

On the little finger of his left hand, Sorensen wore a signet ring whose raised crest was sharply incised and slightly higher than one usually saw. When he fanned out his hand, he pressed the face cards over the surface of the ring to create an indentation that only he would feel and be able to read. By the time he judged enough cards had been marked and it was his turn to deal again, he would know what each man held as surely as if he were looking over his shoulder. Then his winning streak would begin.

Ned wouldn't know until he received one of the marked cards where Sorensen was putting the indentation for each suit and how he was differentiating among the honor cards. The simplest way to do it was to designate one corner of each card for the suit, and then space along it to distinguish between kings, queens, and jacks. Aces were usually marked in the middle.

Whist is played in silence. No one comments; there is never a conversation between partners. Even when bets are made, words are few and to the point. Fingers aren't drummed on the table; throats are rarely cleared; the loudest noise is the slap of cards in the shuffle and the deal. It's a gentlemen's game.

Sorensen wouldn't catch on to what was happening until it was too late. Ned marked every face card that came his way. He figured out Aaron's system by the end of the first two hands, indenting with his own signet ring previously unmarked cards in the wrong place and double marking the ones Sorensen had already singled out.

He and his opponent were the only two at their table not enjoying a good whiskey along with the game. Alcohol and cigars tended to dull the fingertips, so Ned sipped at his cold tea and feigned a slight inebriation. He noted that while Sorensen raised his glass occasionally, the level of whiskey never went down. When Sorensen finally became certain that one of the three other men was attempting the same con he was, he'd toss back his drink and leave the table. Ned gave him an hour, no more than that.

The end came sooner than Ned had foreseen. The elderly gentleman to his left called for a new deck when it came his turn to deal. He knew something was wrong by the feel of the cards, more by instinct than because he could prove tampering. The card room steward quickly supplied what was asked for, and Aaron Sorensen made his excuses moments later and relinquished his seat to one of the waiting players. Ned sat on for one more hand, then also left the table.

"He was definitely marking the cards," he told Geoffrey, who had waited in the club bar. "He's fast and good, but nowhere near the best I've seen."

"Professional?"

"A gifted amateur. Professionals don't lose their control, no matter how the cards run. Sorensen was miffed that things weren't going his way, and it showed. I think the gentleman who called for a new deck would have put the finger on him if he'd known exactly what was going on, but he wasn't certain. My guess is that he wanted to get rid of Sorensen without making a fuss, and that's how he chose to do it."

"Your package, sir." One of the waiters from the card room handed Ned a small parcel wrapped in brown paper.

"The marked cards?" Geoffrey asked.

"I decided it would be a good idea to

remove the evidence." Ned slipped the package into his coat pocket. "We don't want Sorensen's world to collapse until we're the ones who pull it down."

"The patterns are obvious," Geoffrey said. He had filled Prudence in on what he and Ned learned the night before about Sorensen's gambling habit. Now they were planning the next phase of the investigation. "Both his wives are with child in the early days of their marriages, which prevents them from appearing at most social functions. Isolates them."

"If they complained of excessive fatigue or lack of appetite, a physician would order them to bed, making the seclusion more pronounced. Visitors would be limited or forbidden altogether." Prudence spoke with authority. She had read *Compton's Medical Guide* on pregnancy.

"Both wives are heiresses," Geoffrey continued. "Ethel is an only child, while Catherine's sister was a continent away most of the time. And in each case, there is only one parent alive, a father who is either very ill or on the point of dying."

"A mother would be more likely to monitor her daughter's pregnancy, ask questions if she sensed something wrong, but these wives have no mothers, and apparently no other close female relatives nearby." Prudence ticked off the points on her fingers.

"The fathers have to predecease the daughters so the wives inherit and their fortunes are joined to the husband's property, or at least come under his control. When Catherine died, Sorensen was her only heir. Even if a separate provision had been made for the child, the infant was also dead. Ethel's will is probably similar," Geoffrey said.

"We need a copy of Catherine's will."

"It was probated, so it's a public document now. Josiah can get it from city records."

"Was a baby nurse hired for Catherine's child?" Prudence asked. "They usually come to the house to prepare the nursery and lay out the newborn's routine several weeks before the expected birth, especially if it's a first child. They are notoriously unpredictable."

"The children or the nurses?" Geoffrey asked, dark eyes twinkling.

"You know exactly what I mean," Prudence reprimanded him, tapping the cover of *Compton's*.

"The housekeeper would know," Josiah contributed. "If an agency was used, they'd have records. Your friend Mrs. Langston has five children, Miss Prudence," he reminded her. "She's bound to know the best agencies in the city."

"What excuse could I give for wanting the information?" Prudence asked. "She's a terrible gossip, remember."

"We'll make up someone," Geoffrey offered, "an *enceinte* cousin who may be moving to the city."

"She'll want details."

"What do you hope to find out, Prudence?" Geoffrey asked.

"If Sorensen never intended his wife and child to live longer than a few days after the birth, he might have neglected to make the kind of long-term arrangements or purchases that would be expected. Baby nurses, especially nurses hired through an agency, are paid for a fixed term, whether the child thrives or not. If he negotiated for the shortest period of time the agency allows, I would consider that an indication that he knew the nurse wouldn't be needed for very long. He had and continues to have gambling debts. He wouldn't waste any of his hard-gotten fortune paying for services that weren't needed.

"For whatever time she was there, the nurse would have made it her business to find out everything she could about the household. Nurseries are little kingdoms. Baby nurses and nannies are forces to be reckoned with. No one dares interfere with their regimens or contradict them on matters pertaining to their charge's well-being. They are tyrants of the worst sort. I remember how strict my nanny was," Prudence concluded.

"Wouldn't she have reported any irregularities to her agency?" Josiah asked.

"I doubt it. Not if she wants to continue working for the best families. Anyone who complains becomes suspect herself. It's the client who's paying the bill," Geoffrey reminded him.

"I wonder if Ethel Sorensen has engaged her baby nurse yet?" Prudence asked. She had a look in her eye that spoke volumes.

"You don't know anything about taking care of an infant," Geoffrey said. He knew immediately where this was heading.

"There's always *Compton's,*" Prudence answered.

CHAPTER 14

"I'll never get away with pretending to be a baby nurse." Prudence closed *Compton's Medical Guide* with an exasperated thump. "Just reading about infant care gives me a headache. I certainly won't be able to answer the interview questions with any pretense of expertise. Do you know, Geoffrey, I've just realized that I've never held a baby, let alone diapered or fed one."

Josiah and Geoffrey exchanged relieved glances. Neither of them had felt comfortable with Prudence's announced intention of penetrating the Sorensen household in the capacity of hired help.

"But I do think I'd make a very decent lady's companion," she mused, smoothing her face into the agreeably bland expression paid companions typically wore.

"Lady's companion?" Josiah tried to keep the dismay out of his voice.

"I don't think Ethel Sorensen needs a

lady's companion," Geoffrey said.

"Of course she does. Her husband is frequently out of town on those mysterious trips of his, and she's without family in the city. She's alone too much. According to *Compton's,* expectant mothers are particularly susceptible to spells of despondency, which can affect the unborn child."

"You can't just appear on her doorstep," Josiah said.

"I'll pay another call on Georgina Langston and tell her that I've had the most wonderful idea."

"Which is?" Geoffrey asked.

"I'll tell her that a dear widowed friend of mind is reducing her household staff and that the situation of her lady's companion is quite urgent. This young woman would be the perfect antidote to Ethel Sorensen's loneliness and melancholy. I give Georgina a name and an address to which a note can be sent. She persuades Ethel to follow through, and *voilà,* I'm hired."

"I think it's risky," Geoffrey said. He wondered why he was bothering to try to argue her out of the scheme; once his partner made up her mind, there was no changing it.

"We have to move quickly." Prudence ignored his objection. "I'll need a name I won't forget to answer to, but nothing traceable or too memorable. Josiah, you're good with things like that."

"I'll think of one, miss."

"I think it's a very bad idea, Prudence. All kinds of things could go wrong."

"How else are we going to find out what we need to know about Sorensen?" Prudence reasoned. "We may not be running out of time, but his wife is. As soon as her father dies, she becomes vulnerable."

"If he did, in fact, murder his first wife. We have no proof of that," Geoffrey reminded her. "Our case is the investigation of Catherine Sorensen's death."

"Which is exactly what I'll be doing."

"He's had more than enough time to destroy incriminating documents, if there ever were any."

"I've made up my mind on this," Prudence said. She knew why Geoffrey was objecting so strongly to her incognito presence in the Sorensen house, and she was determined not to give in. She had skirted precariously close to death twice before, when the cases they were investigating turned ugly and dangerous. If she allowed him to warn her off whenever a threat loomed, she might as well lock herself in her parlor and throw away the key. That was not the kind of life Prudence was determined to live.

"If I can't persuade you not to do this, Prudence, at least get yourself a good disguise," Geoffrey said, surrendering to the inevitable. "Go to that R.H. Macy and Company on Sixth Avenue and buy yourself a plain, serviceable wardrobe suitable for the daughter of a deceased Episcopal priest or Presbyterian minister."

"Is that who I'm to be?"

"A clergyman's daughter is always respectable and usually genteelly impoverished, which should explain why you're earning your livelihood as a paid lady's companion."

"I can buy my wardrobe this afternoon," Prudence said.

"If I may make a suggestion, miss?" Josiah scribbled a list of items he thought Miss Prudence would need. "New gowns and boots are bound to be noticed and remarked on by the staff. Perhaps even Mrs. Sorensen herself. You'll need items that are a bit worn, but still suitable for your station in life. There are secondhand clothing stores farther downtown that can provide exactly what you require."

"I had no idea, Josiah."

"Your maid will know the best of them, and she'll also be able to bargain to get a decent price for what you want."

"He's right, Prudence," Geoffrey said. "You'd stick out like a sore thumb in one of those places. Better to send Colleen."

"How long do you plan to stay at the Sorensen house, miss?" Josiah asked.

"Just a few days, I think. Definitely no longer than a week. No more time than it takes to gain Ethel's confidence, get a sense of the atmosphere of the house, and search Sorensen's study."

"The servants aren't likely to be of much use," Geoffrey warned. "They'll consider you not quite part of the family, but not domestic help, either. And you can't disappear without an explanation when you've gotten the information we want. That would put Sorensen on his guard."

"I'll leave because of a death in the family. My sister's husband. Also a man of the cloth, like our father. When I'm ready to go, I'll tell Ethel that my unexpectedly widowed sister is distraught. I'm urgently needed to help with the children. Clergymen always have large families. Ethel is sure to ask about my relatives when she interviews me. I can lay the groundwork then."

"I think you should write romances, Miss Prudence." Josiah's comment was frankly admiring.

"I'd rather live them," she said, pointedly ignoring the pained expression on Geoffrey's face.

Prudence's room in the Sorensen mansion was in the family wing, but at the opposite end of the corridor from the suites occupied by Aaron and Ethel. It had been one of several guest rooms that had gone largely unused since the death of the first Mrs. Sorensen's father several years ago, the housekeeper explained. A small sitting room adjoined the bedroom, with a desk suitable for letter writing and a comfortable chair close to the fireplace for reading. Mrs. Hopkins hoped that Miss Mason would find everything satisfactory. Prudence assured her that she would, smiling triumphantly to herself as the housekeeper led her back downstairs to the parlor, where a slightly overwhelmed and very pregnant Mrs. Sorensen was waiting.

Ethel wasn't quite sure how Georgina Langston had managed to make it all come together so quickly. She was more than a little concerned about what Aaron would say when he returned, but she was so grateful for the company of another woman of her own age and background that she determined to put the worries out of her mind.

Not that Miss Penelope Mason came from the kind of wealth that had always cushioned Ethel's life; she did not. But she was the well-educated daughter of a clergyman, which made her almost a social equal. She was widely read, a pleasant conversationalist, and as disinclined to needlework as her employer. All of this Ethel discovered in a few short hours. By the end of her first full day in the Sorensen household, it was as though Penelope Mason had always been a part of it.

"I would so like to see the nursery," Prudence told Ethel as they sat over afternoon tea and sandwiches. The wig Josiah had suggested itched, and the spectacles he'd provided pinched her nose, but she was definitely unrecognizable as Judge MacKenzie's daughter. "It will be wonderful to be in a home with a child in it again."

Ethel looked confused.

"My dear sister has six children," Prudence continued, reading the relief on Ethel's face as she realized that her new companion was not referring to the infant who had died in this house so soon after birth. "I made my home with them after our father departed this life." Unspoken was the obvious inference that the family had run out of room for a spinster aunt. "I would feel obliged to assist in any way, should she ever need me." There. The stage had been set for the lie to come; Ethel seemed to have understood that Penelope's stay might not be a permanent one.

Ethel inched forward on her chair, preparatory to heaving herself awkwardly to her feet. She was three or four weeks away from her *accouchement;* but to Prudence's inexperienced eye she looked ready to deliver at any moment.

"Doctor says a short walk every day will aid the digestion." Ethel smiled, rubbing her belly and trying not to release an unladylike burp. "I'll show you the nursery and you can help me decide what else needs to be done."

"Are you sure you should attempt two flights of stairs?"

"I shall be perfectly all right, as long as we take them slowly."

Left hand on the banister, right elbow supported by Prudence, Ethel climbed steadily to the second-floor landing. She was only slightly out of breath and delighted to have proved to her companion that she was able to accomplish what she'd set out to do.

By the time they reached the third floor,

Ethel was pale and panting. A light sheen of moisture lay across her forehead; the hand that reached for support was trembling.

"I don't think you should go any farther," Prudence said, lowering her gently into an armchair placed beside a marble-topped table holding a bouquet of fresh flowers.

"Perhaps you're right." Ethel held out a small ring of keys. "It's two doors down the hall on the right. I'll join you as soon as I catch my breath."

Trying not to betray her impatience, Prudence walked toward the nursery, stopping once to look back at Ethel as if to ask if she should wait. Ethel shook her head and waved her on.

The key turned effortlessly in the lock; the door opened soundlessly. Prudence stepped inside, reaching for the knob that would turn on the gaslights. The room had a musty, closed-up smell to it. She pulled back the heavy drapes that shut out daylight so baby could nap, and eased the window up a hand's width. Fresh, cold air poured into the room in a thin stream.

This was the day nursery, where the baby nurse or nanny would care for the child and take her own meals apart from the other servants. A cradle sat by the fireplace, beside it a cushioned rocking chair. On the opposite wall stood a chest of drawers, a wardrobe, a table for changing and dressing the infant, a pitcher and basin for bathing. Rag rugs covered the wooden floor, small knit blankets were stacked in the large crib near the door to the nanny's bedroom, miniature pillows covered in embroidered linen cases leaned against the bars of the crib. The walls were papered in a cottage print of imaginary animals peering out from the foliage, and here and there hung cross-stitched samplers bearing exhortations to a virtuous childhood.

But was the room newly furnished or were the crib, the cradle, and the rocking chair reminders of another child, who had not lived long enough to leave her mother's side? It was impossible to tell; there wasn't a speck of dust anywhere. Prudence had never met Catherine Buchanan, and she hadn't known Ethel long enough to be familiar with her tastes and preferences.

The drawers were full of tiny garments, all neatly folded and arranged. Surely, none of them had been intended for that other infant? Was that a question Prudence could even ask?

"What do you think?" Ethel stood in the doorway, one hand steadying herself against the frame.

"It's a lovely nursery," Prudence replied. "May I look into the nanny's room?"

Ethel nodded, absorbed in some mental list she was making.

When Prudence opened the door to the room where the baby nurse or nanny would sleep, she knew that at least one of her questions had been answered. The room was as clean and free of dust as the adjoining nursery, but it had the feel and smell of a room left long unoccupied and not being readied for a new tenant. The furniture looked as though it had been put in place years ago and never moved. The linens in the drawers she opened were neither new nor freshly laundered.

She supposed it didn't matter that the nanny would sleep in someone else's bed, under sheets and blankets meant to be used by that other baby's caretaker. Dried lavender had been sprinkled in the closed-up spaces, so the mustiness was faint. But if she had been that infant's father, that dead mother's widower, she would have ordered the rooms stripped to the walls, everything associated with the dreadful loss burned or given to charity.

Unless the deaths were not unwelcome. Unless instead of mourning a loss, Aaron Sorensen celebrated financial gain.

"My husband says our baby will feel a kinship with its half sister if we leave the nursery untouched," Ethel said. "I suppose he's right, but I wonder if some things should be added." She looked quizzically at Prudence, as if wanting her to agree.

"Have you hired a baby nurse or nanny?" Prudence began.

"Aaron wants to be present at the interviews before I agree to hire anyone. I've contacted an agency, but I haven't made appointments yet."

"Perhaps some new sleeping bonnets," Prudence suggested. "I suppose nannies come with their own lists of what they consider the necessities, but I don't think you could go wrong with head coverings."

"I'm not very skilled with a needle," Ethel confessed ruefully. "I hadn't the patience for it when I was a girl, so I never learned properly."

"We could go shopping," Prudence proposed, expecting Ethel to agree delightedly.

But she did not. "Aaron doesn't like me to go out alone."

"Now you have a companion."

"I'm feeling a little light-headed," Ethel said, abruptly ending the conversation. "Do you mind if we go downstairs? I think I'll lie down on my bed and try to nap."

Prudence locked the nursery door behind them, then turned the key again when Ethel started down the corridor. She'd once had to steal keys to open doors in her own house. She'd learned to take precautions when she thought she might want to return alone to a room.

In the space of a few days, she'd become a prowler, as well as a thief. Geoffrey would commend her new skills.

Ethel Sorensen was not always as even-tempered as she at first appeared to be. When Prudence asked if Mr. Sorensen was expected home soon, Ethel snapped a response and changed the subject. She never knew how long Aaron would stay away and it vexed her to be so ignorant. That evening they dined together in amicable, though awkward, fits and starts of conversation.

It was clear that the household staff didn't know what to make of the new resident; they couldn't place her. She wasn't a member of the family, nor was she precisely a guest, yet she was to be treated in every respect as though she were. Mrs. Hopkins, who had begun her career in service in one of the grander houses of the city, explained the role of lady's companion.

"I wish someone would pay me just to keep her company," said the skivvy whose job it was to clean out the coals and lay the new fires every morning. It was the hardest, dirtiest job in the house, and Sally had to do it without ever being seen. Only the prettiest of upstairs maids could aspire to be noticed.

Three days after her arrival Miss Mason came into the parlor a full hour before Mrs. Sorensen was expected to ring for her morning tea. She laid a five-dollar gold coin on Sally's dirty palm. The skivvy nearly fainted with the shock of holding so much money in her hand.

"Were you here when the first Mrs. Sorensen was still alive, Sally?" Prudence settled herself onto a small sofa, crossing her hands in her lap, tucking her feet under her skirt. Back rigidly straight, she was a picture of the ladylike authority Sally had been trained since childhood to obey.

"Yes, miss. I came before the old master passed away."

"Tell me what she was like."

"The kindest lady you'd ever want to meet. Very beautiful, and with a voice like an angel. Though she never sang after the old master died and the new one forbade it."

"Did you ever hear him tell her not to sing?"

"There were terrible fights, miss. Mr. Sorensen shouted so loud you could hear him all over the house. Mrs. Catherine cried and pleaded with him." Sally brought her fist up to her mouth as if realizing that she was telling secrets she wasn't supposed to know.

"That's all right, Sally. Nothing you say will get you into trouble. I promise." Prudence pried open the skivvy's fingers and laid another five-dollar gold piece in her hand. "Tell me about what happened when Mrs. Sorensen learned she was going to have a baby."

"She was already in the family way before I came, miss. Mrs. Catherine was well along when the fighting just stopped one day. There was no more arguing. After that, they hardly ever talked to each other. He started staying away longer on his trips. Whenever he was likely to be gone for a while, she'd leave the house early in the morning, two or three times a week, and stay away for half the day. We knew something was up. She'd been studying to be an opera singer before she married Mr. Sorensen, but he put a stop to that. What we thought was that she was taking lessons again like she did when her father was alive. We all had our fingers crossed that she'd have the baby and then go off to become famous and leave Mr. Sorensen behind."

"How was it just before the baby was born?"

"Everyone was waiting. You could have heard a pin drop in this house most days. Even when you were doing your work, you'd be listening."

"Listening for what, Sally?"

"For the baby to start coming, miss. It was terrible, what happened to Mrs. Catherine. None of us thought things would turn out the way they did. You could tell she wanted that baby. And she wasn't ill the way some ladies are. Mrs. Catherine was strong, right up to the end."

"Can you tell me about the birth?"

"No, miss. I was never in the room. The midwife came first, and then the doctor. Cook had the stove going to heat water and there was more than enough clean linen. Mrs. Catherine never made a sound that I heard tell of. The first we knew the baby had been born was when we heard her cry. It wasn't any little mewling squeak, either. Little Miss Ingrid hollered so loud, we thought for sure it was a boy. The doctor left, but the midwife stayed on. She said it was too late for her to go home, and she didn't have any other patients, so she might as well spend the night. Miss Ingrid was born early, so the nanny's room was empty. The baby nurse wasn't expected for another week."

"What about Mr. Sorensen? Was he here through all of it?"

"He'd been on one of his trips. None of us knew when he'd be back, and when Mrs. Hopkins wanted to send a telegram, Mrs. Catherine said she didn't know where to reach him." Sally curled her fist tighter around the gold coins. She had more to say, and now that she'd begun talking, the memories were flooding back. "He came home that night, after the doctor had left. We were all still up. The butler we had then said we should drink to the baby's health. So we were sitting in the servants' hall downstairs when we heard the front door open. Mr. Baron went up the stairs as fast as you please, and when he came back down, he had the most peculiar expression on his face."

"Can you describe it?"

"Like he'd bit down on something sour. He'd told Mr. Sorensen the baby had been born, that it was a girl, and that Mrs. Sorensen and the child were both fine. He said Mr. Sorensen stared at him as if he didn't understand what he was talking about, then he started up the staircase to the second floor without saying a word. Not fast, either, like someone happy and eager, but slow, his shoulders stiff and hunched over.

"The next morning, early, he came down and told Mr. Baron to call the photographer. They were dead."

"Where was the midwife?"

"Gone already. And he'd locked the door to Mrs. Sorensen's bedroom. That's where they were, the both of them. No one was allowed in until after the photographer had finished."

"One more question, Sally. Do you know the names of the midwife and the doctor?"

"Mrs. Emerson and Dr. Norbert. The doctor would never have left that night if he'd thought something would go wrong. He'd taken care of both Mrs. Sorensen's parents and Mrs. Catherine, too, when she was a little girl. I can't say any more, miss. I shouldn't have told you anything at all. It's just that no one ever talks about them, Mrs. Catherine and her baby. It's like they never existed. That's not right."

They both heard footsteps on the staircase at the same time. Ethel was making her slow, careful way down to the breakfast room.

The skivvy turned and fled down the servants' staircase to the basement before Prudence could reassure her once again that no harm would come to her for having told so much to a stranger.

Sally left the Sorensen house well before dawn the next day, her two gold five-dollar coins wrapped in brown paper and stuffed in the toes of her shoes. She was no more fearful than the next one, but she hadn't been able to sleep a wink all night. All she could think about was how strange it was that Mrs. Catherine and her baby had died when no one expected them to.

And how angry Mr. Sorensen would be if he ever found out she'd talked about them.

CHAPTER 15

Ethel Sorensen's doctor had recommended a potion called The Expectant Mother's Anodyne and Soporific to help her sleep through the night, the caution being to swallow only a few drops dissolved in sherry to kill the unpleasant taste. It was, Prudence thought, a tincture of laudanum dissolved in herbal extracts and honey. Despite her restless, uncomfortable slumbers, Ethel seldom used it. She hadn't awoken one night in time to reach the chamber pot; the humiliation of wetting her bed like a child had reduced her to tears and near hysterics.

But on Prudence's third evening in the Sorensen household, Ethel doctored her after-dinner *digestif* with the mixture that was guaranteed to give her the rest she so badly needed. She offered some to her companion, who declined.

"I'm afraid I would sleep right through the morning hours," Prudence explained apologetically. "My conversation wouldn't make sense until well past noon." The truth was that even a single swallow of laudanum was as dangerous to Prudence as a loaded gun. What had begun as a doctor-recommended aid to calm the nerves had swiftly become an addiction. By sheer force of will she had weaned herself from the opium mixture; she counted herself one of the lucky ones. But the lure would always be a part of her; she didn't dare give in to it.

"It makes me groggy when I wake up," Ethel confessed, "but I'm desperate for sleep." The skin beneath her eyes was dark with fatigue, she was too tired to sit with back straight and not touching her chair as etiquette demanded, and she was having difficulty focusing her attention on what Prudence was saying. "I can't go on any longer like this." She counted out the drops, then added a few more for good measure.

No hands of whist that night, no reading aloud by the fire in the small parlor. The piano remained silent. Before the long case clock in the foyer chimed nine, Ethel had summoned her maid and climbed into the great bed, where Aaron hadn't visited her since she'd told him she was in the family way.

She sighed contently as she felt a blissful release steal over her. Ethel needed sleep and strength to get through the next few weeks until the baby was born. If Aaron remained true to form, he'd be back from this latest trip in a few days. She dreaded the confrontation that was sure to erupt when she had to tell him she'd engaged a companion. She wondered if she could do it with Penelope at her side. Surely, Aaron wouldn't be so ill-mannered as to berate her in front of a stranger. But as she fell asleep, she knew he would.

Prudence listened for footsteps ascending the uncarpeted servants' staircase that ran from basement to attic. The last ones up would be Mrs. Hopkins, the housekeeper, and the butler, whose job it was to secure the house for the night. They would also be the last to turn out their lights, remaining awake until they were sure the maids and young male servants were safely asleep in their own beds.

By midnight Prudence judged that everyone in the Sorensen house, except her, was deeply asleep. The more she thought about it, the more she had become convinced that for her own safety she had to decamp as soon as she'd searched Aaron's study. Ethel had mentioned several times that she expected her husband home any day now. It was time to finish the job and go.

Prudence wrote a note to leave in her sitting room, being deliberately careless with her handwriting, as though she'd been overcome with emotion and the need for haste when she penned it: *Brother-in-law dead in a tragic carriage accident, sister collapsed with grief, six nieces and nephews desperately needing care.* There was no logical way to explain how she had gotten the news, so she ignored that complication. Someone, probably the housekeeper, would suggest they count the silver. Someone else was bound to announce that he or she had always thought there was something odd about Miss Mason. At least Ethel would be spared having to explain a companion to an irate husband.

Carpetbag in hand, Prudence descended the main staircase carrying her outdoor boots, her stockinged feet noiseless in the deep silence of the house. The only sound she heard after she tiptoed from her room was Ethel's soft, distant snore. Her husband had forbidden her the lapdog she'd begged for, and the kitchen mouser was safely below stairs in the basement, presumably about her nightly prowl.

Prudence had no key to Sorensen's study,

but Geoffrey had taught her how to pick a lock one rainy, clientless afternoon. She had insisted, and he had finally given in when she reminded him that the Pinkerton female detectives were trained in all of the same skills as their male counterparts. She had clapped as gleefully as a child the first time a lock clicked open under the careful probing of the pick Geoffrey supplied. And then she had practiced until hours of sore fingers and ears straining for the sound of tumblers turning had made her nearly as skilled as he.

The lock that secured Aaron Sorensen's study posed very little challenge. Prudence had it open in less than thirty seconds. She slipped inside, closed the door behind her, and relocked it. If someone with a key appeared, she had at least bought herself a few precious seconds in which to hide behind the heavy drapes drawn closed over the windows.

The hallways of the Sorensen mansion were dimly lit at night by low-flamed gaslights, but there was nothing breaking the stygian darkness of the study. She lit a lucifer, locating and lighting the gas lamp on Sorensen's desk, careful to trim the wick to burn as low as possible without extinguishing it.

One of the desk drawers was locked. She picked it open, studied the contents so she would know how to replace them, then lifted them out and placed them on the leather blotter. A bundle of letters bound with a clerk's black ribbon, a narrow ledger, a sheaf of documents stuffed into a large brown envelope. Odds and ends that made no sense. A woman's pearl ring, a gold stickpin, a pocket watch with an inscription she could not make out in the dim light. A folding clasp knife, a silver cigar cutter, an empty leather card case.

She set the small objects aside and opened the ledger, paging through it as slowly as she dared. It seemed to be a record of gambling wins and losses identified by date, place, and initials. *U* and *L* obviously referred to the Union and Lotos, where Geoffrey and Ned Hayes had followed Aaron Sorensen and watched him attempting to cheat his fellow club members. But there were entries that Prudence could not connect to any of the gentlemen's clubs she had ever read about in the social columns of the New York newspapers. One had the letter *P* next to it, as though Sorensen had begun to write another word, then stopped because it wasn't necessary. Philadelphia? Ethel had been born and raised in Philadelphia; her father still resided there. Could he have taken Aaron to his club sometime?

Empty pages were followed by another type of entry. This time the description lines listed items of furniture and artwork. Paintings, sculptures, handwoven Turkish rugs, bolts of French silk for the walls of a lady's boudoir. Fainting couches, fauteuils, tables inlaid with ivory and ebony, Chinese vases, crystal chandeliers, and gold candelabra.

Running down the length of each page were two columns of figures, the price Sorensen paid for each article and the total for which he sold it. There was such an enormous disparity between the two sums that Prudence felt certain she was looking at a list of his fraudulent sales, of the cons he had managed to put over on Americans willing to pay exorbitant amounts for imported European culture. She would have liked to have found a listing of Georgina Langston's yellow silk upholstered Louis XV fauteuils, but she didn't dare take the time to search for a specific item.

All of the letters had been sent to the main New York City Post Office, and none of them bore return addresses. The handwriting on most of the envelopes was decidedly feminine, the contents unremarkably maudlin, until she came to the most recently dated note. This one she read through closely from beginning to close, then set it aside to copy. Though penned in a woman's hand, it was formal, businesslike, and devoid of the protestations of undying love and longing she had expected to find. The writer mentioned a financial request Aaron had stipulated as a condition of their agreement. She assured him that she would soon be contacting her bank on his behalf. She hoped that would settle matters between them once and for all. Prudence thought it sounded as though one of his attempted conquests had gone wrong.

The brown envelope held bank statements, bundles of canceled checks, records of transfers and sales of property. One marriage certificate. One death certificate. Neither had been filled out. She settled down to copy the letter she had read onto a piece of monogrammed stationery. Then a page of gambling debts, another of sales of forged antiquities.

The long case clock in the foyer chimed four. How could the time have passed so quickly? She had been in the study long enough, had copied a dozen names and addresses from documents she didn't dare take. On impulse Prudence slipped the gold stickpin and the pearl ring into her skirt pocket. If Sorensen realized they were gone, there was a good chance he'd believe a dismissed servant had taken them. She made sure the drawer looked exactly as it had when she first opened it, then closed and locked it again. A quick glance into the remaining drawers told her they contained nothing of interest.

Four o'clock in the morning. The servants would be getting up soon; she had to leave.

Poor Ethel.

"I don't think I'll ever want to face her again," Prudence told Geoffrey later that morning. "Running out on her the way I did."

"I think you made a very wise decision," he told her. "It sounds to me as though she was expecting her husband home momentarily. There's no telling what unpleasantness you might have had to endure if he'd taken it into his head to blame you for any newfound independence Ethel might have been reaching for. He's a thief, a swindler, and very possibly a murderer."

"He may also be a bigamist. The letter I copied suggests that he's begun courting Ethel's replacement. And there were communications from at least five or six other women in that bundle. That's why he stays away for two weeks at a time and refuses to tell her where he's going or how to reach him. Some of the entries in the ledger book pointed to recent sales."

"What about your Mrs. Langston's fauteuils?"

"I didn't have time to search for them. My guess is that she may have bought some items from Sorensen, but the fauteuils could have come from a competitor in the forgery business. Maybe someone who gave her a better price."

"This stickpin has what looks like a date on the back," Josiah said. "Is it too much to hope that whoever purchased it for our Don Juan bought it in New York?" He passed the small piece of men's jewelry to Geoffrey.

"Claire might know if Catherine gave it to him as a gift."

"Too easy. And I'm not sure the date works for that marriage," Geoffrey commented. "Even with Josiah's magnifying glass I can't make it out. It's too worn, as if someone fingered it over a number of years. Rubbed the edges smooth, so I can't tell if I'm looking at a three or an eight. The ring should be easier to trace. It's definitely a woman's item, and it's newer. The jeweler who created it might still be in business. It'll take legwork to find him, but it's not an impossible task."

Josiah went into the outer office to answer a knock on the door. They heard him speak to someone and then the rattle of the petty-cash box. One of Geoffrey's small army of informants was being paid for something he'd found out.

"Sorensen arrived home this morning, just a few hours after you'd left," Josiah reported. "A hansom cab driver passed the information on to Danny Dennis. The cabby picked him up at the station about when the early train from Philadelphia pulls in. He was carrying one small bag and a leather case."

"He's sure about the arrival time?"

"He told Danny the man was hurrying, so he figured he'd just gotten off a train and was getting out of the station as fast as he could. The time was right for the Philadelphia train."

"He didn't happen to leave a ticket stub in the cab, did he?" Prudence asked.

"No, miss. I think that only happens in novels."

"One can always hope."

"What else could he tell us?" Geoffrey asked.

"He didn't ring the bell for the butler. Opened the front door with his own key.

The cabby left a boy on the scene and told him to stay until somebody ordered him otherwise."

"Is Danny downstairs?"

"Waiting at the curb. He thought you might need him and Mr. Washington this morning."

"Tell him to keep a boy outside the Sorensen house until further notice. Rotate them every few hours and make sure they change their caps and jackets so somebody doesn't wonder why the same runner is hanging around with nothing better to do than walk up and down with his hands in his pockets." Geoffrey got up from the desk and reached for his overcoat.

"Where are you going?" Prudence looked a little the worse for wear after her sleepless night, but she wasn't about to admit feeling tired.

"I think it's time to track down the midwife and the doctor you told us about. And I need to talk to Ned Hayes."

"I can have Danny take me to Dr. Worthington's office. He may have the information we want. But Ethel isn't due for another month, Geoffrey." She didn't understand why he suddenly seemed in such a hurry.

"In the South, the daughters of tenant farmers who get caught use pennyroyal or slippery elm to abort themselves," Geoffrey said. He didn't add that many of them died along with their unwanted infants. Nor did he comment on how he knew what desperate young women swallowed to induce a miscarriage.

"Ethel wouldn't be aware of it if someone slipped something extra into her drink," Prudence said, following the deadly logic of what Geoffrey was suggesting. "She doses herself with an expectant mother's concoction that probably has laudanum in it. It's bound to be bitter. She wouldn't notice another herbal taste, but a premature birth might very well kill her at the same time as the child."

"Her husband won't profit unless Ethel's father dies and leaves his fortune to his daughter free and clear," protested Josiah.

"What was Sorensen doing in Philadelphia?" Geoffrey asked.

No one answered.

CHAPTER 16

Dr. Peter Worthington had been the MacKenzie family doctor for almost thirty years. He'd delivered Prudence, taken care of her mother during her slow decline and death from consumption, and been both close friend and physician to the late Judge MacKenzie.

He'd never forgiven himself for recommending that Prudence take laudanum to help her cope with her father's passing and then her fiancé's death during the Great Blizzard. For so many females it was the only way to deal with deep sorrow and loss. But for the young woman he thought of as almost a daughter, the drug had induced a dependence that had all the earmarks of the addiction suffered by so many wounded veterans of the war.

She had beaten the awful reliance on laudanum, but not without a terrible struggle and the knowledge that she would never be entirely free of it. So easy to slip into the dream state, where sharp edges blurred into comfortable roundness and the gift of sleep was long and deep.

Now, as he looked at her across his desk, Worthington saw in her face both the determined strength of her father and the warmth of her beautiful mother. He smiled, and then he sighed. The last time Prudence MacKenzie had sat in that chair she'd been seeking proof that her father had been murdered. He remembered the relentless questioning, the challenge she issued that he could not meet. There had been no physical indications that Thomas MacKenzie had died of anything but a massive heart attack. Whatever suspicions he might have had about what brought on the attack, Peter Worthington had had no choice but to insist to the judge's daughter that her father's death was a natural one.

"Her name is Mrs. Emerson, and as recently as a year ago, she was acting as a midwife," Prudence said. "I hoped you might have heard of her."

"I've worked with midwives, of course. Every doctor has. But I don't recall that name, and certainly nothing within the last year or two. Let me ask my nurse. She keeps a list of midwives and baby nurses that we sometimes recommend to patients. They have to have proven themselves or we won't propose them."

"We don't have a long list," the nurse said, showing Prudence the register. "I mostly keep it in case the doctor is tied up with another patient and the mother needs someone with her if he doesn't make it on time."

"I don't think I've missed birthing one of my ladies more than a handful of times in all the years I've been practicing," Dr. Worthington commented.

"Better to be safe than sorry." The nurse, who was also his sister and housekeeper, pursed her lips.

"I can't help you with the midwife, but I do know Dr. Norbert. Knew him, that is. He died about three months ago, of old age and irascibility. The man practiced medicine right up to the last few days he was on his feet, though I don't know that I would have gone to him myself at that point with anything more serious than a hangnail."

"He was old? Perhaps past his prime?"

"Ancient, my dear. Deaf as a post, thick spectacles, and tremors in both hands. But his patients were loyal to a fault. He'd been a marvelous diagnostician in his time, and that talent never deserted him. He claimed he could tell a woman was in the family way just by glancing at her eyes. I don't know how he did it, but he was never wrong."

"Would he have known if a patient was in danger of not surviving her confinement? Say, a year ago."

"He wasn't at his best, but he wouldn't have misread the signs. His decline was precipitous. Very noticeably so."

"Suspiciously rapid?"

"Prudence, not every death is a murder." Peter Worthington's eyes twinkled. "Unless you're the one asking questions about it."

"Did he leave a widow? Perhaps a son who took over his practice?"

"His wife died in childbirth. Forty years ago. It was her only pregnancy."

"How tragic."

"He had a nephew who came into the practice about the time Norbert's tremors made it difficult for him to hold an instrument." Dr. Worthington scribbled a name and address on a piece of paper. "Here. I'll tell him you're asking questions on my behalf." He added a few lines, then signed his name.

"That's very considerate of you, Doctor."

"I think it best to get out of your way when you have that resolute look in your eye, Prudence."

He was immensely proud of her.

Young Dr. Norbert declared himself more than happy to accommodate Miss MacKenzie. The histories of deceased patients were kept separate from the files of the living, a nicety he was sure she appreciated. In this case it meant a bit of a wait while his nurse retrieved Catherine Sorensen's information. Would Miss MacKenzie care for tea while they waited?

"How long did you have the opportunity to practice with your uncle before his death?" Prudence asked politely.

"Not nearly long enough. He was a truly gifted healer, though his medical education was initially sketchy. He said he learned more in the field hospitals of the war than from any lecture he ever attended."

"Some doctors specialize."

"He didn't, though he gravitated toward the care and healing of women after my aunt's death. He never recovered from losing her."

"Will you specialize, Dr. Norbert?"

"I am moving in that direction, Miss MacKenzie, though I won't abandon any of the patients I inherited from my uncle." His face flushed, he changed position in his armchair, and straightened an already impeccably aligned cravat. "I am particularly interested in the treatment of hysteria, which I studied in England and Germany."

Before she could ask him to explain exactly what *hysteria* was, and how it could be treated, the nurse returned with a thin brown cardboard folder. The word *Deceased* had been written across it in thick strokes of black ink.

"If you'll just give me a moment to read through these notes," Dr. Norbert said, opening the folder and skimming the first sheet of paper. "Uncle kept meticulous records."

From where she sat, Prudence could see even rows of fine copperplate handwriting filling page after page, gradually becoming shaky, spiky, and difficult to decipher.

Norbert read rapidly until he reached the final pages. He copied a few words and then whole sentences, frowning over what he was writing. "I assume you want something more definitive than just a description of what my uncle wrote. I regret that I can't let you have the entire dossier."

"Catherine Sorensen and her child are dead."

"They are. Most regrettably so. However, her widower is still with us, and I daresay he would not appreciate his late wife's most private moments being shared. I'm only giving you what I am because Peter Worthington requested that I do so."

"And doctors feel free to talk to one another?"

"Not as much as we probably should, but from time to time we do share interesting or baffling cases." Norbert folded his hands across Catherine's medical record. "I'll summarize in layman's terms what my uncle wrote." He glanced occasionally at the notes he had jotted down for Prudence, but for the most part he spoke from memory.

"Mrs. Sorensen was a healthy woman who had come through her pregnancy with few if any concerns. When her husband mentioned that she complained of swollen ankles, bouts of indigestion, and severe fatigue, my uncle advised confinement to bed, a restricted diet, and a few drops of laudanum in the evening to allow her to fall asleep more easily. He expected her to deliver without complications and make a good recovery. The baby's heartbeat was strong, and its position in the womb where it should be. He wasn't anticipating any problems there, either."

"So what happened?" Prudence asked impatiently.

"He writes that he doesn't know and that

he is quite perturbed at being shut out by Mr. Sorensen. It appears that mother and child died sometime during the night, after my uncle had left. The midwife remained behind, but only because the woman said it was late and she preferred spending the night to going out into the streets at that hour. There was no medical reason that required her continued presence. Mrs. Sorensen delivered a week earlier than expected, but the baby nurse had already been hired and was to arrive in a day or so. A telegram could have been sent to hasten her coming."

"Your uncle wasn't called in the next day to examine the bodies?"

"A photographer and the mortician had done their work before he was notified of the deaths. I think he was very angry, Miss MacKenzie. There are ink spatters throughout the last paragraph he wrote."

"This is a delicate question to ask, Dr. Norbert. Does your uncle say or intimate that there was anything unusual or suspicious about the Sorensen deaths?" She took one of the Hunter and MacKenzie, Investigative Law calling cards from her reticule and laid it on the desk.

"Dr. Worthington said nothing in his note about an investigation into dubious circumstances."

"We are in the very early stage of our inquiry," Prudence explained. "Questions have been raised, and we are attempting to answer them."

Dr. Norbert opened the file folder and read through the final two pages of notes again. "I detect anger, but not suspicion. He would never have signed the death certificates if he had any doubt about the cause of death. But he was furious at being excluded until after the bodies had been coffined. I gather he knew the lady's family well and had been their physician for many years."

"They were embalmed?"

"Apparently, there at the house, as soon as the photographer finished taking his pictures. My uncle writes that when he was finally allowed to see them, Mrs. Sorensen and her infant lay together in the same coffin in the parlor. He noted the faint odor of arsenic not quite camouflaged by the scent of flowers, and concluded that they had been embalmed."

"I'm not asking out of a prurient curiosity, Doctor, but because it might impinge on our findings. How was the embalming done?"

"He doesn't go into details, but I'm sure

it was the same method that came into favor during the war, when families desperately wanted the body of a loved one returned whenever possible. A preservative fluid is introduced into the blood vessels where the arm joins the chest. It's not as thorough as the procedure performed nowadays in mortuary parlors, but it gets the job done."

"And you say that arsenic is used?"

"It's the most important ingredient in the preservative. Arsenic has many uses, Miss MacKenzie. It's essential to modern life." Dr. Norbert handed her the notes he had written.

"I won't take any more of your time, Doctor," Prudence said.

"Do remember me if you should begin to suffer any of the symptoms of hysteria. If you lose your appetite or experience excessive nervousness or the inability to sleep."

"I shall certainly think of you if I fall into a hysterical state," Prudence promised. She had suddenly remembered the most common treatment for female hysteria and understood what the doctor was suggesting. Even though she still had her gloves on, she managed to leave his office without shaking hands.

"Ned thinks he knows a woman who will be

able to give us information about Mrs. Emerson, the midwife."

"I'll go see her as soon as I've written up my interview notes of Dr. Norbert," Prudence said. She hadn't mentioned to Geoffrey the doctor's offer to treat her for hysteria.

"I don't think that's a good idea," he said. "It's best I do this one alone."

"May I ask why? I thought my questioning of Norbert was very thorough."

"I'm sure it was."

"Then why are you shutting me out?"

Geoffrey did not answer.

Ned knows a woman. Not a lady. Prudence's hackles rose. She suddenly had more than an inkling of who it was Ned Hayes had suggested might help them find Mrs. Emerson. There were midwives who did more than deliver babies; they also aborted the unwanted or inconvenient accidents that a certain profession was prone to experience. Madame Jolene. That was who Geoffrey did not want her to interview.

"You can't protect me from what you think is unsuitable, Geoffrey. You're neither my father nor my brother. And you are certainly not my guardian."

"That wasn't my intention, Prudence." He hoped one day to be so much more.

"I suppose if women are ever admitted to the bar, you'll want to limit the types of clients they can represent. Widows trying to reclaim their dower rights, orphans seeking proof of legitimacy, perhaps an odd divorce now and then. Certainly no one accused of a capital crime and definitely no woman who's been obliged by poverty and ignorance to sell her body."

Prudence could feel herself trembling with anger. The detecting they were doing together was just a first step toward her ultimate goal. Geoffrey knew how much she dreamed of becoming the lawyer her father had educated her to be, how avidly she followed the arguments being made in favor of admitting women to the bar. The practice of law would be a farce if she couldn't go where she wanted, take on any case that intrigued her, choose her own clients no matter who they were.

She'd never raised her voice to Geoffrey Hunter before. This had been their first quarrel.

CHAPTER 17

It wasn't precisely a battle, since neither party claimed victory. Geoffrey withdrew from the field because he knew Prudence was right. Hard as it was for him to admit that she was just as entitled as a man to throw herself into a compromising situation, he had to admit she had earned that privilege. No Southern woman of quality would put herself forward as Prudence did, but that was precisely what drew him to her. She was unlike any other woman he had ever known, North or South.

She had never been less than determined and courageous from the first moment he met her, when he'd taken her arm at her fiancé's funeral and rescued her from the clutches of a conniving stepmother. It galled him to think she intended to enter a house where women sold their bodies to strangers, but it vexed him even more to know that if she were a Pinkerton operative, he might have suggested just such a visit. In disguise and incognito, perhaps, which would make it all the more dangerous.

Conflicting emotions weren't something Geoffrey usually tolerated in himself. There were moments when he thought that time spent with Prudence was a threat to who and what he had always been. He felt himself changing, and he wasn't sure he liked it. Until he thought of what life would be like without Prudence. Stating her mind. Saying exactly what she thought. Refusing to flatter him the way so many other women did. Challenging him. Just being herself. Confusing the hell out of him.

Apologies weren't exchanged, but neither did Prudence continue the discussion. She accepted Geoffrey's capitulation with good grace and quickly changed the subject, salving what was left of his masculine pride.

"Will Madame Jolene talk to us?"

"I think so," Geoffrey said. "She was grateful for what we were able to do when Sally Lynn Fannon was murdered, and she has a soft spot for Ned Hayes."

"Maybe we should have brought him with us."

"He's gone off on a tangent of his own. Wouldn't say what it was. But she'll talk to us because she knows Ned will be pleased if she cooperates."

Madame Jolene's brothel was housed in a respectable brownstone on a street just a stone's throw from some of the most expensive real estate in town. It was protected by the New York City Police, whose upper-echelon officers enjoyed the pleasures of the establishment gratis. Ordinary coppers were served at an address that wasn't nearly as posh, and by girls who were a trifle more worn. The madam knew how to butter her bread.

"Good afternoon, George." Geoffrey removed his hat as he stepped into the small foyer that concealed embossed red wallpaper and scantily clad ladies from anyone passing in the street. "Would you tell Madame Jolene that we'd like a few minutes of her time?" He didn't mention Prudence's name. That would have been crossing too far over the line of propriety; he was uncomfortable enough already.

George Bright ushered them into the main parlor, then hurried off to Madame Jolene's office. He was a muscular young man who took seriously his job of bouncer. He'd boxed bare-knuckled and gloved until his ears became injured and deformed, his nose hardly functioned anymore for breathing, and he had a hard time remembering things.

Despite the ears and the nose, he was still handsome enough to make a woman catch her breath at the sight of him. Since George didn't like women in that way, he and Madame Jolene had long ago agreed that the job she offered him suited both their needs.

He passed through the parlor on his way back to his post at the front door, nodding to Geoffrey as he went, ignoring Prudence, which he thought was the only proper way to handle her appearance where she so obviously didn't belong.

Madame Jolene was as elegant as the madam of an exclusive brothel could be. Dressed always and entirely in embroidered black silk, she wore enough paint to conceal her age, but not enough to look raddled. Not a single gray strand disturbed the deep black of her upswept hair, where beads of jet sparkled and a feather waved over her curls. She was as Irish as Paddy's pig, but since she'd spoken only Gaelic when she got off the boat, an immigration officer decided she must be French, and she agreed. It meant she could charge more for her services, since everyone knew that French whores were the best. She'd learned English easily, deformed it with an accent she thought sounded French, and *voilà*, there she was. Renamed, enthusiastically a citizen, on her way to becoming a wealthy woman. She loved everything about America.

"I know you didn't come for the usual," Madame Jolene said, sweeping into the parlor with a swish of silk and a wave of expensive French perfume. She looked at Prudence the way a horse trader examines a mare he intends to breed. "We've managed to go a few months without a murder, Mr. Hunter. So what brings you to my doorstep?"

"We're looking for a midwife," Geoffrey began.

"I don't keep one on the premises," Madame Jolene interrupted. "Aren't you going to introduce your companion?"

"My name is Prudence MacKenzie." She smiled and held out a hand, as composed and polite as if greeting one of the Vanderbilts or Astors.

"You're welcome in my house," Jolene said. She liked a woman who was sure of herself and not afraid to treat a whore like the sister under the skin she was.

"Jolene, the woman we're looking for provided other services to women and girls who found themselves in a bad way. She calls herself Mrs. Emerson." Geoffrey resolutely kept to the business that had brought them to the brothel. Prudence was looking unsuitably curious about her surroundings. He wouldn't put it past her to ask for a tour of the house, a request whose consequences he didn't want to contemplate. Josiah would be horrified.

"And you thought I might be able to tell you about her because of these other services?"

"That's what I thought. So did Ned."

"Smart man. He played fair with me when he was on the force, one of the very few who did."

"Do you know her? Mrs. Emerson? Have you heard the name?"

"Why are you looking for her?"

"We're trying to solve a murder she might know something about," Geoffrey explained.

"And save another woman's life, if we're quick enough," added Prudence.

"Paulina Kowalski is her real name. She uses Emerson because she thinks it's less threatening, less foreign."

"What do you know about her?"

"None of my girls ever used her. I wouldn't allow it. She had a reputation for losing as many as she helped. Rumor was she'd do the job drunk or sober, but mostly drunk. She started out as a legitimate midwife, but she lost her husband and her two kids to the cholera. That's what set her drinking. Nobody wants to be delivered by a woman who keeps a bottle in her apron pocket. But the girls who are desperate will pay anyone who promises to fix them up. That's how she made her living, or at least made enough to keep herself in cheap gin and bad whiskey."

"Do you know where we can find her?"

"I do. But the Mrs. Emerson I'll send you to doesn't drink anymore. I don't know how long she's been sober, or if she goes on a binge every now and then, but from what I've been told, she's a far cry from what she used to be."

"Climbing out of the pit of addiction isn't easy," Prudence said. "Not everyone can do it."

"Paulina's always been odd. When her husband and children were alive, she went to early Mass every morning as regular as clockwork. Didn't go anywhere without a rosary in her pocket. When they died, she blamed God for not answering her prayers, so she took to the bottle and walked away from religion."

"And now?"

"Now she calls herself a spiritualist, one

of them that believes in being able to contact the dead and talk to them. She's not a medium, but I wouldn't be surprised if she decides someday that she's got the gift."

"How do you know so much about her, Jolene?" Geoffrey asked.

"Like I said, I wouldn't let her near any of my girls while she was drinking, but there's no denying she's one of the best when she's sober."

"Anything else?"

"Spiritualists have some peculiar beliefs. Like the one about being able to sense or see the soul fly out of a dying person's mouth on his last breath. There are some who think if they set up a camera, they can catch that soul in a photograph. It's supposed to look like mist or fog in the shape of a person."

"There were pictures of the ghost of Lincoln standing behind his wife," Prudence said. "But they were proven in court to be frauds."

"It's just rumor, mind, but it's said that Paulina makes extra money working with one of the photographers who makes cabinet photos and *cartes de visite* of the deceased. She lets him know when she thinks a woman isn't going to survive delivery for long, or when it looks like a baby is born too early or too weak to survive."

"Surely, no family would let a photographer into their home at such a time," Prudence exclaimed, remembering her father's death and how he lay in his open coffin in the parlor so that friends and relatives could pay their last respects. There had been no photographs taken of Judge MacKenzie's body.

"You'd be surprised. If there'd never been time or money or an occasion important enough to justify having a photograph taken, this is the last opportunity to capture a likeness. She probably makes the suggestion, but has already forewarned the photographer so he arrives right away after the death."

"Perhaps before?"

"That I wouldn't know."

A clock bonged the hour and Madame Jolene rose to her feet, signaling that the interview was over. "I run a business," she said. "Time is money."

The exteriors of the brick rooming houses on West Twenty-seventh Street were as neat and respectable looking as the brothels and businesses that shared the block, their only distinction being the signs in their windows advertising ROOMS TO LET. Mrs. Thompson's establishment was four stories tall, a narrow building with space for only one window on each side of the front door.

When their knock was answered, Prudence and Geoffrey found themselves in a long, dark hallway, with stairs to one side rising to the floors above. Except for a front parlor and the set of rooms Mrs. Thompson kept for herself on the ground floor, every square foot of the formerly single-family, upper-middle-class home had been converted into small bedrooms, where the only furniture was a narrow bed, a chair, and a commode just large enough to hold a water pitcher and basin. It was nearly as cold inside the house as outside in the street.

"I'll fetch her for you," Mrs. Thompson said. "I know she's in because I heard her go upstairs not half an hour ago. You can wait in the parlor."

Clean, cold, and barren of any unnecessary item of decoration, the parlor was a place where a guest would not be tempted to overstay his welcome. Two upholstered wingback chairs flanked a worn sofa, in front of which stood a low table, where a pot of ivy struggled to stay alive. The fireplace held an aspidistra plant, though there were signs that a coal fire had been lit there not too long ago.

They waited in silence, certain that a landlady who recognized her roomers by their footsteps would also be able to overhear every conversation that took place beneath her roof. Prudence took out one of their business cards and slipped it beneath her glove. They would have to decide how much to tell Paulina Emerson after they'd had a chance to size her up.

The woman who came into the parlor and introduced herself was as plump and harmless looking as a storybook grandmother. Her gray hair was twisted into a tight bun, her dress was of sturdy dark blue serge, and she wore an old-fashioned crocheted lace collar. Her landlady had no doubt described the visitors to her; Paulina Emerson showed no surprise that she had been called upon by two well-dressed members of the upper class.

"I remember Mrs. Sorensen," she said in answer to their question. "It wasn't a difficult birth, but the infant wasn't delivered until very late into the night. The mother begged me to stay with her until the baby nurse arrived the next day. That's a bit unusual, but the child was early, so the arrangements for care had to be adjusted."

"And you did spend the night?" Prudence asked.

"Yes. What was left of it. I hadn't been looking forward to walking alone through the streets in the pitch-blackness, so staying for a few extra hours suited me fine."

"Could you tell us about the doctor? Did he deliver the child, or did you?"

"I did," Mrs. Emerson said. A hint of stubbornness shone in her pale blue eyes. "I'd already been engaged by the husband, you see, but the doctor had cared for Mrs. Sorensen's family before she married. I don't know who sent for him when the labor began. It might have been Mrs. Sorensen herself or one of the servants. Mr. Sorensen wasn't there. At any rate there were two of us when there only needed to be one."

"That would be Dr. Jonathan Norbert," Geoffrey contributed.

"The uncle, not the nephew," Mrs. Emerson elaborated. "I don't like to speak ill of the dead."

"We wouldn't ask if it weren't important." Prudence watched as the midwife's strong hands tightened in her lap until the knuckles turned white. *She's planning to lie or to hide something, and she's nervous about it.* "Dr. Norbert passed away a few months later. He was quite elderly at the time. We've been told by a colleague that he had a markedly irascible nature."

"If that means he had a temper, yes. I had more experience with birthing than he could ever hope for, but he ordered me around as if I didn't know what I was doing."

"Why did you stay then?"

Mrs. Emerson flushed a deep, dark red. She tossed her head and clamped her lips tightly shut.

"Was it because you knew Mr. Sorensen wouldn't pay for your services if it was the doctor who delivered the child?" Prudence asked quietly. She nodded sympathetically, as if she knew what it was like to wonder where the next coin was coming from or if there would even be one.

Mrs. Emerson sat in mulish silence.

"Or maybe Mr. Sorensen wasn't the only one who hired you? Is that it?"

Despite the chill in the parlor, beads of moisture broke out on Mrs. Emerson's forehead.

"There are photographers who pay for information about childbirths that go wrong," Prudence continued. "But only if they're called in to photograph the deceased. I think you stayed that night in case something went wrong, as it so often does.

You were planning to recommend a particular photographer, if one were needed. He'd paid you in the past and you'd gotten used to the extra bit of money now and then."

Mrs. Emerson stared coldly at Prudence, then turned to look at Geoffrey. It was plain that she regretted having told them anything.

"Just a few more questions." Geoffrey smiled engagingly.

"I don't have anything else to tell you."

"Mr. Sorensen arrived home after the child was born. We know that. Were you with Mrs. Sorensen when he came into the room to see the infant?" he asked, ignoring her protestation. He smiled again and leaned forward, as though only good manners kept him from picking up and holding one of her hands.

"The housekeeper put me in the baby nurse's room," Mrs. Emerson answered. "I was very tired and it was late, so I fell asleep right away."

"You didn't hear or see anything during the night?" Geoffrey prodded. "An experienced midwife like yourself must sleep lightly when an infant has just been delivered. Even when you're not completely awake, you must be listening for a cry or perhaps a moan of distress from the mother.

Isn't that true, Mrs. Emerson?"

"I did hear someone come up the stairs." Paulina Emerson seemed mesmerized by Geoffrey's hypnotically persuasive voice. "I waited, in case I was needed, but I heard nothing more. Then, after a while, I opened the nursery door just a narrow crack to see out into the hallway, and there was Mr. Sorensen, locking the door to his wife's bedroom. I must have made a sound, because he turned around and saw me."

"Then what?" Geoffrey urged.

"He was furious. I don't know when I've seen a man so angry. He came into the nursery, grabbed me by the arm and demanded to know what I was still doing there. Before I could answer, he told me to get my clothes on and leave his house. Immediately. He waited outside the nursery door until I came out and then he marched me down the stairs and into the street."

"Did he pay you?"

"Yes." She flushed that deep red color again.

"More than you expected?"

"Twice what we'd agreed on. He told me I'd be sorry if I ever came back to that house."

"Have you told this story to anyone else before today?"

Mrs. Emerson shook her head. As she looked at the two strangers, her face suddenly contorted and she bit her lower lip. Fear. Paulina Emerson was terrified of something. Or someone.

She bolted to her feet and was gone from the room before they realized what she intended.

The door slammed behind her retreating back.

CHAPTER 18

"The only time I see you is when you want something," Billy McGlory said.

He poured two fingers of Cascade Tennessee Whisky, one of Ned Hayes's preferred brands of bourbon, and held the crystal glass out to the man who had saved his life at the expense of his career with the New York City Police. For himself he favored an Irish whiskey tapped straight from the barrel and sold for pennies all over Hell's Kitchen. *Uisce beatha* in Gaelic, water of life, though for many it was pure perdition.

"I wouldn't want to ruin your reputation." Ned raised his glass in a silent toast.

McGlory was one of the most notorious casino saloon owners in the city; there were more stories told about him than anyone could keep track of. He dressed like a dandy and ran his empire with merciless efficiency. He'd bought the police and all the judges he needed years ago; his only opposition were the reformers who swarmed out of their churches every few years determined to convert the godless and destroy the cesspits of sin. They could rarely be bought off, but the wave of righteousness never lasted very long. Putting up with them was accepted as part of the cost of doing business.

"I always pay my debts," McGlory reminded him. It was the first thing anyone who crossed his path remembered. "And I collect on them, too."

When you owed your life to a man, the debt never ended. McGlory expected to be doing favors for Hayes until the ex-detective's twin addictions to morphine and alcohol finished him off. He looked good today, though. McGlory's dealers reported that Hayes's buying had changed. Nowadays he rarely purchased enough morphine to make it worth their while to sell it to him, though they made sure that what he did buy was the best that could be obtained. No cutting with rat poison, either. That was part of McGlory's debt.

"I need information about a man named Aaron Sorensen," Hayes began. "Whatever you have, but I'm especially interested in his gambling habits. How much he owes and where. If what I already know is any indication, he's verging on the desperate. A lady's life is at stake."

"I take it he's not a client."

"Hardly."

"Clients have been known to lie."

"Everybody lies, Billy. But Sorensen is not our client."

"I heard you were working with Geoffrey Hunter again."

"Hunter and MacKenzie."

"Miss MacKenzie proved herself as brave as any man in the Joseph Nolan affair. And probably more resourceful. I doubt either one of us would have thought of bringing him down with the knotted waist cord from a religious habit and a large rosary."

"I'm not sure she and Josiah Gregory would have succeeded without the dog. Miss MacKenzie promised Kevin Carney in the carriage that day that he and Blossom would always be welcome to bed down in her stables."

"They'll turn up from time to time," McGlory said. "They're both fond of horses."

"Aaron Sorensen?"

"He's the worst kind of gambler for himself, his family, and whatever business he makes his money in. He doesn't know when to walk away from the table and his card sense gets worse and worse as the night progresses. But he's exactly the kind of loser I like to see walk through my doors."

"How much does he owe?"

"At his clubs or around town?"

"Both."

Billy McGlory scribbled something on a scrap of paper, then handed the message to the bouncer who stood guard outside his office door. He strolled back across the thick Turkish carpets that helped make his private quarters both luxurious and soundproof, dimming the gaslights along the wood-paneled walls as he came. He liked to conduct business in the equivalent gloom of a moonlit back alley.

"Will you ever go back down South, Ned?" he asked.

"Will you ever be tempted to visit Ireland?"

"I was born here. Why go somewhere that's never been home to me?"

"Nostalgia?"

"It's not an emotion strong enough to get me across the ocean."

"My father was a Union man. My mother married North, but her heart didn't come with her."

"Yet you became a Confederate officer."

"I couldn't bear to disappoint her. I was seventeen when I was commissioned. That's not old enough to know anything about real life."

"Still. You were the one who asked the question. I've just turned it around and pointed it at you."

"*Touché,* Billy. I miss the South with about the same intensity as a sufferer from toothache mourns the loss of what caused him so much pain. Which is to say, I wish it were still there, but I'm glad I don't have to put up with it."

McGlory chuckled to himself as he opened the door to the hesitant knock he'd been expecting. A tiny man with the sharp-featured face of a mythical leprechaun sidled into the office. He carried a heavy ledger that rocked him back on his feet. McGlory poured him a healthy glass of the staggeringly potent Irish whiskey and spoke to him in Gaelic.

"He doesn't understand a word of English," he explained to Ned. "And as long as he remains ignorant of the language, he'll have a very well-paying job keeping my books. The minute he learns how to communicate in American, I fire him," he continued, switching to Gaelic and then translating what he'd said.

The bookkeeper smiled, drank down his *uisce beatha* in a single swallow, and opened the ledger. McGlory leaned over Aaron Sorensen's page, asking questions in hesitant Gaelic as he ran a diamond-ringed forefinger down the columns.

"All the old people in the neighborhood turned to Gaelic when they didn't want us kids to know what they were talking about," he said in answer to Ned Hayes's unspoken question. "I don't think it ever occurred to them that hearing the language that often made understanding it become as natural as drinking mother's milk. For some of us. Not all."

The bookkeeper wrote two figures on the same scrap of paper on which McGlory had printed Sorensen's name. He hefted his enormous ledger and left his employer's opulent office with a longing, backward glance at the bottle of Irish whiskey sitting on the table.

"The first figure is what he owes club members at the Union and Lotos. The second is what his less gentlemanly creditors are ready to collect from him, one way or another."

"How much more time will they give him?" Ned Hayes asked.

"How much time do you need?"

"I'm not sure. A month or two."

"I'll see what I can do. I can lean on the

gamblers who owe money to the casinos, but probably not the careful players who confine their wins and losses to within the walls of their clubs. Unless they have other, less acceptable vices."

"I'll be grateful for whatever time you can buy him. He doesn't deserve it, but his wife does."

"That's the lady whose life may be in danger?"

"It is," Ned replied. "He's got her trapped in as tightly tied a Gordian knot as I've ever come across."

McGlory shot his diamond-studded cuffs and sipped from his crystal glass of *uisce beatha.* Sparks of light leaped into the dimness in which both men sat.

"How involved is Miss MacKenzie?" Billy asked. There was something undeniably compelling and stimulating about a young woman who was determined to shape her life exactly the way she wanted to live it. If he'd sired a daughter, Billy would have wanted her to have Prudence MacKenzie's spirit.

"Mr. Hunter and Josiah Gregory are doing their best to keep her safe." Ned shrugged his shoulders. Miss Prudence had a mind of her own.

"Then I'll drink to her good health," Mc-

Glory said. He'd send some men out, too, he decided, just to be on the safe side. Women were unpredictable creatures.

"I'm so tired," Ethel said, setting down the tea she hadn't finished drinking. It tasted bitter. The sound of the cup settling into the saucer was unexpectedly loud.

"You should go to bed, my love," Aaron Sorensen told his wife, one arm around her waist as he helped her to her feet. "We'll talk tomorrow about my trip. I'm afraid my return has fatigued you more than is good either for you or for my son."

"We don't know that it's a boy." She rather hoped it would be a girl who would grow up to cherish and look after her mother.

"I know it's a son, Ethel. You mustn't worry about disappointing me."

She felt something warm and wet trickle down her legs and ducked her head in embarrassment. That had been happening too often of late; as her belly grew larger, her ability to make it to a chamber pot became less reliable. She decided to say nothing, though there was also a most annoying pulling sensation in the small of her back. Ethel thought she had been sitting too long. The baby wasn't due for another three or four weeks, and everyone told her that first babies were always late. Nothing to be concerned about.

Aaron dismissed his wife's maid. He would see to her comfort himself tonight. It was the least he could do after nearly two weeks away. The maid almost said something about the lady's companion who had only been in the house for four days before her brother-in-law's death ended her employment, but then she remembered that the housekeeper had instructed all of the servants not to mention the brief episode. You never knew how Mr. Sorensen would react to news he didn't expect. Better to pretend it had never happened, since it was highly unlikely Miss Penelope Mason would ever return. She closed the door to Mrs. Sorensen's bedroom and went off to her own attic room, where she promptly fell asleep.

When the pains began in earnest, Ethel held tightly to Aaron's hands and drank the bitter brew he held to her lips, then the laudanum that eased the agony and tipped her into sleep. She clasped her legs around the towels he put between them to absorb the blood flowing too fast and thick to be normal, never realizing that her life forces were draining out of her. The babe she carried fought his way toward the future, but the muscles that should have propelled him from his mother's body moved spasmodically, convulsed by the pennyroyal, rendered too quickly flaccid by the laudanum. The boy smothered to death during the passage down the birth canal. Ethel's body was too weak to expel him.

Aaron pinched a thumb and forefinger on either side of his wife's nose, closing off the delicate nostrils she'd occasionally dared flare at him. So much blood lost. So much pennyroyal and laudanum swallowed. Ethel died without a fuss, without a sound.

She had finally done something right.

Two weeks in Philadelphia had been barely enough time to ease Ethel's father out of life, bury him, and meet with the lawyers who had drawn up his will. They understood when Aaron explained that his wife was in fragile health herself, and also with child, so they agreed, of course, that since the estate would pass under his control anyway, there was no reason to insist that Samuel Caswell's daughter make the journey from New York City to Philadelphia. They also understood that it was in her best interests, and to ensure the safe delivery of her child, that her husband choose the time to inform her of her father's passing. Women were fragile creatures.

Aaron Sorensen returned to New York two lives away from a fortune larger than he had hoped for. Ethel would have to die; the child, her heir, could not live, either.

He made his plans on the train hurtling toward the most exciting city in America. He loved New York; he regretted that he would have to leave it soon, but he was a careful man. He had to pay debts that could cost him his life if left unsettled, and then he had to move on to new territory, where past losses would not haunt him. There would be the house to sell; that might slow him down, but the property was too valuable not to cash it in. He wondered if Catherine's sister might want to buy the home in which she had grown up.

The conundrum he faced this morning as he closed Ethel's bedroom door and slowly descended the staircase toward the dining room was whether or not to send for Bartholomew Monroe and his sister. Catherine's cabinet photograph had done precisely what he had intended. Her passing had been mourned by friends and admirers of her talent, the tragedy of two lives snuffed out at the moment of great promise lost on no one. Nor was the deep sorrow of the bereft widower. The key was doing what was expected, not shirking any of the rituals society countenanced. But first the body had to be discovered.

"Tell Mrs. Sorensen's maid to bring her up a breakfast tray," Aaron told his butler.

"I trust you slept well, sir."

"I did. There's nothing quite like one's own bed at the end of a journey." The dining room had a certain glow to it this morning, which was as soothing as the fragrance of the coffee being poured into his cup. The size of his gambling debts had been worrisome, and his own temporary inability to win back the losses had begun to eat away at his confidence. Not to mention the threats that had surfaced and the presence of two vicious-looking thugs he had spied dogging his footsteps. Now all would be well again. Ethel's money would flow like manna from heaven, and he could get on with the life he was meant to lead. Women had proved the surest way to wealth, but they were never the easiest creatures to deal with. Fortunately, they were among the most vulnerable. No one questioned a death in childbirth.

He heard the sound of breaking crockery and panicked footsteps running down the servants' staircase. The butler reappeared in the dining room, his face blanched of color.

"I've taken the liberty of sending for the doctor, Mr. Sorensen," he said. "Mrs. Sorensen appears to have gone into labor during the night and lost consciousness. The housekeeper and her maid have gone up to her."

The doctor? Couldn't the damn maid see she was already dead? But he didn't dare ask, in case questions were posed later on and someone remembered.

Leaving his coffee to cool on the table, Aaron rushed from the room, the butler following close behind. Up the stairs, down the hallway. He could see the door to Ethel's bedroom standing ajar. A wide-eyed maid came out as he approached; she carried a basin heaped with bloody towels.

What would a concerned husband do? He reached out a hand and touched the maid's arm.

"Is she . . . ?" he asked.

"No, sir, thanks be to God. But Mrs. Hopkins says it'll be touch and go, and she may not last until the doctor gets here." The maid ducked her head and spun away, suddenly aware she'd said too much.

"Perhaps it's best not to go in, sir," the butler said.

Aaron allowed the man to help him to a chair. He sank into it heavily, as though the weight of imminent loss had suddenly fallen onto his shoulders.

"I'll bring up some brandy, sir."

"And the doctor, the moment he gets here."

"It won't be long, sir. His sister said he'd been summoned out during the night. He's only a few streets away and the house is on the telephone."

"Who did you call?"

"Dr. Peter Worthington, sir."

"He's not my wife's regular physician."

"No, sir, but we were unable to reach him. Mrs. Sorensen gave me Dr. Worthington's number in case of just such an occurrence. Apparently, he comes highly recommended."

There was nothing else to say.

Brandy in hand, listening intently to the muted sounds coming from within his wife's bedroom, Aaron Sorensen waited for his future to arrive.

Chapter 19

Ethel Sorensen was still alive when Dr. Peter Worthington arrived twenty minutes after being located and told of her plight. The sun had been up for an hour, but the sky was overcast and the temperature wintry cold. He'd come only a short few blocks from the patient with whom he'd spent most of the night, but there hadn't been time for bricks to be heated and put into his carriage. His fingers were icy and his feet numb.

"I don't know what happened, Doctor," Aaron Sorensen told him. "I've been out of town on business, and when I came home yesterday, Ethel was fine. Tired, of course. She told me to dismiss her maid, so I helped her to bed myself. I sat beside her and we talked until she fell asleep. My room adjoins hers, but I'm sure she didn't call out. I would have heard her."

"I'll go right up. Is there someone with

her now?" The husband looked distraught and smelled of brandy, not at all uncommon under the circumstances.

"Our housekeeper, Mrs. Hopkins. I don't think she's left my wife's side since her maid found her and ran for help."

"What time was that, Mr. Sorensen?"

"Not more than an hour ago."

"Try to have some breakfast, especially coffee. I'll send word down as soon as I've examined Mrs. Sorensen and can ascertain her condition." Worthington glanced over his shoulder once as he climbed the stairs to the second floor. The foyer was empty.

He knocked softly on the bedroom door, outside of which a basket of fresh linen sat waiting to be used. The woman who greeted him had the competent air of an experienced housekeeper, one who long ago learned to deal with all sorts of situations. She met him at the foot of the patient's bed, introduced herself in a voice lowered to a whisper, and assured him that anything he asked for could be made available. Then she stood back, and he had his first unobstructed view of Ethel Sorensen.

She lay motionless beneath coverlets, which hardly moved with the barely discernible rise and fall of her breathing. The smell of blood was strong in the room, though the stained linens had been removed and a candle lit to purify the air. Even before he touched her, Peter Worthington knew her skin would be cold from the shock of blood loss. A small blanket-wrapped body lay in its cradle beside the bed. The tiny face had been left exposed after the child had been washed. He wondered whether the mother had been conscious then, and if it was to spare her feelings that the swaddling was that of a live child. Covering the face sometimes brought on paroxysms of grief.

"I found the child half delivered," Mrs. Hopkins said. "He slid out very easily, but he was dead, of course. She was still bleeding heavily. We packed her as best we could with clean linens." She twitched back the towel covering the basin she held out for the doctor's inspection. The torn placenta had left Ethel's body at almost the same moment as her dead child.

"Was she ever conscious?"

"Very briefly." She pointed to the tonic bottle on the bedside table. "Mrs. Sorensen occasionally took a few drops in the evening to help her sleep. I fear that last night she may have awakened and taken more than she should have. Not realizing what she was doing."

"Will you uncover her, please?" He took

off his coat and rolled up the sleeves of his spotless white shirt. "I'd like to examine her."

Mrs. Hopkins on one side of the bed, Dr. Worthington on the other, they rolled Ethel's linens as gently off her body as they could. Thick pads of folded sheets had been placed under her hips and between her legs. The top layers were soaked through with bright red blood.

"Leave them for the moment," Dr. Worthington ordered. He lifted the patient's eyelids, listened to her heart and lungs, counted her feeble pulse and palpated her abdomen.

Mrs. Hopkins watched his every movement, white-faced and tight-lipped with the effort of staying strong while the young woman who had been such a good mistress lay dying before her. Nothing to be done. When a mother bled this much and still bled after the child left her body, it was next to certain that she wouldn't leave her bed alive. The housekeeper took the small mirror from the dressing table and stood with it in her hands, waiting.

"I'll go downstairs and tell Mr. Sorensen that we fear the worst. You can change the saturated linens and replace the covers, but try not to disturb her too much." Worthington refastened his cuffs and put on his coat. "There isn't much time left. Her husband will want to sit beside her."

It wasn't the first time Bartholomew Monroe had been called in while a new mother lay dying, her deceased infant already washed and prepared for burial. When the child was not to be embalmed, a post-mortem photographer had to move quickly. Fortunately, Mr. Sorensen had been pleased with the work done of his first wife and had had the foresight to contact the studio as his second wife's *accouchement* approached. A woman's first infant rarely came when expected. Early or late, but almost never on the date predicted.

"The doctor has informed me that Mrs. Sorensen will not last the day. She has lapsed into a coma." Aaron's eyes were red with grief and unshed tears, his voice thickened with brandy.

"My heartfelt condolences, sir. How tragic to lose two soul mates and not to have a living child by which to remember either of them. My sister and I will do our best to ensure that you will always have an image of their dear faces to console you."

"If you'll follow me, I'll take you to them."

"The doctor is still here?"

"I've persuaded him to rest for an hour in the library. My housekeeper is at my wife's side. Her name is Mrs. Hopkins."

"I think we shall send Mrs. Hopkins down to the kitchen for a restorative cup of tea," Monroe said. "My sister's presence will preserve the proprieties, and if your dear lady should stir, we'll alert you immediately. Perhaps your butler can send a footman out to the carriage for our cases. He can leave them in the hallway outside Mrs. Sorensen's bedroom. We'll bring in only what's absolutely necessary."

"Doctor Worthington thinks she won't see another sunrise," Mrs. Hopkins said as she stirred sugar into her tea, "but I think there's a chance he might be wrong. Her breathing is stronger and steadier and the bleeding has stopped."

"How do you know that?" Cook spread newly churned butter on thick slices of this morning's fresh loaves.

"I looked, didn't I?"

"What did the doctor say to that?"

"He wasn't there. Mr. Sorensen insisted he go take a nap in the library. He's been up all night, poor man."

"What could have happened to her to make everything go so wrong?"

"Laudanum. I told the doctor that she sometimes took a few drops of that expectant mother's tonic after dinner or when she went to bed. And that we think she must have waked up and dosed herself again, but being half asleep, she took too much."

"Have you ever heard of such a thing?" Cook filled the teapot with fresh leaves and more boiling water from the kettle. She brought her cup and saucer to the table and sat down heavily. Her feet seemed to be always hurting nowadays.

"I've never touched a drop of the stuff myself," Mrs. Hopkins said. "And I won't, either. There's too many has come to grief over it."

"How much would it take to make the babe get stuck half in and half out like that?" Cook asked. She liked to know the precise measurements for everything.

"She might have taken a couple of spoonfuls instead of a few drops," Mrs. Hopkins speculated. "There was a teaspoon in a glass by the bottle."

"And how much was left in the bottle?"

"Mr. Sorensen took it away as soon as he came into the room. He put it in his pocket."

"I suppose he couldn't bear the sight of it, knowing the damage that had been done."

"I can't help but think that if that lady's companion hadn't left after only a few days, there might have been someone here to watch over poor Mrs. Sorensen and make sure an accident like this couldn't happen."

"Do we know how to get in touch with her? To let her know?"

"Perhaps there's an address in Mrs. Sorensen's letter book, but I don't think she wanted Mr. Sorensen to know she'd hired a companion. It might have seemed as though she were reproaching him for neglecting her."

"Have another cup of tea, Mrs. Hopkins," Cook urged. "You're going to need it before the day's out."

"She looks so peaceful," Felicia Monroe said. "As though she's already passed over into a better place." She'd found that when death was this close, it sometimes helped the survivors to speak of it as though it had already happened.

Aaron Sorensen held her hand mirror under his wife's nostrils. The glass fogged, cleared, fogged again.

Felicia thought she detected the slightest expression of annoyance flit across his face. She stored away her impression until she could mention it to Bartholomew.

"If you would step outside for just a moment," Sorensen said.

"Of course," Felicia answered. She motioned to Bartholomew, who was consulting the exposure chart he already knew by heart. Until they opened the curtain, the room would remain dim. She thought Mr. Sorensen wanted to be alone for a few moments with his dying wife and dead son, perhaps hold the infant in his arms with no one to witness the tears of a father's heart.

The door opened moments later and Sorensen brushed past them, head down, one hand in the pocket of his jacket. Clutching a handkerchief, Felicia thought.

"Laudanum," Bartholomew said when they were alone in the bedroom. "Can you smell it?"

"I thought he smelled of brandy when we arrived."

"I don't think he was the one who just swallowed a dose of laudanum." Monroe gestured toward the figure on the bed; then he leaned over and inserted a forefinger between her lips. Held it to his nose and then to Felicia's. "He's helping her along."

"It wouldn't be the first time," Felicia reminded him. "I was watching when he held the mirror to her face. He was impatient with the result. Disappointed, I thought."

"Lock the door."

They set up the camera and tripod where the exposure of the dead child lying in his cradle would have the best light. Even with the curtains open and the drapes drawn all the way back, there was not quite enough brightness to capture a good image without the use of a magnesium flash.

"We'll do the infant alone first," Bartholomew decided.

"I don't think these clouds will dissipate," Felicia said. "This is all the daylight we're going to get."

"I'll use the flash. We can put a drape between Mrs. Sorensen and the cradle."

"She's unconscious, Bartholomew. She won't wake up."

"How much is unconsciousness and how much is sleep induced by laudanum? There's no telling how long he's been dosing her or how much she's been taking on her own. If she's already susceptible to nightmares, the flash could cause her to have laudanum hallucinations."

"She's too weak from loss of blood to be able to get out of bed."

"She can still thrash her arms and legs. I'll use as little magnesium as possible. The drape should muffle the effect of the flash."

There was no arguing with him. Bartholomew Monroe was a law unto himself; his sister had learned long ago that it was best to do as he instructed.

Felicia hung the black drape from a portable frame, then turned her attention to the motionless bundle in the cradle. The child was perfectly formed and only a little smaller than he would have been, had he been allowed to grow to term. The woman who washed him had meticulously removed every speck of birth blood and brushed his blond infant hair so it lay neatly across his scalp. The tiny hands and miniature fingers with their perfect blue-tinged nails lay curled at his sides.

"There's a christening gown laid out on the dresser," Bartholomew said. "I think there's a cap there also."

"I'll dress him in those, then."

While Felicia eased the unnamed Sorensen boy into his christening robe and cap, Bartholomew arranged sprays of silk flowers around the cradle and spread a crocheted blanket over its sides. The child would look like he was lying in a cloud of soft wool surrounded by a grove of fragrant lilies. Such a perfect setting that in years to come the father could imagine his son to be sleeping, not dead.

Ethel Sorensen did not stir when the magnesium flash went off. She didn't move even when Bartholomew opened the window to allow some of the fumes to escape into the brisk March air.

"Try the mirror," he told his sister, standing at the foot of the bed.

The surface of the glass clouded over.

"Stay there," Bartholomew commanded when Felicia took a step away from Ethel's side. He moved the camera closer to the dying woman's face, then disappeared under the black cloth that covered everything but the lens. Felicia heard him muttering exposure calculations. She knew what would come next.

"Pinch her nostrils when I tell you to," Bartholomew instructed his sister.

Some spiritualists contended that the soul flew out of the mouth at the moment of death, and that if one believed enough and was present and engaged with the spirits at that precise instant, its passage would be visible. A cloudy substance, not unlike the ectoplasm of longer departed spirits, would take wing and sail into eternity. Perhaps not even entirely shapeless. There were those who claimed to have witnessed the phenomenon, but no one had as yet captured an authentic soul flight through the aegis of photography. It was Bartholomew Monroe's ambition to be the first.

Felicia told herself that what she was about to do was not really murder. Ethel Sorensen was already a dead woman; it was just a matter of when her body would surrender to the inevitable. Her breathing was shallow and erratic; she would feel nothing when it ceased altogether. She had done what Bartholomew requested before, though their opportunities had been far fewer than he had hoped. It wasn't altogether unheard of for a supposedly dead individual to gasp his way back to life while lying in his coffin. Still.

"Are you ready, Felicia?"

Two or three times in the past, she hadn't pinched hard or long enough, and Bartholomew had had to come out from under his black cloth and do the job properly. If a soul had been visible, they'd missed it, and Felicia was to blame. She was determined not to fail him this time.

"I'm ready."

"On the count of three, then." The black cloth settled over his head and shoulders. She could just make out his voice counting off the seconds left in Ethel's earthly life. "One, two, three. Now."

Felicia squeezed as tightly and steadily as

she could, watching Ethel's upper torso so as not to have to see her face should it contort. The end seemed to come almost immediately. She breathed and then she did not. No gasping, no rattling, no sound like a door squeaking on rusty hinges.

But nothing floated from between Ethel's lips, no spectrally pale presence bade farewell to the body that had housed it. Seconds and then minutes ticked by on the clock the housekeeper had stopped when the child was taken from his mother's body. Bartholomew had restarted it when they began their work.

A disappointed sigh came from beneath the black cloth. The sound of the glass plate being extracted.

"You don't suppose the soul had already left?" Felicia asked timidly. Her fingers dropped to Ethel Sorensen's wrist, to the blue vein that no longer pulsed.

"Don't be ridiculous," her brother grunted. "Life ends and the soul departs. In that order." He opened the case where he stored and carried the glass plate negatives, inserted the plate he had just exposed. He would keep and look at it in the darkroom, just in case.

"There's no point leaving when we'll have to come back again," he said. "Go inform her husband that his wife seems to have passed away without our noticing it while we were photographing the child. I'm sure he'll want us to stay and photograph her as well. You might hint that we have other appointments to keep in the next few days."

Aaron Sorensen agreed that it would be best to preserve his wife's postmortem images at the same time as her child's. He also decided that Dr. Worthington's nap on the library sofa should not be interrupted. He could sign the death certificates when he woke up.

A single coffin was ordered and delivered, Ethel's washed body placed inside, the nameless infant boy cradled against her side.

Bartholomew Monroe promised to have *cartes de visite* and cabinet photos delivered the next morning; the viewing would take place in the afternoon.

Aaron left the choice of photograph to Monroe's discretion; appropriate remembrances of the departed were what he was known for.

Dr. Peter Worthington woke up with a thundering headache and a mouth that tasted as though every horse-drawn hansom cab in New York City had rolled through it.

He stood over Ethel Sorensen's open coffin in bewilderment; it was the first time in all of his years practicing medicine that he hadn't managed to stay awake at the bedside of a patient who needed him. How could he have slept away the morning and half the afternoon on the library couch and not responded to repeated attempts to rouse him? It had never happened before. Never. Yet he had no reason to doubt Aaron Sorensen's account of his wife's passing.

Worthington signed Ethel Sorensen's death certificate and attested to the stillbirth of her child. He stood beside the coffin that had been placed atop a cooling table in the large parlor and studied the new mother's face. Calm, composed, pale beneath the paint the photographer had applied. Some heavy floral scent had been rubbed into her skin to disguise the hint of incipient decay, but there had been no embalming. The husband had adamantly refused even to consider injecting arsenic compounds into the bodies of his wife and child. They would go into the family crypt like all of their predecessors, as God intended.

It wasn't until Dr. Worthington was halfway home, hot bricks at his feet, wrapped in a wool blanket to ward off a chill, that he remembered that Prudence MacKenzie had come to his office to ask about the doctor and the midwife who attended the first Mrs. Sorensen. Who had also died in childbirth.

He'd told her that not every death was a murder. *Unless you're the person asking about it.* He'd spoken the words in jest because Prudence was so serious and he'd wanted to see her smile. Now he rapped on the roof of the carriage and told his coachman to take him to the United Bank Building at the corner of Wall Street and Broadway. If Prudence wasn't in the offices of Hunter and MacKenzie, Investigative Law, he'd go to her home off Fifth Avenue.

It suddenly seemed vitally important that Prudence and her ex-Pinkerton partner know about the second Mrs. Sorensen's death.

Chapter 20

"The cabby you sent to bring me here said it was urgent, Prudence."

"His name is Danny Dennis. We have him on retainer. There's no better hansom cab driver in all of New York City." Prudence took a deep breath. She and Geoffrey had debated how to break the news, knowing how tightly wound the singer was. Best to get it over with as quickly as possible. "I have to tell you something I couldn't put in a note, Claire. A doctor brought me the news less than an hour ago."

Claire Buchanan sat motionless, staring at the polished surface of Prudence's desk. Then she raised her head and closed her eyes against what she was about to hear. "You'd better tell me," she whispered.

"Ethel Sorensen has died in childbirth. The infant she carried was stillborn."

Claire opened her eyes and stared straight ahead as if visualizing the deaths. "Poor creatures. Two more of Sorensen's victims." She looked directly at Prudence as she made her accusation. "It wasn't a member of the company who had Lucinda killed. It was him, Aaron Sorensen. I was a fool to believe anything else."

"Geoffrey put one of his ex-Pinkerton operatives on you as soon as he saw the cut rope in Jacob Riis's photographs."

"Aaron must need money very badly," Claire said. "He had to have known that my will named Catherine and her heirs as my beneficiaries. Somehow he found out I hadn't changed it after she died. I made myself a target when I wrote to tell him I was back in New York covering at the Met and that I wanted to see him. He knew I'd be onstage for every rehearsal. All he had to do was find a sailor working the flies who needed money badly enough to agree to cut loose that sandbag. The man is probably long gone by now. Back to sea, out of reach."

"We don't have any proof of that."

"Aaron must have been furious. The sandbag missed only because Lucinda pushed me out of the way. He killed an innocent woman for nothing. Before he could try again, I'd taken steps to make sure he wouldn't profit from my death. I've been safe ever since my lawyer informed him he could no longer expect to inherit any of my estate."

"He has gambling debts. Geoffrey suspects he's been cheating at his clubs."

"He killed her," Claire said. "When he couldn't get my money, Aaron murdered that poor woman he married two months after he ended Catherine's life. She was an heiress, wasn't she, Prudence? She had to have been. He made sure she became pregnant right away so she couldn't escape if she found out what he was."

Prudence didn't contradict her.

"It's my fault she's dead." The torture of experiencing the guilt of being alive at another's expense twisted the features of Claire's face. "If I had died instead of Lucinda, two blameless women would have been spared. He would have had the money he needed. There would have been no reason to kill his wife."

"Ethel was doomed the day she signed her marriage certificate," Prudence said. "And if you hadn't come to us with suspicions about your sister's death, no one would have thought to look into Catherine's passing. Claire, there may have been others."

"Before Catherine?"

She hesitated, tempted to tell her client about the items she'd stolen from

Sorensen's desk. Josiah had begun tracing what she had brought back, but it was far too early in the investigation to expect results. *"Evidence shared is evidence lost,"* her father had often said. *"Don't make a move unless you know what the result will be."*

"It's only a theory," she temporized, knowing how unsatisfactory an answer that was.

"When is the funeral?" Claire asked. She squared her shoulders and held her head high. Tears had streaked, then dried on her cheeks.

"There's to be a viewing tomorrow afternoon, but no funeral here in New York. The bodies are being taken by train to Philadelphia to be interred beside Mrs. Sorensen's father. Our secretary just confirmed the details with the mortuary handling the transportation."

"I'm going to the viewing," Claire said. "It's at the house?"

"Yes. Are you sure you want to meet your former brother-in-law under such circumstances?"

"Someone has to stand in front of him as witness to what he's done. He won't be able to hide it from me. I'll read it in his eyes. I'm going to put the fear of God into what passes for his soul, Prudence. He'll never be able to look over his shoulder again without fearing that I'll be following him."

"If he's the murderer we think he might be, that could be extremely dangerous."

"I won't be alone with him. There will be other people there."

"Geoffrey and I will go with you, but you have to promise you won't provoke him."

"I'm not a fool, Prudence. I know what he could do if I accuse him without proof. I just want him to look at me and understand that he has no secrets. He has to begin living in fear of discovery."

Prudence picked up the speaking tube attached to the side of her desk. "Josiah," she said, enunciating carefully, "where has Mr. Hunter gone?"

"I'm not sure, miss," came the answer. Josiah's voice sounded hollow. "He mentioned something about meeting Mr. Hayes."

"We'll pick you up at your hotel tomorrow afternoon," Prudence said, returning the speaking tube to its hook. "Don't leave without us."

"You can call off your bodyguard," Claire instructed.

But Prudence knew she wouldn't.

■ ■ ■ ■

Knotted swags of black sateen hung above the ground floor windows and over the massive recessed oak door of what had once been the Buchanan mansion in Lower Manhattan. The four-story home, luxurious by the standards of the prewar era in which it had been built, stood just north of the Fifth Avenue Hotel, where Geoffrey Hunter rented a suite. Dimmed gaslight shimmered faintly behind drawn drapes. Men passing by tipped their hats in recognition of Death's presence; women quickened their pace to avoid its menace. Straw had been layered over the cobblestones in front of the house to deaden the sound of horse hooves and carriage wheels.

"We were very happy here for a while," Claire Buchanan said as the carriage approached. "Even after my mother died. It was emptier without her, but still home, still the place to find comfort. I wonder if our voices echo off the walls late at night when no one is awake to hear them."

"Yours and Catherine's?" Prudence asked. She glanced at Geoffrey, who was studiously avoiding any comment that would interrupt their client's reminiscences. Next to him

Josiah, deprived of his usual stenographer's pad, was mentally taking notes. It had been decided that the secretary would accompany Prudence and Claire to the viewing, while Geoffrey waited outside in the carriage, available if there should be a problem, but safely out of sight of the man whose cheating he had thwarted at the Union Club.

"I know I've told you many times what an extraordinary voice she possessed, but you had to have heard her to fully appreciate it. Have you ever worried that the soprano you're listening to won't make the pitch when she reaches for her next high note? No one ever doubted Catherine's ability and range. It was like watching a bird soar effortlessly into the sky and out of sight. Pure delight."

"I cannot imagine how someone so gifted could be persuaded to renounce that talent," Prudence said. "Was it a sudden decision? Did she simply stop singing one day? Without warning or discussion?"

"I wasn't here. So I don't know the answer to your question. I've asked myself the same thing, over and over again. From what Lucinda said, her withdrawal wasn't complete until after our father's death. She stopped taking lessons, she no longer spoke of the roles she would be studying, she very seldom and then almost never left the house when Sorensen was in town. That's all I was able to learn."

"Yet we know she picked up the threads of her professional life after she became pregnant."

"Not right away, Prudence. Lucinda believed it wasn't until shortly before the child was to be born that she began her lessons again."

The carriage pulled to the curb in front of the house where Catherine and Ethel Sorensen and their infant children had died, where a lady's companion named Penelope Mason had disappeared after being in the household less than a week. Prudence lowered her thick mourning veil to hide her features; Claire did not. Her face paled and the ridges of her cheekbones stood out in stark white relief against her skin; her eyes blazed with anger and accusation.

Keeping his back turned to the windows of the house, Geoffrey handed the women out of the carriage, his gloved hand firm and steadying, his tall presence a reassuring bulwark against whatever awaited them. Prudence looked up at him gratefully, then allowed Josiah to lead her to the front door.

Claire seemed oblivious to her surroundings. Her performer's intensity was wholly focused toward the moment when she would finally be face-to-face with the man she believed had murdered her sister.

A greeter from the mortuary parlor ushered them into the two-story central hallway. The house was utterly silent. Felt pads had been attached to the soles of the servants' shoes, ticking clocks had been stopped, and the lid of the grand piano in the music room lowered and locked. Tall vases of lilies and white chrysanthemums stood in every downstairs room. Black crepe covered the mirrors, photographs lay facedown on tables, and family portraits were turned toward the walls.

The butler who escorted them into the heart of the house glanced more than once at Prudence, but her opaque mourning veil concealed her face and she gave no sign of recognizing him.

The parlor was dim and chilly, the coffin resting on a cooling table draped in black to conceal the blocks of ice resting in metal trays beneath. A dozen chairs had been ranged near the coffin, others placed around the room against the walls. Candles burned on every surface, their waxy aroma warring with the heavy sweetness of cut flowers.

Aaron Sorensen was not keeping watch

over the bodies of his wife and stillborn son. He had relegated that duty to his housekeeper.

Mrs. Hopkins, dressed in her best Sunday black, face composed but bearing traces of honest grief, stood beside the coffin. As she moved away to give them a moment of privacy, Josiah nodded politely, but did not volunteer their names. Prudence averted her veiled face and hunched her shoulders to appear shorter than she really was.

Ethel Sorensen had been a small woman in life; in death she had shrunk to childlike proportions. Her lips and cheeks had been lightly rouged, her skin powdered, dark brown hair dressed to frame her face. Eyelashes long enough to cast shadows on the skin, a glimpse of pearl white teeth between lips that were beginning to pull back from each other. Long fingers, buffed nails, her son resting in the crook of her right arm, easily mistaken for one of the porcelain-headed baby dolls little girls were given for their birthdays. Cold air from the melting ice wafted up through the decorative piercings of the cooling table and its thin black linen cover.

On a stand near the coffin lay a guestbook and fanned-out stacks of *cartes de visite* and cabinet photographs of the deceased. Josiah's signature was the first one on the page, penned in an unintelligible scrawl. He slipped several of the cards into his pocket, then handed one of each to Prudence and Claire.

Bartholomew Monroe had done his work well. It was easy to see why he was one of New York City's most sought-after post-mortem photographers. Ethel had been posed seated in a rocking chair, gazing down at the child in her arms as though she had just sung him to sleep. Not a hair out of place, not a fold of her dress disturbed, nothing to suggest that she was not about to place the child in his cradle and tiptoe out of the room where he lay sleeping.

Prudence knew there would be other negatives stored in Monroe's studio, but this was the public face of Ethel's death, the one by which her husband had chosen to have her remembered. Peaceful and serene, she had become the lovely young wife and mother of every family's dream. The tableau was eerily like the cabinet photo of Catherine Sorensen holding her infant daughter.

A hiss of indrawn breath announced Aaron Sorensen's arrival. He stood motionless in the doorway, staring into Claire Buchanan's irate eyes and desolate face. The twice-widowed husband and his former sister-in-law exchanged not a word; then Sorensen swung his gaze toward Josiah and the veiled Prudence.

"Kind of you to come," he murmured as he approached. He plainly didn't know who they were. Wasn't even sure yet if they had accompanied the sister-in-law he'd been avoiding.

Josiah nodded, spoke condolences so softly it was impossible to make out exactly what he said. He stood aside to allow Prudence to precede him into a middle row of chairs, then tugged gently on Claire's sleeve until she also took a seat.

"Watch him," Prudence whispered. "Watch what he does and how he looks."

Aaron Sorensen approached his wife's coffin stiffly. He stood there, motionless, head bowed as if in prayer, one hand resting on the coffin as if loath to let her go. Claire's eyes bored invisible holes into his back. The silence thickened, lengthened.

Movement at the parlor door broke the tension. An older man and his wife drew near the widower, spoke to him, looked at Ethel and her baby, turned and sat down in the second row of chairs. Not family then. Prudence wondered if Ethel had cousins or aunts and uncles to mourn her passing; both her parents were now dead and she'd had no living siblings.

A clergyman in Episcopal clerical collar and black suit stood beside the bereaved husband as he bent to kiss his wife farewell. When Sorensen took his place in the first row, his eyes were dry and empty.

The prayers were brief, though recited with sincerity. The Episcopal priest did not pretend to have known the dead woman well; he spoke of her comparatively recent arrival in New York City, the joy of a couple awaiting the birth of their first child, and the potential sacrifice every mother had to face. He prayed again, inviting the mourners to join him. When he finished, he lowered the coffin lid and blessed for the last time the woman and child who lay within.

Two men from the mortuary staff rolled the coffin out into the foyer of the house, then carried it down the front steps into the waiting hearse. No one was expected to accompany it to the railroad station; no one did.

The older couple left without lingering longer than the few moments it took to shake Aaron Sorensen's hand and whisper condolences again. Prudence stepped back into the parlor and glanced at the guestbook. Mr. and Mrs. William P. Sufferan, New York City. She wondered if they were fond of imported European antiques.

"The house will be put up for sale," Sorensen was saying to Claire Buchanan. "I planned to ask my lawyers to contact you, since it was your family home at one time. You did, however, sell your interest to Catherine."

"I'm aware of that." Claire's voice was coldly precise.

"So while I can extend you right of first refusal, I'm afraid I cannot quote you anything but the market price."

"I wouldn't expect anything other than that from you."

He handed her a card. "My lawyers. We have nothing more to say to one another. I think all future contact between us should be through them."

"We have to go to Philadelphia," Geoffrey said.

As soon as they returned to the office, he sent Josiah out again in search of Philadelphia newspapers, anything he could find from the last two weeks. He came back with four issues of the *Public Ledger,* one of which contained the obituary of Ethel Sorensen's father.

"Here's another article about Samuel Caswell. It's more comprehensive than the obituary. Both his and his wife's family are well-known. Their fortune is entirely inherited. Apparently, Ethel's parents were neither of them strong. The mother died when their daughter was still a young woman, and the father appears to have been a semi-invalid."

"Which would explain why they were such easy prey for someone like Sorensen," Geoffrey said. "A lonely young woman who probably seldom went out into society and an elderly and infirm father living largely in the past with his deceased wife."

"The law firm that managed the Caswell family affairs is mentioned," Prudence said, reaching for a scissors to cut out the article. "The obituary doesn't go into detail about funeral plans. That's unusual. Most of the time people count on these things to tell them where and when to attend."

"A family crypt in Laurel Hill Cemetery. That's according to the information Josiah was able to get from the mortuary company." Prudence scanned the notes their secretary had provided. "Ethel's coffin is being taken directly from the train to Laurel Hill. The mortuary parlor in Philadelphia is Mortensen's."

"We've missed the afternoon train today," Geoffrey said. "I'll ask Josiah to get us two tickets on tomorrow morning's run."

"What are we looking for?"

"Anything that seems out of place or unexpected. We'll interview anyone who talked with Aaron Sorensen while he was there. Definitely the lawyers who handled his father-in-law's affairs and filed the will for probate. If they're still around, any servants in the family home, especially if they were employed during the time when Sorensen was courting Ethel. One thread should lead to another."

"Geoffrey?" Prudence hesitated, unsure whether she really wanted to pursue what she was about to propose. "Ethel seemed very healthy to me during the four days I spent with her. Except for being short of breath after climbing the stairs to the nursery, I would have said there was nothing wrong with her that delivering her child wouldn't cure."

"Go on."

"Dr. Worthington told us she and the baby were already in the coffin when he signed the death certificate. He didn't examine either of them. They'd been washed and dressed and photographed by Bartholomew Monroe while Worthington was taking his nap."

"Which he'd never done before, according

to him."

"He doesn't have any reason to lie."

"Except embarrassment."

"Suppose he had been given something to make him sleep. He did say he had coffee and sandwiches because he'd been up all night. If the coffee was strong enough, it could easily hide the taste of whatever was used to knock him out."

"Laudanum?"

"Possibly, but he might have detected the bitterness, even if only a few drops were used. It was probably something else, something that works more quickly and doesn't have such a distinctive taste. I think he was deliberately kept away from Ethel's body. If that's true, there has to be a reason for it."

"What are you suggesting, Prudence?"

"The bodies need to be examined by someone who knows how to look for signs of unnatural death."

"That would take a court order, which we have no grounds to request. And neither body has been embalmed. We'd have to move quickly."

"We'll be in Philadelphia tomorrow."

"Are you suggesting what I think you are?"

"Can you think of anything else? We had only a few moments to look at Ethel and the baby before Sorensen came into the parlor, and there wasn't anything to see except their faces and hands."

"The crypt will be locked."

"That shouldn't be a problem for either of us," Prudence said. "Aaron Sorensen has profited financially from two wives who died in childbirth." She fanned out across the desk the *cartes de visite* and cabinet photographs created by Bartholomew Monroe.

"Are you thinking there may have been others?" Geoffrey asked.

"I am."

"Then maybe it's time we set about proving it."

CHAPTER 21

Laurel Hill Cemetery was on the northwest side of Philadelphia, seventy-four acres of rolling countryside overlooking the Schuylkill River. Modeled on Père Lachaise in Paris, the cemetery was a themed garden of narrow, winding roadways and landscaped meadows dotted with commemorative headstones, elaborate crypts in iron-fenced family plots, and sculpted statuary as large and ornate as anything commissioned for a public park. Thousands of visitors thronged to Laurel Hill every year: some to visit the tombs of family or the famous, others to enjoy the swaths of green grass beneath towering trees.

Prudence and Geoffrey hired a small buggy and joined the procession of horse-drawn vehicles winding its way through the cemetery grounds.

"This reminds me of Central Park," Prudence said. "I hadn't thought of a cemetery as a place one comes to amuse oneself. Look, Geoffrey, they're picnicking over there." She pointed to a family group seated on blankets spread out on the grass. If they had come to pay their respects to a deceased relative, they certainly seemed lighthearted about it.

"I don't know that we'll be able to do what we planned," Geoffrey said, flicking the whip lightly over the back of the horse. He was careful to make a snapping sound, but not touch the animal's coat.

"I doubt we'll be noticed," Prudence countered.

"An empty buggy in front of an unlocked family crypt?"

"That's why I brought flowers and the tools." Prudence had purchased several floral displays from a shop near the cemetery gates. At a mercantile store she bought a broom, a bucket, and a pair of secateurs, all of which she planned to display prominently once they found the Caswell mausoleum. The man from whom she bought them asked if she was on her way to Laurel Hill. When she replied in the affirmative, he volunteered the information that he, too, had family interred there. He slipped a small trowel into her bucket with his compliments. It seemed that although the cemetery's landscaping services were excellent, relatives of the deceased always added a few touches of their own.

The Caswell family slept in a miniature Greek temple faced with four Ionic pillars beneath a triangular typhanon adorned with winged symbols of flight. Heavy metal doors, locked against intruders, guarded the interior.

While Geoffrey secured the buggy's brakes and put a feedbag on the horse, Prudence carried the flowers and tools to the temple's porch, stacking them in plain sight. She moved with efficient purpose, as though she had been to this tomb before and knew exactly what needed to be done. She hoped that none of the passersby would know and remark on the fact that a coffin had been placed inside only the day before. Glancing around as she moved between buggy and crypt, she decided that they didn't seem to be attracting any undue attention. It was a bright, sunny, early March day, just warm enough to herald the promise of spring to Philadelphians seeking an escape from the indoor winter fug of cramped, coal-heated rooms.

Geoffrey positioned his body to shield the lock on which he was working. Prudence stood close beside him, holding a floral arrangement that further hid what he was doing. "They must have oiled this recently," he said, his pick soundlessly working the tumblers. "Probably when Samuel Caswell was interred." The heavily embossed metal door swung loose in his hand. "Leave a few things outside," he instructed, "so it looks like we've nothing to hide. I'll lock the door behind us, just in case."

The interior of the mausoleum was damp and cold. A row of windows just beneath the roofline allowed enough natural light in to let them get their bearings. A ring in the floor told them that a burial chamber had been excavated below ground. Six names were chiseled into the marble blocks around it; dates indicated that at least three of them belonged to men who had gone off to war and met their deaths on the battlefield. A small marble altar surmounted by a pair of weeping angels stood opposite the doorway, three granite shelves to each side. Two of the shelves had been sealed off, names and dates carved into the marble facing. The coffin in which Ethel Sorensen lay rested on a raised bier just in front of the altar, her father's coffin beside it.

"The custom in some places is to leave the deceased where the coffin can be touched and wept over until the first anniversary of the death. Then it's moved onto one of these upper shelves and sealed in or entombed down below." Prudence's father, interred in the MacKenzie family crypt, had recently made that final step on the journey to eternity.

"We do things faster in the South," Geoffrey said. His memories were of brick vaults and bodies that were hastily buried as soon as the coffin could be knocked together. Summer was an especially bad time. So long ago, yet he'd forgotten not a single sight or sound. The only thing that saved him was the rigid control he exercised over the worst memories; even the best ones were too painful to be permitted to surface.

Ethel's coffin was of highly polished oak, its hardware gleaming brass. The nameplate that included her birth and death dates told them she had been twenty-three years old. *Male infant* was engraved on a smaller brass plate. Aaron Sorensen had not bothered to attach a name to the child who never drew breath.

The lid had been screwed down in six places to keep the wood from warping during the year the coffin might be in view. Geoffrey moved methodically from one brass screw to the next, slipping each into his pocket as he removed it. "Light the lantern," he instructed. "What's coming through those windows isn't bright enough for us to see what we're looking for."

Prudence held the lantern at shoulder height while Geoffrey lifted the coffin lid. Ethel and her child looked just as they had the day before, laid out in the parlor of their home surrounded by banks of flowers. A faint whiff of decomposition hung over their bodies, not unpleasant yet, but hinting at the putrefaction to come.

Geoffrey took out a handkerchief and dipped it into the water that dampened the bottom of the floral arrangement. Bending over and holding his breath, he wiped the makeup paste and powder from Edith's nostrils.

"What are you looking for?" Prudence asked, holding the lantern steady so he could see what he was doing.

"There," Geoffrey said. "Do you see those faint purple marks on either side of her nose? Someone pinched hard on the nostrils while she was still alive. If you look closely enough, you'll see bruising around her mouth where a hand was pressed down on her lips to keep her from opening her mouth." He rolled back the lid on one of her eyes. Tiny red pinpoints indicated burst capillaries. They had seen them before in the photographs made from the glass negatives Prudence had stolen from Bartholomew Monroe's studio.

"I smell laudanum. Even under all of the other odors, that acrid bitterness is unmistakable."

"Her body is beginning to break down and release it. If I were a poet, I would say it's giving up its secrets."

"She was murdered."

"Helped along by doses of laudanum she probably never knew she was being given. And when that didn't accomplish the deed quickly enough, deprived of the air she needed to breathe."

"Dr. Worthington told me the baby died during birth because Ethel didn't have the strength to push him out. From what I know of its effects, laudanum could interfere with a normal labor if enough was ingested to stop the muscles from contracting. *Compton's Medical Guide* warns of just such a danger."

"Are you sure you don't want to enroll in the Women's Medical College instead of battering at the bar?" Geoffrey asked.

"I might do both." Prudence smiled as she said it.

Geoffrey lowered the coffin lid and screwed it tight again. Then he turned toward the mahogany casket holding the remains of Samuel Caswell. "Ethel's father has been dead for two weeks," he said. "Sorensen is careful not to allow his victims to remain able to accuse him. He refused to allow Ethel to be embalmed. He would have done the same if he had anything to do with this death. The sooner the bodies of his victims decompose and become skeletal remains, the safer he feels."

"Catherine was embalmed, Geoffrey. Old Dr. Norbert wrote that he was furious because she and baby Ingrid were coffined before he signed the death certificate. I'm positive he said they were both embalmed. I remember his nephew telling me that it was done right there at the house, and that arsenic was used. It's what they did with the battlefield dead they managed to ship home during the war."

"I wonder if the mortuary attendants assumed the husband wanted the bodies preserved and began the procedure without checking with him. Sorensen never would have allowed it to happen, had he been able to stop it. He wants the physical evidence of his guilt to disappear."

"I think we should open the coffin, Geoffrey. It's the only opportunity we have, and if we don't do it now, we'll never know."

He handed Prudence a clean handkerchief and tied the one he'd used on Ethel's face over his own mouth and nostrils. The odor they expected began to seep out as soon as the first few screws were removed and the coffin lid loosened. It wasn't pleasant, but it wasn't as bad as they'd feared.

Ethel's father was a painfully thin man with the knobby knuckles and twisted fingers of someone who suffered from rheumatism. The flesh had loosened around his facial bones, his mouth sagged open, and the lids over his eyes had begun to sink. He may have been handsome in his younger years, but age and affliction had taken their toll. Death could not have been unexpected; he might even have welcomed it.

Geoffrey moved quickly, lifting the eyelids while Prudence held the lantern as close as she could. Samuel Caswell's eyes showed more damage than his daughter's; in addition to pinpoints of blood they could clearly see the spiderweb effect Jacob Riis had described in the crime scenes he had photographed.

"What do you think?" Prudence asked.

"I think Sorensen repeats what's been successful. He may have drugged Ethel's father just enough to make it difficult for him to resist, but he certainly cut off the man's air.

If he was already a semi-invalid, he may have received his son-in-law's visit from his bed. If that's what happened, I'd hypothesize a pillow over the face and strong arms to hold it down. No one the wiser, once the sheets were straightened and the pillow slipped back under the victim's head. Sorensen could tell a housekeeper or butler that the master was sleeping peacefully and be gone from the house hours before it was found that Caswell had died."

"And if he was as ill as everyone believed him to be, the death would not be a surprise. I can almost hear someone saying it was a blessing he went peacefully in his sleep."

Geoffrey screwed the coffin lid shut again and Prudence extinguished the lantern. Both handkerchiefs went into Geoffrey's coat pocket before his pick unlocked the crypt door. As soon as it opened and they stepped out into the fresh air, Prudence reached for the broom she'd left leaning on the outside wall.

Now that they were safely out of the crypt, she shuddered with a delayed reaction to what they had done and seen. Geoffrey had tried to prepare her, but the reality was only slightly less shocking than what her imagination had pictured. "Have we attracted any attention?" she asked, head down, sweeping energetically.

"Not as far as I can tell," Geoffrey answered, "but I don't think it's a good idea to linger." He looked around, then quickly placed the flowers at two neighboring graves. The bucket and secateurs went into the buggy, followed by Prudence's broom. They'd dispose of them somewhere along the road winding out of the cemetery. "We don't want to leave evidence that anyone was here," he said.

"I wonder how many laws we broke today," Prudence mused as Geoffrey clucked the horse into motion.

"Probably only a few, but that doesn't count flouting city ordinances, cemetery regulations, and social customs. Have you considered that you're in danger of being disbarred before you're even admitted to the practice of law?"

"You'll be disbarred with me," Prudence said.

"I was a Pinkerton. We don't get caught."

"How sure are you of what you've just told us?" Malcolm Caswell was a senior partner in the law firm of Caswell, Benton, and Farrell. He was also the late Samuel Caswell's cousin and godfather to Ethel Sorensen. Halfway through Geoffrey's recital of suspicions, he asked his son to join them. "Arthur did most of the legwork on the estate," he explained. "If there are irregularities, he'll know where to look for them."

Geoffrey had taken the precaution of telling Claire that he and Prudence planned to visit the Philadelphia law firm that handled the Caswell family affairs. She immediately gave her written consent to disclose whatever information might be needed to persuade the lawyers that the deaths of the two wives were not isolated events.

"Can you tell us how Ethel met Aaron Sorensen?" Geoffrey asked. "How long they knew one another before they married? What her father thought of his son-in-law? Anything that will allow us to draw parallels."

"I can probably tell you more about Ethel than my father can," Arthur Caswell said. "For a while we were as close as brother and sister." He paused for a moment before continuing. "By the time I came home from Harvard Law, she'd just about withdrawn entirely from society. Her father didn't notice because he began cutting off social contacts years ago. He had been ill nearly all his life and he missed his wife more than any other man I've ever known. So he simply gave up. He turned Ethel over to the care of housekeepers and governesses and thought that fulfilled his fatherly responsibilities. Isolated as they were, neither of them had any defenses against someone like Aaron Sorensen."

"You had reservations about him from the beginning?"

"I did," the younger Caswell said. "No one in the family met him until it was too late. He was clever that way. He used his business travel to make excuses not to meet us. Ethel told me that he spun her some romantic nonsense about not wanting their special love to be diminished by having to share it with others. He convinced her they should be married in private because a society wedding would be injurious to her father's health. I don't think he told her they would be living in New York City until after the honeymoon. She never came back to Philadelphia after the marriage, not even when it became obvious to all of us that her father's health was worsening. Aaron came in her place, to spare her the rigors of travel. He got her with child almost immediately, and if what you say is true, it was all part of a scheme to rob her of her inheritance."

"Did she ever write you?"

"If she did, Aaron would have seen to it that her letters never made it into the mail.

He cut her off from her family so effectively that she might as well have been living in another country. I went to visit her in New York once, but there was no way to be sure he was out of town when I did. He welcomed me as though there'd never been an effort to keep her apart from us, but I didn't see Ethel that afternoon. She sent word via her maid that she was too ill to come downstairs, and when I said I'd go up to her, the maid sputtered out some story about her mistress being asleep. It was as plain as the nose on your face what was happening. I never thought he meant her harm, though. I wouldn't have left her there with him if I suspected that. I thought he was overprotective and perhaps jealous of anyone she was fond of, but I wanted to believe he would mellow after they'd been married for a while. After the child came, he would have another human being to distract him. If you're right, I'll never forgive myself for being so wrong and so blind."

"Can you tell me what happened to the family fortune?" Geoffrey asked.

"My cousin's will has been probated, so it's public record —" the senior Caswell began.

"Even if it hadn't been, I'd tell you everything I know," his son interrupted. "Samuel may have been living in his own world of illness and loss, but he'd never been anything but careful with the wealth he inherited. He considered it to be in trust for future generations. He was diagnosed with rheumatism as a very young man, so he never expected to live a long life. He made provisions for Ethel before she was born."

"Everything was in a trust that was worded so as to safeguard her from the predations of exactly the type of husband she ended up marrying," the senior Caswell explained.

"I don't understand then how Aaron Sorensen could get his hands on the Caswell money," Prudence said. Her own experience with a greedy and unscrupulous stepmother had taught her a great deal about the world of trusts.

"Our firm was the original trustee of the estate, but the power to name a successor trustee rested with Samuel during his lifetime."

"He named Aaron Sorensen as trustee to replace you." Geoffrey knew that would have been a swindler's logical next step.

"It was one of the few times I ever argued with my cousin," Malcolm said. "We both lost our tempers and said things we couldn't take back or forget. In the end Samuel had his way. There was nothing I could do to stop him. He had the legal right to name the trustee and he did."

"In the wording of the trust, all monies and properties would revert to the trustee after the death of Samuel Caswell and the last heir of his body."

"Ethel's child," Prudence said.

"Exactly. The provision was put in so the estate would default to the family firm if Ethel died without issue, the understanding being that the family fortune would be disbursed to family members as the trustee saw fit. When Aaron Sorensen became trustee, he also became heir if his wife and any children of her body predeceased him."

"Her father had to die first, so the way was clear for Ethel to inherit."

"We may not have liked him, but at that point we had no reason to doubt Aaron's affection for Ethel. If anything, we thought it excessive and him overprotective. So when he came to Philadelphia when Samuel died, bringing with him Ethel's power of attorney, we suspected nothing. We knew she was carrying a child, and given her parents' history, we believed him when he said she was too frail to travel. Everything was in order, Mr. Hunter."

"You said he came to Philadelphia when Samuel Caswell died."

"I misspoke. He arrived the night before my cousin passed away, though he had no idea at the time that Ethel's father was so close to the end. None of us did. His doctor, who's been treating him for years, had warned us that there wasn't a great deal of time left, but he thought it likely that Samuel would live to see the birth of his grandchild. It's not the first time a physician has been wrong."

"We'd like to speak to him."

"My secretary will give you his address."

"We'd also like to talk to any of the servants who remain in the house."

"Sorensen put it up for sale within days of Samuel's death. From what you've told me about him, I can't help but wonder if he told Ethel what he'd done."

"I have reason to think she was never told of her father's death," Prudence said. She wouldn't mention her short career as a lady's companion; lawyers were used to unnamed sources of information.

"You said that Sorensen arrived in Philadelphia with his wife's power of attorney." Geoffrey tented his hands in the universal posture of a man deep in thought. "Why? Why did he bring a power of attorney with him on that particular visit? How could he have known he would need it?"

"I think we should engage the Pinkerton Agency," Malcolm Caswell said. "What do you advise, Mr. Hunter?"

"Not yet," Geoffrey said. "Our investigation is making headway, though it's still early days. Another team of operatives would muddy the waters and possibly tip Sorensen off that we're onto him."

"Will you keep us informed of what you find out? For the sake of confidentiality we could put you on retainer."

"We have a client, Mr. Caswell," Prudence said. "She's already empowered us to share information with you. I don't see a problem."

"I still think we should call in the Pinkertons." Arthur nodded his agreement with his father's repeated suggestion.

It was on the tip of Prudence's tongue to tell him that one of Allan Pinkerton's best operatives was already working the case, but she swallowed the boast, sensing that Geoffrey had decided not to share that portion of his life.

Judge MacKenzie believed that law partners who worked closely together over a period of years were eventually able to read each other's minds.

Prudence and Geoffrey had met barely a

year ago. Something other than time was happening between them.

CHAPTER 22

A discreet sign in the window of Ethel Sorensen's childhood home advertised that it was for sale. Nothing indicated that this had recently been a house of mourning.

"The butler's name is Nelson," Prudence reminded Geoffrey as they climbed the steps and rang the bell. "I hear footsteps."

The man who opened the door to them wore an overcoat and gloves. He carried his hat in his hand, as if he had just come in or was on his way out. "If you're here to inquire about the house, you'll have to contact the firm that's handling the sale," he said, stepping out onto the stoop and pointing to the sign in the window.

"Mr. Nelson?" asked Prudence.

"Yes, I'm Micah Nelson. May I ask how you happen to have my name, miss?"

Geoffrey handed him one of the firm's business cards.

"My name is Prudence MacKenzie. Mr.

Hunter and I have just come from the offices of Caswell, Benton, and Farrell. We spoke to the two Mr. Caswells. They said you were the most likely person to be able to answer some questions for us."

"I'm no longer butler here, Miss MacKenzie. I came back today to check that the house had been thoroughly cleaned after the furniture removal and to put my keys through the mail slot for the estate agent when I leave."

"We need information about Aaron Sorensen," Geoffrey said. "It's in connection with a possible crime."

Micah Nelson studied his hat as though he'd never seen it before; then he made up his mind. "The heat's not on, so the house is cold. But I haven't closed the door behind me, and maybe I shouldn't until after you've told me more of what this is all about." He stepped back through the doorway; Prudence and Geoffrey followed.

"There's nothing to see except empty rooms," Nelson said. "Everything's gone."

"Sold at auction?" Geoffrey asked.

"Organizing that would have taken too long to suit Mr. Sorensen. No, he called in a company that appraised and bought all of the furniture in one afternoon. Packed every last item in the house into barrels and hauled them to their warehouse."

"Personal things?"

"As far as he was concerned, nothing was personal. It all went."

"I take it you aren't fond of Mr. Sorensen," Prudence remarked.

"Did you say you were investigating him in connection with a crime?" Nelson looked at their card again. "What exactly is investigative law?"

"Are you familiar with the Pinkerton Agency, Mr. Nelson?" Geoffrey asked.

"Who isn't?"

"We investigate, just as the Pinkertons do. But I'm also an attorney, so I can represent my client in a court of law as a consequence of what I discover."

"What is Mr. Sorensen supposed to have done?"

"He hasn't been accused of anything yet," Geoffrey compromised.

"I was Mr. Samuel Caswell's butler ever since he and Mrs. Caswell set up house after they were married. Twenty-eight years, Mr. Hunter. Miss Ethel was born in this house. Mr. Samuel and I drank to her health that very night, and I held her in my arms many a time as she was growing up. If Miss Ethel is in some kind of danger from what Mr. Sorensen has done, then I'll do anything I can to help her."

Prudence laid one hand gently on the sleeve of Micah Nelson's coat. "I'm sorry to have to be the one to tell you this, Mr. Nelson. I wish it could be different, but there's no changing what happened. Miss Ethel died in childbirth three days ago. Her little boy never drew a breath. They've been laid to rest next to her father. It breaks my heart that no one told you."

Micah Nelson stood very still, aging before their eyes as he lost all hope of ever seeing again the child and young woman to whom he had given the love and devotion her natural father had been unable to bestow. The butler was a proud and disciplined individual; he would grieve later, in private. Now he would help destroy the man whose greed and self-indulgence had contributed to Miss Ethel's passing.

"There's a coffeehouse not far from here," he said. "It won't be crowded this time of day and there'll be a warm blaze in the fireplace."

"We have a buggy outside, Mr. Nelson."

"Would you like to see the house before we go?"

Not so much because there was anything to see as to afford him a final farewell, Prudence and Geoffrey trailed behind him as

Micah Nelson led them from room to room of the large, empty house. Their footsteps echoed on the bare wooden floors; dark rectangles on the wallpaper showed where giltframed mirrors and family portraits had once hung. When the butler paused to stare out into the garden, it was because he was seeing in his mind's eye the figure of a little girl playing happily on the grass, watched over by her governess.

By the time they settled themselves in the buggy, and Micah Nelson had dropped his keys through the mail slot of the front door, it was clear that he had locked away his memories and was prepared to help them shape Aaron Sorensen's future.

"I'm disappointed," Prudence said as the New York–bound train pulled out of the Philadelphia station. "I'd hoped he could tell us more than he did."

"Sorensen's actions may be coldhearted and reprehensible, but we haven't found anyone yet who's observed anything overtly criminal."

"You and Ned caught him trying to cheat at cards."

"But we stopped him before he succeeded. That night, at least. We know he runs up debts as though there's no tomorrow, and he uses his wife's fortune to pay them off."

"I thought the Married Women's Property Act was supposed to protect against that."

"It does, as long as the wife is able to stand her ground against her husband. In practice, however, I doubt that much of anything has changed in the forty years the Property Act has been in existence. What's his is his, and what's hers becomes his through social convention or intimidation. If she doesn't consent to allow him to control her property, a wife's only recourse is divorce."

"Which can put a woman out on the street and deprive her of her children," Prudence said.

"As long as the law firm controlled the trust, Ethel was protected. Once her father appointed her husband as sole trustee, everything that supposedly belonged to his wife was actually his to dispose of as he saw fit. He didn't have to seek her approval or even tell her what he was doing."

"All Micah Nelson could tell us was that he always distrusted Sorensen."

"Servants can sense a man's true feelings before anyone else. Their livelihoods depend on an employer's whims."

"The only piece of information that points

to murder is the coincidence of Sorensen visiting Philadelphia just before his father-in-law died."

"Less than twenty-four hours before," Geoffrey reminded her. "Nelson said he arrived at the house in the afternoon. Unexpectedly. No advance notice, though he claimed to have written a note to say he was coming and blamed the butler for mislaying it. Samuel Caswell died that night."

"The death certificate was signed the next morning."

"In addition to his rheumatism, Ethel's father had suffered from a weak heart for more than twenty years." Geoffrey consulted the notes he'd taken during their brief conversation with Samuel Caswell's doctor after they'd left Micah Nelson. "He'd had numerous episodes within the past two years that brought him close to death."

"And which became more frequent after his daughter married Aaron Sorensen."

"Sorensen is careful. There's no way to prove a connection with any visits he might have made to Philadelphia and his father-in-law's declining health."

"Nelson said he was closeted with Mr. Caswell for hours at a stretch whenever he came, and that he permitted no interruptions. What was Sorensen doing all that time?"

"Lying. Assuring Ethel's father that his daughter was happy with her new home and her new husband. Probably painting a false picture of her health so her father would agree that she shouldn't be bothered with visits or correspondence. It's a quick and logical step to naming him sole trustee of his wife's property. Who better to care for a woman than the man who loves her and fathers her children?"

"Do you think he had anything to do with Mr. Caswell dying when he did?" Prudence asked.

"I think he's hastened six deaths that I can count; whether by his own hand or someone else's doesn't matter. In Mr. Caswell's case, when a man is expected to die of a heart ailment his doctor is treating him for, there's hardly any risk in adding something to the potions he already takes."

"My father's bedside table had half a dozen bottles on it," Prudence recalled. "We suspected he was murdered, but we couldn't prove it."

"Nelson said there were never any quarrels between Ethel's father and his son-in-law that were loud enough to be overheard."

"Mr. Caswell knew he was dying. I doubt

he was anything but immensely relieved to believe he'd provided for Ethel's future. His only child fell in love with a handsome, apparently well-to-do man who whisked her away from staid Philadelphia to the whirl of New York City social life," Prudence said.

"And made sure she was promptly with child so she couldn't take advantage of that glittering promise."

"What bothers me most is that Ethel and her child died *after* we began investigating Sorensen."

"She was marked for death the moment she met him, Prudence. A rich woman victimized by an unscrupulous and greedy man. The only thing that could have saved her was if she'd left him. And we know she wasn't strong or suspicious enough to have done that."

"Catherine was preparing for a return to opera, but she was careful to keep her plans secret. That sounds like a woman who intended to make a new life for herself and her child."

"But she waited."

"I can only speculate about the feelings of a woman who is carrying new life, Geoffrey. But when I try to put myself into Catherine's place or Ethel's, I think I would be weakened by a sense of physical and emotional vulnerability until after the child was safely delivered. If that's true, it made them the perfect victims for a predator like Sorensen."

There seemed little more to be said. No matter how many times they went over everything they'd learned about Aaron Sorensen, they slammed against a brick wall. Everything was damning, but it was all circumstantial.

Gradually, as their train thundered toward New York City, Prudence and Geoffrey fell silent.

"He's moving quickly. I think he senses he's being investigated," Ned Hayes reported when they met to discuss what Prudence and Geoffrey had learned in Philadelphia. "He's paying off the gambling debts, at least the ones McGlory could verify. I'm assuming that if he's taking care of those obligations, he's also clearing his club tabs."

"You went to Billy McGlory?" Geoffrey asked.

Ned's relationship with one of the city's most notorious dive-keepers was both dangerous and fascinating. McGlory caused things to happen that couldn't be traced back to him; he lived by his own code. He never failed to pay what was owed, and he always collected on a debt.

Ned shrugged his shoulders, neither confirming nor denying his visit to Armory Hall Saloon and Casino.

"It sounds as though Sorensen is planning to leave town," Geoffrey said. "He wants to be able to disappear or set up again in another city without embarrassing questions following him."

"We know he's getting rid of the house. He mentioned it to Claire and offered to sell it to her before he put it on the market." Prudence's voice shook with indignation. "He's also disposing of Ethel's childhood home. It's been emptied to the walls."

"He'd be a very wealthy man if he didn't have to settle the gambling debts." Ned consulted a set of figures McGlory's bookkeeper had given him. "He'll need to find another wealthy wife. Soon."

"He's never seen my face," Prudence said.

Silence spread around her like ripples from a stone tossed into a pond.

"I wouldn't have to actually marry him," Prudence reasoned. "If he's short of money, he's already looking for a new victim. All I need to do is delay him here in New York long enough for us to find the proof we need that he murdered Catherine and probably Ethel."

"How do you propose to do that, Prudence?"

"I'm not sure, but he must know about the loss I suffered last March during the Great Blizzard. Charles's death was reported in all the newspapers. When Victoria died and Donald was murdered, reporters dragged out the story all over again. Aaron Sorensen reads the society columns, I'm sure of it. What could be more attractive to someone like him than an orphan heiress who lost her fiancé and is about to come out of mourning?"

"You have to be properly introduced and chaperoned," Geoffrey said, "which means attending social functions." The Pinkerton in him liked the plan she was proposing; the man did not.

"I don't think so. He'll be more interested if he believes I want to keep the developing relationship a secret. There's also less chance of my finding out about his recent widowhood."

"Being alone with him is dangerous, Prudence."

"Only if it's not in a public place. New York City has enough museums and galleries to keep us busy for months."

"Do we know anything about the items Prudence took from Sorensen's study?"

Ned asked.

"Not yet," Josiah said, laying a list of jewelry stores on the conference room table around which they had gathered. "All we've established so far is that the workmanship and condition of the stickpin indicates that it dates well before the war, but so far the operative who's doing the legwork hasn't located a jeweler who recognizes it. The pearl ring is newer and much more valuable, but again, the jewelers who have examined it haven't claimed it as their own or been able to suggest the name of the craftsman who fashioned it."

"And the letter?" Ned persisted.

"The woman's name is Damaris, but the postmark on the envelope wasn't legible," Prudence said. "I tried as hard as I could to decipher it, but the ink was smudged too badly to make it out."

"I asked an informant at city hall about the marriage and death certificates Prudence told us about," Josiah said. "They were probably genuine. The right price will buy you anything down there. Sorensen may have intended at one time to fake a marriage rather than actually wed his victim, and perhaps he entertained the idea of presenting a phony death certificate to claim an inheritance. That's the best we could come up with."

"We have to keep Aaron Sorensen here in New York City. I don't think any of you would quarrel with that," Prudence said. "If he leaves, we may never be able to track him down again." She looked around the conference table from one worried face to another. "I can buy us the time we need—"

"Miss Prudence," Josiah interrupted, momentarily putting aside his stenographer's notebook and pencil. "He'll be suspicious the minute you approach him. Everybody in the city knows about Mr. Hunter taking over Mr. Conkling's law practice and the two of you partnering in Hunter and MacKenzie, Investigative Law. Stories about it were in all the gossip and society columns. He's bound to have seen them."

"He's right," Geoffrey said. "And if Sorensen missed an item in one of the newspapers, there was plenty of talk in every club and at every women's tea. Your conduct has been close to scandalous, Prudence."

"Then I'll meet him in disguise and under a different name," she declared. "I'm not giving up on this idea. All of you know it's a good plan and maybe the only way to keep him from getting away from us. I refuse to be wrapped in cotton wool for my own protection." Her cheeks flamed red and she sat very straight in her chair.

"You'll be recognized the first time you attend a social gathering. You're too well-known, Prudence." Geoffrey knew he was right.

"I can be someone's cousin from Boston," she said. "The important social events of the winter season are over. Lent begins next week. No one will be hosting anything but small dinner parties."

"No young lady leaves her home unaccompanied, Miss Prudence." Ned admired her independence and determination as much as Geoffrey did, but he knew that what Prudence was suggesting was a chancy adventure at best. What Aaron Sorensen would do to her if he discovered the scheme didn't bear thinking about.

"Lydia Truitt," she said, turning excitedly to Geoffrey. "She's perfect."

Prudence was right. They could have no more objections. She knew she'd won.

CHAPTER 23

"As it happens," Lydia said, pouring another cup of tea to go with her excellent seed cake, "Father is deep in deciphering a new code. He's having more difficulty than expected, so his temper is not the best. I'd be glad for an excuse to leave the house for a few hours every day."

"Are you sure he can spare you?" Prudence asked.

Ben Truitt was a blinded veteran of the war that had devastated the country for four long years. He was also a cryptographer, whose exceptional skills were much in demand by the government and private clients. Ably helped by his war-widowed daughter, he had built a successful business out of cracking the codes governments and commercial empires used to keep their dealings secret from one another. Lydia was his eyes and his feet, reading aloud to him the alphabetic symbols he could no longer see, creating transcriptions in pinpricked Braille letters, donning disguises and delivering envelopes of documents wherever they needed to go.

"He has a bodyguard now," she answered. "Another wounded soldier who decided the woman he hoped to marry couldn't love a man with half a face. I don't know how he tracked us down, or what he and Father said to one another when they first spoke after so many years, but Clyde moved himself and his haversack into our spare room that afternoon. He's been with us ever since. That was three months ago."

"A bodyguard?"

"That's what he calls himself. Clyde isn't someone you want to contradict. He's never without a whittling knife in his hand. I get the feeling he'd as soon use it on a human being as the piece of wood he's working on. He only lets Father out of his sight when he goes into the yard to smoke or do a reconnaissance of the neighborhood. I have no idea what or who he's on the lookout for, but Father seems to take him seriously."

"I need to make the acquaintance of a man we suspect of killing at least two wives and their infants and convince him to make me his next victim," Prudence blurted out. She'd rehearsed what to say all the long drive from Manhattan to Lydia's home in Brooklyn, but the bare statement was as bald as though she'd never practiced at all.

"I assume you don't intend to go as far as marrying him," Lydia said. "I don't think even Allan Pinkerton demanded that of his female operatives during the worse days of the war."

"Our client is the sister of one of his victims," Prudence continued. She'd come to appreciate Lydia's dry wit and trenchant comments when Geoffrey had asked for Ben Truitt's help on an earlier investigation. Though worlds apart in social status, the two women had much in common. Both were intelligent, fearless, and often frustrated by the restrictions society placed on them because they were female. "We've reason to believe he's preparing to move on before we can gather enough evidence to prove a case against him. Geoffrey and I suspect there may have been others."

"Delightful creature," Lydia commented. "I smell money, as well as the stench of murder."

"Both women were heiresses," Prudence confirmed.

"As are you."

"As am I."

"What does Geoffrey think of this plan of yours?"

"He doesn't like it."

"But you've no doubt persuaded him that it might be the only way to trap the fellow."

"I need a companion to be believable."

" 'A lady never leaves her home unaccompanied,' " Lydia quoted from *The Manual of Proper Etiquette for Young Ladies Desiring to Secure Their Places in Society.* "Which is why I've never aspired to so lofty an appellation."

"My only hope of succeeding is to attract his attention while staying well out of the reach and sight of everyone I know in the city."

"I would say that's impossible, Prudence."

"He's greedy, Lydia. He's just paid off a shocking number of gambling debts, so he's looking to recoup his losses. That may make him careless."

"How much time does Geoffrey need? I suppose Ned Hayes is in on this, too?"

"He is," Prudence confirmed. "I wish I knew how long it will take, but I don't. It could be as little as a few days, or it might stretch into weeks. I have to convince him that I'm rich, lonely, and foolish enough to have fallen in love at first sight with a handsome stranger."

"Then what?"

"He'll likely try to persuade me to elope with him. Geoffrey thinks his gambling is ruining his chances of remaining acceptable to New York society. Sooner or later some of the men he's cheated will catch on and make sure he's ostracized. He has to have another wealthy wife before that happens."

"And what's my role to be in all of this?"

"I thought you could be an impoverished cousin taken into my household as companion after the tragic deaths of my parents."

"And to safeguard your reputation I stick by your side everywhere you go."

"Precisely."

"Except that I drift out of earshot often and long enough for him to get on with his courting."

"We'll be going to museums, galleries, rides through Central Park, afternoon tea in places where I'm unlikely to run into anyone who might recognize me."

"Shouldn't you have a mansion somewhere?"

"Geoffrey suggested a suite at the Fifth Avenue Hotel. I'll pretend to be visiting the city from somewhere upstate. Syracuse, perhaps."

"On a shopping spree to the finest New York houses of fashion. How very like an heiress."

"And if I have a suite, I can entertain him at tea as long as my faithful chaperone is there with us."

"What is this monster's name?" Lydia asked. She could feel herself entering into the excitement of what Prudence was proposing. Things had been decidedly quiet lately, despite the sudden appearance of her father's self-appointed bodyguard.

"Aaron Sorensen. He passes himself off as a private dealer in European antiquities. We think they're counterfeits."

"So he's both a swindler and a murderer. He should be stopped, Prudence."

"I hoped you'd say that."

The New York City Post Office stood opposite City Hall Park on a trapezoidal block that snarled traffic and created monumental delays as delivery wagons, drays, carriages, and hansom cabs vied for passage on badly congested Broadway. Barely eight years after its completion, the post office building was already derided by New Yorkers for its pretentious French Second Empire design and Doric columns that were out of place in busy, bustling Lower Manhattan. An enormous mansard roof formed its fifth story and would have graced the Paris skyline; in America it had come to define the building people ridiculed as Mullett's Monstrosity.

Josiah Gregory loved it.

"The boxes have combination locks," he told Geoffrey Hunter. Sometimes he dropped off the firm's outgoing mail rather than giving it to the carrier just so he could linger in the splendor of the building's interior. "And there's a uniformed guard walking up and down in front of them, keeping an eye on the customers."

"You'll have to distract him," Geoffrey said. "Just for a few minutes. It shouldn't take me long."

"It's noisy," Josiah warned. "The floor and the walls are tiled in marble and the ceiling is vaulted, so there's always an echo."

Geoffrey took a small black tube flared at both ends out of his pocket. It was the most useful weapon in a safecracker's arsenal, but it was also exactly what an alert guard would be watching for. Very few cracksmen could break a combination by the sensitivity of their fingertips alone. No matter how acute their hearing, even the best of them needed to magnify the sound of the brass or steel cams clicking into place as he turned the dials.

"I'll drop my carrying case," Josiah offered. "Unlatched. The noise of it hitting the floor should make him look in my direction. If I have trouble picking up the papers that spill out, he'll come over to help. That's another thing about the post office. It's never empty, always full of people and lines in front of every window. If I stand still, someone's likely to bump into me. The guard will want to get me out of the way."

Geoffrey handed him the piece of paper on which Prudence had written the information copied from the envelope she hadn't dared steal from Aaron Sorensen's desk. No name, no return address, just a post office box number penned in an elegant, feminine hand she'd done her best to duplicate. "This is the number we're looking for."

"There are hundreds of boxes," Josiah said. "When the light strikes them just right, it looks like a wall of gold with crystal inlays."

"Brass facings with small glass windows where the numbers are written," Geoffrey interpreted. "Do you have any idea where this number is located?"

Josiah thought for a moment, picturing the wall of boxes. "If I had to guess, I'd say nearer the left than the other side. And probably in one of the middle rows."

"Let's hope you're right."

■ ■ ■ ■

The post office guard wouldn't remember much about the fussy little man who spilled the contents of his carrying case onto the floor when the morning crowd was at its busiest, except that he tipped him generously for helping clean up the mess he'd made. The fellow was clumsy, repeatedly dropping half of what he picked up, clucking worriedly over the state of the papers that landed in mud tracked from outside. By the time he'd reclaimed the last of them and secured the case's leather strap, the tall gentleman the guard had glimpsed heading for the mailboxes had finished his business and gone.

Once they were safely back in Danny's hansom cab, Geoffrey showed Josiah the three envelopes he'd removed from Aaron Sorensen's box. "I couldn't take everything or it would look suspicious if he stops by. I don't think he's gotten his mail in at least a week or so. He's bound to pick it up soon."

"He's been doing other things," Josiah said. *Like murder.*

"You can take them back as soon as we're finished with them." Geoffrey chuckled at Josiah's alarmed expression. "You won't have to break into the box," he said. "I'll give you the combination."

"This one has a return address," Josiah said, holding the envelope at arm's length to read what was written on it.

"It's a law firm. The letter Prudence copied for us mentioned that the writer would be contacting her bank on Sorensen's behalf," Geoffrey reminded him. "If the sum she requested was excessive, the bank might have alerted its lawyers." He handed Josiah a smaller envelope addressed in a woman's handwriting. "This looks very much like the sample Prudence tried to reproduce. It may tell us who she is."

"I'll put the kettle on as soon as we get back. We'll have them steamed open in no time."

"Miss Prudence will be at the Fifth Avenue Hotel booking a suite this afternoon. We won't wait for her."

"I can have copies finished by the end of the day and the originals back at the post office before it closes," Josiah said. He knew Danny Dennis was listening through the trapdoor in the hansom's ceiling; he'd show up in plenty of time to get Sorensen's mail back into the box where he expected to find it.

Twenty minutes after clambering out of

the cab, Geoffrey was reading the letter from Damaris Tavistock's lawyers while Josiah copied the note written in a feminine hand. Something had gone wrong at the bank; her guardian had been notified of the uncharacteristically large transaction she had initiated. The envelope she had addressed to Aaron's post office box had been found, but despite vigorous questioning, she had not revealed Aaron's name. Nor would she. She trusted that her silence would be partnered by his own. In closing she urged him to burn this, her last communication to him, as she had destroyed all of his letters to her. She signed it *Damaris T.* The Tavistock who had signed the letter from the law firm was obviously a relative and her guardian.

The third envelope contained a list of items now available from someone who signed himself *Philippe* and provided no other identification. The stamp was French, the blue stationery cheap, flimsy, and foreign. Josiah clucked worriedly to himself as he struggled to decipher the curlicue numbers and oddly slanted handwriting. "I think I've got it all," he finally said, waving the copy to dry the ink. There was still time before Danny would be back to take him to the post office, but it never hurt to be ready well in advance. Being late, in Josiah's opinion, said a great deal about a man's character. Or lack thereof.

Regluing the envelopes might leave a telltale unevenness, so Josiah held them one by one over the still-steaming kettle, securing each flap with a single quick, heavy stroke, then laying a thick law book atop the weakened but still effective seal. When they dried, there'd be nothing to indicate that anyone had interfered with them.

"Will you go to visit Miss Tavistock?" he asked, pouring his employer a cup of strong coffee.

"There's just time to catch the afternoon train, if I hurry," Geoffrey said. The return address for Miss Tavistock's lawyers was Saratoga Springs, almost two hundred miles north of New York City.

"Shall I send a telegram?" Josiah asked.

"No. The element of surprise may be the only advantage I have," Geoffrey said. "Can you make another copy of each of the three letters? I'd like to take these with me, but I want Miss Prudence to read them before she beards Sorensen, and there's no telling how many days I'll be out of the city."

"I'll make a shorthand transcription and write her out a copy as soon as I can," Josiah said, his pencil flying over the pages of his stenographer's notebook. Learning the new Gregg shorthand was one of the smartest things he'd ever done. It cut copying time by at least half.

Geoffrey checked the bag he kept packed and stored at the office, then wrote a note to Prudence. "I'll hail a hansom," he told the still-furiously-scribbling Josiah. "Let Mr. Hayes know where I've gone and why." He folded and pocketed the letters Josiah handed him. He'd read them again many times on the train, trying to tease out hidden meaning from between the lines. He suspected he'd learn more from young Damaris Tavistock's legal guardian than from the targeted victim herself.

He was gone before Josiah thought to tell him to be careful. But that wasn't a sentiment to which Geoffrey Hunter would pay attention anyway.

Chapter 24

"Mr. Hunter isn't going to be happy about this, Miss Prudence." Josiah winced as the judge's daughter took two of the three envelopes destined for Aaron Sorensen's post office box and set them firmly aside.

"You can take Philippe's list," Prudence told him, "but I have the germ of an idea sprouting and its success depends on replacing the Damaris letter with something that will set the stage to our advantage. Don't you think so, Lydia?"

"It would be a shame not to use the opportunity when it's dropped in our lap."

If Danny Dennis had sent word up five minutes earlier that he and Mr. Washington were waiting down at the curb, Josiah would have been safely away, following Mr. Hunter's instructions to return the stolen letters. He groaned.

"I'll explain everything to him when he gets back," Prudence soothed. "He knows that once I make up my mind, there's no changing it." Geoffrey also knew that Josiah was no match for Prudence on a mission. Perhaps no one was. And that's why he worried. Interesting thought. Prudence put it aside to examine later.

"Josiah will be back soon," she said, watching from the window as the secretary climbed into Danny Dennis's hansom cab. She led Lydia toward the private office, which gave her confidence every time she entered it. "There's no need for him to know all the details. He'll fuss and try to meddle."

"What is this germ of an idea you told him you had?"

"In addition to Damaris ending whatever was between them, suppose she tells Sorensen that she's agreed to marry the young man who is her guardian's choice for her?"

"Make it even stronger. She was already engaged when she met Sorensen and now regrets the infatuation. That way he has no hope at all of changing her mind. He has to let her go."

"But she recommends him most heartily to her good friend or distant cousin, whatever we decide I am, who is visiting New York City and is every bit as rich as she and even lonelier. It's obvious from what she writes that he had asked for some type of financial help or proof of her commitment, but since that has obviously gone sour, we have her throw him another victim to take her place. As desperate as he is, he'll swallow the bait."

"We can't risk his not picking up the mail that's waiting in his box," Lydia reasoned. "Didn't you say Ned thought he was preparing to leave New York City for good?"

"That was his impression. Most of the gambling debts have been paid and the house is for sale. Ned believes Aaron is playing it safe."

"Then time is definitely running out. We have to lure him to the Fifth Avenue Hotel with the promise of a wealthy, vulnerable heiress from another city as soon as we can. And if she's already predisposed in his favor because a friend or cousin has spoken highly of him, I don't see how he can resist."

"Our fake letter has to go to his home, but he's apparently given Damaris a post office box number as her only means of contacting him." Prudence tapped impatiently on her desk. "Think logically, Lydia. How would she get his address?"

"Look at the letter from the law firm," Lydia advised.

" 'Dear Sir.' No name, just the post office

box number." Prudence sighed. "From which we have to infer that even though Damaris's guardian found out about Sorensen, she's kept her promise and not revealed his name. Or what he told her his name was."

"Making things all the more difficult for us."

"How logical is it that Sorensen would have used a false surname?" Prudence asked.

"There are arguments for and against," Lydia began.

"If Damaris has access to the New York City newspapers, he wouldn't want her recognizing his name in the gossip columns."

"Or the obituary notices," Lydia added. "Beloved husband of . . ."

"But there would be problems when it came time to apply for a marriage license or transfer property from his wife's name to his."

"The best scam is the simplest one. The more lies, the harder it is to remember them and the easier it is to make a mistake."

"So we'll take a chance that he didn't use a false name?" Prudence asked.

"Agreed," Lydia said. "I think Sorensen's greatest weakness is his belief that he's untouchable, that he's created the perfect fiddle."

"We send the letter to his home."

"He'll wonder how Damaris got his address, but when she makes it plain that he's not to contact her, he'll have to let it go. He won't risk endangering the new con."

"The letter should be on the table with his breakfast coffee."

She would move into the Fifth Avenue Hotel in the morning, but tonight Prudence had chosen to remain in the house on Fifth Avenue.

She hadn't thought she would sleep, and she didn't. Not for many hours.

Exactly one year ago she had stood at her bedroom window and watched the beginning of what came to be known as the Great Blizzard, a devastating snowstorm that had obliterated New York City and killed two hundred of its residents. Charles had died in the Great Blizzard; Prudence's life changed forever.

Orphaned the previous Christmas, addicted to laudanum, bereft of the childhood friend who was also her fiancé, and controlled by a murderous stepmother, Prudence MacKenzie's future had been bleak . . . if she had anything to look forward to at all. Then she met Geoffrey Hunter.

She had learned to fight her own battles and escape the traps set for her, but always with the assurance that should she need him, Geoffrey would be there. Renewed trust in herself had been hard-won; even now there were moments when she doubted. But they were short-lived and growing weaker as she strengthened.

It was time to let go of Charles Linwood forever. Relinquish wondering what might have grown between them, had they married. She had used her fiancé's death as a protective wall behind which she could hide when she felt Geoffrey drawing too close. If there hadn't been the photograph of Charles that still stood on her dressing table, she would have forgotten what he looked like. He had become a handsome, fair-haired stranger.

Very gently Prudence turned the silver-framed likeness facedown. And felt tension she hadn't known was there flow from her shoulders.

She opened the window, as she had on that freezing night a year ago, and breathed deeply. New York City had its own distinctive smells. She wondered what scents Geoffrey was inhaling in Saratoga Springs tonight. She knew he was awake and picturing her looking out over Fifth Avenue. He would understand why she could not sleep, and he would not push her. He would wait until she was ready.

Prudence smiled out at him across the two hundred miles that separated them and felt a kiss of warm air brush her cheek.

She took one last look at the dark stillness of the city, then closed her window and climbed into her four-poster bed.

And fell asleep almost as soon as her head touched the pillow.

The suite Prudence engaged at the Fifth Avenue Hotel was a floor below Geoffrey's luxurious apartment. Tall windows in the parlor looked out over bustling Fifth Avenue; each of the two bedrooms contained a carved four-poster bed draped in silk hangings and a French armoire inlaid with rosewood and ivory.

"Sorensen is coming for tea at four o'clock," Prudence said, holding out his acceptance of her invitation.

"Will I do?" Lydia asked. Her tall, willowy figure was wrapped in layers of dusty black wool over a rigidly corseted bodice. Cheap lace framed her neck, there were visible darns on the cuffs of her sleeves, and her skirts rose over a bustle too large for the current Parisian styles. The boots peeking out from beneath her skirts were scuffed and sturdy.

"You look like everyone's idea of the poor relation who can't be hidden in a back room and won't go away," Prudence said. "Perfect."

They had decided that Prudence's name would be Miranda Prosper; it had the awkward ring of old family and safe money. If Aaron Sorensen attempted to research Damaris Tavistock's friend in Syracuse, he would find a graveyard full of Prospers and precious little else to reveal Prudence as the fraud she was.

Lydia had chosen a pale gray dress for her friend. "It matches your eyes," she explained, "but it makes your skin look like a day-old corpse. Which is what you want."

"Definitely not a beauty, but very wealthy." Prudence's looped skirt had been sewn from yards of expensive watered silk, the buttons on her bodice were star moonstone, and around her throat hung an exquisite ivory cameo. Everything she wore screamed money, yet the overall effect was of unrelieved dowdiness. The gown had hung in a dressmaker's workroom for months, one of her few failures; when Lydia declared it exactly what they needed, the woman had been only too glad to be rid of it for the cost of materials and labor.

"Slump your shoulders," instructed Lydia, "as though you're used to taking and obeying orders."

"A lady doesn't slouch," Prudence objected.

"Just a hint of subservience. Not too much."

Prudence burst out laughing as she struggled to overcome years of training in proper deportment.

"Giggling and babbling are what we want," Lydia declared. "You have to appear silly. Not quite stupid, but definitely vapid. I suspect from what you've told me that Catherine was more than a match for Sorensen, especially if she was secretly preparing to leave him. He chose Ethel for her passivity. He won't make the Catherine mistake again."

A rap on the door announced a waiter with the tea cart.

Prudence settled herself in a too-large armchair to add to the impression of awkwardness, folded her hands meekly in her lap, and waited for her prey to appear.

Lydia opened the door to Sorensen, stepping back immediately so he had an unobstructed view of the pale, self-conscious, and socially inept young woman he had come to meet. He'd expected a lady's maid or companion; after one quick glance at Lydia's glaringly impecunious state, he ignored her.

"Miss Prosper." He bowed, not quite clicking his heels, crossed the room and bowed again. "How good of you to invite me." Like most European men, he was a master of the elegant art of hand kissing, a skill American gentlemen never seemed able to learn.

Prudence managed an appropriate nervous simper. "Do please be seated," she said. "I've ordered tea." She poured, managing to spill a few drops into the saucer she handed her guest. "This is my first visit to New York City," she explained. "Dear Damaris insisted there was no one better able to advise me on what I absolutely must see while I'm here. I hope I'm not being forward, but she spoke very highly of you."

"I understand she's engaged to be married," Sorensen said.

"The wedding was put off once," Prudence contributed vaguely. "I'm not sure what the problem was, but it seems to have been resolved and the banns have been announced. They're leaving for a long honeymoon in Europe in two weeks. Isn't that delightful?"

"Wonderful."

"It's to be a private ceremony. Both her parents have passed on, you know. There's only her guardian, and he's not someone who puts up with what he calls ostentatious show." Prudence sipped her tea and glanced at Lydia, bent over some unidentifiable piece of knitting. "She's my dearest friend and the closest I'll come to having a sister. We write nearly every week." She paused, then added, "When was the last time you were in Saratoga, Mr. Sorensen?"

It was the question whose answer they hoped would provide a clue to at least one of the mysteries about Aaron Sorensen. Had he found and wooed Ethel's replacement months before she died? There was no record of his initial trip to Philadelphia, and thus no way to know whether Catherine had still been alive when he smooth-talked his way into the Caswell household. Proof of premeditation could be evidence against deaths attributed to childbirth. If he believed Miranda Prosper and Damaris were frequent correspondents, he'd have to assume Damaris might have written about their first meeting.

"Several months ago," he said.

"Though, of course, you had already met," Prudence said. She felt Lydia stiffen and knew she had taken a chance they hadn't discussed. But it felt right, and sometimes acting on intuition got results.

"I was there for the races last summer."

More likely trolling for your next victim, Prudence thought. She doubted she'd get any more information out of him. "There's no need to say any more, Mr. Sorensen. I'm sure the memories are painful."

"I wish her only the best."

"Of course you do. Dear Damaris is not always as forthright as she should be. She reads novels. I blame that on her not having a mother to guide her in her formative years. No matter how strict one's governess, it's not the same, as I very well know. And her father was hopeless. We won't talk about her."

"That's very kind of you, Miss Prosper."

"Now you must help me decide how best to spend the next week and a half. That's all the time I have. I promised Papa I'd be back at his bedside before he could begin to miss me."

"Your father is unwell?"

"For almost two and a half months now."

"Might I inquire what type of illness?"

"The horse he was riding lost its footing on an icy road. A few days before Christmas. Papa was thrown and badly injured. The horse had to be put down."

"How worrisome that must be for you."

"He'll make a full recovery, but it will take time."

For the next fifteen minutes Prudence skittered from one frivolous topic to another. She asked his advice about visits to museums, shopping expeditions, evenings at the opera or the theater, carriage rides in Central Park. She rambled on, pausing only to ask if he would care for more tea, another crustless cucumber sandwich. Finally, just before the rules of etiquette dictated that Sorensen take his leave, she inquired if he might know of a suitable dealer in antiquities from whom she could purchase a small, portable writing desk. "Preferably French," she said. "Papa is confined to his bed, which he finds most annoying. I thought the gift of a writing desk he could balance on a pillow would revive his spirits."

The gleam in Sorensen's eye came and went quickly, but Prudence caught it. So did Lydia.

"As it happens, I have contacts in Europe from whom I'm often able to import exactly what might suit your needs."

They would talk more about it tomorrow, when Aaron came to escort her to the Metropolitan Museum of Art on Fifth Avenue.

"Miss Durant will accompany us," Prudence said as Sorensen bent over her hand to take his leave.

"She'll be most welcome." But the look he shot in Lydia's direction was anything but congenial.

Chapter 25

Saratoga Springs in mid-March was bleak, chilly, and empty. Most of the hotels and boardinghouses that catered to the race crowds and health seekers were shuttered and silent. Inside the Grand Union, the United States, and the Adelphi hotels scurried armies of carpet and upholstery cleaners, window washers, laundresses and seamstresses, painters and plasterers. Hordes of spring and summer visitors had wrought havoc on the inlaid parquet floors and furnishings. They'd be back again this season, expecting everything to be perfect.

The last time Geoffrey had been to Saratoga Springs, he had been working for the Pinkerton National Detective Agency, tracking a pair of light-fingered con artists who traveled the resort circuit from the West Virginia mountains to Niagara Falls. Their favorite victims were honeymooners too engrossed in one another to pay much attention to what was going on around them.

Crossing Broadway, he paused to look up and down the wide avenue that during the season was crowded with every imaginable type of horse-drawn carriage. Only a few vehicles braved the damp cold today. The tree branches stood out bare and black against a gray sky and the flags atop the Grand Union Hotel whipped in the gusty March wind. Geoffrey turned up the high collar of his overcoat as he walked the final few blocks to his destination.

It had been nearly dawn before he'd managed to catch a few hours' sleep; he hadn't been able to get Prudence and today's anniversary out of his mind. He wondered whether she was still determined to set herself up as Sorensen's next victim. Whatever happened here in Saratoga, he intended to be back in New York City before she could get herself into trouble.

He had no appointment, but the Hunter and MacKenzie, Investigative Law business card got him into the office of one of the small law firm's two partners.

A broad, heavyset man, with old-fashioned muttonchops and a thick mustache curling down over his upper lip, Mortimer Tavistock had been expecting someone to answer the letter he'd sent to the post office box number in New York City. It was the only address he'd been able to cajole and then threaten out of his stubborn niece. From what he'd learned during his nearly thirty-year practice of the law, men who preyed on women were usually cowards when called on the carpet to answer for their actions. He didn't for one moment think Geoffrey Hunter belonged to that particular breed of rogue, but he considered it likely they were both chasing the same scoundrel.

"I can't divulge anything about my client," Geoffrey began, "but I can tell you that we believe the individual I'm tracking has a long history of defrauding the women he courts. We suspect him of the worst kind of violence."

"Suspicion isn't proof," Tavistock said.

"Your letter is clear. You warn the person to whom it is written that he is to stay away from an unnamed young lady or risk incurring consequences he will regret. You used the word *rue.*"

"By your presence here I surmise the missive reached its destination."

"It did," Geoffrey said. He laid a sheet of paper on the lawyer's desk.

"This is a copy." Tavistock touched the facsimile lightly with one knobby forefinger.

"It is," Geoffrey agreed.

Both men understood that he would say no more about the original, how it had come into his possession, and where it was now.

"He covers his tracks very well," Geoffrey began. He had decided not to mention the letter by which he had learned Damaris's first name and her probable relationship to the man sitting across the desk from him. "Our investigation has found nothing that will stand against him in court. Actions on his part could be construed as circumstantial and ethically problematic, but no more than that."

"The bank alerted us," Tavistock volunteered. He offered a silver box of fine hand-rolled cigars and, when Geoffrey declined, prepared one for himself with an initialed double-guillotine silver cutter. There was no mistaking who was on his mind as the razor-sharp blade clipped and trimmed. "The estate of the young lady in question is overseen by our family bank. She made a mistake, which we were able to correct before any real damage was done."

"Yet you don't have his name," Geoffrey commented.

"She refused to reveal it. The transaction she was attempting was interrupted in the earliest stages, before the paperwork could be completed. One could wish that the bank officer who stepped in had waited just a bit longer."

"I'd like to speak to your client," Geoffrey said.

"Out of the question," Tavistock replied. A cloud of cigar smoke hung above his head.

"You have no guarantee that he won't approach her again. And perhaps succeed in obtaining what he wants." Geoffrey tapped Josiah's copy of the law firm's letter. "Marriage and access to her fortune. It's already happened twice that we know of."

With measured deliberation Tavistock laid the burning cigar in a crystal ashtray. He straightened in his luxurious leather chair, rested his elbows on the polished surface of his desk, and leaned forward. "Tell me," he said.

"Do we have an agreement?" Geoffrey asked.

"I'll take you to meet her myself."

"She's already refused to answer your questions."

"The best I can do is to give you an hour alone with her. I can't guarantee that she'll tell you what you want to know."

"His name is Aaron Sorensen. We're aware of two wives who died in childbirth, although in each case there were no warning signs of potential medical complications. We believe he selects his next victim and begins to court her before he's rid himself of the spouse from whom he plans to inherit. Your client could provide us with proof of that."

"Two wives that you know of. Were there others?" Tavistock rasped. He'd prosecuted or defended every kind of wrongdoing from trespassing to murder, but he'd never been as angry as he was now. His client was also his niece, and, for the next six months, his legal ward; he considered his brother's child the daughter he never had. Unmarried himself, he'd gone to great lengths to find Damaris a suitable husband, only to have the girl tell him she wasn't ready to marry yet. She'd lied to him. If she hadn't made the mistake that gave her away, he didn't doubt she'd have ruined herself by now.

"We don't know," Geoffrey replied. "We think he repeats what's worked for him in the past; that's one of the reasons I need to speak to your client. So far she's the only concrete lead we have. No one else can tell us how he operates, what promises he makes, how he manages to convince these young women they're in love with him."

"Damaris is twenty," Tavistock said. "Both her parents died when she was a child. I've been her guardian ever since."

"Was she sent away to school?"

"Governesses. I kept her home. With me. But she hasn't been lonely. She has cousins, aunts, and uncles on her mother's side. I made sure she's always had everything she wanted."

"I'd like to catch the afternoon train back to New York City," Geoffrey prodded.

Tavistock heaved himself to his feet, cigar clenched between his teeth. "Let's get this over with," he growled.

Damaris Tavistock was not what Geoffrey anticipated. Catherine had been a talented beauty, Ethel delicate and fragile. The young woman he suspected Sorensen had picked out to be his next wife was squat, fleshy, and so decidedly unattractive that the words *ugly duckling* sprang to mind the moment he saw her. The lace-mittened hand she extended to him was thick-fingered, the corseted waist far from the desirable hourglass silhouette fashion dictated. Yet, as he took the chair she offered in her guardian's opulent parlor, Geoffrey caught a glimpse of a deliberately concealed intelligence behind the blank expression and unremarkable features.

"I shall return in an hour," Mortimer Tavistock said. His introduction had been brief and to the point. The man from whom he had rescued his niece in the nick of time had a history and was contemplating the ruin of another young lady. He had to be stopped. Mr. Hunter had promised that the family name would be protected.

"So you've blackmailed my uncle into agreeing to cooperate," Damaris said. She closed the parlor door her guardian had left cracked open an inch for propriety's sake, then turned the key in the lock.

"That may be an exaggeration," Geoffrey said mildly. His first impression had been correct. This young woman was neither stupid nor easily duped. He wondered what hold Aaron Sorensen had had over her.

"I knew it wasn't my person that attracted him," she continued, seating herself again, smoothing out her skirts, folding the mittened hands in her lap. "I'm not a fool. I know what I look like. I also appreciate that wealth conceals a multitude of flaws."

She looked at him with the kind of frank, determined gaze young ladies were usually at pains to conceal. Geoffrey was reminded for a fleeting moment of Prudence.

"Why did you persist in not naming him?" he asked.

"I was vulnerable, Mr. Hunter. I still am. Aaron Sorensen is not to be trusted. I learned that lesson in a very hard way, but I learned it well. My mistake was in wanting to believe his lies, in allowing myself to fall into a situation in which I was entirely at his mercy. Once I extricated myself from his grasp, I couldn't allow my guardian to pursue and catch up with him. Aaron would tell everything to save himself. And for the sheer malicious pleasure of doing me harm."

Geoffrey was trying to read between the lines of what Damaris was telling him. He knew she wouldn't reveal whatever she had gone to such pains to hide from her uncle, but he also sensed that she wanted him to find his way to the truth she had resolved to put behind her. Maybe, if he could repeat her words accurately, Prudence would be able to pierce through the thicket of hidden meanings.

"He's a dangerous man," Geoffrey began.

"I know that now," Damaris agreed.

"He may be responsible for the deaths of two women."

"And I would have been number three?"

"We think in each case he began courting a new wife before he was widowed."

"Convenient."

"He's a gambler."

"Which means he's always in debt," Damaris said. "We know a lot about gambling in

Saratoga Springs."

"If you could tell me how he approached you, and when, it would do a lot to help us build a case against him."

"Am I the only lead you have?"

Geoffrey nodded.

"I'll deny telling you anything," Damaris promised. "I won't testify in a court of law. I won't identify him as being anyone I've ever known."

"I understand."

"Don't bother giving me your word because if you're a man of honor, I already have it, and if you're not, a promise means nothing." Damaris pitched her voice low, as if to ensure that what she was about to say could not be heard by someone standing outside the parlor door.

"I met Aaron Sorensen here in Saratoga at the beginning of September, the last week of the racing season. I remember because it was a glorious early-autumn day, cool and fresh after the heat of summer. Once the racetrack closes, the only visitors we have are people who come to bathe in the springs and drink the water. The hotels are nearly empty, you can cross Broadway without fear of being run down, and we permanent residents look forward to a quiet, snowy winter."

"Did he have an introduction?"

"No. I should never have spoken to him. I wouldn't have, if I'd been anywhere except the racetrack. I can't explain why exactly, but there's an entirely different atmosphere in the paddocks. Owners who wouldn't socially cross each other's paths mingle and drink together, the jockeys are brought out and shown off like pet monkeys, and ladies forget to be aloof and distant. My uncle has his own silks, and last season he had the most promising entry his stables had been able to put forward in years. Under other circumstances he would never have left me on my own."

"What happened?"

"I'm not sure. Looking back, I think Aaron engineered the whole thing. He pretended to be one of the investors who owned that day's favorite. He admired my uncle's horse and it seemed natural to drift into conversation. What strikes me now is that he made an excuse to leave the paddock area just as my guardian was coming back toward the stables. It didn't make an impression then, but I'm positive I saw my uncle from a distance and said something about introducing Aaron to him. When I turned back around, Aaron was gone. It was just that quick. I never mentioned him to my guardian, because I knew that talking to a man who wasn't a relative or old friend of the family was something I should never have done."

"And you hoped he would follow up that initial meeting."

"Yes, I did. He was so charming, so sincere. A week later . . . I received the first letter."

"Was it sent to your home?"

"Just that once. He begged me to rent a post office box here in Saratoga Springs and to write to him at a post office box in New York City. He said he traveled so much that he never knew from one week to the next which hotel he would be staying at. As for me, he didn't mince words. He said he knew my guardian would never agree to a friendship between us, and for that reason and no other, he urged me to keep secret the 'mysterious and exhilarating feelings' that had taken hold of him when he first saw me. Feelings he didn't doubt I shared. I remember almost every word of that initial letter, Mr. Hunter, though I burned it according to Aaron's instructions. I was thrilled, drowning in emotions I'd never felt before, crazy to deceive my uncle and forge a new life. Every time we met was like being caught up in a whirlwind. I was powerless to refuse whatever he asked of me."

"What went wrong?"

"I think I've told you enough. Aaron approaches a young, vulnerable woman at a public function, isolates and then flatters her, draws her into a relationship that is all the more powerfully compulsive because elaborate precautions have to be taken to keep it secret."

"You tried to arrange for substantial funds to be made available to him."

"Now that he's ending up with nothing, I think asking for that much was a mistake he must bitterly regret. But gamblers often make unwise decisions when they're threatened with physical injury. I've heard stories that would freeze your blood about some of my uncle's clients."

"And that's how your guardian discovered what was going on."

"And made me sever the connection."

"Did you save any of Sorensen's letters?"

"None. I burned each one as soon as I'd read it."

"Gifts? Did he send or give you any tokens of his affection?"

"A pair of earrings. Antique jade wound with gold thread worked into a lover's knot. He said a ring would be noticed, but no one remarked on what a woman wore in her ears."

"Do you still have them?"

"Why?"

"It's possible they could be traced to a jeweler who might have a record of who originally purchased them."

Very slowly Damaris took a small velvet drawstring bag from her skirt pocket. "I tried to throw them away. Many times. I don't know why I couldn't. It wasn't out of any excess of sentimentality. I despise Aaron Sorensen and what he tried to do to me, the harm he succeeded in inflicting." The emerald green velvet glowed on the white lace of her mittened hand. "Take them, Mr. Hunter. Maybe this is the only way I can finally be rid of them. Of him."

Geoffrey slipped the earrings into his coat pocket just as the door handle rattled and an angry male voice called Damaris's name. Before she could rise from her seat and turn the key in the lock, he whispered, "Is there anything else, Miss Tavistock? Anything you can or want to tell me?"

He thought she hesitated, as though some terrible secret had fixed itself in her throat and she was struggling to dislodge it. The moment passed; she shook her head. Opened the parlor door. Ended their private time together.

"My carriage will take you to the train station," Mortimer Tavistock said.

CHAPTER 26

"You can't be alone with him." Geoffrey paced away from where Prudence sat demurely on the pale blue silk sofa of her Fifth Avenue Hotel suite. It was all he could do to keep from clenching his fists and pounding them against something. Preferably a wall or Aaron Sorensen.

"I won't be. Lydia is my lady's companion. She's sticking to me like glue," Prudence said. "Sorensen came here yesterday for tea in answer to my invitation, and this afternoon we're going to the Metropolitan Museum of Art. I have to pretend I've never been there before."

"I don't like your not being able to use your own carriage and coachman. Kincaid is a good man in a crisis."

"Danny Dennis has promised to be at the head of the hansom queue when we come out of the hotel. He has two other drivers lined up for future excursions so Sorensen doesn't get suspicious. There isn't much that can go wrong, as long as I confine our outings to public places," Prudence explained. She'd proven her ability to handle herself in tough situations; now she chafed under what seemed an obvious lack of confidence. "I suggested meeting at the museum so we wouldn't have to ride in the same hansom." She took a deep breath. "I *have* been careful, Geoffrey."

"What did you learn in Saratoga?" Lydia asked. The spark she'd always sensed between these two was still there. And getting stronger, she thought.

"Damaris Tavistock was holding something back," Geoffrey began, turning from the window overlooking Fifth Avenue. "Maybe you can figure out what it is." He took the jade-and-gold earrings out of their velvet pouch and placed them on the table in front of the sofa where Prudence sat. Lydia joined her.

"These are beautiful," Lydia remarked, twirling one of the earrings so the miniature cage of interwoven gold threads shimmered as they caught the light.

"They look to me as if they were designed to complement the gold nets women used to hold their hair in place before the war," Prudence said. "You don't suppose . . . ?"

She stopped, appalled at what she was thinking.

"If we had them appraised, I think we'd learn they aren't very valuable," Lydia said. "But they could be family heirlooms."

"There's no point attempting to find the jeweler who might have sold them to Sorensen. He didn't buy them." Prudence laid one earring on the palm of her hand and held it out before her. "Claire has green eyes. I noticed how pure and clear they are the first time we met. You don't often see eyes that color, with no trace of hazel." She closed her fingers over the earring she believed had once hung from Catherine's ear. "If Claire recognizes them, I'll know I'm right."

"Catherine inherited them after their mother's death," Lydia said. "A woman's jewelry is divided between her daughters after she dies," she explained to Geoffrey.

"I wonder why Sorensen didn't sell them," he commented. "We know he always needs money."

"Jade isn't an expensive stone. He may have decided it wasn't worth the bother when he could put them aside until he needed them." Lydia shuddered with distaste. "To give to someone else."

"You said Miss Tavistock in Saratoga was

holding something back," Prudence reminded him. "What made you think that?"

"Just before I left, when her guardian was about to put an end to the interview, I had the feeling she was on the verge of confiding whatever it is she's been so determined her uncle not find out."

"Can you remember exactly what she said?" Lydia asked.

"I made notes once I got to the train." Geoffrey consulted the small leather-covered book he carried with him everywhere. He caught the smiles the two women exchanged and knew what they were thinking. *Pinkerton training.* As best he could, he recounted the hour he had spent with Damaris Tavistock.

"She got caught," Lydia said without hesitation. "Nothing else makes sense. She may have miscarried very early on, perhaps before she could be certain, but at some moment she realized that Sorensen wouldn't stand by her."

"Ethel was still alive," Prudence said. "He couldn't risk a bigamous marriage in the same state where Ethel's death certificate was going to be filed."

"We may never know exactly what happened," Lydia continued. "The only thing we can be certain of is that she decided to buy his silence."

"Damaris Tavistock is not a stupid woman," Geoffrey said. "She must have known that by giving him money, she was putting herself in his power. Yet you believe she was willing to risk it."

"I do," Lydia said. "But to make it work she had to convince Sorensen that she was willing to expose him if he went back on the deal — despite what it would do to her reputation."

"He may have realized she was the mistake that could topple his house of cards," Prudence said. "So it made sense to walk away."

"Then he let his greed or his desperation get the better of his caution. I'd lay odds he promised silence for a larger payment than she anticipated." Geoffrey had known men more clever than Sorensen ruin a scam because they didn't know when to quit.

"And that's where he tripped himself up. The amount alarmed someone in the family bank who notified the guardian," Lydia summed up.

"He might have gotten away with it if he'd asked for less."

"Damaris made one terrible mistake, but she was able to pull herself out of the abyss before it swallowed her." Lydia grimaced. "Sorry. That makes it sound poetic and romantic when it's actually a very ordinary tale of misplaced affection and callous seduction."

Prudence unobtrusively replaced the earrings in their velvet bag and handed it to Lydia, who quietly left the room. She didn't think Geoffrey noticed she hadn't given the earrings back to him; mention of pregnancy discomfited even the most worldly of men.

"We don't want to be late," Prudence said, arranging a fur stole around her shoulders and pulling on her gloves. "After the museum I'm going to ask Aaron to escort us to Monroe's gallery." She expected Geoffrey to react explosively and she wasn't disappointed.

"Of all the places in the city you could go, Prudence," he bellowed. "Why there?"

"Other than the fact that they each died as a result of childbirth, we only have two commonalities between Catherine's death and Ethel's," she explained patiently. "I talked it over with Lydia and she agrees. Sorensen is the obvious shared link, but the other one is less apparent. It's the photographer Bartholomew Monroe. He was one of the first people at each deathbed, either immediately before or after the doctor or the undertaker. Surely, that bears investigating."

"It doesn't surprise me that he should be

in both homes," Geoffrey said. Society people tended to use the same florists and caterers, hire their household staff from recommended agencies, and frequent a limited number of butchers and green-grocers.

"Have you forgotten what Jacob Riis said? He thought Monroe might have touched up Catherine's eyes without instructions from Sorensen. Blackmail could be the motive. He saw the petechiae, decided something was not as it should be, and covered up the evidence so he could use it later to his own advantage."

"That could be another reason Sorensen is desperate for money." Lydia had come back into the parlor without drawing attention either to her absence or her renewed presence. It was a gift she had for disappearing in plain sight. Now she shrugged into a rather worn black wool jacket.

"Proving it is the problem." Geoffrey scribbled something in his leather notebook. "He may not be the only one Monroe is shaking down."

" 'Shaking down'?"

"It's street slang for *extortion,*" Geoffrey explained. *"Blackmail."*

"We thought it would be instructive to observe how the two men speak to each other," Lydia said.

"No more than that?" Geoffrey frowned.

"That's all we can hope for at the moment," Prudence said. "If we can be reasonably certain of a connection, we should be able to use one of them against the other."

"I'd feel better about this if you had someone else with you," Geoffrey said, reluctantly conceding to the logic of what the two women proposed. "I can't do it. Sorensen would recognize me from the Union Club. Ned is out because he foiled his cheating scheme at the Lotos."

"And Josiah spoke to Sorensen at Ethel's viewing," Prudence said. "I'm telling you, Geoffrey, there isn't any danger. I was as thickly veiled the only other time I was in the gallery as I was at the viewing. If Sorensen hasn't recognized me, neither will the gallery attendant. And I've never come face-to-face with Monroe." She opened her reticule to show her partner the derringer he insisted she carry everywhere she went. "But I won't hesitate to use this if I have to."

"Lydia?"

"I'm always armed," Lydia said matter-of-factly. "Most of Father's clients have very few scruples."

"There's something else, Geoffrey," Prudence said, one gloved hand on the suite's polished brass doorknob. "Josiah counted the months between the marriage and the death dates. Catherine was a pregnant bride."

"The father knew. That's why he didn't try to have it annulled after they eloped," Lydia added.

Geoffrey stared at them. A man who stole the virtue of an unmarried lady was the worst kind of cad. Thank God he'd had a word with Danny Dennis. Prudence and Lydia might think they were alone, but Danny would have someone watching them every moment.

"I'm fascinated by postmortem photography," Prudence said as she alighted from the hansom cab in front of Bartholomew Monroe's gallery. She posed a hand lightly on Aaron Sorensen's extended arm. "Are you familiar with what some of the spiritualists believe about the possibility of capturing an image of the soul leaving a body at the moment of death?"

"I've heard something to that effect. But no one has succeeded in doing it."

"Well, that's what I shall certainly ask this photographer about when we talk to him. Miss Durant called this morning to request a consultation," Prudence said.

"The young man I spoke to assured me that Mr. Monroe would be available," Lydia confirmed. She settled her skirts and looked curiously toward the photographer's display windows.

"I've made a reservation for tea at the Astor House when we're finished here." Aaron Sorensen leaned solicitously toward Prudence, excluding the unwelcome chaperone from the conversation.

"I'm sure that will be lovely," she murmured. She would have to manufacture some plausible excuse when the time came; the risk of taking tea at the Astor House without someone recognizing her was too great.

"Shall we go in?" Lydia asked. She huddled into her well-worn jacket and skillfully inserted herself between Prudence and her suitor, managing to separate them without seeming aware of what she was doing.

A different young man than the one who had shown Prudence and Josiah the glass negatives of Catherine Sorensen bustled out into the gallery through the heavy black curtains separating the viewing space from the rear workrooms.

"Mr. Monroe is expecting us," Lydia informed him. She sensed Sorensen's looming discomfort behind her. "I called this morning."

"We've really come to acquaint ourselves with what is on display. There's no reason to disturb Mr. Monroe if he's busy," Aaron contradicted her.

"But if he isn't, I would certainly like to meet him," Prudence chirped. "Such masterpieces of dignified sorrow." She waved an eloquent hand at the enlarged photographs surrounding them.

"All of the subjects in this gallery have passed over." The man parting the black curtains paused as if a camera lens were focused on him and he needed to stand absolutely still to ensure an unblurred image. He was taller than the unusually tall Sorensen, dressed entirely in unrelieved black. The stickpin in his elaborately knotted neckpiece was gold and onyx. When he smiled, the whiteness of his teeth shone against the olive cast of his skin. He wore his hair long, black locks curled and brushing against his shoulders. His eyes were too dark to have any depth; Prudence thought immediately of the opaque blackness of obsidian.

"The name I was given was Prosper," Monroe said as he approached the group. He seemed undecided about recognizing

Sorensen.

"I have the privilege of escorting Miss Prosper this afternoon," Aaron said. He moved forward to clasp the photographer's hand. "It's a pleasure to see you again in circumstances different from our previous meetings, Mr. Monroe."

"Indeed."

Lydia moved closer to the two men. "I hope it was not an occasion of personal grief to which you're referring, Mr. Sorensen. Was it 'meetings,' you said?" She waited for an answer to her question. Nothing was going to budge her.

"I had the honor to provide Mr. Sorensen with a *memento mori* of his late wife," Monroe finally said when it became embarrassingly obvious that his client was not going to satisfy the obnoxious woman's curiosity.

"Late wife?" Prudence pitched her voice high. For added effect she managed the suggestion of an agitated tremolo.

Lydia stepped aside, the better for Prudence to note the expressions passing across Monroe's and Sorensen's features as Aaron reluctantly confirmed his widowhood.

"Such lovely ladies," Lydia commented when Monroe led them past a set of panels where young mothers smiled wistfully down at the tiny bundles they held in their arms. "It must be such a comfort to their families to be able to remember them this way."

Sorensen tried to detach himself from Lydia's remarks and Monroe's relentless tour of the gallery's highlights, remaining close by Prudence's side, occasionally murmuring something to her that no one else could hear. Very gradually Prudence allowed her frown to lessen and then disappear. Finally she placed a gloved hand tentatively on Sorensen's arm and agreed to be steered away from Monroe and Lydia.

Prudence and Aaron stood apart, talking quietly as Lydia's eager exploration ended. Before Monroe left the gallery to return to his workrooms, Sorensen flashed him a look that was nothing short of triumphant, Lydia would later tell Geoffrey. Whatever signals had been passed back and forth between the two men, it was obvious to her that Sorensen believed he had come out the victor.

"We'll have tea another day," Prudence decided before climbing into Danny Dennis's hansom cab.

"Tomorrow?" Sorensen asked. He held Prudence's hand a fraction longer than was customary.

Two could play at this game, Prudence decided. She gave no answer, merely turned away to settle herself beside Lydia. At the last moment she raised a hand to her eyes.

Let him think the tears were for him, let him believe his loss had touched her tender heart. Everyone knew that a woman's greatest attribute was her ability to comfort a grieving man.

"He didn't volunteer any information about Catherine or the two dead infants," Prudence said, "and very little about Ethel."

They had gathered in Prudence's hotel parlor, where Geoffrey joined them after assuring himself that no one saw him enter the suite. Josiah ordered tea and fussed over the tray as efficiently as though he were back in the firm's offices, while Lydia wrote notes of everything she had heard and observed. Like Geoffrey, she was a great believer in the importance of preserving impressions before they could be forgotten.

"He said Ethel had urged him not to mourn her, should she die in childbirth, and that he'd promised he wouldn't. 'Made a solemn vow' was the way he phrased it. That was his explanation of why he's so obviously and eagerly looking for a replacement. The dead wife told him to." Prudence shuddered. "He's repulsive, Geoffrey. The most disgusting man I've ever met."

"Murderers usually are," Lydia commented.

"I think I've accomplished what I set out to do." Prudence accepted the cup Josiah handed her and sighed contentedly at its warmth and fragrance. "He believes I'm thoroughly besotted with him and that I've swallowed his pack of lies about Ethel. He had the gall to tell me that the greatest compliment he could pay her was to marry again. 'Only a man who's been happy in a marriage seeks to return to that blissful state.' Or some such platitude."

Lydia capped her pen and tidied the sheets of hotel stationery on which she'd written her notes. "He ignored me completely, so I had no difficulty watching him assess our dear heiress. Every time Prudence did that fluttery gesture with her fingers, I could see his estimation of her intelligence fall a bit further."

"Bravo, Miss Prudence!" Josiah called.

Prudence fluttered her fingers at him.

Chapter 27

"He writes that he's planning to move into the hotel when he returns. He's reserved a suite." Prudence crumpled Aaron Sorensen's note in one angry fist. "That's much too close for comfort."

"You'd better let me read the entire thing," Lydia said. She smoothed out the heavy stationery and positioned a pair of gold-rimmed spectacles on her nose. "He'll be gone for two days and counts on finding you still in residence when he returns. That's odd. I wonder where he's going."

"Philadelphia? To see to the final settlement of Ethel's estate?"

"I suppose so. He's given his servants their notice and a removal company will be emptying the New York house of its furnishings tomorrow."

"Hence the hotel."

"Everything he explains is very logical," Lydia said, removing her spectacles and tapping them on her knee. "He took an early train out of the city this morning."

"Which means that if the servants were dismissed, there's no one in the house."

"Until tomorrow."

"We should probably tell Geoffrey," Prudence said, beginning to unbutton the bodice of her pale pink silk morning gown. "I brought my dark gray secretary's suit." She stepped out of the high-heeled satin slippers, which were made to be worn only in a lady's boudoir, and grinned at her companion.

"Wear a shawl instead of a coat," Lydia advised. "And screw your hair into a bun. If anyone sees us at the back door, we'll look like additional household help."

"I don't know what we're searching for, but I can't bear the thought of not using this last opportunity to find whatever Sorensen may be hiding."

"Anything we take away can be assumed to have been packed or discarded by the removal company. It's the best cover we could ask for."

"I should call the office," Prudence said. She looked questioningly at Lydia, who raised her eyebrows and shrugged her shoulders. "I don't really want to waste time arguing, though, and Geoffrey is bound to try to talk me out of this."

"Josiah?"

"Can't keep a confidence if his life depended on it. And he's worse than Geoffrey when it comes to worrying that I'll encounter something or someone I can't handle."

"It's not as though you'll be alone," Lydia reasoned. "There are two of us."

"Done!" Prudence decided. "We'll inform them after the fact."

"If we don't find anything, there won't be any reason to confess our housebreaking at all."

By mutual agreement they waited until mid-afternoon before setting out for Claire's childhood home. Danny Dennis, waiting outside the Fifth Avenue Hotel in the hansom cab line, saw them emerge onto the crowded pavement and reached for his whip to flick Mr. Washington into motion. Prudence shook her head in his direction; arm in arm with Lydia, she strolled down the avenue as though nothing more important than looking in shop windows was on her mind.

"Is he following us?" she asked.

"I don't think so," Lydia said, glancing back over her shoulder.

"He won't let us out of his sight. Geoffrey's orders. But there's a hat shop on the corner. We'll let him see us admire what's on display and then go inside. They're bound to have a back door that opens onto the alley."

"As soon as we're inside, I'll look annoyed. You mumble something about a bothersome suitor. By the time Danny decides to get Mr. Washington moving, we'll be long gone."

Neither of them paid attention to the urchin in ragged cut-down men's tweeds who scooted past them to hold open the door to Madame Estelle's Parisian Hat Fashions. He pocketed the coin Prudence gave him, then ran for all he was worth around the corner and down the alleyway.

Once through the back door of the hat shop, they walked half the distance to Sorensen's house, then stopped for a late tea with sandwiches, taking their time as evening twilight deepened into dusk. Prudence had written a note to Geoffrey before they left the hotel: *Going shopping, then dinner in the suite and an early night.* A bellboy had slipped it under her partner's door. Even though Danny Dennis would not have seen them leave Madame Estelle's and return to the hotel, neither man would worry. A shopping woman was not to be interfered with.

And *early night* could be understood as feminine code for not wanting to be disturbed because of an embarrassing physical condition no man allowed himself to think about.

They thought their biggest challenge would be sneaking back into the hotel and up the stairs without being seen coming in at night unescorted.

"He must have ordered the furnace turned off before he left," Lydia said, tightening her grip on the wool shawl she'd wrapped around herself during the cold wait they'd forced themselves to endure until Prudence's watch read nine o'clock.

Full dark. Society dining out or in their boxes at the theater or at the opera. Their staff starting to climb the long flights of stairs from basement workrooms to attic sleeping quarters. The best time for two women in dark clothing to approach the back door of the residence where it would be presumed they worked, should anyone glance out a window while drawing the curtains. Late enough, but not so late as to be suspicious. The locked door had opened as smoothly under Prudence's pick as if she'd used a key.

The kitchen and below-stairs servants'

rooms of Aaron Sorensen's home were silent, frigid, and pitch-black. Not daring to light a lamp, Lydia and Prudence felt their way up the servants' staircase to the first floor, where someone had left a dim gaslight burning in the central hallway. It was just enough to allow them to get their bearings.

"The four most important rooms are the nursery, although I've been there once before," Prudence said, "Sorensen's bedroom, Ethel's bedroom, and the library. We can leave the library until last."

"We'll need light," Lydia said.

"Make sure all of the drapes are pulled tightly closed, and keep your lamp as dim as you can. We'll have to take a chance that no one knows the house is supposed to be empty."

"The bedrooms first?"

"I'll show you where they are." Prudence picked up one of the small gas lamps lined up atop a table in the central hallway, lit it, then turned the flame down as low as possible without extinguishing it. Her companion did the same. "I don't know why we're whispering," she said nervously, "we know no one can hear us."

"Empty houses echo," Lydia said.

"Sorensen's suite is just there." Prudence pointed toward the door opposite the staircase on the second floor. "There's a bedroom, a dressing area, and the master's private bathing room, complete with water closet."

"How do you know that?"

"A maid who used to work here. She had the skivvy's job of lighting all the fires in the house."

"Used to work here?"

"I think she decided she'd told me too much. Mrs. Hopkins complained to Ethel that the girl left without giving notice and therefore didn't deserve a reference, should she be foolish enough to ask for one. Mrs. Hopkins was the housekeeper during my short-lived career as a lady's companion."

"Should you be here at all, Prudence?" Lydia asked. "I'm having second thoughts about this. If the housekeeper or the butler came back to the house tonight, you might be recognized."

"No one's coming back. They've all been given notice. I can't imagine any servant feeling so loyal to an employer like Sorensen that he's willing to spend an extra night in an empty house just to ensure no one breaks in before the removal van arrives."

"I still don't like it."

"We'll be quick. Not to worry, Lydia." Prudence hugged her friend, then gave her a gentle push toward Aaron Sorensen's bedroom. When Lydia disappeared through the door, Prudence turned toward the suite belonging to the mistress of the house, the rooms in which both Catherine and Ethel had breathed their last.

The bedroom was draped in a pale Federal-blue velvet, which reflected tones of smoky gray in the lamplight. The same Federal blue, executed in satin coverlet and bed hangings, set off the deep mahogany luster of a four-poster that was the largest bed Prudence had ever seen. Chairs covered with a tangled green-leaf design were scattered around the walls, as if an audience were expected to gather. It didn't feel like a room in which a woman slept alone, except for the few hours a night when her husband sought her out until his seed took root. Prudence wondered whether this had been the suite occupied by Catherine's parents and then her father, until he ceded it to his newly married daughter and her tall, handsome husband.

She pictured Ethel bleeding out her child and her life as the hours passed and she drifted in and out of consciousness, perhaps unaware of exactly what was happening to her, puzzling over the pain, then floating into unconsciousness. Surely, everything

Prudence had managed to find out about Ethel's slow death pointed toward the oblivion of laudanum or a purer form of morphine.

The drawers of the bedside tables were empty, their surfaces waxed to a high gleam. Nothing remained of what Ethel had kept beside her during the night or what someone else had placed there. Dropping to her knees, Prudence stretched her arm out between the two mattresses, sweeping back and forth for anything that might have been hidden there, moving from the head of the bed to the foot, around to the other side, and all along the length of the mattress. She hadn't really expected to find anything, and she didn't. She thought the housekeeper would have seen to it that the upper mattress was turned when the soiled linens were changed.

There was nothing beneath the bed, not even the cat's-paw dust balls that gathered under furniture in most households. Still, obeying Geoffrey's oft-repeated Pinkerton dictum to be thorough, she ran her fingers over the legs of the bedstead and then along and under the edges of the carpet. Just where one leg of the bed pressed so tightly against the wall that she couldn't pass the palm of her hand behind it, Prudence felt something slender and smooth wedged in the claw-foot. She pulled, pushed, and prodded until it popped loose and rolled across the carpet into her fingers. A vial — a tiny, cork-stoppered glass vial. When she held it against the chimney of her lamp, she could see that it contained at least two teaspoons of a dark, viscous liquid.

Anyone else would have pulled out the cork stopper to sniff the contents of the vial. Not Prudence. She knew what it contained. Laudanum in a form more concentrated than that usually employed by ladies desperate to calm their nerves. Laudanum was deadly dangerous to Prudence; the slightest whiff could set off a craving that would leave her twisting in the agony known only to addicts who managed to live their daily lives without its succor. Or worse. She might upend the vial and swallow its contents. Backing out from beneath the bed, she slipped the minuscule glass vial into her skirt pocket, then scrambled to her feet.

A moment later, Prudence froze, every muscle rigid with concentration. What was that she had heard? The snick of a well-oiled lock as a key turned its tumblers? The soft hiss of a door opening? Head pounding, fingers trembling, she turned down the flame of the lamp and waited, motionless, remembering to control her breathing as Geoffrey had taught her. Moments, then minutes passed. Nothing broke the silence of the empty house, except the tick of the long case clock in the downstairs entry hall and the occasional swish of Lydia's skirts in the room next door. If Lydia was continuing her search of Aaron Sorensen's bedroom, it must mean she had heard nothing. Prudence had let her always-active imagination run away with her.

She made quick work of the dressing room with its armoires still full of Ethel's clothing. The velvet-lined drawers in which the mistress of the house would have kept her jewelry were empty. Her writing desk contained nothing but blank sheets of initialed letter paper and matching envelopes. Nothing remained that would cast a light on the personality of the individual who had lived in these rooms. Even the round crystal dish for face powder had been emptied and washed, its feathered puff thrown away.

She made her way back into the bedroom, trying to put herself in Ethel's frame of mind, turning slowly as she scanned one last time for a spot where Ethel might have hidden something she didn't want her husband to see. Every wife had secrets, but if she was prudent, she destroyed old love letters and keepsakes *before* she married. She'd already looked behind every framed picture and painting, run her hand over the wide hems of the drapes, lifted the corners of the Oriental rugs to check for telltale scuff marks in the fine dust that housemaids never quite removed. Hopeless. Either Ethel hadn't hidden anything, or her husband had found whatever it was and removed it.

Prudence glanced at the watch attached to her bodice. They'd been in the house for more than an hour. Time to move on to the other rooms she'd chosen to search. She wondered if Sorensen had swept his suite as clean as he'd obviously ordered his wife's to be.

Wait. There it was again. A noise that shouldn't be there. This time it was the unmistakable sound of a footfall, not against the checkered marble of the entryway, but nearly absorbed in the thickness of carpeted stairs. Someone was climbing inexorably toward where Prudence had no business being. She turned the key of the gas lamp, plunging the room in which she stood into blackness. Had she been in time to hide the narrow stream of light that must have streaked out beneath the bedroom door into the hallway? Had the person climbing the stairs been high enough to have seen it? All she could do was flatten herself between the protective bulk of a large armoire and the concealing folds of the drape that brushed against its side.

One last thing to do: She had to alert Lydia. She could hear her moving nearly soundlessly in the master's suite, unaware of the approaching danger. Prudence knocked once, twice, on the padded silk that lined and softened the walls of Ethel's retreat. The rustle of Lydia's skirts stopped abruptly. Prudence heard a soft exhalation of breath. Good. Lydia had blown out her lamp. She'd understood Prudence's warning.

The footsteps reached the second-floor landing, paused for a moment, then drifted away. Strain as hard as she could, Prudence couldn't be certain which direction they'd taken. Upward toward the third floor? She didn't hear them resume, but common sense suggested a servant. A footman, or perhaps even the butler himself, paid extra to remain in the empty house overnight. Returning from an afternoon bending his elbow or arranging for new lodgings until he could find another position. If they waited until he fell asleep, which couldn't be long, the way down to and then out the kitchen door would be clear. Sorensen had undoubtedly made sure nothing incriminating remained in either the nursery or his library. Prudence decided she'd been twenty times a fool to believe otherwise.

This was one daring adventure Geoffrey need never know about.

From the first moment he entered his house, Aaron Sorensen knew something was wrong. No one in his employ wore the expensive perfume whose faint traces floated through what should have been empty, unscented air. Miranda Prosper smelled of that special blend of sandalwood and old roses, but he dismissed that thought without examining it.

Mrs. Hopkins wore a faint lily-of-the-valley toilet water he'd smelled on many older women. So it wasn't his housekeeper who had trailed that tantalizing aroma through the ground-floor rooms. Yet she was here, probably sound asleep in her narrow bed up on the fourth floor. She had assured him that after her brief visit with the sister to whose home outside the city she was relocating, she would return to spend one final night under his roof and greet the removers when they arrived in the morning. Once they had taken charge, she would leave for good. Perhaps Mrs. Hopkins had

had a sudden attack of nerves at being alone in the great house all night; perhaps the sister had accompanied her. That was the likeliest answer.

It had taken the threat of withholding a letter of reference, and the payment of a significant bribe, to ensure her cooperation, but at the time he'd believed he would not be able to do the job himself. Circumstances had changed since then.

When Sorensen arrived at his destination at midday, he'd been told the paperwork that should have been ready for his signature would not be complete for several more days. Enraged, he'd demanded to know why, only to be met with lawyerly shoulder shrugs and a wall of stubborn resistance to his demands that they produce what was ready so he could get on with it. *"All in good time,"* he'd been told with maddening calm, *"all in good time."*

He'd slammed out of the offices and back to the railroad station, where he'd caught the afternoon train just as its wheels began to roll. He'd fumed the whole way back, then gone to the Union Club for a restorative dinner and an evening of poker. Nothing had worked out as he'd planned. The whiskey he drank before dining hit him hard; he fumbled his silverware, and the waiter had been slow to refill his wineglass. Coffee sobered him enough for admittance to the card room, but he'd begun losing as soon as he sat down at the table. His luck hadn't changed. He'd had to sign more notes, just when he'd thought his way was clear. Long before he wanted to leave, the other players at his table made it clear his presence was no longer desired. When he turned the key in the lock of the house that had come to him after Catherine's timely death, he was in a foul mood.

Now he smelled a recently extinguished gas lamp as he stepped into his bedroom. Mrs. Hopkins had been showing her sister around the mansion in return for her company during the night; he'd have words to say to her in the morning. If it hadn't been for the risk of running into Miranda Prosper at the Fifth Avenue Hotel when he'd told her he would be out of town, he might have bullied the staff into giving him a suite two days early. He never would have come back to this cursed place. Elegant, sumptuously furnished, still known as the Buchanan House, it had never fit Sorensen the way it should have. The house recognized him as an interloper and refused to enfold him in its welcoming embrace. Catherine had loved the place; even Ethel declared herself content within its walls. Aaron couldn't wait to get it sold, pocket the money, and move on.

Without a valet to help him with his clothes, he struggled to remove his shoes. He let his trousers, coat, shirt, suspenders, and cravat lie on the floor where they fell or he tossed them. He wasn't in the mood to clean his teeth or wash his hands. Aaron pulled back the covers, let himself sink into the feather mattress, and extinguished the bedside lamp.

Waves of whiskey fumes roiled in his stomach and crept up his throat. He piled extra pillows against the walnut headboard and propped himself up. He'd slept many a night in that position. But even though he closed his eyes and concentrated on what he needed to do the next day, his legs twitched and the whiskey fumes burned. He forced himself to lie still, not to twist and turn and punch angrily at the pillows. He knew that eventually sleep would come.

In the meantime he let his imagination picture the size of Miranda Prosper's fortune and the whiteness of her breasts and belly.

Chapter 28

Prudence's urgent knock set Lydia's pulse racing as she eased shut another empty drawer in Sorensen's dressing room. She blew out the lamp's flame, then realized the mistake she'd made when a puff of smoke rose into her nostrils.

Lydia closed the door that opened into Sorensen's bedroom, hoping the smell hadn't had time to drift, then groped for the door connecting the two dressing rooms. She crossed her fingers that Prudence had hidden herself somewhere in Ethel's bedroom and was waiting for her.

A hand clutched Lydia's arm the moment she emerged from the blackness of the dressing room. She stifled a scream as Prudence's voice hissed a warning.

"This way," she whispered, "behind the drapes. Take tiny steps so you don't bump into anything."

The two women inched their way along

the wall, then behind a set of floor-to-ceiling drapes. Faint lamplight from the street below lit their faces with an eerie yellow glow, but at least they could see. Neither of them dared put down the lamp she was carrying for fear of knocking against it, cracking the glass bulb, and spilling the lamp oil onto the floor. They stood straight, still, and silent against the windowpanes, careful not to let the velvet drape outline their bodies. They were hidden, but trapped inside a soundless, nearly airless space. For who knew how long?

Prudence looked down at her feet, then touched Lydia's arm and pointed. What they were watching for was a shaft of light from the hallway to shine through the open bedroom door, indicating someone had entered or looked into the room. They waited, ears straining for the slightest sound, eyes glued to the half inch of space between drape and carpet. Nothing happened. No light appeared; they heard no sounds of movement.

"I'm almost positive someone came into Sorensen's bedroom as I was leaving through the dressing-room door," Lydia whispered into Prudence's ear. "I thought I heard the bed creak as the person sat down on it."

"It can't be Sorensen," Prudence whispered back. "We know he's out of town."

"One of the servants Sorensen paid to remain here tonight? Maybe he decided to sleep in his master's bed instead of an uncomfortable iron bedstead in the attic."

"We'll give whoever it is an hour," Prudence said. She pulled out the tiny watch she wore pinned to her bodice in a jeweled case and read the timepiece by the murky gaslight filtering in through the window.

Lydia nodded. She leaned back against the wall and settled herself in to remain alert but motionless. If she turned her mind to figuring out how the pieces of the Aaron Sorensen puzzle went together, the time would pass quickly.

It was almost midnight before Prudence nudged Lydia and moved out from behind the drape, looping it back from the window so the streetlight illuminated the bedroom enough to outline the furniture. Shapes of lighter and darker gray, with here and there a reflection off glass or polished brass. Enough to allow them to make their way to the door without bumping into anything. They would have to carry the two oil lamps they had used in their search of the bedrooms down the main staircase and place them back on the side table where they had gotten them. The house seemed to be fitted with gaslight wall fixtures throughout the family living quarters, so perhaps the lamps were no longer used on a regular basis. Whoever was sleeping in Sorensen's bedroom had obviously not missed them. Probably hadn't even noticed they were gone.

Prudence eased open the door of Ethel's bedroom. A gas wall sconce lit the central section of the wide, carpeted hallway, though the far corners were in deep shadow. The house was so quiet, she could hear the faint hiss of the gas as it streamed into the mantle and burned.

Prudence planned to tiptoe across the hallway and make her way down the great staircase as Lydia waited in the doorway to Ethel's bedroom. Neither woman could remember whether the steps had creaked under their combined weight when they climbed to the second story, but there was no sense taking a chance. Once Prudence was safely on the ground floor, Lydia would follow. A few moments later they would be in the servants' stairwell. From there, through the kitchen, out the back door, up the steps into the cobbled back courtyard, and through the carriage gate into the alleyway — where they could breathe deeply again and hurry back to the Fifth Avenue Hotel.

Adventure completed and no one, but the two of them, aware of it.

Mrs. Hopkins had tossed and turned ever since hearing Mr. Sorensen enter the house and climb the stairs to his bedroom. The man came and went at all hours, often without giving warning of his plans. She remembered the horrible night when Mrs. Ethel had labored unconscious and all alone while the household, unaware of what was happening, slept around her. He had come home unexpectedly that night also, though it hadn't done his wife any good. If memory served, he'd put her to bed himself, then firmly closed the door between their adjoining rooms and slept through the hours of her long, futile labor.

Housekeepers knew more about their employers than they ever let on. Like butlers, they reprimanded junior servants for gossiping, enforced the rules of appropriate behavior, covered up what couldn't be condoned, and carried on as though nothing were amiss. Not until he or she had secured another position was it safe to think about a former employer's missteps. Not that they would ever be talked about openly.

Mrs. Hopkins, twisting and turning beneath her inadequate blanket, would be glad to be shut of Mr. Sorensen. He'd already written the good reference he'd promised and been surprisingly generous with what he'd paid her for this one extra night. Waste of money, since he'd come back himself, not that he couldn't afford it. Rich as Croesus when Mrs. Ethel died, or so the rumor ran, and he'd inherited from another wife, too.

The thought of two dead wives haunting the soon-to-be-empty house didn't make it any easier to fall asleep. Tired as Mrs. Hopkins was, her eyes refused to stay closed. Maybe she'd feel more secure if she got up and locked the door at the foot of the staircase that led from the family bedroom corridor to the servants' sleeping quarters in the attic. The butler had seen to that every night, which was why she hadn't thought to secure the passageway herself tonight.

Not that Mr. Sorensen posed any threat, she thought as she climbed out of bed and shrugged her arms into her dressing gown. And not that a locked door would keep out ghosts if they chose to roam. But there was something about turning a bolt that made you feel safe. She put her feet into a pair of embroidered slippers; the floors in the servants' quarters were uncarpeted and always cold.

Mr. Sorensen had left the gaslight burning in the corridor outside his bedroom. She could see the yellowish glow of it as she started down the bare wood stairs toward the open door. Maybe she should step into the hallway and turn it down a bit. She never felt comfortable when too much gas burned during the night.

She could see the bolt clearly, below it an additional lock, its key firmly in place. At least there was a railing to hold on to, Mrs. Hopkins thought as she inched her way down. Some servants' stairways were death traps.

Prudence reached the bottom of the wide, curving staircase without making a sound. She'd hugged the outer edge of each step; Geoffrey had told her once that a board was more likely to creak in the middle than at either end. She'd had to let the narrow skirt of her secretary's suit drag on the carpet behind her and hope the slight rustle was too faint to penetrate Sorensen's bedroom door. One of her hands held the oil lamp, the other gripped the banister. She set the lamp down on the narrow sideboard, then turned to signal an "all clear" to Lydia.

Kerosene lamp in hand, Lydia crept through the door of Ethel's bedroom and turned to close it tightly behind her.

A scream echoed the length of the hallway. Lydia lost her grip on the lamp. The crash of shattering glass mingled with another scream, and then the sharp stench of lamp oil filled the air. Without thinking, Prudence rushed up the stairs just as Mrs. Hopkins ran toward the female intruder she had seen when she turned the corner from the servants' staircase. They collided in mid-corridor, the housekeeper shrieking and beating with both hands at the woman who fell on top of her.

A shot rang out, and a man's deep voice shouted for everyone to stand still. Not to move. The smell of hot gunpowder mingled with the lamp oil.

Lydia froze, staring in horror at the half-naked man pointing a gun at the two women on the floor. She thought of edging back into Ethel's bedroom before he noticed her in the semidarkness, but it was too late. Blue eyes took her in at a glance and the gun motioned her away from the wall.

"Miranda?" For a long moment Aaron Sorensen stared at Prudence and said nothing else. "Miranda, what are you doing here?"

"Her name is Penelope Mason." Mrs. Hopkins was panting as she struggled to her feet, drawing her dressing gown around her and tying it tightly at the waist. Her eyes glanced at her employer's broad, blond-haired chest and bare legs. "I recognize her, though her hair was a different color and she wore spectacles when she passed herself off as a lady's companion to Mrs. Sorensen. Poor lady, may she rest in peace." Her right hand sketched a quick sign of the cross.

"My late wife never had a lady's companion," Sorensen corrected her.

"She did, sir, just for a few days when you were out of town on one of your trips. Miss Mason wrote a note saying she had to leave because her sister's husband died and there were children to look after." She patted stray hair into place and tugged at the long gray braid reaching to her waist. "We all thought it very strange at the time, but Mrs. Ethel cautioned us not to say a word about it. I think she suspected she'd been duped and was embarrassed. Nothing was missing, though, thank the Lord. We counted all the silver pieces."

Sorensen looked at the housekeeper as if she'd lost her mind. He stared hard at Prudence, then came to a decision.

"Mrs. Hopkins, take the cords off the

drapes at the end of the hallway and tie their hands behind their backs," he ordered, punctuating his commands with sharp jabs of the silver-plated revolver. "Good, tight knots."

The housekeeper scurried to the end of the corridor and returned with two lengths of twisted crimson cord. When Prudence refused to put her hands behind her back, staring defiantly at Sorensen, he swung the gun around to point it at Lydia's head. The message was clear. Prudence had no choice but to do what she was told.

Mrs. Hopkins wound the cord around her wrists the way she'd been taught to truss a chicken when she'd been starting out in service as a kitchen maid. Around, over, under, between, over again, around once more for good measure. When she pulled it tight and tied the knot, Prudence knew her hands would soon begin to tingle as impeded blood flow made them useless. She watched Lydia's face as her hands were also tied. Their eyes met, then skittered away. The last thing either of them wanted was for Sorensen to realize that they were more than unlucky con artists caught in what they'd believed to be an empty house.

"Now that you've done that, Mrs. Hopkins, you can take yourself upstairs, get your things together, and leave the premises. I counted on you to protect this house from exactly what appears to have happened. I want you out of my sight."

"Sir, I . . ."

"No excuses. Get dressed, pack your carpetbag, and be gone. You have ten minutes. Then I'm contacting the police to take these miscreants away. If you don't want to be accused of complicity, you won't be here when they arrive."

"Mrs. Hopkins . . . ," Prudence began.

"Not a word from either of you," Sorensen snarled. "As a householder defending his property, no one would fault me for shooting either or both of you dead."

Mrs. Hopkins disappeared up the servants' staircase to the attic. Less than her allotted ten minutes later, she was out the front door and halfway down the block, carpetbag and reticule bouncing against her legs as she ran through the night. Mr. Sorensen hadn't thought to ask for his extra money back. By the time he remembered that she hadn't earned it, she'd be at her sister's house. Where she'd be safe. She'd intended to leave him a note in the morning, just in case he needed to get in touch with her about the removal people. The paper with her sister's name and address written on it crackled in her skirt pocket.

Imagine that Miss Mason turning out to be a housebreaker. It just went to prove that you couldn't trust anyone, no matter how proper they looked or how well they spoke.

Sorensen hustled Prudence and Lydia down the stairs and into the library, gun always at the ready. He was clever. When Prudence lagged, he pointed the revolver at Lydia and cocked it. They both understood the threat.

"On the floor," he ordered. "Fold your legs crosswise in front of you."

It was all they could do to keep their balance, sit upright, and not fall over. Leaping at him in an attempt to knock the gun out of his hand was impossible from the position he'd made them assume.

"You'll tell me who you really are and what you're doing in my house," he said. "But first I'm going to make a call. Wonderful invention, the telephone."

Sorensen laid the gun down on the desk and picked up the candlestick phone. He gave a number to the operator, then waited. In the silence of the library, they could hear it ringing.

"Monroe," Sorensen said. "I need you. Bring laudanum and your van."

Chapter 29

Lydia was quickly and deeply affected by the laudanum. Minutes after Bartholomew Monroe held the brown bottle to her lips and forced her to swallow, while Sorensen trained his gun at Prudence's head, Lydia began to sway. Her pupils contracted as her head lolled on her neck and she rolled over on her side, hands still tied behind her back.

"Not too much," Sorensen cautioned.

"I know what I'm doing," Monroe replied. He jammed the bottle against Prudence's lips, forcing them apart. When she shook her head violently from side to side, he grabbed her by the hair, forced her head back, and pressed two fingers so hard into the hollow of her throat that she gasped for breath. Almost immediately she tasted the well-remembered bitterness of the drug. The two fingers dug into her throat again; involuntarily she swallowed.

The laudanum rushed into every cell of

Prudence's body; it was like sinking into a warm, comforting bath. Her head fell forward and she dropped into a boneless heap beside her friend.

Every nerve ending tingled, begging for more of the opium mixture, but Prudence feigned unconsciousness, knowing it was her only hope of saving herself and Lydia. She was an addict who had built up a tolerance for laudanum during the months after her father's and then her fiancé's murder a year ago. No one knew how long the craving lasted, but the phenomenon of requiring more and more of the drug was a well-documented fact. Countless wounded soldiers who had been introduced to laudanum during the war regularly consumed amounts of the drug that would kill a first-time user right up to the moment of their deaths many years later.

"You gave them too much," Sorensen complained. "They can't walk."

"Or scream for help." Monroe gathered up Lydia in his arms. "I'll leave the other one to you," he said. "Whoever she is."

"She's Judge MacKenzie's daughter," Felicia Monroe said, lighting a lamp in the gallery basement, then untying Prudence's hands. "The cord has left marks on her wrists. You tied it too tightly."

"How do you know who she is?" Sorensen snapped. The underground storage room of Monroe's gallery and studio was like every other space of its kind on Manhattan Island, darkly ominous, smelling strongly of mold, and so damp his skin quickly grew clammy. But there was nowhere else they could bring their two captives; leaving them in the Buchanan mansion was out of the question.

"She was pointed out to me. I was delivering more *cartes de visite* to a viewing. I think it was that set of twins who died of diphtheria before Christmas. Miss MacKenzie was leaving just as I was coming in. One of the funeral parlor attendants told me her story." Felicia rubbed Prudence's wrists, nodding in satisfaction as the blood returned and the cold white flesh warmed up. "That's better," she said. "You can hardly see where the cord was now. Her full name is Prudence MacKenzie. She scandalized society by going into business with an ex-Pinkerton. Investigative law is how they describe what they do, but it's plain old snooping, if you ask me."

She reached for Lydia's hands.

"No, leave her," Monroe said. "She's staying here."

"Arsenic?" Felicia asked, turning to a tray

full of chemicals, needles, and tubing.

"I haven't decided yet. And it won't be until after we've dealt with the MacKenzie woman. I want to take my time with her."

"She may wake up," Felicia warned.

"Put a gag on her and tie her feet together. We have a better chance of capturing what we're after if she's not as drugged as she is now. There will only be a second or two in which to catch the soul's image." Monroe's voice rang with excitement. It was rare to be present at the moment of death without family members hovering nearby. He began calculating the contrast of light and dark and the precise timing of the exposure. So much could go wrong.

Sorensen and Monroe carried Lydia to a battered cot on which lay a thin, stained mattress and a blanket that stank of mildew. Monroe thumbed her eyelid and grunted in satisfaction. The woman was unconscious, but her breathing was steady and the pupils of her eyes, though constricted, were still clear. He covered her to the chin with the blanket, being careful to tuck it tightly around her shoulders in case she came around and started thrashing to free herself. He didn't want an accident to rob him of what could be the greatest achievement any photographer had ever attained.

"We have to take Miss MacKenzie back to the Fifth Avenue Hotel," Sorensen said. He kept his eyes on her as he talked; she was as insensible as her friend. "Do you have anything that reverses the effect of the laudanum?"

"Smelling salts," Felicia offered. "But they only work for a few minutes. She'll fall back unconscious again, unless the laudanum is wearing off naturally."

"Spill some strong wine on her skirt where it won't be noticed, except for the smell. Just in case we run into another guest," Monroe said. "We'll prop her up between us and get her upstairs as quickly as we can. Felicia can go in first and distract the desk clerk. He'll probably be half asleep."

"How do I keep him from seeing you?" Felicia asked.

"Tell him you're a new maid on the night shift and that the staff entrance around back is locked and no one answered your knock. He'll be furious that you've come into the lobby, so he'll hustle you out of sight right away. All we need are a few minutes to get to the staircase."

"I don't have a uniform."

"You can say you were told the hotel was providing the uniform and cap. Better yet, don't open your coat." There were times when Bartholomew Monroe thought his sister's basic intelligence was questionable. If he didn't need her to chaperone deceased females, he'd be tempted to shove a needle in one of her veins and focus his camera lens on that stupid mouth of hers.

"The timing is important," Sorensen said. "And how we set it up will determine what the person who finds her thinks happened. Once a plausible story is accepted, the investigation will peter out of its own accord. She has to be half dressed, as though she climbed onto the bed intending to rest for a while. Do we leave the laudanum bottle in her hand?"

"No," Monroe decided. "Leave it on the bedside table with a glass and a spoon. We grab whatever jewelry and money are in the suite so it will look as though the lady's companion coaxed her employer to take a nap, gave her an overdose, then absconded with everything of value. The companion disappears, so there won't be any evidence to contradict that assumption. And Miss MacKenzie doesn't wake up. I hate not taking advantage of an opportunity like this, but I can't lug camera equipment into the hotel in the middle of the night."

Sorensen coiled the drapery cords that had been used to bind Prudence's hands and feet. "Burn these," he ordered, handing them to Felicia.

She nodded, laying them atop the coal scuttle. They were too pretty to be burned, she decided. As soon as the two men had gone upstairs, she'd hide them somewhere. She thought the rich crimson color would look beautiful in her own modest bedroom. Bartholomew was so parsimonious when it came to rewarding her little whims that Felicia had to take what she could get. He had no idea how many souvenirs she'd secreted away over the years.

"I still think we should take a bottle of this champagne down to Miss Prudence's suite," Ned Hayes said, rolling some of the vintage golden liquid over his tongue. "It's much too early for anyone of good taste to retire for the night."

More than anything else, Ned enjoyed an evening of witty conversation that began at dusk and continued to dawn. Prudence's friend Lydia was one of the most intriguing women he'd met; something about her hinted at dark secrets and a mind that might be the equal of his own. Which was a singularly odd thought, given the fact that well-bred women were not encouraged to develop their intellect. Still, her father was arguably the best cryptographer in the country. Some of that fascination with solving enigmas seemed to have rubbed off on her.

"I suppose I could ring," Geoffrey said. The Fifth Avenue Hotel had modernized to an astounding degree; many of the suites were equipped with individual telephones, a convenience not even most homes could boast of having, though the craze was rapidly spreading.

He might as well acquiesce to Ned's several-times-repeated suggestion. The former detective of the New York City Police had obviously settled in for the evening. He slept very little, and if he were to continue reining in his twin addictions to alcohol and opium, he needed distraction.

Earlier tonight, when Geoffrey answered the knock on his door, Tyrus, Ned's minder and former slave, had marched purposefully in behind his master. Now he dozed in a straight chair he'd set in a far corner of the parlor. Every now and then, one ancient eye opened, assessed the state of Master Ned's sobriety, then closed again.

"There's no answer." Geoffrey murmured his thanks to the operator, then replaced the candlestick telephone on his desk. "I think they've made good on their plan to have an early night."

"How boring," Ned said, taking a deck of cards out of his jacket pocket.

"Is that the deck you took from the steward at the Lotos Club?" Geoffrey asked. "It's marked, Ned."

"You need practice reading the cards with your fingertips," Ned replied, shuffling and fanning so fast that Geoffrey couldn't follow the cards he was palming and inserting exactly where he wanted them in the deck.

Tyrus rose from his chair in the corner and sauntered slowly to the table where Ned was dealing out three hands of poker. "You ain't gonna get away with none of them fancy tricks tonight, Master Ned. Mister Geoffrey see right through you." The eighty-two-year-old ex-slave settled into one of the cushioned chairs with a sigh of satisfaction. He cracked his knuckles and nodded his head in delight. "Master Ned, I'm gonna have to teach you a lesson. Yessir, I surely am."

Prudence let her legs go loose and her feet drag as Sorensen and Monroe lifted her out of the photographer's van onto the pavement. They were half a block away from the entrance to the main lobby of the Fifth Avenue Hotel. Streetlights glimmered, pools of darkness spreading out between them. Every other streetlight had been extinguished by the lamplighter making his rounds after midnight; no point running up the city's bill when respectable folk were home sleeping in their beds.

"Take the van around into the alley," Monroe instructed his sister. "Then get yourself back out here as fast as you can."

Felicia nodded, flicked her whip, and drove to the end of the block and out of sight.

Sorensen leaned Prudence against a lamppost and pressed his body close to hers, as though she were a lady of the night and he her customer.

"Here she comes," Monroe said. Felicia had nearly reached the hotel's huge main doors. She stopped for a moment, jerked her coat tightly around her body, then disappeared.

"Let's go," Sorensen whispered. He slipped one arm around Prudence's waist, let her head rest on his shoulder, and signaled Monroe to take his place on her other side. Together they alternately lifted and dragged her down the block. To anyone passing by, including the beat copper, they were two gentlemen helping a lady in distress make her way home. And whatever happened after that was nobody's business but theirs.

Felicia had done her job. The hotel foyer was empty, the desk clerk gone off somewhere with the incompetent new maid. Sorensen and Monroe met no one as they climbed the staircase to the third-floor suite Miranda Prosper had rented. Where she had entertained an eager suitor at tea. Where Prudence MacKenzie had dared try to make a fool of Aaron Sorensen.

Monroe hung Prudence's secretary's suit neatly in the armoire, arranged her shoes beneath it, left her stretched out on the bed in loosened corset, petticoats, and stockings.

"It should look as though her companion helped her disrobe, then gave her a drink laced with laudanum. She lies down on the bed, where she's given another dose." Monroe had staged so many death scene photos that he knew exactly how to achieve the effect he wanted.

"The overdose has to look accidental," Sorensen reminded him.

"It will. Laudanum is tricky. The police see this kind of thing every day." It was on the tip of his tongue to tell Sorensen that Prudence MacKenzie's widowed stepmother had died of a laudanum overdose, but at the last moment he decided to keep that bit of information to himself. Felicia had whispered into her brother's ear the few particulars she'd remembered from the newspaper account nearly a year ago, wondering if the two deaths might not seem too coincidental when the stepdaughter's true identity was discovered. As it would be. Monroe had scolded her for letting her nerves run away with her, and she'd quickly fallen silent. Half or more of the women he photographed died with a small brown bottle on their bedside tables.

"All right," Sorensen agreed, emptying the contents of Prudence's jewelry box into a sack he'd brought from Monroe's basement. He took the bills and coins out of her reticule, ran his hand over the top of the dressing table as though a search had been made, opened a few drawers and scattered some of the contents onto the rug. "One last thing." He held the brown bottle against Prudence's nose so that a few more drops of laudanum slid down her throat and pooled on her lips. "That should do it," he said, stepping back to admire his handiwork.

Prudence had moments of clarity when she was fully aware of what was being done to and around her, but she also drifted in and out of a light laudanum sleep. *Don't fight it,* she told herself. *They have to be convinced you're unconscious.* She clung to the belief that her tolerance to laudanum would save her, that she'd be able to summon help. *Please don't let them disable the telephone.*

There had never been any doubt in her mind that Sorensen would kill her if she tried to resist him. She wasn't strong enough to beat off either of the men, let alone two of them working together. If she forced his hand, Sorensen would strangle her or run a knife into her belly. Her only chance to escape was to swallow every dose of laudanum he gave her, then force herself to vomit up as much of it as she could the moment she was alone. She was counting on Monroe's eagerness to get back to the cellar, where he had left Lydia. So confident would Sorensen be, so eaten up by his own hubris, that instead of waiting until Prudence breathed her last, he would yield to Monroe's impatience. What could go wrong? Hadn't he already disposed of at least two wives with no one the wiser?

She focused her thoughts on Lydia. Her friend's life depended on how quickly Prudence was able to summon help when her attackers left the suite. She had heard enough of what they discussed in the cellar to remind her that Monroe was one of those photographers who believed it should be possible to capture the image of a departing soul at the moment of death. He would keep Lydia alive long enough to set up his experiment. She suspected Lydia had been aware of nothing after the first large dose of laudanum had rendered her unconscious. When she awoke, she would have no idea what lay in store for her.

"One more look around," Monroe said. He had a photographer's eye for details, a sharp instinct for what belonged and what didn't belong in a photograph. Or in a murder scene dressed up to mislead the police.

Sorensen leaned over Prudence. "She's still breathing," he complained.

"We can't wait. We need to be off the streets and back at the gallery before the early-morning deliveries start. We don't want anyone remembering that he saw us or the van."

"I don't like it."

"How much more did you give her?"

Sorensen lifted Prudence's head and emptied the bottle of laudanum into her mouth. He smiled. "Enough."

"Then let's go. Unless you think you've botched it."

Sorensen's hand crept to the revolver in

his pocket. He yearned to put a bullet into Bartholomew Monroe's hard and greedy excuse for a heart. But he didn't dare. The noise would wake up half the guests on this floor. They'd be out in the hallway demanding to know what was going on before he could reach the staircase at the end of the corridor.

There was another reason he couldn't kill him yet. Monroe had stolen a piece of evidence from Catherine's deathbed that would send Sorensen to the gallows. The photographer had demanded the first blackmail payment six months ago. And every month thereafter. Gambling wasn't the only thing that had bled the widower dry.

Aaron Sorensen walked out of Prudence's suite without another word.

Bartholomew Monroe followed, a broad smile on his face.

He locked the door behind him and pocketed the key.

CHAPTER 30

Wake up. Wake up, Prudence. Crawl to the phone. Call Geoffrey. Call Geoffrey.

Prudence rolled onto her side, pulling at the sheets with her fists to help her body twist its way to the edge of the bed. If she passed out again it would be forever. Her eyelids began to close; her fingers relaxed their grip on the bed linens. *Fight! Fight it! Keep moving!*

She knew what she had to do. She'd repeated the commands over and over; as she swam in and out of consciousness, the words danced in front of her eyes. *Wake up! Wake up! Keep moving! Fight it! Fight it!*

She obeyed the voice barking orders inside her head. Prudence clawed her way across the bed. When her body would have rolled off onto the floor, she pushed and grabbed at the mattress, forcing herself not to pitch forward, letting just her head hang over. She jammed two fingers into her throat, felt the nails scratch as they probed their way down past her tongue. Her gorge rose; her stomach convulsed. A wracking pain surged past her heart and lungs as laudanum gushed from her stomach into her mouth and out onto the rug. Her abdomen contracted until it felt like her belly slammed into her backbone. A mixture of acid digestive fluids and laudanum spurted between her lips and from her nostrils. She pounded with clenched fists against her gut, thrust fingers past her teeth and into her throat again, thrashed like a landed fish trying to escape the hook.

When the spasms no longer produced fluid, Prudence allowed herself to slide from the bed. She crawled toward the delicate writing desk on which sat the suite's brass-plated candlestick telephone. So far away. Drawing closer by inches as she struggled toward it. She tried to hoist herself into the chair in front of the desk. It overturned, crashing down on the arms she raised to protect her head. She could feel tears of anger and frustration leaking from her eyes. *Don't give up. Never give up.*

If she couldn't reach the phone, she'd have to bring it to where she lay on the floor. Prudence tugged on the cord, trying to slide the phone off the desk as gently as she could. But it was getting harder and harder to force her muscles to obey her commands; what was meant to be a steady pull turned into intermittent jerks. The phone fell, the heavy base striking her on the side of the head, sending waves of pain to all the sensitive places behind her eyes. Clutching the shaft of the apparatus in one hand, she pressed a finger up and down repeatedly on the cradle where the earpiece hung. The operator's voice asked her what number she wanted.

She tried to speak. And couldn't. Garbled a string of incomprehensible sounds that were meant to be words. She lay on her side, lips inches from the phone's daffodil-shaped mouthpiece, earpiece wedged between the carpet and her head, powerless to make herself understood to the woman at the other end of the line.

Over and over, the operator asked what number she wanted. Then she called her supervisor to listen. The two women conferred. Again Prudence was asked her party's number.

"Someone has knocked the receiver off its cradle," an authoritative voice said. "Children getting into mischief or someone's dog. Break the connection."

A loud click as the cable linking Prudence

with the outside world was pulled from the telephone company's switchboard. Then nothing.

Little Eddie nearly fell asleep waiting for the big Scandinavian and the even bigger black-headed man to come out of Miss Prudence's hotel suite. He'd been embarrassed for her when he saw how much help she needed to climb out of the photographer's van that appeared out of nowhere in the middle of the night at the rich man's house. He was used to seeing men much the worse for drink, and women of the streets also, but not a lady like Miss Prudence.

Danny wouldn't be happy when Eddie made his report, but at least she was safe in her bed now and the two swells had left her alone. He didn't know what he would have done if they'd tried to interfere with her, but they hadn't. Not enough time, and the glimpse he caught of her face didn't show any bruises. Her clothes looked all right; no rips or gaps in the row of tiny buttons still in their loops. Who would have thought a fancy lady like Miss Prudence MacKenzie would turn out to be susceptible to a gentleman's flattery and liquor? Danny would make him keep his mouth shut. Too bad. It was the kind of story that could buy you awestruck respect from the pack of other runners who never saw anything half as interesting.

When Little Eddie got to the stable where Mr. Washington was boarding, every lamp except one had been extinguished. Danny Dennis sat on a three-legged stool, a book of poetry no larger than the palm of his hand resting on his knee. He knew all of the poems by heart, but he liked the feel of the green leather cover embossed with a golden harp. The smooth pages with expensive gilt edges. He was humming the tune of "A Nation Once Again," every now and then singing a verse as if to remind himself that although he'd come to America, there was a struggle building across the Atlantic. Young Irelanders, they were called, gifted in language, brave of heart, on fire with dreams of freedom.

"Sorry to be so late, Mr. Dennis," Little Eddie said, sidling toward the huge white horse, whose enormous rump stretched from one wall of his stall to the other.

Danny raised a finger to his lips, rose from his stool, and smoothed a reassuring hand over Mr. Washington's hindquarters.

"We'll talk over there, boyo," he said, motioning toward the open door of the tack room.

In one of the empty stalls slept a large red dog and his small master. Blossom and Kevin Carney. Rumor on the street had it that Kevin had stopped bedding down in Miss Prudence's carriage barn because he was having more bad days than good. Danny would know what to do for him when the time came. His beardless face looked flushed against the sunset pillow of Blossom's flank. The dog thumped her tail once, but didn't disturb Kevin. She knew he needed his sleep.

"Now where have you been all day?" Danny asked. He poured the boy a cup of hot tea, added two teaspoons of sugar and a slug of milk.

"I didn't let her out of my sight for a minute," explained Little Eddie, gulping the scalding brew. "Not neither of the two ladies."

"The blond man's name is Sorensen," Danny said when Little Eddie had finished detailing where Miss Prudence and Miss Lydia had gone after they thought they'd escaped his surveillance. "And the other one, the dark-haired photographer, is Bartholomew Monroe. Now tell me again what you saw. Without all the distractions and the extra details."

"Miss Prudence and Miss Lydia had a

long tea, then they waited until dark and went into the big house on the corner. I stayed outside. Mr. Sorensen came home, then a woman ran out the front door and up the street. Mr. Monroe drove up the alley in his photographer's wagon and parked it in the back courtyard. The two gentlemen carried the ladies out and put them in the van —"

"Are you sure they carried them?" Danny interrupted. "They weren't just lending an arm?"

"Carried them like this." Little Eddie demonstrated.

"All right, go on."

"They went to Mr. Monroe's gallery, but around back, in the alley. I saw a lamp lit in the cellar. There's a window at the sidewalk level, but it's too dirty to see through." He waited, but Mr. Dennis didn't interrupt again. "Then they went to the Fifth Avenue Hotel, where the gentlemen and Miss Prudence got out. Another lady drove the van around the corner, then came running back and went into the hotel before they did."

"It couldn't have been Miss Lydia?"

"No, sir, it wasn't. I've seen Mr. Monroe before. Lots of times. It was his sister, Miss Felicia. She waved at him as she went up the hotel steps."

"Tell me about Miss Prudence."

"I'm sorry to say it about such a fine lady, Mr. Dennis, but she had to be helped to walk by Mr. Sorensen and Mr. Monroe. She was that far gone."

"I don't believe it."

"I smelled the wine on her. Her skirt was soaked with it."

"Something's wrong."

"They took her right upstairs and into her suite. I hid at the end of the hallway. Then they were back out and away. It didn't take long at all. Not more than a few minutes."

"And where was Miss Lydia?"

"I never saw her again after they got to the gallery. Maybe she was too sick to go back to the hotel?" It sounded lame, even to Little Eddie.

He watched, fascinated, as Mr. Dennis grabbed an instrument off the wall and began shouting into it. He'd heard of telephones and seen their wires strung all over the city, but he'd never seen one actually used before.

Ned Hayes nearly dropped the cards he was dealing when the infernal contraption an arm's reach away from him shrilled into his ear. "I don't ever want one of those things in my house, Tyrus," he said. "And don't you try to talk me into getting one. I don't know what this hotel was thinking of, Geoffrey, putting a telephone in every suite. It's the most intrusive thing I've ever had to put up with."

"You didn't protest when I used it to call Prudence," Geoffrey said, getting up from the table to pick up the earpiece and put an end to the ringing.

"That was different. It was you doing the calling. I'll bet you a dollar some fool gave the operator the wrong number."

"Call Worthington," Geoffrey shouted, breaking the connection and shoving the candlestick phone in Ned's general direction. "Tell him to get here as soon as he can. It's Prudence."

He flung open the door. "Sorensen got to her!" he yelled over his shoulder as he raced into the hallway.

Then he was gone, feet pounding a tattoo down the stairs to the floor below where Miss Miranda Prosper had entertained a murderer at tea three days ago. Tyrus followed close behind him, moving faster than he had in years.

Geoffrey hurled his body against the double doors of Prudence's suite. They gave way with a thunderous crack of breaking wood. He shoved his way past the wreckage, eyes searching frantically for what he dreaded to find.

He was holding Prudence cradled in his arms when Tyrus tottered into the parlor, his old legs trembling with the effort of getting down the stairs. He smelled the laudanum vomit as soon as he crossed the threshold, took in the rumpled bedclothes and the phone on the floor. "She done the best she could," he told Geoffrey. "That girl's smart as a whip. Now let's get her up on her feet and start walking her around."

Geoffrey nodded. Somehow Sorensen had forced Prudence to swallow a lethal dose of the drug, and she'd known it. Gambled on being able to survive if she could empty her stomach. Tried to call for help, but it had been too late. No telling how long Sorensen stood over her waiting for the laudanum to take effect. Lingering as long as he dared. Gloating as it began to kill her. He and Monroe.

Figuring out that twisted relationship would have to wait; Geoffrey's whole being was focused on not losing the woman he'd fallen in love with. Not allowing her to let go and leave him.

"He's coming," Ned Hayes said from the doorway. "Dr. Worthington's only a few blocks away and there isn't any traffic this time of night, so he won't be long. What happened?"

"Master Ned, you need to get on that phone and order us up some black coffee," Tyrus said. The kitchen wouldn't take orders from a man of color and they both knew it.

Ned wheeled around and ran for the newly installed elevator that would take him to the basement kitchens faster than the stairway. A voice over a telephone wire wouldn't be enough. He'd have to bully and bribe whatever skeleton staff was napping downstairs to get what was needed. At least three big pots of the strongest brew they could concoct. Money would have to change hands to ensure silence. If word ever got out that Prudence MacKenzie had nearly killed herself in a hotel room, there'd be no end to the gossip. Her reputation would be in tatters; she'd be years trying to sew it back together.

"Keep her walking, Mr. Geoffrey," Tyrus said, staggering under the weight of the slender young woman. "We got to keep her moving."

"You did the right thing to keep her on her feet," Peter Worthington said, taking a long tube with a suction device attached to it out of his leather medical satchel. "But we can't take any chances."

"This hotel's got hot running water," Tyrus volunteered.

"Warm is what we want," Dr. Worthington instructed. He'd heard about the old man who'd kept Ned Hayes alive when everyone else thought the ex-detective would lose his war with liquor and opium. If anyone had experience with what Worthington was about to do, it was Tyrus. Ned still alive was proof of his skill and dedication.

"You may not want to stay for this, Mr. Hunter."

"I'm not leaving her, Doctor."

"All right, then. Lower Miss Prudence to the bed, prop her on her side, and hold her there. You got that warm water ready, Tyrus?"

"Yessir."

"I'm inserting the tube now. As soon as I tell you, start pouring the water into that funnel. Not too much all at once and not too fast."

"I done this a time or two, Doctor."

"I'm sure you have. Nice and slow. That's good. We want to get as much as we can into her before we suction it out again."

Geoffrey held Prudence firmly in his arms

as the warm water passed through the tube Dr. Worthington had inserted into a nasal passage. It wasn't the first time he'd witnessed or helped with emptying out someone's stomach, but the procedure was never easy to watch. He listened to the rise and fall of Prudence's breathing and held one finger against her neck to monitor the steady rhythm of her heart. She was strong, he knew that, but the drug she'd been given was notoriously unpredictable. There was no telling what other substances had been added to the mixture Sorensen had forced into her.

"Again," Dr. Worthington said. "Once more should do it. We don't want to cause injury to the esophagus or the lining of the stomach."

"She might not have all that much laudanum left in her," Tyrus agreed. "Looks to me like she managed to get most of it up all by herself." He thought Miss Prudence's color was better. Mr. Geoffrey was the one who looked like he was knocking on Death's door.

By the time Ned Hayes arrived with a harried waiter pushing a cart loaded with coffee urns, Prudence had regained consciousness and was on her feet again. Geoffrey and Tyrus resolutely walked her around the suite, while Dr. Worthington packed up his instruments. She wasn't able to talk coherently yet, but the pupils of her eyes were larger and she seemed to be aware of her surroundings.

Ned paid the waiter, then spun him around and hustled him out of the suite before he caught more than a glimpse of a woman held up between two men. The waiter could have told them it happened all the time, guests overindulging, but then they wouldn't have paid him as much to keep his mouth shut.

"I caught a glimpse of Mr. Washington at the curb when I was in the lobby," Ned told them, pouring coffee and drinking it down himself before he remembered to hand it to Geoffrey. "Danny is probably on his way up."

"What were you doing in the lobby?" Geoffrey ceded his place at Prudence's side to Peter Worthington.

"The night clerk claims he never saw Miss Prudence come in, but he refuses to admit he ever left the front desk."

"What about Lydia?"

"Same thing."

"I let myself in," Danny Dennis announced from the doorway. "Is Miss MacKenzie going to be all right?"

Beside him stood a small, scruffy boy wearing a set of ragged tweeds meant for a much larger frame.

"I know where the other lady is," Little Eddie said, doffing his cap, staring open-mouthed at the pretty young miss lurching unsteadily around the room. "I saw where they carried her in. She's still down there."

"Bartholomew Monroe's gallery," Danny contributed. "Eddie says he saw a light come on in the basement."

"Go," called out Peter Worthington. "Tyrus and I will see to Miss Prudence."

"Don't you worry none," Tyrus assured them. "She gonna be just fine."

Resolutely Geoffrey turned his thoughts to Lydia. "How quickly can you get us to Monroe's studio?" He shrugged into the shoulder holster containing his loaded Colt revolver, nodded in satisfaction when Ned opened his jacket to show he, too, was armed.

"Mr. Washington's ready to go," Danny told him. "You know how fast that horse can move when he needs to."

He wasn't sure she felt it, but before he left the suite, Geoffrey brushed his fingers lightly along one of Prudence's beautiful cheekbones.

Whatever else happened tonight, Aaron

Sorensen would pay for the life he'd tried to take.

Chapter 31

"I don't understand why you need me for this," Sorensen said. He looked around at the dank basement, which smelled of photographic and mortuary chemicals, and shuddered. Simple murder never bothered him, but Monroe's obsessive determination to capture the image of a human soul leaving its body struck him as macabre. Dangerous because it wasn't logical.

Sorensen didn't believe in souls, human or otherwise. He had no patience with people who claimed to have heard voices from the beyond, felt the cold breath of the departed, or seen with their own eyes the ectoplasm that made up the ghostly entity. Rubbish. Superstition. The ultimate con. The only thing he had any faith in was the power of money. He enjoyed the women who brought it to him, but only until the uniqueness of a new conquest turned into the boredom of daily living. Pregnancy made every female creature a captive of her own body; it was a tool he used well. The infants he sired to keep their mothers docile meant less than nothing to Aaron Sorensen. He disposed of them with as little emotion as he rid himself of the mothers who bore them.

He didn't quarrel with killing the woman who had swum out of her laudanum haze and told them her name was Lydia Truitt. She knew too much; if allowed to live, she would ask questions. He thought Monroe's plan to bury her under another name and in someone else's coffin was both sensible and amusingly creative. What annoyed him, what had set his teeth on edge, was the man's maddeningly slow preparations for the taking of her life. And Monroe was infuriatingly verbose, explaining every step of what he proposed to do as though the victim were not there listening, with growing fear and horror widening her eyes.

"The exposure has to be precisely calculated," he explained. "It's possible that the image will be blurred, but I think that will be acceptable. As long as it is clearly the soul that's seen to be in flight." He fussed with the camera, with the box of glass plates, with the black drape waiting for him to duck beneath it.

Felicia prepared Lydia as best she could, given that her brother had refused to allow anything more freeing than the retying of her hands in front of her body rather than behind her back. The prisoner groaned with relief and then pain when Felicia loosed the cords and massaged some life and blood into her wrists. Tears trickled down her cheeks. She asked for water, which Felicia held to her lips when Bartholomew nodded his permission. Lydia couldn't hold on to the glass; Felicia tipped the liquid into her mouth as if she were a child.

She retied Lydia's wrists, but not tightly. Then she smoothed the dark hair and straightened her clothing. Not that it mattered. But Felicia was used to posing a subject as perfectly as possible so as to obtain an image that would please and comfort family members for years to come. That Bartholomew would retouch the photograph to blur parts of Lydia's face and make her unrecognizable was regrettable, but necessary. Still, Felicia knew her brother would only be pleased with the most presentable model she could provide him. From the box of paints and powders that were the same as those used by mortuary parlors, she chose a faded rose tint for Lydia's cheeks and a slightly brighter hue for her lips. She was already so pale that powder did not seem appropriate.

"I don't understand why I have to be a part of this," Sorensen repeated. The longer he stayed in this wretched basement, the closer it came to the time when Prudence MacKenzie's body would be discovered in her hotel room. He wanted to be on a train and well out of the city when that happened. He'd removed all of his papers from Catherine's family home before the last, unproductive trip to Philadelphia, but he hadn't emptied his box at the main post office yet. Two things had gone wrong: Ethel's family lawyers had dragged their feet and Miranda Prosper had turned out to be an imposter. Time was running out. He had to disappear for a while. Whatever was in the post office box would have to wait.

"I need you," Monroe replied. "I've changed my mind about the remains. I'm now of the opinion that once the essential photograph is taken, it will be too dangerous to keep Miss Truitt here indefinitely. Felicia tells me we have no prospective match on the books. It could be weeks before one becomes available. I suggest the river. With a piece of Miss MacKenzie's jewelry snagged in her skirt pocket so the implication is clear."

"You don't require me for that."

"Oh, but I do, Mr. Sorensen. You must earn your daughter's pillow."

"The agreement was that you would destroy it. I paid you what you asked."

"So you did. But the price has gone up. Show it to him again, Felicia."

Monroe's sister produced a white silk carrying pillow, lavishly embroidered, with silk tassels attached to each corner. She held it where Sorensen could see, but not touch it. When she was sure he recognized the pillow, she turned it over. Bloodstains had stiffened the white-on-white silk embroidery. They were brown with age, but all the more recognizable for the clear outline of desperate lips and teeth.

"The bitch bit her tongue," Sorensen complained.

"That's what my sister and I believe. And so will anyone else who sees it. We photographed your daughter lying on the pillow, but we didn't see the bloodstains until we turned it over. Fortuitously, I would say. The blood was still fresh. Still red."

Sorensen reached for the pillow that had been a gift from Catherine's friend, who had died under the weight of a swiftly descending sandbag. Monroe jerked it out of Felicia's hand and flung it behind him to land on the steps leading up to the gallery.

"When we're finished here. When you've earned it," Monroe said.

When you and your fool of a sister are as dead as Prudence MacKenzie's friend, Sorensen thought. The gun in his pocket that he'd used to capture the two women held six bullets. He'd fired one. Five remained, and he was a very good shot.

Lydia's feet were as numb as two blocks of wood; if she attempted to stand on them, she would fall. Escape was impossible, but she didn't have to die without putting up a fight. Feeling had returned to her hands; she flexed the fingers surreptitiously until the pins and needles stopped prickling and tingling. She thought she could hold on to an object, grip it tightly enough to use it as a weapon. She might do some damage before they wrested it away from her. That's all she wanted. Not to go quietly like a dumb animal to its slaughter.

She watched Felicia insert a thick needle into the end of a glass-and-metal syringe. Then Monroe's sister removed the cork from a bottle labeled PERPETUAL LIGHT EMBALMING FLUID and drew enough of the liquid through the needle until the syringe was entirely full. Arsenic. Lydia had listened to enough of her father's battlefield stories to know that arsenic had been the main ingredient in the embalming fluids used during the war. And still was. If a mortuary parlor owner got to a corpse before an autopsy could be performed, there was often no way to tell if the deceased had been poisoned with arsenic or just well-preserved by it. Death could come quickly, if enough arsenic was used, or slowly, over time, if the intent was to mimic the symptoms of any one of a number of fatal diseases or conditions.

For Monroe's purposes, if she had interpreted correctly his ramblings about photographing departing souls, the dosage would be enormous. Lydia wondered if her organs would cease to function before the horror of vomiting, cramps, loosening of the bowels, and unimaginable pain took hold of her.

Felicia smiled reassuringly and patted Lydia's hand. It would be quick then. She returned Felicia's smile vaguely, as though she were not looking at the face of her killer's willing accomplice. Her fingers twitched as she imagined them grabbing the syringe and plunging the needle into Felicia or Monroe, whichever of the two picked it up to use on her.

Sorensen remained in the shadowy area

by the staircase, waiting to be told what to do next; he'd lost all interest in Lydia as a person. She was an obstacle he was impatient to have removed.

Danny Dennis reined in Mr. Washington while the cab was still a block away from Monroe's gallery. His hooves struck sparks from the cobblestones as he pawed the roadway. He was a horse who didn't like to be halted once he'd set his stride.

"They'll hear him for sure if we go any closer," Dennis said, climbing down from his high seat above the passenger compartment. He held a whip in one hand and a club in the other. Little Eddie, who had perched beside him during the furious ride along Fifth Avenue, clutched one of Mr. Washington's enormous and well-worn steel shoes, thrown just a day or so ago and stowed temporarily in the driver's well. It didn't fit his hand like a good pair of brass knuckles, but he figured it could do at least as much damage.

"The entrance to the alley is over there," Eddie said, pointing with the hand holding the horseshoe. He scampered off without giving anyone the chance to tell him to stay behind with Mr. Washington and the hansom cab. He had a feeling that exciting things were going to happen very quickly.

Both Geoffrey and Ned were armed, each with a repeating revolver. Geoffrey had used the same double-action Colt for years, while Ned had recently bought himself and Tyrus a pair of new Smith & Wessons. Each man carried extra ammunition, though neither thought there would be time to reload. If they lost the element of surprise before they could get to Lydia, they expected a firefight. Little Eddie had reported hearing a shot fired inside Sorensen's mansion, and half the residents of the city kept arsenals in their basements. Both killers would be armed, neither one willing to risk capture and the state's brand-new, and as yet untried, electric chair.

Geoffrey's skill with his picks had the lock to the delivery chute open in less than a minute. If Monroe's basement was like most of the others beneath businesses, the coal chute would end in a dark and filthy furnace room, with a stout door to separate it from storage areas and keep the coal dust confined. Strips of wood had been nailed to the side of the chute so a deliveryman could descend without slipping and sliding.

Geoffrey led the way, Danny behind him, Ned following. Little Eddie danced his way among the men, his bright blue eyes sparkling with excitement, his feet silent in the rags he'd wound around shoes so worn his skin scraped the sidewalk through holes in the leather. As soon as Ned cleared the ramp, Little Eddie scooted halfway up to ease the delivery hatch down. Except for a faint strip of light beneath the door leading to the rest of the cellar, they were in inky, dusty blackness.

Geoffrey opened the door and stepped out into a storage room lined with photographic props, discarded furniture, and mounted postmortem portraits from past exhibits. A faint murmur of voices led them toward where they hoped to find Lydia. A woman spoke, but Ned shook his head. Not Lydia. Probably Felicia Monroe. They froze, each man readying himself for what came next. Geoffrey's left hand reached out for the brass doorknob picking up a faint gleam from the light shining beneath the door. He turned it. Slowly and silently.

Then he jerked his head in a quick nod and threw his body against the wood.

Felicia rolled Lydia's sleeve above the elbow. She wound a length of cord around the wrist until it was immobilized against the arm of the chair, where Bartholomew had tied her. For the sake of the photograph, the restraints were hidden under a crocheted shawl, and as soon as Sorensen depressed the plunger and sent the arsenic-laced embalming fluid into Lydia's body, Felicia would draw that corner of the shawl over the exposed arm. Nothing could distract from the flight of the soul escaping Lydia's body. The death had to look natural.

"Felicia can do this," Sorensen said, but a furious rumble from under the black cloth covering the camera and the man crouching behind it made him move closer to the tray and its lethal syringe.

"I have to watch her face," Felicia explained. "I'll call out her expressions as they change so Bartholomew will know the exact moment to take the exposure. He can't see as well under the cloth as I can if I stay close to her, but just a step or two out of range." She spoke in the gently instructive tones of a patient teacher. "We hope it won't take long."

"I don't think she's conscious," Sorensen said.

"She's drifting in and out, but perhaps that's for the best. I put a few drops of laudanum in the water I gave her to drink. I could tell by the look in her eyes that she knew what I'd done, but it was too late. She'd already swallowed it."

"Why? I thought he said he wanted her alert so the soul could release itself without impediment to its essence." Gibberish, but Sorensen was playing the cooperative conspirator to keep Felicia and her murderous brother at ease and unsuspecting. He'd chosen the moment when he'd pull the gun from his pocket and shoot them both. Right after he depressed the plunger to release the arsenic into Lydia Truitt's vein. Both of them would be staring hard at their victim, anticipating the instant of death and the flight of the soul. The last place they would be looking would be at him.

One bullet each to take them down. Another to finish them off. They could experience their own souls fly out of their mouths. No more questions. No more mysteries. They'd know it all.

Geoffrey shot the syringe out of Sorensen's upraised hand; Little Eddie tackled the legs sticking out beneath the black cloth. Danny raised his club and politely asked Felicia to kindly put her hands up over her head. For a moment it all seemed too easy. It was.

Monroe kicked viciously at the boy, who'd wrapped one skinny arm around his legs and was pounding on his feet with what felt like an odd-shaped hammer. The heel of one heavy boot smashed into Eddie's mouth, releasing what few good teeth the boy had onto the floor, where they floated in a pool of blood and mucus. He passed out from the pain, still holding tight to Mr. Washington's large shoe. Danny pulled him away before Monroe could kick him in the stomach and groin, blows that might rupture something inside and kill him.

By the time Danny picked up his club again, Monroe had shaken off the dark cloth and decided he was badly outnumbered. Grabbing a rifle from a full gun rack, he made for the staircase.

"Get him out of here!" Geoffrey yelled to Danny, pointing at Little Eddie curled in a fetal position on the floor. Blood was coming out of the boy's mouth and ears.

A woman's piercing scream rang through the basement. Felicia had picked up the syringe loaded with Perpetual Light Embalming Fluid and was calmly approaching Lydia, as if all hell had not broken loose around her and the soul-capturing photograph still had to be taken. Ned took aim, but at the last moment Felicia turned and smiled at him. She held the deadly needle in upraised hands, the universal gesture of surrender, but her eyes roamed the basement. When they settled on her brother, she smiled again and began to move.

Ned shot her. He took no chances. The bullet pierced Felicia's torso and lodged against her spine.

Aaron Sorensen had crawled away from Lydia, feigning weakness and confusion, cradling his injured fingers, none of them broken. He saw Geoffrey glance at him, then bend to untie Lydia's hands and feet. He was getting out of this cellar, and he was going to make sure there were no witnesses to rat on him. Felicia had not let go of the syringe when she fell, but her eyes were glazed over. As she shuddered and convulsed, her fingers loosened.

With the deadly syringe in the injured hand and his revolver in the other, Sorensen scrambled to his feet. Monroe had reached the top of the staircase, but the door into the studio area was locked. He was too close to risk a ricochet, so he slammed the butt of the rifle against it repeatedly; splinters of wood flew beneath his fingers. The door was about to give.

Sorensen clawed his way up the staircase, knocking Monroe off balance, sending both of them tumbling to the basement floor. The photographer tried to stand, sliding in his own blood as it poured from his head wounds. Not understanding what had happened, he reached out an arm for Sorensen to grab and help hoist him to his feet.

Only when he felt the stab of the needle, and the fiery wash of the arsenic-impregnated embalming fluid, did he realize that he'd made a foolish and fatal mistake. There was no such thing as partners in crime. He should have remembered that. Facedown at the bottom of the staircase, bubbling out his last breaths as the arsenic burned a path through his vital organs, Bartholomew Monroe wondered if he could keep his eyes open as he died. If he'd see his own soul take wing.

Aaron Sorensen had almost reached the top of the staircase and freedom. Two more steps and he'd push open the damaged door to the gallery, wedge something against it from the other side, and be out on the street and away from the carnage below. He turned to fire at whoever might be coming after him, saw Ned taking aim, raised his revolver, and stepped sideways into shadow. Stepped on the soft white silk embroidered pillow he'd held over Catherine's face, and lost his footing. Dropped the gun as his arms flew out to hold him upright on the narrow stairs.

Geoffrey's bullet caught him in the neck; Ned's drilled a neat hole in the center of his forehead. When Aaron fell, he dragged the beautiful tasseled pillow with him. And when his body rolled to a stop, his bloody face was pressed against the stain a dying Catherine had made to bear final witness against him.

CHAPTER 32

"I've had this in my skirt pocket for a week," Prudence said, placing the tiny vial of laudanum she'd found under Ethel's bed on the long table in the Hunter and MacKenzie conference room.

Josiah had ordered pastries from the German bakery and brewed both coffee and tea. Bowls of whipped cream and rich brown sugar sat beside a stack of dessert plates, folded linen napkins, and sterling silver forks and spoons. Fine bone china cups nestled in translucent saucers. The firm might have just closed a rather sordid case of multiple murders for profit, but appearances had to be kept up. It was how you did the ordinary things that defined you. And he was determined that Hunter and MacKenzie, Investigative Law would always do things right.

Ned touched the laudanum vial with a long, elegant finger, then turned solemnly to Prudence. "Congratulations," he said. "That must not have been easy."

"I had to prove something to myself," she answered his unspoken question.

"You'll have to keep proving it, you know. Over and over again. I wish I could tell you that it gets easier, but I don't think you'd like me to lie to you."

"You just go at it one day at a time, Miss Prudence." Tyrus refused to pull his chair up to the table. He'd take his pastry and coffee into the outer office when the time came, but he hadn't been able to say no to Master Ned's flat-out order that he accompany him today. It was time to reexamine the case and evaluate the results.

Tyrus wasn't sure it did anyone any good to pick over things once the problem had been resolved, but he'd learned a long time ago that life was easier if white folk were allowed to do whatever came into their sorry heads. "Worry something to death" was what Tyrus called it. Not much point to it, seeing that the folks that caused the problem were all dead. He took the cup of coffee Master Ned handed him and wandered out into Mister Josiah's office. He'd rather have a piece of that fancy imported chocolate with his coffee than an apple fritter. He knew where Mister Josiah kept them hidden.

"Shall we wait for Danny?" Prudence asked.

"He's not coming," Geoffrey said. "He's teaching Little Eddie how to groom a horse. Says the boy needs to have a trade if he's ever to get off the streets."

"He must be healing well if Danny is putting him to work."

"Apparently, he's younger than he let on. All those teeth he lost when Monroe kicked him would have fallen out anyway. He's black-and-blue all over, but only a few of the cuts needed stitching, so, yes, I'd say he's healing very well."

"Danny has a soft heart."

"Don't let him hear you say that. He'll admit to caring for Mr. Washington, but he finds his fellow humans extremely wanting."

"I suppose you got Little Eddie to tell his story one more time?" Ned asked.

"Josiah did."

The secretary opened a folder lying on the table and took out a neatly transcribed witness statement. All the whipped cream and German pastries in the world wouldn't make up for not being part of what had happened in the basement of Bartholomew Monroe's gallery. He wondered if he should be writing all this down the way that British doctor had recorded the strange case of the odd-mannered detective whose Baker Street flat he shared. Josiah wrote himself a note to contact an acquaintance in the publishing business.

"I'm sorry to be late. Someone named Tyrus let me in." Claire Buchanan leaned over to kiss Prudence on both cheeks, shook hands with Geoffrey and Ned, and nodded politely at Josiah. Her cheeks were a polished apple-red hue from the cold March wind, and her green eyes sparkled. From her ears dangled the jade-and-gold earrings once worn by her mother and then by her twin. She shrugged out of her coat and helped herself to coffee. "I have wonderful news. The house is definitely mine. It should never have gone to that beast Sorenscn in the first place. Catherine wrote a later will when she decided to leave him. She hid it in one of those boxes you can rent at some banks nowadays. When the fee hadn't been paid for more than a year, they opened it."

"Will you live there, Claire?" Prudence asked, hoping the answer would be yes.

"I've been offered a company contract with the Met, and not as a cover singer," she said, beaming. "I'll keep the apartment in Paris, but my real roots are here."

"Can you bear it? Knowing the crimes Sorensen committed in those rooms?" Ned existed in a world of memories and ghosts. He often wondered how other people managed to avoid them.

"I hired a medium. Please don't frown like that, Mr. Hunter. She walked through all the rooms, and when she finished, she told me that the only auras she sensed were good ones. The spirits who lost their lives there don't linger, but they do return occasionally, so I shouldn't be surprised if I sense their presence. Catherine and Ethel. I've nothing to fear from either of them. Or their babies. There's no trace of the evil that was Aaron Sorensen."

"Shall we begin?" Geoffrey asked. Talk of ghostly spirits brought back painful memories of the North Carolina plantation house where he had spent his early childhood.

Josiah opened his stenographer's notebook and laid two freshly sharpened pencils beside it.

"From the evidence we have, there's no doubt that Aaron Sorensen married for one purpose only — to kill and inherit. The young woman in Saratoga Springs, Damaris Tavistock, is the only one to escape him that we've been able to identify. There were others, I'm sure, and if we put our minds and a considerable amount of energy to it, we might be able to track them down. A few of them, at any rate."

"I told Geoffrey that I saw no point to it. Not now that he's dead. We paid for an obituary to run in most of the state newspapers every day for a week. I should think women who gave him gifts of money, but were able to pull away before it was too late, would be reading those obituaries every day, hoping to find his name. They're safe from him now. They should be able to get on with their lives without our interference." Prudence looked inquiringly at Claire.

"I agree," Claire said. "I had no idea what a Pandora's box I was opening when I asked you to investigate Catherine's death. But I'm glad I did. The only thing I bitterly regret was that Lucinda lost her life because of it."

"Two of the sailors who worked the flies when the sandbag fell are also dead," Geoffrey said. "The rest of them, the ones we've been able to interrogate ourselves or could hire someone in another city to question, either have good alibis or claim no knowledge of a cut rope. The police department has closed the case, concluding 'death by persons or circumstances unknown.' " He omitted mentioning that Detective

Phelan had inquired after Claire by name, then abruptly changed the subject when his face flushed red. "There is always the possibility that whoever severed the rope either did so without deliberate malice or for a personal grudge unsuspected even by Lucinda. I don't think you should blame yourself, Miss Buchanan."

"You're saying it might have been a spurned lover, or perhaps even what I first thought it was, someone in the company consumed by jealousy and spite, warning me off, trying to frighten me into returning to Europe?"

"It's possible," Geoffrey hedged. "We also checked the Met's hiring records. Several performers have moved on to other companies, two contracts expired and were not renewed, and there's been turnover among the stage crew."

"We're wanderers," Claire said. "Opera gypsies. It's one of the reasons we're good enough to entertain in society, but never to be a part of it. It's always a scandal when a fatuous young gentleman or an elderly fool marries one of us."

"Will you want the other photographs Monroe took of Catherine and Ingrid? Jacob Riis says he can get the glass negatives and print them up for you."

"Yes. I want to look at all of them one last time. I'll decide which to keep and then destroy the others. Prints and glass negatives alike." Claire looked down at her hands, the fingers of which had begun to twist themselves into a knot. "I asked one of our dressers if she could clean Lucinda's pillow. They work marvels with the company costumes. She tried, and she was able to get most of Sorensen's blood out, but she said the other stain had been set for too long. I burned it. I couldn't bear to leave Catherine's blood mingled with even a drop of Sorensen's."

"She wanted you to know what happened," Prudence said. "More than that, she was leaving proof behind in the only way she could."

"How is your friend?" Claire asked, changing the subject.

"Much better, but still recovering. She had an unusually strong reaction to the laudanum they gave her. Dr. Worthington said it will take some time to work its way entirely out of her system."

"Is there anything I can do for her?"

"She's working for her father again, and Ned has been to see her."

"Perhaps tickets to some of our performances? When she's feeling up to it?"

"I'll ask," Ned said. "We haven't talked much about music, but I have a feeling Miss Lydia would enjoy the opera very much."

Still in the outer office, enjoying Josiah's chocolates, Tyrus cleared his throat loudly. Ned flushed and muttered something unintelligible under his breath.

"I must go," Claire said. "We have a rehearsal this afternoon." She raised her eyebrows in Josiah's direction; he nodded his head. Hunter and MacKenzie, Investigative Law had been paid in full.

"I think I'll always wonder about Felicia Monroe," Prudence said when Claire had left. "Sorensen was twisted by greed, Bartholomew Monroe obsessed by his quest to become the first photographer to capture an image of the human soul. But Felicia?"

"She kept a souvenir from many of her brother's clients," Geoffrey mused.

"But they weren't all jumbled together," Prudence said. "I think the ones she kept apart from the others, the dozen or so that had initials inked onto them, those must have had a more personal meaning for her."

"There were times in the hospital during the war when orderlies carried a dead soldier out to where the graves were being dug, and before they could lay him in a coffin, somebody would notice he was still breathing," Ned contributed.

"You think she killed them?" Prudence asked.

"It wouldn't be the first time bereaved family members heard the death rattle and assumed it meant what it sounded like. Monroe could have emphasized how important it was for him to be at the bedside immediately after death. He also could have paid hired nurses to warn him when the end was near."

"I think there were instances when she helped prop a not-quite-dead subject in place and then stood by until Bartholomew had done his calculations and drawn the black cloth over his head," Geoffrey said. "And when he did, when he signaled he was ready, she leaned over the victim and pinched shut the nostrils and held her hand or a cloth over the mouth. Then she stepped back out of the picture while he uncovered the lens so the departing soul could get its portrait made. She was as guilty as either Monroe or Sorensen."

"If she'd lived, would she have gotten the rope?"

"It's supposed to be what they're calling the electric chair," Geoffrey reminded her. "A more humane method of execution, if you can believe that electricity is always that reliable. They haven't tried it out yet."

"She'd be lying paralyzed on a cot in an asylum for the criminally insane," Ned decided. "With my bullet still stuck in her spine." There wasn't a trace of compassion or pity in his voice.

"In that case I think it's better she didn't survive," Prudence decided. She'd visited the Tombs with Geoffrey a few months ago. Bad as the city jail was, an asylum was bound to be a hundred times worse.

"Telegram, Master Ned." Tyrus stepped into the conference room, empty coffee cup in hand, a barely discernible trace of imported Belgian chocolate on the dark skin just below his lower lip.

"It's addressed to Miss Prudence," Ned said, passing the flimsy pale yellow envelope across the table.

"Are we expecting anything, Geoffrey?" Prudence asked as she slid the blade of one of the silver knives beneath the glued flap. "Josiah?"

"Nothing on the books at the moment, sir."

Prudence groaned, then flashed a rueful grin at the only other person in the room who would understand the gravity of what was about to descend on them. "It's Aunt Gillian, Geoffrey. She's decided to come to

America to chaperone me, and it's too late to stop her. You know how she is. Once she makes up her mind, there's no changing it. 'By the time this reaches you, arrangements will be well under way. Final plans to follow.' "

"Who is Aunt Gillian?" Ned asked.

"My mother's sister, the Dowager Viscountess Rotherton, for the past twenty-two years a pillar of English society. Geoffrey and I stayed at her London home in December. I'm sure I must have mentioned her to you."

"Not a word."

"We'll have to be sure people know to address her as *Lady* Rotherton," Josiah said. "And your servants will have to call her *my lady,* Miss Prudence."

Prudence stared at him. "You are such an Anglophile, Josiah," she said.

"I'll do my best to ensure that her ladyship has a favorable impression of America," he replied. Something had gone wrong with his familiar New York City accent.

"She's American," Prudence said. "At least she was."

Geoffrey left the conference room and disappeared into his office. When he returned, he was carrying glasses and a bottle of the bourbon Ned Hayes had introduced him to.

"I think we can all use something a bit stronger," he said, pouring each of them a neat tot and raising his glass. "To Lady Rotherton."

"To Lady Rotherton," echoed a mystified Ned.

No one understood what Josiah said. It was very British.

"To us," Prudence said. "We're going to need it."

AUTHOR'S NOTE

Candlestick telephones were not invented until several years after the action of *Let the Dead Keep Their Secrets* takes place. I decided to bring them into Prudence's 1889 world because they were too elegant to resist, and such a wonderful addition to the final scenes. I usually try not to take liberties with historical fact, but this one time, I couldn't resist. *Mea culpa,* dear reader.

Thanks as always to Jessica Faust, my patient and inspirational agent, and to John Scognamiglio, whose edits are always spot on.

My Tuesday morning critique group keeps me honest in more ways than I can count. I don't know how any writer can survive without a group of loyal and accomplished critics.

As always, my family supports and soothes the twitchy writer in me. Their constant reassurances are invaluable.

ABOUT THE AUTHOR

Rosemary Simpson is the author of two historical novels, *The Seven Hills of Paradise* and *Dreams and Shadows,* as well as historical novels in the Gilded Age Mystery series. She is a member of Sisters in Crime, International Thriller Writers, and the Historical Novel Society.

The employees of Thorndike Press hope you have enjoyed this Large Print book. All our Thorndike, Wheeler, and Kennebec Large Print titles are designed for easy reading, and all our books are made to last. Other Thorndike Press Large Print books are available at your library, through selected bookstores, or directly from us.

For information about titles, please call:
(800) 223-1244

or visit our website at:
gale.com/thorndike

To share your comments, please write:
Publisher
Thorndike Press
10 Water St., Suite 310
Waterville, ME 04901